# Down and Dirty

*Berkley Sensation titles by Sandra Hill*

ROUGH AND READY
DOWN AND DIRTY

# Down and Dirty

## Sandra Hill

BERKLEY SENSATION, NEW YORK

**THE BERKLEY PUBLISHING GROUP**
**Published by the Penguin Group**
**Penguin Group (USA) Inc.**
**375 Hudson Street, New York, New York 10014, USA**
Penguin Group (Canada), 90 Eglinton Avenue East, Suite 700, Toronto, Ontario M4P 2Y3, Canada
(a division of Pearson Penguin Canada Inc.)
Penguin Books Ltd., 80 Strand, London WC2R 0RL, England
Penguin Group Ireland, 25 St. Stephen's Green, Dublin 2, Ireland (a division of Penguin Books Ltd.)
Penguin Group (Australia), 250 Camberwell Road, Camberwell, Victoria 3124, Australia
(a division of Pearson Australia Group Pty. Ltd.)
Penguin Books India Pvt. Ltd., 11 Community Centre, Panchsheel Park, New Delhi—110 017, India
Penguin Group (NZ), 67 Apollo Drive, Rosedale, North Shore 0632, New Zealand
(a division of Pearson New Zealand Ltd.)
Penguin Books (South Africa) (Pty.) Ltd., 24 Sturdee Avenue, Rosebank, Johannesburg 2196,
South Africa

Penguin Books Ltd., Registered Offices: 80 Strand, London WC2R 0RL, England

DOWN AND DIRTY

A Berkley Sensation Book / published by arrangement with the author

PRINTING HISTORY
Berkley Sensation mass-market edition / November 2007

ISBN: 978-0-7394-8982-6

BERKLEY® SENSATION
Berkley Sensation Books are published by The Berkley Publishing Group,
a division of Penguin Group (USA) Inc.,
375 Hudson Street, New York, New York 10014.
BERKLEY SENSATION and the "B" design are trademarks belonging to Penguin Group (USA) Inc.

PRINTED IN THE UNITED STATES OF AMERICA

This book is dedicated to my good friend Sharon Martin, and to all those out there who are lifelong fiction readers. There is nothing in the world like a good book.

And to my good friend and fellow author Trish Jensen, who has proven over and over through her illness and many surgeries that bravery and love and, yes, even a sense of humor do not just occur in our books.

And last but not least, to my husband, Robert, who motivates me with his never-ending ability to laugh at all life throws his way. A stockbroker, Robert gets a kick out of telling people that he models for my covers and inspires the wicked love scenes.

To you many dedicated fans who continue to buy my books, I love you.

*There once was a Viking smitten.*
*By a modern "witch" the troll was bitten.*
*Some say love comes to those*
*who need it most.*
*Some say love comes when*
*least expected.*
*Some say love is a gift*
*from the gods.*
*But mayhap 'tis just*
*a form of bewitching.*

Sandra Hill, a variation on Bolthor's saga from
THE BEWITCHED VIKING

# Chapter 1

**Sometimes life throws a rock in your path, sometimes a boulder . . .**

"Stinkin' American pig!"

"You don't smell so good yourself, kiddo."

"Don't call me kiddo, you toad-sucking son of a camel's ass."

"Whoa! That's some potty mouth for a five-year-old child."

"I'm not a child."

"Yeah? Can you spell brat?"

"Go hump a goat."

"No thanks."

"Take me back to my grandfather, and I'll tell 'im not to chop off yer head. Jist put a bullet through yer eyes. It won't hurt much . . . I don't think."

U.S. Navy SEAL Lieutenant (J.G.) Zachary Frank Floyd stood, walked around the small fire, and loomed over the dirty urchin who didn't have the sense to flinch, not even when another round of munitions exploded off in the distance. They were hiding in a former Taliban cave in the mountains of Tora

Bora. *What does it say about the kid's life, that he's so inured to the sounds of battle? At his age, I was playing with Legos.* "That'll be enough, Sammy!"

The boy practically growled, baring his teeth . . . teeth that were stark white against his grimy skin. Zach had been forced to restrain the boy's wrists and ankles with plastic cuffs for fear he would run away. *Just call me Marquis de Floyd.* A wool blanket was wrapped around him like a shroud. Although it wasn't as cold inside the cave as it was outside, it was cold enough. The kid had been shivering moments ago. "Don't call me that name. I'm not yer son."

*I wish!* Zach shrugged and plopped back down on the other side of the small cave, the anger seeping out of him. Hell, he had no more desire to be a father to this gremlin from tango hell than the kid wanted him for a father. *Tango* was a SEAL word for terrorist. "That's not what your birth certificate says. Your mother named you Samir Abdul Hassim Floyd. Doesn't matter that your grandfather dropped the Floyd and added Arsallah. Either way, that's too much of a handle for any man, let alone *a little boy*. So, Sammy it is, unless you can give me a better nickname." *Like Samir the Snot.*

"My mother is dead." For the first time since the boy had been handed to him yesterday by an Afghan friendly, resulting in Zach being separated from his SEAL squad, he heard a quaver in the boy's voice. "I been livin' with my grandfather for a long time."

Zach supposed that six months was a long time for a child.

"Grandfather came for me when my mother died, praise Allah!" The implication was, *Where were you, Daddy dearest?*

"That's only because I didn't know about you sooner. Your grandfather is a butcher, and his hidey-hole is no place for a boy." Mullah Ahmed Arsallah put on a religious face in public, all pious and phony-baloney, but everyone knew he was behind some of the worst Taliban attacks in history. It was one of his very camps that SEAL Team Thirteen, along with some Army Rangers and Air Force hotshot pilots, had just shot to smithereens as part of Operation Maggot. Thank God, the kid had been taken out beforehand. Unfortunately, the grandfather had escaped and no doubt set up camp somewhere else. These al-Qaeda tangos were like roaches. You killed them in one spot, and they showed up somewhere else, in greater numbers.

Sammy let loose with another volley in what Zach presumed was either Pashto or Dari, the primary languages of Afghanistan. He would have to get help from one of his fellow SEALs back at Coronado, Ensign Omar Jones, product of an Arab father and a Native American mother, who had been a linguist and college professor. Sammy had no doubt learned the expletives from Arsallah's band of terrorists or the English-speaking mercenaries who worked with the rebels.

In the meantime, the kid's English was pretty good, due to his mother's teaching. Esilah had been a student at UCLA, but her premed studies had been interrupted when she'd returned to Afghanistan to fight against the hated Taliban, including her father, who disowned her. Zach had met her in Afghanistan, and, yeah, they'd had adrenaline sex in the middle of a bloody firefight.

The kid—who had Esilah's black hair and Zach's blue eyes—was still ranting on in a mixture of Arabic and English, but Zach just tuned the brat's tirade out and checked his watch again. His buddies should be here soon to rescue him, or at least try. Their motto was and always would be "No man left behind."

The wire bud, which had remained in his ear nonstop since yesterday, remained silent, as expected, after the initial message he'd sent pinpointing his hiding spot. It was best not to talk any more than necessary on an open line to avoid the enemy tracking his position.

"Why do they call you Pretty Boy?" the kid asked out of the blue.

"Who told you that?"

"My mother."

Zach shrugged. "Because I'm pretty?" Although he couldn't look too good now with his filthy desert BDUs and face cammied up.

"I think you're ugly."

*I don't look that bad.*

"I have to piss," Sammy said.

*Isn't that just swell?* Zach narrowed his eyes at the kid. He'd tried every trick in the book so far to get away, and Zach wasn't in the mood for more of his shenanigans.

"I mean it."

Muttering with disgust, he walked over and picked up the kid with both hands on his waist. He was skinny and weighed no more than a pillow, which made Zach feel kinda queasy. Walking to the back of the cave, he stood him on his feet and proceeded to tug his pants down. He wasn't wearing any underwear. That, too, made his stomach roil.

"Hey, untie me. I can't piss like this."

"You'll piss like that or piss your pants. Your call."

The kid made that growling sound again. "Don't you know nothin'? A man's gotta hold his cock when he pisses."

*Aren't kids supposed to say tinkle or pee?* He turned his back on the scamp. *Mom would have killed me or Danny if we'd ever said piss in front of her. And cock . . . man oh man, we would have been tasting Irish Spring for a month if we ever used that word.*

He turned around to see the kid glance up over his bony shoulder, an evil glint in his blue eyes, which, fortunately or unfortunately, mirrored his own. "What do you think of it?"

"Of what?"

"My cock."

*Holy shit!* Zach yanked the kid's pants back up, then returned him to the blanket.

"Well?"

"Well what?"

"Is it big enough?"

*Oh, boy!* "For what?"

"You know."

*God must be punishing me for something. Maybe it was the time I . . .* "Are you kidding? That little worm? You've got a few more years to worry about that."

"How big is yours?"

*I do not frickin' believe this.* "Big enough."

"Well, my cousin Taj says his is as big as a bull's, but he's seven, and he lies sometimes. Is yours as big as a bull's?"

"It's not good manners to ask someone that." *Pretty Boy Floyd giving etiquette lessons? Hope the sky doesn't fall down.*

"Uncle Masood slapped my face when I asked him."

Zach went stone still at that news. Was that bruise on the kid's chin caused by a clip, too? And why was the kid so damn skinny? "I'll answer any questions you have about anything . . . but not now."

Thankfully, Zach's earpiece staticked before the kid had a chance to argue with the delay.

"Raven to Eagle. Do ya read me, Eagle?" It was his good friend Justin "Cage" LeBlanc on the other end. Military men always used code names when on a live op, over communication lines that could be intercepted. In this case, with Operation Maggot, it seemed apt that they take on names of the worm's natural enemy . . . the worm being al-Qaeda, of course.

"Eagle here."

"Helo on its way. Oh nine hundred. Are y'all ready to boogie?"

Zach set the timer on his watch for fifteen minutes. "Roger."

"There are tangos all over the place. Be careful."

"Gotcha." Zach was already standing and preparing his gear, including the collapsible stock on his M4 carbine, which he slung over his shoulder. It had an M203 grenade launcher underneath, which he hoped he wouldn't need. He checked to see that he had two magazines left, which amounted to more than fifty rounds of ammunition. He would leave his backpack behind so that he could carry the kid, but he took out a couple extra grenades and his KA-BAR knife. The next inhabitant of this Better Homes & Caves dwelling could have the MREs.

"Pigeon, Tweety, and me will be on the ground, covering your six. Y'all have to make it to the ascender. Quick, quick."

"Uh, problem here. Passenger. Need harness."

"Whaaat? A prisoner?"

"Not exactly. A little boy."

Sammy made a snorting sound, still trying to be the little man.

"No way! Ya cain't take any unauthorized person outta the country, *cher*." Cage slipped into his Southern Cajun dialect when he was nervous, as he had every right to be now.

"Bull!"

Cage sighed. "Who is it?"

Zach hesitated, but then said, "My son."

There was silence on the line after that. Zach didn't know if they'd been cut off or if Cage and the guys were stunned speechless. Probably a bit of both. Master Chief Sylvester "Sly" Simms was no doubt on the Motorola in the chopper right now, relaying all this info to CENTCOM. He would bet his Budweiser, the Navy SEAL trident pin, that there would be a band of MPs awaiting him when they landed at Kabul. On the other hand, Sly was a good man . . . a friend. Maybe he would let Zach do his own communicating on this issue.

"I have to put a gag in your mouth, Sammy. No, don't give me any more lip. I can't take the chance that you'll shout or give my location away. I'll remove it as soon as we're on the copter."

"Copter? We're goin' on a helicopter?" The kid's eyes went wide, then immediately reverted to their usual surly cast. "I ain't leavin' here."

"Wanna bet?" Zach gagged Sammy with a handkerchief and lifted him over the shoulder of his nonshooting arm, though he could actually shoot just as well from either hand.

The kid squirmed and grunted stuff under his gag, but Zach had a firm hold. He waited at the entrance of the cave, his heart pumping so loud it felt as if it might lunge out of his chest. But then he heard the thwap, thwap, thwap of the Blackhawk's propellers, followed by Cage's cue, three short bird calls. "We've only got two minutes to get out of here and in the copter, kid. So work with me, huh?"

With those words, he dashed for the hanging rope and harness about thirty feet away. Out of his side vision, he saw Cage and Luke "Slick" Avenil off on either side of him and Sly in a crouch, rifle raised near the rappelling rope, ducking and firing at the tangos coming in on all three sides. Zach and these three guys had suffered through Class 500 of BUD/S training together seven years ago; a SEAL might change teams or squads as ordered, but he always identified with his class number. The members were bonded for life.

The terrorists, still a considerable distance away, were firing at the copter and the other guys, not him, because presumably they saw that he was carrying the boy and had orders not to aim for him for fear of collateral damage . . . collateral in this case meaning Arsallah's grandkid. At one point, a bullet zinged a rock near Slick's foot. With a curse, Slick did a ninja-style roll, landing on his feet. Cage was crab running toward the helo, urging him to hurry. "Go, go, go!"

Zach strapped a terrified Sammy into the harness and wrapped himself around him on the rope, which was already being raised up to the copter. Meanwhile, Cage, Sly, and Slick were shooting off rapid rounds. Just before they started ascending the rope, each of them lobbed a grenade in three different directions. The helo took off by the time the explosions hit. Sly had a thigh wound that would need care as soon as they landed, and Cage's palms appeared raw from rappelling down the rope. He must have forgotten his gloves, or else the action had worn through the Kevlar. Other than that, they were in good shape.

They all sat on bench seats, breathing heavily, adrenaline

almost popping out of their pores. Sammy sat on Zach's lap, too stunned to protest . . . yet. Finally, when their heart rates were down to about a hundred beats a minute, each looked at the other, grinned, then said as one, "Hoo-yah!"

Zach took off Sammy's gag but not his hand and wrist restraints. Immediately, the brat launched into a tirade that involved fuck, shit, ass, snot, piss, bastard, hell, damn, cock, prick, and dick in a dozen combinations, both in English and his native tongue.

The guys continued to grin.

"Are you going to introduce us?" Sly asked.

"This is Samir Abdul Hassim Floyd. My son." Zach exhaled on a loud whoosh. "You can call him Sammy. Or the Snot."

"You sure 'bout that, *cher*? I mean, that he's yer son?" Cage was only looking out for his best interests, but Sammy didn't see it that way and let loose with another volley of expletives.

Ignoring him, Zach said, "Pretty sure."

"I already wired ahead to a nurse I know. She'll do DNA tests for you right away so at least you'll have that defense." Slick knew more ways to avoid the law than a corporate lawyer.

Zach nodded.

"You do realize you're in trouble from so many angles you're gonna look like a target riddled with bullet holes by the time they're done with you." This was Sly's astute opinion.

He nodded again. "For the past two years, I've been miserable, mooning over Britta," he told them. Britta was the one woman who hadn't succumbed to his charms—and, yeah, he had plenty—and in the dead of the night, she was the one he fantasized about. "But, man, I sure wish I was back there with her right now."

Cage laughed. "Nah! You'd just be tradin' one misery fer another."

"I suppose so." Zach sighed and glanced down at his personal, present-day misery.

His misery stuck his tongue out at him.

## NORTHUMBRIA, 1015 AD
### Just call me Xena, Warrior Nun . . .

Britta Asadottir, far-famed Norse warrior woman, was a novice in St. Anne's Abbey . . . a Saxon nunnery, for the love of Thor! And she blamed the world's biggest fornicator, Zack-hairy the Pretty Boy.

Not that she had ever fornicated with the lout, or wanted to, but the man had ruined her life. If she ever got her hands on him, she would throttle him with glee.

Britta had met Zack-hairy at The Sanctuary, a women's refuge in the Norselands, more than two winters past. He and his comrades had been there only a few sennights, helping to rid the country of the villain Steinolf and beguiling the gunnas off every woman that crossed their paths. The whole time, the godly handsome man had pursued Britta relentlessly, trying to lure her into his bed furs. Which was strange in itself, because she was not known as Britta the Big for naught. As tall and well muscled as many men, she intimidated males who were e'er sensitive about being the stronger sex. Not the rogue with the snake-slick tongue, however.

But then, Zack-hairy, his comrades-in-arms, and The Sanctuary's mistress, Hilda Berdottir, had disappeared one day. *Poof!* Everyone surmised that the group had been caught in an avalanche that swept their bodies all the way to the fjord and then to the North Sea. A sad ending, to be sure.

The oddest thing, though, was that once the lout had gone, she'd developed the most intense yearning for him and the mating. Thank the gods she had not been so inclined when he had been here. Otherwise, she would have been rutting with him like a boar in heat. The scoundrel must have put a spell on her because no longer had she been satisfied with serving as chief guard and archer for The Sanctuary. Now that the danger of Steinolf was gone and now that the lout had ignited these irksome fires in her loins, she had fooled herself into believing she could live safely outside the bounds of the fortress, perchance even find a man to douse those woman-fires.

A big mistake!

Her father and brothers had found her.

Her father, Jarl Eyvind Tunnisson, wanted—nay, *needed*—her back under his sadistic control again. It turned out that one of his larger and more prosperous Norse estates, Everstead, in truth of law belonged to her . . . or it would once she wed, and then it would belong to her firstborn daughter. On her death, if there were no issue, everything would go to St. Anne's Abbey. And so Britta took refuge here with the good nuns. Her father was only biding his time.

Problems with her father were not new. Any woman's virtue was forfeit in her father's holdings. He and her three brothers slaked their lust on anything wearing a gunna, regardless of age or beauty, regardless of consent. As a result, there were dozens of Tunnisson bastards hither and yon, from the Norselands to Britain to Iceland and beyond. It had been a huge embarrassment for her mother, a highborn lady, afore her death ten years ago.

Her father considered women chattel, good only for bed-sport and the coin brought by prospective husbands. He had been enraged at Britta's refusal to wed the various men he'd brought to her.

Her brothers had the same attitude toward women, and worse. They were demented and cruel and had been from an early age. When she was eight, Trond had skinned her favorite kitten, whilst still alive. When she was twelve, Erlend had held her down with a knife to her inner thigh, forcing her to spread and show his filthy friends her nether parts. She had a scar there still where the knife had drawn blood. But it had been Halvdan's attempt to mount her himself that caused Britta to go to their ancient castellan and beg for instruction in the warrior arts.

From that day forward, Britta's life path took a new direction. No longer could she nurture the usual womanly dreams of home and hearth and family. Taller than the average male, she had begun to develop muscles . . . Not an attractive marriage package, as her father had told her on many an occasion. Although men did not like having a wife towering over them, they could live with that; however, when said wife could best her mate in swordplay, that was beyond acceptable. Or so had said the many prospective husbands her father paraded before her.

The final indignity had come when her father gave consent to a Danish jarl for rape as an incentive to force her to bend to his will, a rape that she managed to evade. Her jaw still ached on occasion, an eternal reminder of his rage that time . . . a fist to the chin that had knocked her senseless and no doubt jarred her jawbone out of place. It had been then that she had known she had to flee, her fighting skills not nearly enough to fight them all.

For years, she had moved from place to place in the Norselands, hiring out her fighting skills, until she'd found The Sanctuary, a special place for women. She had been content there being the head archer until that lout Zack-hairy had stirred her blood. When he'd left, without warning, she realized that she wanted so much more. She wanted a man who loved her, and she wanted children. So she had left The Sanctuary, thinking herself safe because of her now-honed military prowess.

What a witless exercise in vanity!

Almost immediately, she had fallen into her father's clutches again. When, five months later, she'd escaped, battered and gaunt from nigh starvation, it had been from a dungeon in his castle awaiting marriage to the most vile man imaginable.

"What is amiss *now*, Lady Britta?" Mother Edwina, the

abbess, asked with a long sigh, calling Britta back from her
straying thoughts.

Britta, who disdained the title, glanced up from where
she'd been kneeling for more than an hour on the stone floor
of the chapel. "Penance."

"Again?"

"Father Caedmon likes to give me penance, as much as
he likes hearing my confessions." She rolled her eyes for
emphasis.

"Child, your attempts at humor do not amuse me."

*Child?*

The nun was no older than forty winters, but she carried a
world-weary, stern demeanor under the strain of her position. She motioned for Britta to join her in sitting on one of
the hard wood pews.

"'Tis not my fault that the priest gets pleasure out of
hearing me create sexual experiences to confess to him."

"Create?" Mother Edwina arched an eyebrow.

"Didst think I really know how to ride a man like a horse?
Or get pleasure from a fat candle? Or jiggle my breasts apur-
pose to entice the tinker . . . yea, the one with rumbling bow-
els? Or sleep naked in the hayloft so the straw would rub my
private places?"

With each of Britta's fantasies, the good nun's jaw
dropped lower and lower. Finally, she said, "Britta!" The
chastisement was belied by a grin tugging at Mother Edwina's lips. "St. Bridget's bones! Why would you confess
lewd acts you have not committed?"

"Because Father Caedmon likes me to. And not just me.
Ask any of the novices. We have made a game of who can
dream up the most outlandish examples of bedsport. Whew!
Sister Ignatia wins hands down on that score. Who knew that
turkey feathers—"

"Britta! That will be enough."

*Not nearly enough.* "Really, Mother Edwina, think how
boring my confessions would be otherwise. I am a trained
warrior. 'Tis what I do best. But there is naught to defend

here at the abbey, other than a wayward bull or angry bees. Truly, my confessions would go thus: Bless me, Father, for I yawned during compline. Bless me, Father, for I cursed when the chapel bell rang for the tenth time during the night. Bless me, Father, for I want to nigh scream if I hear another Kyrie or Sanctus. Bless me, Father, for laughing at Sister Benedictus when she broke wind hitting the high note of "Gloria." Bless me, Father, for I would rather lop off an enemy's head than pray for him. Bless me, Father, for wishing my father and my brothers to the fires of Muspell. Bless me, Father, for drinking too much of Sister Margaret's mead."

The only income source the abbey had was the sale of Margaret's mead in the trading stalls of Jorvik. And good mead it was, too, the secret ingredients passed on by the same Northumbrian family who sent a daughter named Margaret to be a nun each generation from ten decades past.

"You must learn to accept your lot in life."

"Why?"

"Because it is the way of the Lord."

"And who is to say that the Lord prefers I be a nun than a warrior? Remember Boudicca, the Celtic queen who led an army against the Romans."

Mother Edwina made that tsking sound she usually employed when Britta had asked an unanswerable question.

"I grow weary of the tedium," Britta complained. "How can you bear the quiet and the same routine every day, month after month, year after year?"

"Inner peace is its own reward."

Britta, feeling anything but peaceful, grabbed at her own hair with frustration, then pressed her lips together, pondering. "Methinks there may be another way."

"I will no doubt regret asking, but what other way?"

Britta looped an arm over the mother superior's shoulder and confided, "Returning to my father's rat's nest of a keep is impossible. The only way I can leave this nunnery is if I am dead. Or if my father thinks I am dead."

*"Thinks?"*

"Yea. I will do naught to jeopardize the nunnery. But I must needs come up with a fake death."

"And that fake death would be?"

"It must be a death where there would be no body as evidence."

"Like a fire or a drowning?" Mother Edwina's face brightened with understanding.

"Yea, but I am not about to risk either of those. How about if I have suddenly gone barmy?"

Mother Edwina muttered something about her already being barmy.

"For the next few sennights I could do some demented things so that word will begin to spread of my mind's demise. Then when I jump off a cliff—you know, the cliff on the way to Jorvik—everyone will say I committed suicide in the midst of one of my fits."

Mother Edwina's jaw gaped with astonishment. "You would truly die if you jumped off that cliff. There is naught but sharp rocks and deep waters below."

"I would not really jump. I would just pretend. And I would leave pieces of my ripped clothing on the rocks, with a bit of blood doused here and there. Oh, do not look askance at me. 'Twould be chicken blood."

"May the saints preserve us!" Mother Edwina made the sign of the cross over her ample chest. "Where would you go?"

"That is the best part. I will hide in Sister Margaret's mead wagon next time she goes to the market stalls in Jorvik. From there I will arrange passage to Iceland and from there go to that new land called Greenland. Or else I could go to the Rus lands and become one of the Varangian Guard."

"Have you lost your senses, girl?"

"Mayhap I have, but you must see that I have no choices left. Have you considered that Sister Bernice's disappearance last sennight might be related?"

"Never!"

"My father has threatened to get me, even if he has to assault the abbey walls."

"He cannot breach sacred walls. 'Twould be a sacrilege."

Mother Edwina was so naive. "As if my father would care about that!" Britta muttered.

"Sister Bernice will return. She no doubt went to visit her family in Nottingham."

Britta shrugged. She was not so sure.

"And for you, pray, my child. God may yet have a religious vocation in mind for you."

The next day, a driverless, mule-drawn cart pulled into the abbey courtyard carrying Sister Bernice. So brutally tortured had the young nun been that there was a communal horror and a vast wailing inside the convent walls.

After the funeral, Britta approached Mother Edwina again. "Can you see now that I must leave?"

Mother Edwina nodded reluctantly. "If there is no other way, I suppose your plan could work."

For the next few sennights, Britta did indeed convince more than a few nuns, a lusty priest, and several passing travelers that she had gone barmy from her confinement in a nunnery. Spouting a gibberish sort of language that she made up. Pulling at her hair. Dancing with Sister Serena's broom. Bursting out in ribald song in the midst of Mass. Even walking naked in the moonlight.

So, when the day came for her "demise," her sanity was indeed in question. The only problem was, she needed some fortification as she and Sister Margaret wended their way slowly toward Jorvik. And what better fortification than Margaret's mead?

By the time Britta stood at the edge of the cliff, she and Sister Margaret were both a bit *drukkinn*. As a result, she nigh killed herself climbing down the steep incline to place the bloody scraps of fabric. Instead of helping her or urging caution, Sister Margaret sat in the grass singing a song about farm maids and randy soldiers.

"Well, that should suffice," Britta called back to Sister Margaret. "We can be off now."

"Are you sure?"

Britta started, not realizing that Sister Margaret had come up behind her. Sister Margaret screamed as Britta teetered on the edge, vainly attempting to get her balance. She slipped and fell head over tail, desperately managing to grab the branch of a bush sticking out of the cliff side. Her hands were bleeding, as were various other parts of her scratched body, but she was alive, thank the gods. At least she was no longer under the influence of mead, the fall having shocked the fumes from her brain.

"Have a caution," Sister Margaret yelled, peeking carefully over the lip of the cliff. "Are you all right?"

*Odin's breath! Is she blind as well as drukkinn?* "Nay, I am not all right." Her hands had a firm grip on the bush about three body lengths from the cliff edge, but her arms and shoulders burned with the strain.

"Should I pray?"

*Oh, that will help!* "Can you pray and throw me a rope at the same time?" Britta tried to get purchase with her booted feet, to no avail.

"Yea, I can." Sister Margaret disappeared, then soon returned with a coil of thick rope, then disappeared again.

Britta peered upward carefully but could see nothing. Presumably, Sister Margaret was tying the rope to a rock or a tree.

"Catch," the good nun said then, tossing out the heavy coil of rope. Unfortunately, the coil of rope did not immediately uncoil. As a result, it knocked Britta in the head, tearing her loose from her hold on the branch. "Yiiiiiiikes!" She went careening downward once again.

Britta screamed her outrage to her father, Sister Margaret, and the pretty man who'd caused the chain of events that led to this final catastrophe. For some reason, though, she blamed the pretty man most of all. Unfair? Possibly. But who could care about fairness now? If the lout had not laid a burden on her heart and loins, she would still be at The Sanctuary, safe and sound.

"'Tis all your fault, you loathsommmmmmmmme . . ."

# Chapter 2

**My punishment will be . . . WHAT? . . .**

Zach had been back in the USA for two weeks, but this was the first time he'd been summoned to discuss his "problem" in detail since the original, not-too-pleasant debriefing, which had been more like a "Chew Floyd's Ass" session. He pushed open the office door in the training compound, knowing full well that he was late.

Lieutenant Commander Ian MacLean ran his fingers through his receding hair, which had been recently trimmed into the traditional military high and tight, and glared with disbelief at him. "I swear, you would arrive late for your own funeral. Do you have any clue what kind of trouble you're in, Lieutenant Floyd?"

"Yes, Commander, sir," Zach answered, standing at attention before the commander's desk. "But there was an accident involving my . . . uh, babysitter, and—"

"Lieutenant Floyd!" the commander interrupted.

Protocol required his speaking to a higher ranking officer

only in response to questions or when given permission to speak freely. "Sorry, Commander, sir."

MacLean breathed in and out, clearly trying to calm his temper, which Zach knew was formidable. MacLean had been his BUD/S instructor, and he hadn't been known as Lean Mean for nothing. "At ease, Lieutenant."

Zach relaxed his stance and folded his hands behind his back.

"What happened?"

"Here or in Afghanistan?"

MacLean literally growled. "Don't screw with me, dickhead. I can make that hot water you're dog-paddling through turn to boiling and peel your stupid skin off. While I'm at it, I might as well burn off that wayward dick of yours."

*Okaaaay!*

Picking up a pile of pink telephone message slips, he began to flick through them, making a comment about each:

"John Sylvester from the State Department. Wants a meeting with you ASAP.

"Mullah Ahmed Bejah from the L.A. chapter of Muslims for Peace. They're demanding that the boy be returned because of his religious background.

"Admiral George Wilson, CENTCOM. He wants your ass in the brig.

"Your grandfather, General Floyd, is trying to make it all go away, which is of course impossible.

"A representative of the Afghan embassy in Beirut—we no longer have one in the United States—is demanding immediate and unconditional return of Samir.

"Aljazeera TV. Five calls from them.

"One each from Larry King, Katie Couric, and Diane Sawyer. Not to mention *People* magazine and the *New York Times*.

"If you dare talk to any media, I swear, I will personally take the hide off you. Oh, and did I mention some image consultant at the Pentagon thinks you would make a great poster boy for recruitment . . . once this brouhaha all dies down?"

Zach tried to look suitably surprised and outraged, but, frankly, he'd had just as many calls, some even wackier, and some downright scary. Like death threats. How they'd gotten his unlisted number was even scarier. That didn't count the two attempts to kidnap Sammy, once in D.C. when he first came back to the States and several days later at the airport in San Diego. That was before he'd taken security measures.

The commander inhaled and exhaled deeply, presumably to tame his temper. "What happened today?"

"My son kicked the babysitter, who already had a bruised hamstring. We had to call an ambulance because he was unable to walk, possible shin fracture, and then I had to get a backup babysitter. By that time, I was already late, and I did call in, but—"

Commander MacLean raised a halting hand. "The babysitter with the bruised hamstring? You wouldn't be referring to Ensign Omar Jones, would you?"

"Roger that. Omar has custody of his little girl, you know, but she's visiting his parents in Arizona this week. I figured he has experience with kids. Hah! Lotta good that did. Actually, I begged Omar after the first five babysitters quit. My son is not the most pleasant gremlin on the planet. Omar is multilingual, as you know, and a SEAL, both positive attributes when dealing with an Afghan version of Attila the Five-Year-Old Hun."

His humor—his whole frickin' monologue—didn't go over big with MacLean, who continued to frown at him. "I thought your mother came here from Florida to help with the kid."

"She did, but she quit two days ago. Her exact words were, 'You made your bed, sonny, now sleep in it.' Besides she had a modeling gig . . . something for the AARP magazine, I think."

Still not a hint of a smile.

So, he blathered on, "My brother, Danny, is on leave from his Iraq deployment. He's an Air Force pilot. But he just laughs at me. People do that a lot lately."

MacLean frowned. "Who's the backup babysitter?"

Zach hesitated before revealing, "Your wife."

"Madrene?" MacLean's eyes about bulged from their sockets.

"I couldn't think of anyone else to ask."

"And the kids?" The commander and his wife had two children, three-month-old and two-year-old sons, Ranulf and Ivan, the latter better known as Ivan the Terrible. He had been given that name before anyone had met Sammy. Now he was considered a saint by comparison.

"They are there, too. My son seems to behave better in their company, under your wife's iron control."

The commander gave him "the look," the one that put him in the same class as dipwad newbie tadpoles. "Your babysitting woes—in fact, your being late—are the least of your worries, boy."

Zach knew things were bad when MacLean referred to him as "boy," seeing as how the commander had only a few years on him.

"I will not send him back . . . Commander, sir." It was telling how often he referred to his son as "him" or "the kid," he realized with an odd sadness.

"I understand that. You better have bodyguards around the kid, though, because, believe me, Mullah Arsallah has friends in low as well as high places. He won't give up."

"Two of SEAL Team Thirteen's inactive members are stationed outside my building, sir, for the time being. Including Scary Larry Wilson."

His boss didn't find that reference as amusing as Zach did. Scary Larry watching over Sammy the Snot. Whooboy! Actually, Wilson was a nice guy . . . a thirty-something SEAL who was on temporary suspension for breaking some ass-backward Navy rule. He'd hired him in the interim to help guard his son.

"I promise I'll get this resolved soon."

MacLean rested his elbow on the desk and put his chin in

one hand, staring at him as if he were mud under his boon-dockers. "The Pentagon wants to know why—and how—you had sex during a live op in Afghanistan six years ago."

Zach grinned. "Under a tarp in the mess tent."

"Pfff! I'll be sure to tell them that. Not!"

"I didn't ask for this situation, sir, but I take responsibility for all of it. And I *will* resolve all the . . . issues."

"Floyd, you've got as much sense as an armadillo cross-ing a four-lane highway." MacLean shook his head at him. "What a cluster fuck! I hope you have a good lawyer."

"I do, sir. My grandfather retained Jack Delaney for me." His grandfather, Army General Frank Floyd, retired, was a notorious World War II ace pilot who still served in the Pen-tagon as a consultant, despite his advanced age. Delaney was a D.C. attorney with a reputation for winning at all costs.

The bill, which would be monumental, was being footed by his father, an aging lothario who still thought he was Hol-lywood's answer to Cary Grant, playing just such a role, Dr. Lawrence Bratton, in one of the long-running TV soap op-eras, *Light in the Storm*. Incredibly, the old blowhard thought he could still give George Clooney a run for his money.

His mother, who'd divorced his father about twenty af-fairs ago, back when they all still lived in Bangor, Maine, had her own life as a senior citizen model. She'd kill him if she ever heard him refer to her that way.

His family, dysfunctional as it was, were there for each other in times of need. And, man oh man, Zach sure was needy now.

MacLean nodded at the mention of Delaney. "Well, for the time being, you're assigned here at Coronado as an instructor."

Zach had expected that. In fact, he'd expected far worse punishment as he'd worked out every day, waiting for his sentence . . . uh, assignment. Gig Squad, at the least.

"Don't look so smug, Floyd."

*Uh-oh!* Zach didn't like the smirk on his commander's face. *Incoming bomb about to zing me.*

"You are the brand-new assistant commander of the Navy's half-assed, birdbrained, in-your-face WEALS, boy."

"WEALS? Oh, no! No, no, no! Not that SEAL wannabe bunch of women!"

"Exactly. Women on Earth, Air, Land and Sea. The latest BUD/S class just ended, and another won't start for three months to accommodate this program."

"What the hell do I know about teaching SEALs or WEALS or anyone, for that matter?"

"SEAL instructors aren't professional teachers, as you well know. It's a temporary duty billet like any other. Behave yourself, and you might be put back on the teams."

*So much for that argument!* "Who's the commander?"

MacLean's face flushed a bright red. Even his partially bald head was red.

"Wha-hoo! What did you do wrong to get this assignment?"

"Nothing. I was just in the wrong place at the wrong time."

Zach knew how that could happen. Best to make yourself as invisible as possible in the military. "Man, I never thought I'd see the day that they'd allow women into the teams."

"They're not. Listen, terrorism has escalated so much in the past five years that we can't keep up with the demand for SEALs out in the field. Same with all the other special forces units in other branches of the military. Women can fill a need."

"You're talking about lowering the standards, aren't you?"

MacLean nodded. "Let's face it. There's no way a woman, no matter how strong, would be able to withstand a real Hell Week. For example, I think we'll pass on log PT. Those telephone pole buggers weigh three to four hundred pounds each."

"So do IBSs." Inflatable Boats, Small, were heavy rubber boats, an integral part of BUD/S training. "You gonna eliminate those, too?"

He shook his head. "No, we're gonna give them a try. Somehow they seem more manageable. I don't know. We're playing by ear . . . or muscle. But don't worry, we'll push them to their limits. They'll have to work harder than they ever have in their lives to survive . . . till they can kick ass and take names like any special forces unit."

"And afterward?"

"Once trained, they'll be incorporated into the new U.S. Liberty Teams."

Zach frowned. "That antiterrorist squad? I heard about it starting up a year or so ago, then nothing."

"It's still in the works. Just ran into a few snags, which could be expected when you try to combine SEALs, Green Berets, Army Special Forces, and every other Rambo-like idiot warrior group in the world, not to mention, now, WEALS."

"I can see dozens of complications with this WEALS program. Sex, as in instructors and officers hitting on the women. Serious distractions, like breasts bobbing all over the place. Female periods. PMS, for chrissake!"

"That's not the half of it. In pretraining last week, we were doing duck squats when one of the women accidentally farted. F.U. and one of the other instructors laughed. She burst out bawling with embarrassment and ended up ringing out."

Any SEAL trainee, or WEALS trainee for that matter, could DOR, drop on request, at any time. All they had to do was walk to the northeast corner of the grinder where there was a ship's bell, place their personalized helmets on the ground, and ring the bell three times. In fact, there was a 40 percent dropout rate during the first phase of BUD/S. He had no idea how high it would be for WEALS, which had started with ninety-five women.

"And there's more. The Navy has appointed a female ombudsman, Captain Lenore Feldman, to handle complaints from the WEALS trainees. Think anal with a capital A. Her big thing is memos." The commander picked up a memo as if it were something repugnant. "Look at this," he added, shoving a pink slip his way.

### MEMO

**From: Captain Lenore Feldman**
**To: Commander Ian MacLean**
**Subject: WEALS**

**PMS is a legitimate medical condition according to Code 722, Article 7.**

Zach shook his head at the absurdity. "I can only imagine the scenario: 'Please, Instructor Floyd, sir, can I be excused from PT today? I'm in a bad mood.' "
"Here's another one. Can you believe it?"

### MEMO

**From: Captain Lenore Feldman**
**To: Commander Ian MacLean**
**Subject: WEALS**

**Excessive hollering in some circumstances can be considered harassment. No nexus, but open to interpretation, case-by-case basis.**

"You know, SEALs are not the most politically correct beings on the planet. Next they'll be giving us sensitivity training. Find our inner female, or some such crap. This is going to be a nightmare," Zach concluded.
"More like a field of land mines. We'll have to be careful where we step, but I'll be damned if I'll change special forces training just to accommodate these women. If they want to join the game, they're gonna have to play by our rules. Anyhow, we'll have a briefing later this afternoon. All SEALs, SEAL trainees, and any testosterone-oozing body within a mile radius of the compound will know by tomorrow what they can or cannot do."

*Including no laughing at farts. Unbelievable!* Zach nodded. "So this is going to be my punishment."

"It'll be fun."

Zach was too appalled to say anything but, "Hoo-yah!"

## A woman's gotta do what a woman's gotta do . . .

Britta figured that she must have landed on her head when she fell over the cliff, knocking her unconscious. Or was she dead? Could this be the famed Other World? If so, its glory had been vastly exaggerated, in her opinion. There was not a gold sword or one-eyed god in sight.

Or mayhap this was Muspell. It was certainly hot enough. But, nay, Britta did not think she had done anything so bad in her lifetime to merit those eternal fires.

*Still, I must be in bad odor with the gods. Naught goes right with me anymore.*

When Britta emerged from the haze she found herself in, it was not her head that throbbed but her backside. She wasn't impaled on the sharp rocks but sitting in a flat, sandy arena.

A man wearing short, thigh-exposing braies and a short-sleeved *shert* leaned over her, his clean-shaven face florid with anger. To her shock, she realized that she was dressed in a similar fashion, right down to the heavy skin boots. Into her ear, the man shouted, "Lady, get yer butt in gear and climb back up that cargo net. NOW!" He had a ruddy complexion, which got redder, a clear sign of his anger.

Best he be careful. She knew a man, Snorri the Red, who'd had a similar ruddiness. One day in the midst of one of his yelling fits, he just dropped over, dead as a lutefisk.

"Move it, move it, move it!" the man continued to scream.

"What?" She glanced upward and saw not the cliff face but a high wall made of rope. And women, in similar attire, were climbing upward. Could they be Valkyries? Nay. None of them looked goddesslike in beauty. And, truth to tell, if they were all virgins, she would bite her best sword. Not in that scant attire.

One of them fell down, dusted herself off, and immediately started over. Some men, blowing metal whistles, smirked as they stared at the women's fabric-strained buttocks sticking out like obscene boulders above them.

"You heard me, birdbrain. And you know the correct response. Yes, Master Chief Uxley, sir. Say it with the proper respect."

*Birdbrain? Is he calling me birdbrain?* "What did you say?" Britta was about to clout the insulting man aside his head, which had been shaved nigh bald, but then she reminded herself that she was in some strange place. Mayhap she should play along till she got her bearings.

"Are you mocking me? Are you mocking me? Drop, sister, and give me ten," the man hollered, spittle pooling at the corners of his mouth, as he jabbed her in the chest with a forefinger.

"What?" she said again. *What has got the miscreant's bald head in a blaze?*

"You heard me. Push 'em up, sweetie." He said "sweetie" as if it were a slur and pointed to a woman behind her who was raising and lowering her body, which was level with the ground, but never quite touching it. She assumed this was what he wanted her to do when he mentioned "pushing-up."

"Yes, Chieftain, sir," she said, dropping down to the sand. But what she thought was, *Go swive a goat, Chieftain, sir.*

Anger flared in his eyes. "Master chief. Not chieftain. Now give me thirty for insubordination."

*I would like to give you something, you witless cur, but it has naught to do with pushing-ups.* Gritting her teeth, Britta decided that compliance was the wisest course of action till she determined where she was.

Thus it was that she found herself raising and lowering her body like a lackwit, along with a half dozen other women. If this was meant to be punishment, she had news for the man with the flaming face. Flogging was punishment. Kneeling on a stone floor for a day was punishment. Eating gammelost was punishment. Being imprisoned in a nunnery was punishment. Raising and lowering the body in sand was not punishment.

The whole time she and the other women did the pushing-ups, the chieftain kept goading them. "Are you sure you don't wanna ring out? Nothin' wrong with bein' a quitter. It's only your first day. You gotta have a fire in the gut to succeed here, ladies. I don't see a spark in a blasted one of you."

One woman muttered, "I got fire," and the rest echoed her refrain. Britta did, too, figuring it must mean something significant.

"Do you really wanna put yourselves through this pain? Wouldn't you like a nice manicure about now?" the miscreant leader continued.

"For a certainty, it would be nice to have a man to cure me."

The chieftain's face got ruddier, his eyes bulging.

That was her cue to remain silent, she suspected. Since none of the other women were quitting, she followed suit. When in doubt, just follow your instincts; that had always been her philosophy. When she completed the exercise, which was more difficult than it appeared, no doubt due to her recent bout of mead madness, he ordered her once again to climb the rope wall.

She started to climb, then turned back to stare down at the chieftain. "Dare to look at my arse, you bloody lecher, and you will find your face in the sand when I come back down."

His sputtering and the other men's laughter could be heard as she climbed up the rope netting, not an easy task, since it swayed and moved to and fro with the climbers. It would have been easier if she were barefooted. Leastways, she could grip the ropes with her toes. This way, her skin boots could get no purchase. But anger fueled her, and she soon reached the top, which she straddled, as best she could, panting for breath. She had not realized how high it was . . . more than two floors of a fortress castle. She tried her best not to look downward.

Glancing around, Britta realized that from this vantage

point she had a bird's-eye view of a vast region. She should have recognized the scent of salt water in the air, but still she was surprised to see the blue ocean on one side with extremely large metal ships not so far away. Not a low-riding wood dragon ship in sight. Was it a harbor of some kind? If so, where was the market town that usually catered to the incoming and outgoing traders on longboats and knarrs?

There were people running on the beach, both singly and in groups. Was someone chasing them?

On the other side of the arena where Britta sat, high up, there were many buildings, but none resembled the timbersided keeps she was accustomed to or the rare stone castles that the Normans favored. Nor were there farmsteads and grazing animals. Not even the wattle and daub cotters' huts. These buildings were rather ugly, although they did hold precious glass windows.

But wait. In the distance she saw a white castle with a red roof. How odd! Why would anyone want a white dwelling? It must get dirty. She figured the king must live there, since only a king would have staff enough to keep the building clean.

And the people . . . Thor's toenails, there were hundreds of them walking about, most of them in uniforms of brown or white, even women. She also saw what appeared to be horseless carriages traveling hither and yon, but mayhap she was mistaken about that. She must be.

Another woman swung her leg over the top, facing her. She was not panting at all.

"Whose castle is that over there?" She pointed to the white building with the red roof.

"Huh? Oh, you mean the Hotel del Coronado." Grinning at Britta, she said, "Hey, did you just get here? You must be my partner."

*Partner? We are partners?* "Uh, what is your name?"

"Teresa Evans. You can call me Terri." The petite woman with red curly hair and dancing green eyes was a head shorter than Britta but just as well-muscled, especially her upper arms and thighs.

Britta's forehead creased with bafflement, but then she shrugged. The man with the red face had mentioned this being their first day, so Britta's failure to recall her partner's name might be understandable.

"And you're Britta Asado, right? I was told that my swim buddy would be the foreign exchange officer from the Norse navy."

*Since when do I need a "buddy" to swim? And since when does the Norselands boast its own knave-he . . . whatever a knave-he is?* Britta could understand what these strange people were saying in a strange tongue, but the odd words here and there were a puzzle to her. She was about to tell the woman her last name was Asadottir, not the shortened Asado, but then decided she liked the sound of it.

"Where are we?" Britta asked.

The woman eyed her even more curiously. "Coronado, California. At the special forces training compound. Trying out for the new team."

*Ah! A military training area.* Britta nodded her understanding, even though she did not understand one bit.

"We were told last night that the Norse officer, Olga Svensson, had rung out before even arriving. She apparently eloped with her boyfriend, right? Good thing you were available for a last-minute replacement."

"Yea, 'tis a good thing," Britta said quickly. Until she got her bearings, she figured it was best to blend in. "I was just a mite muddleheaded from hitting my head."

Terri laughed. "I thought it was your bottom you hit, not your head."

Britta laughed back. "Both."

"Do you know Olga very well?"

*Olga? Oh, that Olga! Nay.* "Of course."

Terri gave her a questioning look, waiting for her to elaborate.

*Think quick, Britta. Make up a story.* "Sweet Frigg! Olga ever was the fey one, dancing from one man to another. But when the lustsome Gunnar cast his wicked eyes her way, well,

Olga did not stand a chance. When given the choice of serving her country or serving her man, she chose—"

"Her man," Terri finished for her with a laugh. "Wicked eyes will do it every time."

"Yea, but 'tis more than that with Gunnar. He has word-fame for his impressive . . . endowments. A manroot the size of a gourd . . . a big gourd." She spread her hands apart to show just how big. *By the runes! Where do these ideas come from? Mayhap I have a gift for lying.*

Their attention was diverted then by a man down below who took hold of the ropes and scaled them with surprising agility up the wall, over the top, and down again to demonstrate how it should be done. "That's the way, girls. Easy as Friday night hooking," he said, winking at one of the women closest to him.

"You oughta know. It's the only tail you get," a woman shot back.

Another man yelled to a nearby woman on the ground, "Hey, Sanchez, yer so small, if we tied a string to yer ankle, you'd be a kite. Ha, ha, ha! Why dontcha fly on over and ring out?"

The woman named Sanchez said something in a language Britta could not understand. It was not English. But she suspected the words were foul, as evidenced by the widened eyes below.

*Good!*

Down below, the men continued to yell orders up at her and Terri, something about getting their sorry arses down the ropes so they could move to the obstacle course.

*Hah! I would think this rope wall is obstacle enough.*

"Yo, GI girls, wanna jump? I'll try to catch you." One of the men leered up at her and Terri.

Another yelled, "Hey, honey, want me to come up and hold your hand?"

The chieftain, whose face was now purple, nigh screamed, "Either come down or ring out. Make up your friggin' minds."

"Those guys are jerks, aren't they?"

Britta nodded, figuring that jerks must be comparable to crude, lust-filled males, which they definitely were. All men were, for that matter. "Yea, just because they have dangly parts somehow makes them think they are superior."

Terri laughed. "I know they're trying to get us to quit. None of them want women in the SEALs, but dammit, I'm not going to give them the satisfaction."

"SEALs?" Britta homed in on that one word. She had heard of SEALs afore. They were an elite military force in a far-off land. "Dost mean we are in Ah-mare-eek-ah?"

The other woman's forehead creased even more. "Are you okay? The sun is hot. Maybe you're getting sunstroke."

Britta shook her head. *Nay, I just fell off a cliff, am suffering from the world's worst ale-head, must needs avoid my father and his hirdsmen who want naught more than my sword dew on their blades or my maiden blood on a husband of their choosing's cock, and then I might just find out if I am dead or alive. Being hot is the least of my concerns.*

Then Terri said, "Oh, my God! Who is that? What a hunk!"

"A hunk of what?" Britta started to ask as she swung one leg over the top and was about to descend back down the rope wall. She glanced beyond the side of the sandy arena where a man was approaching with fire in his blue eyes . . . eyes she would recognize anywhere. Gesticulating wildly, he stopped to talk with another man who was laughing so hard he held his sides.

It was the lout, the very same loathsome lout who was responsible for all her troubles. Well, not all. But enough. Zack-hairy the Pretty Boy. He was a hunk, all right. A hunk of trouble.

*Oooh, I am going to give him a piece of my mind . . . if I ever manage to get down off this bloody damn rope wall.*

That was when she slipped, causing the rope wall to shake even more than it had been, and all twelve of the women climbing up and down the wall fell to the sand with a thud, shrieking with dismay. Most of the expletives were aimed at her.

"You women are the most clumsy dingbats I have ever had the misfortune to meet," the chieftain sputtered. All the other men were laughing instead of helping the women to their feet or checking for injuries. Chivalry must be dead in this country. "Somebody is going to pay for this fiasco, ladies."

And he gazed directly at her.

# Chapter 3

**Kiss me, baby . . . and that's an order . . .**

Zach was stomping his way from the bachelor officers' quarters to the grinder after having changed into his PT clothes: khaki shorts, a blue T-shirt with gold trim and the SEAL emblem, and heavy socks folded down and over the tops of his boondockers.

The grinder was a blacktopped area used for a structured regimen of hard physical workouts. Almost totally surrounded by buildings, some two-story, it resembled a penitentiary yard, which was not totally without intent, he supposed.

Along the way he ran into Cage and Merrill "Geek" Good, the Beaver Cleaver of Navy SEALs. Zach was explaining his new assignment to them and enlisting their help.

Suddenly, there was a communal scream by about two dozen female voices as the women fell clumsily off the cargo net. This was followed by a series of squeals, groans, expletives, and at least one woman bursting into loud sobs.

He started to shake his head at the sorry examples of what

the government expected them to turn into rough, tough military babes. But then he was blindsided, big-time.

On a day in which one disaster after another had piled on him, like NFL tackles on a quarterback, he was now faced with the biggest disaster of all.

Britta.

Among those women was the one woman who'd rebuffed him . . . the one woman who was like a thorn in his heart . . . or ass. Pick one. The implications were staggering, and they were hitting him like thousand-pound dominos. Whack, whack, whack!

*Oh, my God! Britta is here.*

*Sonofabitch! Now, I have a thousand-year-old girlfriend to contend with. Ha, ha, ha.*

*Well, not really a girlfriend, but she would have been. Eventually. Probably.*

*Shit! She looks as if she's baited for bear . . . and I'm the big ol' grizzly.*

Zach couldn't help but grin at the picture he saw. For an eleventh-century, six-foot-tall, Viking warrior goddess kind of gal, Britta sure did look fine in a perspiration-dampened drab green T-shirt, nylon running shorts, and beat-up boondockers. The Navy had probably dismissed the idea of white T-shirts for the women because once sweaty they would become, well, wet T-shirts. Which might give the male instructors inappropriate ideas, ideas that were always close to the surface. Her blonde hair was pulled off her face into a single, straggly braid that hung down to the middle of her back. Her legs were sinfully long, giving a guy—this guy, anyhow—some really vivid ideas. Her breasts were nicely rounded; they gave him ideas, too. Even with sand on her face and her rump, she looked good enough to eat. And he meant that literally.

Unfortunately, Britta didn't regard him in quite the same way. The first thing she did was shove him in the chest.

He didn't budge. "What are you doing here, honey?"

"Do not honey me, Zack-hairy."

His grin at her mispronunciation of his name did not amuse her.

"What am I doing here? How do I know? You tell me."

"Well, I did sort of pray for you to come here and help me out one night, but I was drunk and didn't know any better."

Britta didn't even crack a smile. She ought to join Lean Mean's frowny-face club.

"You wish-prayed me here?" Her voice was so shrill, he hit the side of his head with the heel of his hand to make sure an eardrum wasn't broken. "For what purpose?"

"Uh, to babysit." The second those words were out of his mouth, he wished he could take them back.

"Babysit? Are you barmy? You actually thought I, a trained warrior, would play nursemaid to your whelp?"

"Well, I did mention that I was drunk, didn't I?" He flashed her one of his too-innocent smiles.

She was obviously in no mood for humor or flirtation. "And your wife? Did she wish-pray for me to be a nursemaid, as well? By the by, you told me you were unwed, you slimy fornicator. Didst think of your wife on those numerous occasions when you attempted to get me in your bed furs?"

"Uh, I'm not married." *Oooh, boy! Another slip of the tongue.*

Britta threw her arms up in disgust, which did amazing things to her breasts. "Why am I not surprised? Dost have any idea how like my father and brothers you are? How many other children do you have, on how many women?"

Zach drew himself up straight, suspecting that comparison to her father and brothers was not a compliment. "There are no others." *That I know of.* "Listen, we need to talk . . . in private. Stay here."

He walked around her and went over to one of the low platforms surrounding the grinder. Instructors stood there to oversee the exercise evolutions. "Master Chief Uxley, you are relieved of this billet. I'm here to take over."

"About time, asshole." Master Chief Frank Uxley, better known appropriately as F.U., was one of the more obnoxious members of SEAL Team Thirteen. A good soldier but a speed bump on the evolutionary superhighway.

"Yeah, I can see you've been doing a bang-up job so far, dog breath."

Close to a hundred women—dirty, battered, and panting like warhorses—stood about fifteen feet away. They were the sorriest class of trainees he had ever seen.

"So, you hittin' on one of the trainees already?" Uxley inquired in his usual snide manner, motioning his head toward Britta, who had come up behind him. "Can you say sexual harassment suit, big boy?"

"Go away, Uxley. I'll take over now."

"My pleasure. Think you can handle a big 'un like her? If not, I'll be glad to lend a hand."

Before Zach had a chance to answer, Britta picked up Uxley by the waist and tossed him into the sand. Uxley was fairly short—only five-nine—but he was built like a bull. He had to weigh a solid hundred and sixty. Standing over him, hands on hips, Britta said, "Be forewarned, Chieftain, I am a Viking warrior, more than you ever wagered for in your flea-bitten life. Dost still think you can *handle* me, knave?"

At first, there was a stunned silence. Then Zach turned to the group and yelled, "Ah-ten-shun!"

Everyone stood in rigid formation, hands at sides, chins forward. Except Britta. He turned to glare at her. At first she balked, but then she went over to stand in line. All of them ignored Uxley as he got to his feet, cursing, and headed toward the Naval Special Warfare Center—or NSWC. He would no doubt file a complaint against Zach.

*Welcome to the club, buddy.*

"I am Lieutenant Zachary Floyd, the assistant commander of this first class of WEALS. These two gentlemen . . . ," he said, pointing to his two buddies strolling toward them, ". . . are Petty Officer Justin LeBlanc and Ensign Merrill Good." He'd enlisted them to help him. He also introduced the other instructors standing around.

Zach saw the flicker of astonished recognition on the part of Britta toward his two fellow SEALs and vice versa. They'd all met before in another time and place.

Cage and Geek were grinning like fools as they gave little waves to Britta, but at least they kept their fool mouths shut, except for Cage muttering to Zach under his breath, "You are in *such* trouble, buddy," and Geek muttering, "I can't wait to see how you wiggle out of this one."

"Now, each of you identify yourselves," Zach urged the ladies.

One at a time, they did so till they came to Britta, who announced proudly, "Britta Asado." Her real surname was Asadottir. She glared at him, as if daring him to disagree with her shortening of her name.

*Not bloody likely. She'd probably punch out my lights.* "Petty Officer LeBlanc and Ensign Good will take over for a short time. Ms. Asado, come with me to the command center. There seems to be some missing . . . paperwork."

Luckily, she followed his order, and he took her not only into the building but into a basement storage room. He slammed the door and turned on her. "What the hell are you doing here?"

"What the hell are *you* doing here?" she countered. Lifting her arms, she pushed errant strands of blonde hair off her face. The gesture caused her breasts to press against the thin fabric of the T-shirt.

*Pssssh!* Like a deflating balloon, every logical thought in his brain shooshed out under testosterone overload. Finally, he shook his head like a wet dog. "You've got to ring out. I'll take you over to do it right now."

"And then what?"

*We could sneak off to the nearest motel, where we can have wild monkey sex. Maybe. Or maybe not.* "What do you want to do?" He wasn't about to suggest babysitting again, or wild monkey sex. Besides, with her attitude toward him, she would be a bad influence on his kid, who had a bad enough attitude already.

"What are all those women doing out there?"

He waved a hand airily. "It's a new experimental program for females. Like SEALs, but different. They'll be called WEALS."

"Like wheels on a cart?"

He laughed. "No. It stands for Women on Earth, Air, Land and Sea."

"Female military?"

"Yeah."

"Good. 'Tis what I want to do."

"No, no, no! You don't understand. This program is going to be brutal. Absolute torture."

"Dost think I cannot endure hardship?"

"I didn't say that." *Not exactly.*

"You wish-prayed me here. If I do not become a wheel, you are responsible for me. Dost want that responsibility?"

"Hell, no, but—"

"You cannot have it both ways. Ah, do not trouble yourself, lout. I will take care of myself. I will be a wheel, but, Holy Thor, I hope no one intends to roll me down a hill or attach me to a wagon, especially with this ale-head."

He laughed again. "Britta, we don't have much time. I don't think you understand what has happened here. You, my dear, have traveled through time one thousand years." Folding his arms over his chest, he waited for her reaction.

It was quick in coming. "You. Are. An. Idiot."

"Believe it or not, that's what happened. Same thing for all of Max's family . . . the Ericssons and the Magnussons." Max was the SEAL nickname for Torolf Magnusson. "They'll tell you that if you meet them. And Hilda, too. Not to mention Geek and Cage and JAM."

"Yo, Pretty Boy!" Cage yelled from an upstairs stairwell. "Haul ass, buddy. Lean Mean is lookin' fer you."

Okay, convincing Britta about time travel would have to wait. Hell, he wouldn't believe it either. Wasn't sure he did even now. "Let's make a deal here, honey. You ring out of

WEALS, and I'll find a way to send you home to the past."

"Nay, let's make this deal, *honey*. I do not ring out of WEALS, and you learn to live with the fact that I am to become a woman warrior in your land."

He bit his bottom lip to keep from making a derogatory remark.

"You are not aware of this fact—not that you would care—but my father wants me wed to one of his evil toads, or dead. I have been hiding in a nunnery for more than a year. There is no reason for me to go back."

*Britta? In a nunnery?* He clapped a hand over his mouth to keep from saying something he for damn sure shouldn't.

Suddenly, her face brightened as something seemed to occur to her. "Didst say that Hilda is in this land?"

He nodded. "She and Max are married. In fact, they have a son named Styrr, named for her father. He's a little over one year old."

"That is wonderful. See. One more reason why I should stay."

"I could take you to her. She runs a kind of women's shelter."

"So you can dump your responsibility for me on Hilda? I do not think so."

"Britta, you have no clue what torture you're going to have to endure to get your body in shape." *Although, truthfully, I like your body just the way it is.* "And I'm going to be one of the task masters wielding that whip." *Whips? Hmmm.* "Do you think you can take orders from me?" *I can think of a few that might be fun.*

That last question seemed to give her pause. The stubborn wench! "Orders regarding military matters?"

*Well . . .* "Of course."

"Yea, I can."

"So be it." He threw his hands up in the air with resignation. *It's your funeral, honey.* "Here's your first order. Come over here and give me a kiss."

She laughed. "Still trying to seduce me, lout?"

"Oh, yeah!" He backed her up against the wall and nuzzled her neck.

She tried to twist away.

Which gave him better access to her neck. He gave the inner whorls of her ear a quick lick.

She gasped.

"I've missed you," Zach said.

"Liar."

"I wish."

"You wish, why?"

"I don't want to miss you. I have enough problems in my life right now without falling in love."

That one knocked her speechless.

It knocked him speechless, too.

Which gave him the opportunity to swoop in and lay his lips on hers. And, man, she was so sweet. Just like he remembered.

With a moan, she opened her lips to his kiss, and he took advantage, deepening the kiss, tasting her.

Suddenly, she went stiff as, uh, let's say, his you-know-what and shoved him in the chest. "You tricked me," she accused.

"I did?"

"Yea, you did," she said, glancing down to see her nipples sticking out of her T-shirt like pointy sentinels. Quickly, she glanced up at him to see if he noticed her condition.

He did. Hell, his you-know-what was also sticking out like a sentinel of a different sort.

"You use your charms—tempting words and wicked fingers—to bestir wicked yearnings in me. But you will not succeed. I would fain stay here than return to my other life, and it has naught to do with you."

Zach liked the fact that she considered his words tempting and his fingers wicked. And he *really* liked those wicked yearnings he was stirring up. Good signs, both, in his opinion.

As she opened the door, about to storm off, presumably

back to the grinder, he called out to her, "Just for the record, Britta, I kissed you for one reason, and one reason only."

She paused, turning back to look at him. Her brown eyes were huge. Her full lips were rose red from his kisses.

"Because I wanted to," he told her. "And I'll probably do it again. And again. And again. And—"

She was gone, but his words echoed after her. Heaven was just a few smooth moves away, he promised himself. Just a few tastes of his well-honed seduction techniques, and she would be his. It was arrogant of him to be so self-confident, but he had years of success with women under his belt . . . so to speak.

Just then, his cell phone rang. He flipped the lid on the second ring, still smiling about Britta, when he noted his home phone number on caller ID. His smile disappeared.

"Pretty Boy, you will not believe what your kid did now. You know that stash of condoms you used to have in your bedside table?" It was Omar, who must have been back from the hospital, helping Madrene, bless the man.

"Uh-huh."

"Let's just say, a few of your neighbors are about to have heart attacks because of the water balloons pelting their windows."

Forget heaven. It was more likely that hell was just a few steps away.

### I know how to make you feel better, baby . . .

It was the end of the day . . . well, end of the afternoon, though it felt like the longest day of Zach's life.

He'd already showered and changed, prepared to go home for the day. There would be another team of instructors taking over the evening run on the beach for the WEALS class.

But then he noticed Britta standing on the grinder. All alone.

Even though he'd advised the stubborn woman to ring

out, over and over and over, he had to concede that this first day of exercise had to be even worse for Britta, who was not only in a strange place but in a different frickin' time. Today's evolutions hadn't been as difficult as first day for first-phase BUD/S, but they'd been damn grueling. A lot of men broke under less.

And much of the pain had been delivered by him, a regular Marquis de SEAL.

The other women and some of the instructors had left for the chow hall across the Strand highway. He'd thought Britta went with them. Apparently not.

She was leaning against a device made of logs that SEALs had long ago aptly dubbed the Dirty Name. Perspiration covered her from her scalp, which had to feel itchy, to her toes, which probably pinched by now in her nasty boondockers. She pretended to be relaxing but probably couldn't move. If experience proved true, every muscle, bone, and sinew in her body ached, even her eyeballs.

"Are you all right?"

Britta did not even open her eyes. "Nay, lackwit, I am not all right. Didst come to gloat?"

He thought about telling her that the correct way to address an officer was "No, Lieutenant Floyd, sir," but only for a second. "C'mon." He tried to take her hand.

She shoved his hand away with her fist.

*Beware of women with fire in their eyes.* "A fist? You going to punch me, or something?"

"If I unclench my fingers, I might collapse."

*Oh.* "You can't stay here, sweetheart."

"Why not?" She must be tired if she didn't argue with him about not being his sweetheart.

"Because you'll be performance dropped in a flash if the commander or F.U. sees your condition. Unless you want to go ring out?" *And be my babysitter.* He added that last hopefully, to himself.

She opened her eyes and looked as if she actually would like to punch him. "I will not quit, Zack-hairy. And if anyone dares attempt to drop me, they will find just how hard I can drop them." Then she seemed to notice something about his appearance. "Why is your hair wet? And your clothing clean? You even smell good . . . like mint, whilst I smell like a randy goat." Her eyes narrowed with suspicion. "You have bathed," she accused him as if he'd committed some heinous crime.

He laughed.

Now her fists resembled claws.

He made sure he wasn't within clawing distance. "Okay, if you're not going to quit, how about a shower? A nice hot shower should make you feel better."

She sighed. "I know what a shower is. There were several in that amazing bathing room in the women's sleeping chambers. We were shown around after the noon meal. I would love a shower."

When she did not move, Zach raised his eyebrows at her.

"I cannot move," she admitted. "My knees and elbows have locked."

"Oh, baby."

"Why dost thou refer to me as baby? I am no baby."

"It's an endearment, like darling, or sweetheart, or hot stuff."

"That is ridiculous." She put a hand to her forehead. "I am not hot."

*Wanna bet?* While she was pondering how ridiculous he was, he put his right arm around her waist and arranged her left arm over his shoulder so that her body weight was leaning on him.

"Whaaaat?" she screeched trying to escape his hold.

"I'd pick you up and carry you, but someone in the command center might notice. Then both our asses would be in a sling."

"I have not the strength to fight you now or ask how two of our arses could be put in a sling, but this is all your fault."

"You said that before. How do you figure?"

"When I stood on that cliff with Sister Margaret, drinking her famous mead—"

"Margaret's mead." He hooted with laughter.

She flashed him a scowl of annoyance for his interruption. "—I intended only to fake my death, not to swish through time. Not that I believe I have actually time-traveled."

"So how is this my fault?"

"I was content with my life afore you meddled."

"Meddled?"

"Yea, you came sniffing at my woman's fleece with sweet words and stolen kisses, tempting me."

His grin was full-blown now. "My nose was nowhere near your . . . woman's fleece. Believe me, I would have remembered that. And, oh, baby, did you say I tempted you? Whoo-ee!"

"Have a caution, rogue. Continue to make mock of me, and you may find my boot planted betwixt your thighs."

He glanced down at his crotch. "I love it when you talk sexy to me."

She rolled her eyes.

"Back to that temptation business . . . ?"

"You started a fire in my loins . . ."

"Whoa, whoa, whoa. First woman's fleece, and now there was a fire, and I didn't know about it."

"The fire did not ignite till you were gone."

"Isn't that always the case?"

"After you, your comrades-in-arms, and Hilda left The Sanctuary, I was no longer satisfied with life there. I made the mistake of trying to live a normal life outside the walls."

While she talked, he led her, limping, toward the building on the other side of the grinder. It was closer than taking her to the women's quarters or the chow hall. "This is the strength training and rehab facility," he explained, turning the knob, then kicking the door open before easing her inside and propping her against the wall. "Get lost, Peterson," he ordered the young newbie SEAL who was lifting free weights.

Surprised, Peterson dropped the weights to the padded floor and said, "Yes, Lieutenant Floyd, sir," before scurrying away.

Zach locked the door after him, then turned to her. "We only have an hour at most before someone comes banging on that door. Can you take your clothes off yourself, or should I do it for you?" *Please, God, let one good thing happen today.*

"Huh?" Britta would have stiffened with outrage at his suggestion if she weren't already stiff as a pole. "Do not dare."

He grinned. "Sweetheart, there's one thing you will learn here, if nothing else. Never, *never*, dare a Navy SEAL." With those words, he picked her up, carried her over his shoulder into the large communal shower room where a half dozen showerheads stuck out from the tiled walls. Before she could squirm out of his embrace, he turned on one of the faucets. With the water pelting her face and body—his body, as well, for that matter—he made quick work of removing her shirt and shorts, leaving her in standard-issue Navy female underwear: cotton bra and panties. Most women eventually used their own undergarments, but Britta wouldn't know that. And, yes, he knew what Navy women wore under their uniforms, thank you very much.

A niggling voice in the back of his brain—the one he usually ignored—warned that removing a trainee's clothing was treading a fine line between being helpful and sexual harassment.

He stepped back out of the range of the shower spray, watching with fascination as Britta's underwear turned transparent under the water. It would probably be polite of him to look away, to not gawk at her practically nude body. Good thing he'd lost his politeness gene. Polite people missed the best opportunities. "Beautiful," he murmured, "abso-fucking-lutely beautiful."

"Is that a compliment?" she asked, eyes closed.

"Oh, yeah."

Britta was tall, probably six feet to his six foot three. There wasn't an ounce of fat on her body, except maybe those full, pink-tipped breasts, which begged to be licked, or her high, curved butt, which also begged to be licked, but she was not model thin. No, her shoulders were wide, and muscles delineated her arms and abdomen, belly and thighs.

At any other time, Britta probably would have been uncomfortable—or spitting mad—under his scrutiny, with him kneeling on the tiles, removing her boots and socks, with his face practically touching never-never land. But the hot water, while soothing her sore body, was distracting her, as well.

"Someday you're going to look at me like that," Zach said, handing her a bar of soap.

Peeping at him through wet lashes, she asked, "How?"

"Like you're having an orgasm."

"Orgy-as-him?"

"Never mind. Want me to help lather you up?"

"Are you daft? Nay. Go away."

"Not a chance."

"Stop ogling me."

"Not a chance." He was leaning against the tile wall, watching her. Her underwear was plastered to her magnificent body, and he felt his blood thicken and pool in his groin with delicious torture. His balls were heavy and begging to burst.

Coming out of her trance, Britta loosened her braid, then ran her fingers through her blonde hair. Finally, she seemed to notice his scrutiny and gave him back an equal examination, her brown eyes widening at the bulge in his shorts.

He shrugged. "Can't help it, baby. You are one hot mama."

"Crude troll!"

When she was sufficiently clean, Zach turned off the faucet and picked her up again. This time she'd gotten her energy back and struggled hard, still to no avail.

"Keep squirming, honey. You're making my hard-on very happy."

She stopped immediately. Hard-on must be one of those universal language things.

Carrying her into the next room, he stepped up to a large

tub filled with gurgling water. "The whirlpool is going to feel too hot at first, but it's the best thing for those sore muscles." When he eased her into what must seem like boiling water, she tried to rise, sputtering her indignation, but then she relaxed when she realized that the water was actually soothing. In fact, she murmured, "Heavenly!"

Soon he returned with a clean T-shirt, shorts, and socks, similar to what she'd had on before. She made him turn around while she put them on. Once she was dressed again, he took her by the hand. "I'll walk you to the chow hall."

When he unlocked and opened the door, they both got a big surprise.

Standing there, arms folded over his chest, was Commander MacLean sporting the world's biggest frowny face.

"Lieutenant Floyd, they oughta gold-plate that dick of yours and put it on display at Ripley's. You surely have a death wish. And you, Ms. Asado, surely you can't think that the way through WEALS is paved by this guy's overused cock."

Zach was about to object to MacLean's crudity, not to mention his mistaken notion that they'd been doing the deed.

Britta gasped. "You missay . . . I take exception to . . . ," she began.

But MacLean put up a halting hand at both of their sputtered protests and said, "Since you two are so fond of each other, maybe you'd both like to work out together tomorrow. Let's say, oh four hundred for surf appreciation."

"Surf appreciation" was a SEAL exercise meant to be hated, not appreciated. It involved the icy waters of the Pacific Ocean, where victims were required to sit, arms locked, in water up to their shoulders as waves crashed over them. It usually only lasted six minutes, but it felt like six hours. Occasionally they were ordered to run into the waves, then run back to shore where push-ups in shallow water were de rigueur. Each time the body lowered, the person would be covered with water.

"And Ms. Asado," MacLean added, stepping around them and walking into the room, then returning with Britta's bra and panties dangling from each forefinger, "could these be yours?"

Britta glared at Zach.

MacLean glared at Zach.

Zach was in deep shit, even deeper than before, and now he'd dragged Britta down there with him.

Could life get any better than this?

### MEMO

**From: Captain Lenore Feldman**
**To: Commander Ian MacLean**
**Subject: WEALS**

**Discourage flirting. Article 83b.**

# Chapter 4

**Beer: A clueless man's answer to any of life's problems . . .**

Zach was sitting at a table, sipping suds, in the Wet and Wild, an off-base bar that catered to SEALs and other Navy personnel.

It was early, so the usual nighttime crowd wasn't around. No band. No sprinklers at the entrance to wet the female T-shirts. No horny men, well not too horny yet. And no wild women. Mostly old or married fuddy-duddies on their way home. Like him. Except he was only thirty-two, and he sure as hell wasn't married.

He checked his watch for the fifth time since they'd arrived. It was only five thirty, but he needed to relieve Madrene pretty soon or Lean Mean would be after his butt. He wasn't worried about any immediate danger to Madrene or Sammy. Hell, his town house had been made more secure than a virgin with a chastity belt, and more help was on the way. Nah, it was his kid who worried him. The boy had more than earned the nickname Sammy the Snot after only two weeks in this country, and he was probably revving up his engines to pull more mischief on him the minute he got home. He had news for the brat. He was in a foul mood. One false move, and he was wrapping him in duct tape, especially his mouth.

His buddies, Cage, Sly, and Jacob Alvarez "JAM" Mendozo were sipping suds, too, and grinning at him. Geek, their resident genius on the team, was on base trying to teach some four-star generals how to use a computer. Omar was at home nursing a bruised shin, on top of his prior bruised hamstring. Slick was in a Malibu court trying to fight his ex-wife's latest effort to empty his bank account. Max was on liberty for two weeks while his wife Hilda opened her new women's shelter up near Hog Heaven, a motorcyclists' trailer park, of all things.

"What?" he inquired at their continuing grins.

"It's jist hard ta believe, *cher*, that a player like you could be so . . . domesticated." Cage, named for his Cajun heritage, enjoyed poking fun at him. They all did.

"I am not domesticated," Zach protested.

"Oh, yeah? What time do ya have to be home, Mr. Pussy-whipped . . . I mean, Kid-whipped?" Sly asked. Sly was a big black dude who once modeled tighty whities for *Esquire* and other hoity-toity magazines.

"A half hour ago." He grimaced as the truth hit home.

They all gave him a pitying shake of their heads.

JAM, who used to be a Jesuit priest, or at least he had studied in a Jesuit seminary, wasn't any more sympathetic. *Too many years of yours truly rubbing my sexual conquests in their faces.* "You are so screwed. You've suddenly got a kid, you're on the Taliban shit list, and now a thousand-year-old girlfriend shows up. How lucky can one guy get?"

*That's all I need, a reminder that an eleventh-century Viking woman has landed in my lap. A sexy-as-sin Viking woman, thank you very much.*

"Were you really nailing a female tadpole in the rehab center on the first day of training? And what the hell is this thousand-year-old reference?" Sly asked. Sly hadn't been with them on that ill-fated trip to Norway.

"Even fer you, first day hanky-panky, thass remarkable," Cage observed. "Talk about!"

"I wasn't nailing anybody." *Although the thought did enter my mind.* "I was just helping Britta to shower and get rid of first-day kinks."

"Kinky. Did ya say kinky?" Cage grinned at him.

Zach stopped talking when he realized his buddies were all smiling and that his explanation was more incriminating than what had actually happened. Besides, he couldn't think about Britta right now, or he would go crazy. "Back to my problems with Sammy, they should soon be over," he said. *I hope.*

"How do you figure?" It was Sly getting his digs in now.

"My lawyer is handling the Afghan government and U.S. legal process proclaiming Sammy my son. My dad is hiring professional bodyguards to keep the kid from being kidnapped. And Geek is helping me investigate boarding schools."

"Boarding school for a five-year-old? That is cruel." It was JAM speaking, but the others nodded their heads in agreement. "I was sent to seminary when I was twelve, and that was painful. He's only five."

*Five going on fifty.* "What else can I do? I'll be back on active duty soon, and I can't just leave him with a babysitter for weeks at a time."

"Dum-dum-de-dum," Sly sang.

"Do y'all smell weddin' cake?" Cage added.

"Whaaaat? Marriage? Are you two nuts?"

"Listen, mah friend. If ya get hitched, ya have sex whenever ya want and a resident babysitter. As my maw maw usta say, 'Ya gotta jump the fence iffen ya wanna taste the berries.'" Cage had a thing about hokey Cajun sayings, which he attributed to his grandmother but probably made up himself.

"That makes absolutely no sense. And I'd like to meet the woman who would want that job." Actually, he'd already offered it to Britta, sort of, and she hadn't been interested.

"I don't know," Sly said. "There are a lot of chicks who would love to park their Jimmy Choos under your bed."

"Not anymore."

"Who's Jimmy Choo?" JAM asked, frowning with confusion. "Why would a woman want to put another man under Pretty Boy's bed?"

"Shoes. Jimmy Choos are shoes, you moron. Dontcha know anything about fashion?" Sly jabbed JAM in the arm.

"Apparently not," JAM said, jabbing him back.

"Back to my plan. I've got to get out of this WEALS instructor billet. ASAP. Arsallah, Sammy's grandfather, is one of the worst tangos in al-Qaeda. He pretends to be all religious and Allah-be-praised in public, but he's the bastard who beheaded those Marines last week."

"Why does Arsallah want the kid?" JAM asked. "I mean, under normal circumstances, yeah, I could see a grandfather wanting his own blood kept close to home. But these fundamentalist Muslims would consider him an infidel, wouldn't they?"

Zach nodded. "I suspect this is all just a power play. The Ugly Americans steal our children, that kind of thing."

"Reminds me of that Elián González case," Cage mused. "Remember the Cuban kid whose Miami family wanted him to stay here, but his dad wanted him back with him in Cuba?"

Zach nodded again.

"I might be able to use my situation to draw Arsallah out of his hiding hole. I can't do that when I'm teaching misguided women how to do jumping jacks."

"You'd use your son as bait?" JAM was staring at him as if he were lower than a snake's belly.

"No, knucklehead, I wouldn't use Sammy. He would be in deep hiding by then."

"We'll do whatever we can," Sly said, "but in the meantime you've got to keep your nose clean. Do jumping jacks till your balls are in shell shock. Otherwise, you're gonna be leadin' females off to war, buddy."

He nodded.

A waitress walked up to the table and put a hand on Zach's shoulder. "Want a refill, Pretty Boy?"

He peered up over his shoulder at Maudeen. "No thanks, honey. Gotta leave soon."

"Hiiiii, Maudy darlin'," Cage drawled, his voice dripping with innuendo.

"Go screw one of your gators, redneck boy," she snapped.

They all laughed.

Maudeen was a five-foot-two bundle of sexy curves and a smile that would light a black op sky, not to mention a mouth that could turn a sailor's tongue blue. She was also the ex-wife of a world-class spouse abuser and was a single mother of twin toddlers. She was trying to get a teaching degree. Sexual harassment wasn't a word in her dictionary; she just gave back as good as she got with the horny sailors who hit on her.

"How's that education loan coming?" he inquired, patting the hand that still rested on his shoulder.

"Great. Thanks for recommending that counselor at San Diego State."

After a bit more chitchat, Maudeen left, and he turned back to the table where all his buddies were gawking at him. "What?"

"Do you know how many men have been trying to get in Bawdy Maudy's pants this past year?" Sly asked.

"I haven't been anywhere near Maudeen's undies."

Cage made a snorting sound of disbelief. "Didja notice, *cher*, that she dint ask any of the rest of us if we wanted a re-fill?"

"Oh." He shrugged. "She probably forgot."

"Earth to clueless Navy SEAL," Sly remarked. "Maudy has had the hots for you from the get-go."

"Probably," he admitted. No false modesty here. Attracting women had never been a problem for him.

"What a shock to see Britta on the grinder today!" Good ol' JAM to the rescue, changing the subject.

"Tell me about it!"

Zach, along with JAM, Cage, Max, and Geek, had fallen into the most bizarre situation two years ago. They'd been on a reproduction Viking longship on some godforsaken fjord in Norway when they somehow landed in the eleventh century. Yeah, yeah, it sounded insane. It had been. While there for a few weeks, they'd defeated some tango named Steinolf, Max had met Hilda, the love of his life, whom he brought back to the future with him, and Zach had fallen for the infamous Britta the Big, whom he'd left behind. Or so he'd thought, until today.

"I don't understand," Sly said. "How do you all know this Amazon babe?"

Every one of them shifted uncomfortably.

Sly narrowed his eyes. "Is this tied into that crazy-ass trip you guys took to Norway?"

*Oh, yeah!* "Sort of."

He and his buddies never talked about the experience. If they didn't analyze it, they could pretend it never happened. Plus, they'd all find themselves strapped to a table in a mental hospital or under some scientist's dissecting knife if word got out. At the very least, they would be living in a bubble. Instead, they chose to believe it had all been a communal bad dream, a hallucination.

But now there was Britta, bringing it all to the forefront again.

"What're you gonna do about Britta?" JAM asked.

"Why should I be the one to help Britta? Why not you guys?"

" 'Cause yer the one that chased her tail twenty-four/seven two years ago."

"Really?" Sly appeared skeptical. "I've never seen Pretty Boy chase a woman before. Wish I'd been there."

"It wasn't pretty, especially fer *Pretty* Boy." Cage ducked the pretzel Zach threw at him.

"I called Max and Hilda and left a message on their answering machine. I'm sure he and his family will be able to do something to help Britta . . . uh, transition," he told them. "In the meantime, I'm just going to play it by ear."

"Or by ass," Sly contributed.

"Transition, my ass!" That was Cage's opinion.

"In other words," JAM interpreted, "he doesn't have a clue."

Zach stood and tossed some bills on the table, preparing to leave.

A group of six Navy nurses, still in uniform, sat down at a table nearby and placed orders for hot wings, a pitcher of beer, and an extra helping of celery sticks with blue cheese dressing. He'd forgotten that tonight was wing night.

"Hey, Sheila," he said as he passed their table. Then he greeted the others, "Candy. Fran. Dot. Beth. Wanda."

He heard JAM mutter behind him. "Frickin' unbelievable!"

"He's like a chick magnet," Sly responded.

"I'd lak ta have a few of his leftovers." Cage sighed with exaggeration.

As if any of the SEALs had trouble getting dates!

And, yeah, he knew all of these women, but it was Sheila he knew best. They had shared an incredible night making love in the sand following a beach party a few years back after having drunk about two gallons of Dirty Gin. The most memorable image in his mind of that night was Sheila showing him her new breast implants. They had looked like bleepin' torpedoes. God bless silicone! He wouldn't mind picking up where they'd left off, though why he hadn't made a move since then, he had no idea.

Well, yes, he did.

Britta.

He'd stopped calling lots of women because he'd been hung up over Britta for a long time. Maybe it was time to get back in the game.

But just then, his cell phone rang. The caller ID indicated it was his home phone.

*Uh-oh!* "Hello."

"I wanna go home," his five-year-old son screamed.

Zach held the phone away from his ear. "You don't have to yell. Besides, you *are* home."

Sammy said a really bad word, for a kid, something about mother-something dickhead, meaning him, he supposed, and he heard Madrene in the background say really bad words for an adult around a kid, something about "bloody damn spoiled rotten bratlings and fathers who tup way too many wanton ladies." Sammy did tend to bring out the worst in people.

"I wanna go to my real home."

"What happened this time?"

"The witch," he started . . . *witch* being the name he reserved for Madrene, who took none of his crap, "she made me eat grass."

"It was a salad," Madrene yelled out.

"Spinach." Sammy's voice held all the disdain a five-year-old could muster.

He laughed to himself. He wasn't too fond of spinach himself.

"And white worms."

"Bean sprouts," Madrene corrected.

"And she hit me just 'cause I pissed in her cat's dish. Then she hit me 'cause I said her cat looks like a fat hairy hog. Then she hit me 'cause I tol' her you prob'ly screwed five hundred women and didn't even remember my mother. Then she hit me just 'cause I farted in the grocery store."

"I did not hit you, you snotling. I just swatted your little arse with my palm." It wasn't like Madrene to lose her temper like this around Sammy. It must have been a particularly bad day.

"And what's with this Scary Larry guy?" Sammy continued. "He looks like he eats little kids for breakfes'. Shiiit! What kinda father sends a scary monster to watch his kid?"

Zach had to smile. Wilson could be a little, well, scary, even to adults. The man never smiled, and he had strange grayish green eyes that sort of looked through a person, like ice.

"And I don't need no watchin' anyways. I can take care of myself. I been doin' it for a long time."

*Oh, yeah! Six months is a long time. And you weren't alone, kiddo. You were with good ol' grandad.*

He heard shuffling sounds then as Madrene took the phone from Sammy.

"You best come home *now*, you lustsome knave, or I will be paddling your arse, too," she said, banging down the phone.

Zach headed off then for home and the madness that had become his life.

### Children are a gift? Says who? . . .

Samir lay in his bed, eyes scrunched shut, arms arranged at his sides, like a corpse, pretending to take a nap. It was a trick his cousin Taj had taught him one time, 'cept they had been pretending to be dead in case the Evil Americans attacked.

He still could not get used to the idea that he was part American. Did that mean he was evil, too?

*Maybe, praise Allah, my father will forget some of the things I did today if I "sleep" long enough.*

Despite his protests, he knew Zach was his father. Even before he'd been shown photographs by Grandmother Floyd—or Nana as she'd told him to call her—he'd known the truth. His Grandfather Arsallah had slapped him every time Samir reminded him that he was half-American, whether it be the color of his eyes, or a slip into the English language, or mention of his mother, whose name was not allowed to be spoken. Because of the way his grandfather treated him, his uncles and cousins felt free to treat him just as badly, or worse.

*A bastard, that's what I am. Don't matter what my father says 'bout me bein' his son. I'm just a dirty little bastard. I don't care if no one likes me. I don't care if my father likes me.*

Sometimes he wondered why his grandfather wanted him back so bad. He'd never acted like he cared when Samir had been there.

And his father would be giving him up soon. Samir knew better than to get too close. He knew he was on his own. He had been for a long time, even when his mother had been alive. She'd said she loved him, but most times she paid more attention to her fighting pals than she did to him. She died on his birthday.

"Sammy."

It was his father opening the bedroom door. Samir shut his eyes tighter and braced himself for the slap or punch that was sure to come. Or even worse, a whip. Oh, he hoped it wouldn't be a whip.

The mattress shifted as his father sat down on the bed. "You've had quite a day today, haven't you, kiddo?"

Samir was confused. Why wasn't his father yelling? Why was his voice so soft? A trick . . . it was probably a trick. *I am not going to talk. If he thinks I am asleep, he will go away. I hope.*

"Why do you do all these snotty things?"

*Because I like to?*

"Do you want me to think you're bad?"

*I am bad, bonehead. Didja forget I'm half-American?*

"I'm thinking about taking you to a psychiatrist. That's a . . . uh, head doctor."

*Oh, no, you don't. No one's cuttin' up my head.*

"There's got to be some reason why you're acting out like this. I can't believe you would want to go back to your grandfather."

*Where else would I go?*

"As far as I can tell, you weren't treated very well in his camps."

*What do you know, Mr. Pretty Boy? Where were you when my mother died? Where were you when my grandfather's men killed my nanny and dragged me into the desert?*

"You do know that your mother wanted you to come live with me, don't you?"

*Why is he talking? Why isn't he hitting me? That's what everyone does when I do something bad. Even when I don't do anything bad.*

"Are you testing me? Trying to see how far you can push me before I explode? Ah, I can see by the flickering of your eyelashes that I'm getting close. Do you want me to explode? Then you can blame it all on me?"

*Explode? My father exploding? Yeech, I don't want any guts on me. What's that name for what happens when a body explodes? Oh, yeah. Pink mist. That's just what it looks like, too.*

"I'm running out of people to take care of you when I'm at work. I don't want to send you away, but I'll have to if you don't shape up."

*See. Only two weeks and he's ready to send me away.*

He heard his father sigh heavily before saying, "I'm hungry. I'm thinking pizza, Pepsi, and a video game before bed. But you're probably too tired to get up. Maybe I'll save you a cold piece for breakfast. Unless you would prefer more spinach salad."

*Pizza . . . my favorite! He's gonna eat my favorite food while I'm sleeping. What a pig!*

Samir cracked open one eyelid. His father was already headed toward the door.

"Okay," he said, sitting up.

He expected his father to smirk when he turned around or say something nasty, but all he said was "Okay what?"

"Okay, I'll eat if I have to."

"Have to?"

"I'm not playin' that *Dora the Explorer* game, though, I'll tell you that right now. What do you think I am? A baby? I wanna play *Firing Range: Blood and Guts.*"

His father laughed. "In your dreams, short stuff."

Samir made a face, but he kinda liked it when his father

called him "short stuff." He said it in a way that Samir thought other fathers might talk to their sons. "How 'bout *Ghosts and Ghoulies*?"

"Give me a break."

"I still hate you."

"That's just great.

Samir stood and adjusted his shorts.

"What's wrong?"

He continued to pull at the waist and legs of his shorts. "Those stupid Superman underpants you bought me are stuck in my crack."

"Way more intel than I need to know! What did you wear when you were in Afghanistan?"

"Nothing."

"You're kidding?"

"Nope. When you gotta piss in the middle of a firefight, you don't wanna take the time to pull your underwear down."

His father's jaw dropped open.

"What do *you* do in the middle of a battle?"

"I wear underwear, and don't you dare try going commando around here. You'll give Madrene a heart attack, and the little girls in the neighborhood will be filing sexual harassment lawsuits."

"That witch needs a heart attack. An' all the little girls round here are nothin' but whiny-ass split tails." Anyhow, that's what his uncles called most girls.

"That was not nice."

He shrugged.

"Were you around actual fighting very much?"

"There was always bombs and guns goin' off. Bam-bam-bam-bam-bam! Never knew when one would hit. A bomb hit our house one night. Ka-boom! Then we lived in a cave."

His father stared at him as if he might be thinking about hugging him.

Samir ducked around him and started down the stairs.

"Kid, you're gonna be the death of me yet."

# Chapter 5

**A woman can have multiple WHAT?...**

Britta was facing a difficult dilemma, unlike any she'd ever experienced afore.

Should she attempt to go back to the place where she'd fallen off the cliff, knowing it would mean a life in the nunnery? If reversal of this bizarre experience was even possible.

And if she could go back, should she just yield to her father's demand that she accept wedlock to one of his toadish puppets?

Or should she take up Zack-hairy's offer to deliver her to Hilda and her sanctuary here? That would mean she was depending on another person; she misdoubted Hilda and her women needed her warrior skills here.

Or should she continue to participate in this strange female unit, the WEALS? It would be difficult, but really, it was what she was: a fighter.

Sad of mood, Britta began to think she really had died when she'd gone over that cliff. She just could not credit Zack-hairy's time-travel theory.

But then the paths of destiny were in the hands of the Norns, beyond the comprehension of mere humans. Besides, the Norse culture was an ancient one, steeped in fanciful notions: gods, spells, trolls, giants, dwarves, sea serpents and other fierce creatures, Valhalla with its golden halls, the Valkyries themselves. But this was even more incredible than all the sagas.

*Let tomorrow bring what it will,* she finally concluded.

America was an enchanted land where carriages carried people without the use of horses, where metal structures flew across the skies, where water flowed freely inside buildings, where rooms were lit not by candle or torch but tiny magic wall levers, where women had little cylinders of fiber which they inserted inside their bodies to collect their monthly flows, where women's arses were tattooed, where tiny pellets could be swallowed every day to prevent a man's seed from taking root in a woman's womb.

Then there was the food in this land. So much of it and so varied! People ate here for pleasure, not just to fill empty stomachs. She could love this land for its chocolate alone. Chocolate cake. Chocolate pie. Chocolate cook-hes. Hot chocolate beverage. Chocolate sweetmeats, known as fudge. Chocolate iced cream.

And, finally, it was a land of freedom and equality for all, even women. A land where women could have multiple orgy-as-hims, whilst a man could only have one. *Finally some fairness in this world!*

When Zack-hairy had mentioned orgy-as-hims to her earlier today, she had not known what he meant. She did now. Since then, the women had spoken at length about their various orgy-as-hims. Explosions, splinterings, heated frenzies, shatterings . . . all confusing terms, except for the fact that the women liked these orgy-as-hims. Immensely. Despite being a virgin at her advanced age of twenty and seven, it did not take long for her to comprehend the idea of a pleasure so intense it was like a little death. Apparently these orgy-as-hims were best delivered in the company of a man.

Right now, it was hardly dark, but she and the women who shared her sleeping chamber were all talked out and preparing for bed. They would have to get up very early, but especially her as punishment for fornicating with the pretty lout . . . which she had not even done, let alone have an orgy-as-him.

As the women continued to talk on this subject, Britta said, "By Odin, I vow, I am going to have one of those someday."

They all looked at her, dumbfounded, then laughed. Her partner, Terri, gave her a one-armed hug and whispered in her ear, "Honey, you and I are going to have such fun!"

She hoped so, because thus far her experiences had been far from fun, more like torture.

Britta wore a long sleeping shirt of Terri's, which would have hung down to Terri's calves but hit midthigh on her. In the front was a painting of a frog with its middle finger raised. It must be some odd hand signal in this country.

Terri had been a physical education teacher in a school for young adults, called a high school. She had been a gymnast in her earlier years. Gymnasts were people who bent their bodies in various contorted ways, for what reason Britta had yet to fathom. Although she had now seen thirty winters, Terri claimed to still be able to do a "kick arse backbend," which was apparently a much-to-be-desired talent in this country. Britta vowed to try this, as well.

"Now dish, girl, what's with you and that pretty SEAL? Man, I wouldn't mind him putting his boondockers under my bed." Terri waggled her eyebrows at Britta.

The other three ladies in the room—there were four pallets in each sleeping chamber—agreed.

Donita Leone, a tall, slim woman with ebony skin and tight black curls like a cap, said, "I heard that Lieutenant Floyd is the poster boy for hottie Navy SEAL . . . you know, screw everything with breasts.

Britta gave Donita her full attention. "I have noticed that Zack-hairy and some of the other leaders carry the title lewd-tenant. Is that not an odd choice of naming? Though perhaps not so much for the pretty boy with the lewd fingers."

"Huh?" Donita said.

Terri had told Britta earlier that Donita was an aging—at twenty-seven—Olympic swimmer who had suffered a great scandal years ago when she was accused of "drugging," whatever that was . . . a form of cheating. The Olympics were something like the old Greek games. The charges had been proven false but never lived down. In recent years, she had been diving from a high board through fire into a pool of water at circus events. That was something Britta would like to see.

The fourth woman, Marie Delacroix—a Cay-jun, just like Cage, whom she'd met afore—summed up the questions for everyone. "Did ya do the deed with the pretty bad boy, *chère*?" Marie, a Marine, was the only one of them with previous military experience, except for Britta. She had good reason to want to fight terrorists, her father having been one of those affected by a bombing that took place at some far-famed towers.

Britta was fairly certain she knew what "the deed" meant, having been accused of and punished for it by the commander. "I did no such thing, even though the rogue has tried repeatedly."

"Whoa! You knew Lieutenant Floyd before?" Terri asked.

"I met him and some of his comrades-in-arms—Torolf, JAM, Geek, and Cage—two years ago." Britta was unsure of her position here in America, and some instinct warned to be careful how much of her past she exposed. "In the Norselands."

"And he tried to jump your bones?" Terri asked.

"Nay, he ne'er tried to hurt me."

Terri shook her head as if Britta were unbelievable. "Did he try to make love with you?"

"Yea, Zack-hairy did try to lure me to his bed furs. To no avail."

"Why, for heaven's sake? Are you . . . were you . . . married?"

"Nay."

"Engaged?"

"Dost mean betrothed? Nay."

"Are ya gay, darlin'?"

"Betimes. But what has my gaiety to do with anything?"

Marie giggled and said, "I don't think she understands. Gay means a lesbian, a woman who loves women, not men."

At first, Britta frowned. Then she understood. She had heard of such women but never met any. "Nay."

"Don't you think he's good-looking?"

"Hah! He is so good-looking he makes my bones ache."

"Holding out for love?"

"Of course not. At my advanced age, I am long past dreaming of those softer sentiments." Well, that was not quite true. Betimes Britta ached deep in her shuttered soul, but she had learned to ignore the pain.

"How old are you?"

"Twenty and seven."

"Good Lord! And you think that's old?"

She shrugged. "I concede, I am not yet in my dotage. Still . . ."

"Is it like a religious thing? No sex before marriage?"

She shook her head. " 'Tis not that, precisely. What bothers me most about Zack-hairy . . . Lewd-tenant Floyd . . . is that he waves his manpart hither and yon. I suspect he has swived an army of women. Just like my father and brothers. They tup anything in a gunna that walks by with no care for the many by-blows they produce."

They all nodded their understanding.

As they bedded down, dark now, conversation evolved to other subjects, mostly involving the grueling days ahead in WEALS. Cushioned by these newfound friends, Britta resolved to make this, WEALS, her new life path. And as for the soul-ache, she had survived worse.

### I like your sugar, cookie . . .

*"I don't know but I been told,"* the women running on the beach sang out lyrics in what Britta had come to recognize

as grody jody calls. What an odd military they had in this country that sang as they performed battle exercises.

*"Navy men are mighty bold,"* Terri, her swim partner, called out the cadence.

*"Navy men are mighty bold."* The rest of them repeated the refrain.

The five SEAL instructors who were leading the WEAL program wanted them to sing traditional Navy running songs, but the women had their own ideas.

The men, damn their hides, barely broke a sweat on these long runs. In truth, she suspected they slowed themselves down so the women could keep up. The whole time the women ran their hearts out, the instructors trotted amongst them, making both encouraging and harassing remarks.

At first it was difficult to sing and run, huffing and puffing, at the same time, but Britta along with the other women—those who had not yet "rung out"—were better able to perform various tasks at the same time after several days of brutal torture of their bodies, that torture taking the name of PE, or physical education.

The only one unaffected by the excessive running was the nimble-footed Donita, who ran like the wind, her long legs nigh flying over the sand. The rest of them staggered by the end of the ridiculously long runs. "For strength and endurance," their instructors kept saying. Britta girded herself with resolve to persevere, but she was not sure how much longer she could endure the pain. Leastways, for now, she could run and sing at the same time, and that was no small thing.

*"But Navy women are better than gold."*
*"But Navy women are better than gold."*
*"They can fight and they can flirt."*
*"They can fight and they can flirt."*
*"They can make a grown man hurt."*
*"They can make a grown man hurt."*
*"Men can grin and strut their stuff."*
*"Men can grin and strut their stuff."*

*"But women know they ain't so tough."*
*"But women know they ain't so tough."*
*"Boobs and butts, latex rubber . . ."*
*"Boobs and butts, latex rubber . . ."*
*"Turn bad ol' SEALs to drooling blubber."*
*"Turn bad ol' SEALs to drooling blubber."*
*"Sound off, one, two . . ."*
*"Three, four."*

There was a small satisfaction in seeing the five men gape with astonishment at the lewd lyrics, then scowl their opinion. She especially liked making the pretty SEAL scowl.

Britta had been in this strange land only four days, and she was more tired, sore, bewildered, and angry than she'd ever been in all her twenty and seven years. It was so bad she half wished she could return to St. Anne's Abbey.

But, nay, she would run and then run some more if that was what it took. Bad as this was, she had no wish to return to the life she had back at the nunnery. Which was no life at all.

Commander MacLean, the leader, was married to Madrene, though Britta could hardly credit a strong-willed woman such as Madrene tolerating this arrogant man. Right now, said arrogant man raised a halting hand for them to stop running and yelled, "Time to cool down before lunch. A little surf passage should do the trick."

The women groaned, knowing that their being nigh drowned in the pounding waves of the cold ocean water would soon prove punishment, not relief. If that were not bad enough, when they all came staggering out of the water, it was to see the five brutes staring at their drenched bodies to which their scant clothing clung. Men! They were the same everywhere. Show them a bit of breast or arse, and they became like rutting beasts. Especially that one master chieftain called F.U. who'd taken a particular delight in tormenting her.

"How about some sugar cookies now, snuffie?" Chieftain F.U. said, standing practically toe to toe with her. "Snuffies are the lowest rank in a training compound, in case you didn't know, and you ladies are the lowest of the low."

In her weakened condition, Britta could barely take her usual pleasure in noting that he was a half head shorter than her. That was no doubt why he picked on her. "Petty Officer Asado, why don't you show us how it's done?" Petty officer was the rank given to all the women who had not come up through their regular military. They would have assigned her the same rank she had in the Norse navy, which she had learned was a type of military. Instead, she'd demurred and accepted the same as the others. Besides, being an officer in WEALS gave no special privileges. All of them were treated alike. Badly.

She flopped down to the beach for the exercise called "sugar cookies" and rolled over so that the sand clung to her skin, her clothing, her hair, and in fact some unmentionable places that sand should never be. The other women followed her example.

"No, no, no, sweetheart. Put your face in it." Chieftain F.U. placed a boot on the back of her neck so that sand went into her mouth, her nose, and her eyes. Then he used the same boot to tip her over to her back. "Now wiggle your hips a little, like a worm. That's it. Pretend you're getting nailed, and you like it a lot. Oh, yeah, baby. Now you look just like a sugar cookie. Good enough to eat."

Britta did not see the humor in his joke, but several of the men laughed.

"That'll be enough for now," she heard someone say behind her.

"Says who?" Chieftain F.U. asked.

"Says me, maggot. Pick up your gear and meet me and the commander in his office at eleven hundred. And, ladies, at ease. You can go to your rooms to shower before lunch, then report back to the grinder at oh two hundred." Under his breath, the same man murmured something about "inappropriate conduct for an officer."

It sounded like Zack-hairy coming to their defense, but it was hard to tell with all the sand clogging her ears.

Moving clumsily to a sitting position, she blinked repeatedly, trying to get the sand out of her eyes. Unable to see, she took hold of the hand stretched out to her. When she was standing, she saw that it was indeed Zack-hairy, and for once he was not grinning.

"You exceed yourself, lout, coming to my defense. I can protect myself."

"Bullshit!"

"Crude oaf!"

"Come on," he said, still holding on to her hand and leading her back into the water.

"No," she squealed, trying to pull out of his grasp, to no avail. "No more salt water."

"It's the best way, honey."

Still, she resisted.

But then he lifted her in his arms, something the brute persisted in doing, though Britta could not recall any man but him being able to do it since she'd gained her full height at sixteen winters. "Here we go," he said, tossing her into an enormous oncoming wave, which hit her like a stone wall, knocking her over, then tumbling her head over heels, repeatedly.

Britta was not sure how much more punishment she could take, especially from this man. Now she had salt water in her mouth and nose and ears and throat, in addition to the sand. She was on her hands and knees crawling toward the beach minutes later, coughing, too tired to raise herself to a standing position.

Zack-hairy sat on the beach, arms resting on raised knees, watching her. If he dared to laugh, *she* might very well pick him up and dump *him* in the ocean. And she could do it, too, in the mood she was in.

When she got close to him, she managed to maneuver herself into a sitting position. And, actually, Zack-hairy's maneuver *had* helped remove the sand from her eyes and some of it from her other body cavities.

She was too exhausted to chastise him, like she usually

did, but she could look. The man was too pretty for words. He matched her in height and then some. Wearing only running shorts—they had special garb for running in this country—he was slightly brown all over, except for his blond hair. His muscled chest. His long muscled legs. His perfectly sculpted face.

*And I look like a drowned rat.*

"Why don't you just ring out, Britta?"

"I am not a person who quits."

"Yeah, but you didn't sign on for this, honey."

"Do not call me honey or sweetling or dearling or any of your other slick words."

"Sweetheart, you don't need to go through all this," he said, totally ignoring what she'd just said.

"Yea, I do. You have to understand, I have no skills in the womanly arts. I cannot do needlework or run a castle household. I can count the times I have been in a scullery. Herb gardens look like weeds to me. As for babies, they are stinksome, and their cries make me wince. But give me a bow and quiver, and I can shoot an arrow straight and true. Swordplay comes second nature to me."

"Your point?"

"A warrior is all I am or can ever hope to be. I cannot fathom where I am or why, but I am where I should be. For now. Leastways I have work here." Which she no longer had in the past.

"I could find you work." He reached over to pick a bit of seaweed out of her hair, and she slapped his hand away.

"Hah! As a nursemaid for your bratling? I declined that offer afore." She suspected the job would involve more than care for his child, more like care for the father . . . in the bedsport. And she was ill-trained for either job.

"I could take you to Madrene's family."

"You have told me there is danger in others knowing of my supposed time travel. Wouldst have me expose them to danger?"

He shrugged. "They've time-traveled, too. Yeah, the more

people associated with them in this crazy business, whatever it is, the greater chance someone will find out. And, believe me, there is danger in that. Still . . ." He shrugged again. "There are Ericssons and Magnussons all over the place, but mostly at Blue Dragon Vineyard."

"And what, pray tell, would I do at a vineyard? Watch the grapes grow? Methinks that would be nigh as bad as being in a nunnery."

"You were in a nunnery?" The expression of incredulity on Zach's face was a mite offensive.

"I told you that afore, half-wit. What? You think I have no godly traits?"

"I didn't say that." He laughed. "But, sweetie, a body like yours would be wasted in a convent."

"Why dost say such things? I have long become resigned that I do not have the womanly traits that draw men. Frail, soft-shinned, sweet-tempered women are the ideal, and I am none of those."

"Are you kidding? You're the hottest woman I've ever met."

Now it was Britta's turn to stare at him with incredulity.

"Slick words! There has not been a woman I've met in the past four days who does not pant after your overly hand-some form. And you well know of your allure."

To his credit, he did not pretend false modesty. Just nod-ded, then replied, "That was not just a line, if that's what you're trying to say. When you were watching me being hit on by those women, did you see me show any interest in any of them? Except for you?"

"Please, do not insult me by claiming celibacy."

His face flushed.

"You are renowned for your excesses, Zack-hairy."

"My name is Zach or Zachary."

"I prefer Zack-hairy. It has a crude sound to it." She glared at him for changing the subject.

Laughing, he stood and pulled her up beside him. They started to walk across the training grounds.

"I'm not a saint, Britta. I like women. I like sex." He smiled as if to include her in his likings. "I like the things I fantasize about doing to you."

She shook her head at his persistence.

"So you like it here?" Another change of subject.

"I cannot say that I like this country. It is confusing, and nay, do not start telling me of time travel again."

"What other explanation is there?"

"I do not know."

"Me and the guys have decided it must be a miracle performed by God."

"Your One-God. Hmmm. For what purpose?"

"We haven't figured that out yet." He laughed. "Is there nothing you like about this place and time?"

"Oh, there are many things I like. What woman wouldn't like indoor water and privies that flush away wastes, or wonderful boxes that wash and dry clothing? And they do not even have to hunt for their game here. Didst know they have ointments in this country that control odor under the arms?" Before he could answer, she lifted an arm and said, "Smell me."

He grinned like she'd made some great jest and leaned down, sniffing. "Yep, your pits smell just great."

"Some of the women even take all the hair off their nether parts," she confided to him. "Do men do that, too? Are you hairless *there*?"

"Some men might, but not me." He was still grinning.

"If I do get sent back to the nunnery, there is one thing I would like to have experienced afore I go," she said with a sigh.

"What's that?"

"I do not want to be tupped, by you or any other man . . ."

*Holy Thor! What a lamebrain way of starting! Mayhap I should tighten my loose tongue afore I embarrass myself.*

"Okaaaay. Not that I asked to, uh, tup you . . . lately."

*It is in your eyes even when you do not say the words, rogue.* She disregarded his teasing words and continued, her flapping tongue out of control. "But . . ."

"But? Oooh, *but* is a very tantalizing word. I think I'm gonna like this. But?"

She hesitated. Now she was really regretting having brought up the subject.

"You don't want to get laid, but?"

*Too late now. Best to finish what I have started.* "But I want to have some of those . . . you know . . . things. And I thought mayhap you might recommend a man."

"Why would I recommend a man for this, uh, thing? Why not me?"

"Oh, nay! Not you! Nay! I need a man with no feelings toward me. Not that you have feelings. I mean . . . oh, forget I brought up this subject."

"Not on your life!"

Her face felt warm and not from the sun, especially since he stared at her with a mixture of confusion and anticipation.

"Okay, let's back up this train, baby. You want me to recommend a man . . . for what *things*?"

"Multiple orgy-as-hims."

"Do you mean orgasms?"

" 'Tis what I said," she snapped.

His grin turned into a full-blown, watch-yourself-wench smile.

**MEMO**

**From: Captain Lenore Feldman**
**To: Commander Ian MacLean**
**Subject: WEALS**

**Women must wear good running bras.**

# Chapter 6

**Come, fly away with me . . .**

Zach was cruising along in his mint-condition red Firebird convertible.

The car had been a gift from his dad seven years ago when he'd gotten the trident pin denoting his acceptance into the hallowed ranks of Navy SEALs. An expensive gift, yeah, but then his father had just renewed his contract with the soap opera *Light in the Storm* for big bucks. In fact, he'd bought his brother, Danny, a frickin' plane and his then-girlfriend a diamond the size of a golf ball.

His dad had many faults, but stinginess was not one of them. When Zach had come in third in the first race of his short-lived NASCAR career, before becoming a SEAL, the old man had given him a custom motorcycle that once belonged to Evel Knievel. His grandfather, on the other hand, who preferred to be called General and not Grandfather, was not miserly, but he believed in a much more austere, military lifestyle. His gift had been an antique gun. Then there was his grandmother, who considered herself the D.C. military hostess equivalent of Martha Stewart. She'd once given him, when he was in college, a set of Egyptian cotton sheets that he was afraid to sleep on because they cost as much as all the secondhand furniture in his apartment. He still had the blasted things. His ever-stylish mother gave him silk underwear and designer T-shirts and gift certificates for facials and pedicures. He'd like to see the day he showed up for a live op smelling of a strawberry facial peel and wearing clear polish on his toenails. When he'd told his mother just that, she'd shot back, "Your pores need a good cleaning, son, and your toenails are disgusting."

*Okaaaay!* His mother never was one to be subtle.

But all that was beside the point.

He was driving in his spiffy Firebird over the Silver Strand that connected San Diego County, via Imperial Beach, with the Coronado peninsula. The weather was balmy on this early evening in September. The view was spectacular. It was Friday . . . enough said! Life should have been good.

But riding in back was a sulking He-Who-Thinks-He's-Too-Big-for-a-Car-Seat, flanked by two laughing SEALs, Cage and JAM, who were egging the snot on. They were all packing heat, just in case Arsallah sent any goons their way.

"Why are you guys tagging along with me? Why aren't you down at the Wet and Wild celebrating Wet T-shirt Friday?"

"We thought you'd get lonely without us," JAM replied.

"I see you every day."

"Besides, I'm lookin' fer new blood to f—" Cage glanced at the kid and saved his butt by quickly amending, "flirt with."

"Any more 'blood' and they're gonna put your you-know-what in Ripley's Believe It or Not."

"You should talk!" JAM remarked.

"Do y'all have a girlfriend yet, Sammy boy?" This from Cage, of course.

"Girls suck," Sammy snarled.

*"Mais, oui,"* Cage drawled, "but thass the bes' part."

"Cage!" Zach cautioned. God, he hated that he had turned prig, but someone had to rein in the guys' language. The kid already knew more blue words than any five-year-old should.

"Ya know what my maw maw allus says, Sammy." Someday someone was going to clobber Cage over his cornball Cajun sayings. "Maybe the girls you've met so far ain't spicy enough yet."

"Cage, you are an idiot," JAM said.

*Great! Now the kid will be calling everyone an idiot.*

"I'm jist sayin'." Cage shrugged and winked at JAM. "A girl without spice is like a gator without a snout."

"Does alligators have snot?" Sammy asked.

"Not snot, kid. Snout," Cage explained, patting Sammy on the knees.

Sammy tried to kick his hand.

"Stop the car. I hafta poop," Sammy announced.

*At least he didn't say shit this time. Maybe I'm actually making some progress.* "You do not," Zach said, studying him in the rearview mirror. "You went to the bathroom before we left the house. Just cut it out, Sammy. You've gotta use a car seat; it's the law. We're not stopping again."

"I don't wanna go to any farty party."

Zach rolled his eyes. "We're going to Madrene's damn— uh, I mean, darn—party whether you like it or not, big shot. And you better behave, or Madrene might just put you over her knee and spank you." She'd threatened it enough times. "Or maybe she'll hug you and kiss you."

Sammy appeared horrified at the latter prospect. "Yeech!"

Another glance in the rearview mirror showed his buddies grinning from ear to ear. The guys were getting a huge kick over his being a father. Who knew he would ever be keeping track of a kid's bathroom habits or watching his language?

He slowed down through the security gate, waiting for

the signal to pass through onto the base. Soon he was in front of the women's quarters. "I'll be back in a sec with Britta."

"Is she expecting you?" JAM asked.

"No, but she'll come."

JAM grinned.

"Man, I'm glad I came," Cage remarked to JAM. "This oughta be good. Better even than oglin' Bawdy Maudy in a wet T-shirt."

Then they both grinned at him.

Pointing at Sammy, Zach ordered, "Don't move."

When he got inside the building, he told the woman sitting at a desk in the entryway, a chief warrant officer, "Can you give Petty Officer Britta Asado a buzz? Tell her Lieutenant Floyd is here to pick her up."

At first, the woman was all afluster. He had that effect on women sometimes, and he wasn't above bleeding it for all it was worth. With that in mind, he smiled.

The woman practically swooned and pressed the button on the intercom, relaying his message. Within seconds, her face turned red, and she told him, "Petty Officer Asado says . . . uh . . . begone."

No way was she going to blow him off now. "Give me that phone."

The woman tried to hold it out of his reach. "Hey, you can't do that."

"Wanna bet?" He took the phone, punched in the same number he'd seen the petty officer use, and said, "Britta, honey, we're going to a party. Either you come down, or I come up."

"Go away, lout. I am tired. I am sore. And I am not going anywhere—"

"You're on liberty for a day and a half, honey. You don't have to muster till Sunday morning." This was the only liberty WEALS were going to have for three weeks. "C'mon, take advantage of the little free time you have."

She said something nasty in Old Norse. He could tell it was nasty by the tone of her voice.

He was already going up the stairs, three steps at a time, with the officer screaming after him, and him yelling "Briiiiitta! Where are you?"

Doors were opening. Women half-dressed, many of whom knew him, called out greetings and hoots of encouragement. When he got to Britta's room, he saw her three roommates—all hottied up for a night on the town, he would guess—but Britta was lying on her cot, propped up on her elbows.

She wore low-riding black jeans that covered about a mile of her legs and exposed a patch of skin around the cutest belly button God ever gifted a female. On top was a stretchy red tank top that matched her red sandals. She was wearing a bra—*Darn it!*—and, yeah, he could tell, even from across the room. He wondered irrelevantly where the modern clothes came from. She was taller than most of the women, which precluded borrowing. He shrugged, figuring they were either from the mysterious missing Norse officer, or God, who was surely responsible for this whole time-travel scenario. But, really, would God dress her in siren red?

Britta had probably intended to join her friends as they went clubbing . . . a prospect he did not like at all for what he considered *his* Viking babe. Despite he and the commander being relatively easy on the WEALS this week, compared to first week of BUD/S for regular SEALs, it must have seemed brutal to them. In fact, there were bruises galore up and down Britta's arms and a half-healed cut on her chin, all of which went with hard PT. Five women had rung out already, and he guessed ten times that number would ring out eventually. The women trainees had no idea how much worse it was going to be next week when the program went into full gear. Yep, Britta had probably fallen to her bed with exhaustion and couldn't get back up.

But hey, he was a SEAL, and a SEAL on a mission never failed . . . or hardly ever. He'd get her up, all right.

Her hair, damp from a shower, was twisted into a single braid that hung below her shoulder blades. Even though the women slathered on sunscreen all day long, they all sported suntans. That included Britta, whose healthy tan contrasted sharply with her pale blonde hair.

Man, she was so sexy she could jump-start a Taliban corpse. If he wasn't already in full-blown, hot-tilt boogie lust with her, he would be now.

"Okay, sweetie," he said, checking his wristwatch, "you've got exactly two minutes to get up and haul ass before the MPs get here."

"Why me? There are women aplenty smitten with your charms. Ask them."

"I think you're smitten, too. You just don't wanna admit it yet. Playing hard to get, that's what you're doing." He waggled his eyebrows at her.

"Methinks you need a good dose of meekness, you misguided clodpole."

He still stared at his watch. "One minute."

"Desist!"

The three woman gawked at her as if she was crazy. Usually he didn't have to coax women to come with him, let alone order them around.

He sighed dramatically. "Do I have to carry you again, Britta?"

"Oh, please," Terri said, putting a hand dramatically over her heart, "let me watch you carry her."

"You would not dare," Britta seethed.

"Tsk-tsk-tsk! Haven't you learned not to use that 'dare' word with me?"

"Not that it matters, but where do you want me to go?"

"A beach barbecue. Cage and JAM and my . . . uh, kid are going with us."

"Bar-be-cue?" Britta frowned her confusion.

"An outdoor feast," he explained.

"I am not dressed for a feast."

"You're dressed fine for this feast. Look at me."

She did. "You look ridiculous."

"What? You don't like my shirt?" He wore khaki cargo shorts, a Hawaiian shirt, and flip-flops. He thought he looked pretty damn good.

Some of the other women agreed, even those peering into the room from the hallway. One of them said, "Be still, my heart."

Britta rolled her eyes. Then she let out a whooshy exhale of surrender and rose to her feet. "I give my free consent. You may take me to the feast this one time, but you must promise not to touch me."

*Are you kidding me?* "Sure, baby, sure."

"Let me help you put some makeup on, hon," her swim partner, Terri, offered.

"She's fine the way she is," Zach said.

He took Britta's hand and led her from the room, her three roommates gawking after them. Avoiding the front stairs, they went down the back way and around the building to the front. When they got to the car, he noticed Cage and JAM laughing wildly at something his son had said. There was a female MP leaning against the car, laughing, too.

"Hey, Georgine," he called out.

Georgine shook her head at him, as if he was pushing the bounds of what she could overlook.

He winked his thank-you.

Britta snorted. "Yet another of your women?"

Opening the passenger door, he indicated that Britta should get in.

She balked. "What is this?"

"A Firebird."

She dug in her heels even more. "You expect me to put myself inside a fiery bird and fly away? You really are barmy."

"We won't be flying. In the sky anyway." He grinned.

"And do not try to seduce me with your charm, either. I am uncharmable today."

He grinned some more and put a hand on her upper arm to guide her in.

"Unhand me, troll." She slapped his arm.

"We don't have time for this." He picked her up, placed her on the seat, and buckled her in, all before she had a chance to whack him a good one.

Resigned, Britta turned and greeted JAM and Cage, then said, "And who is this princeling sitting on his very own throne?"

Zach buckled himself in and turned as well. Actually, Sammy did look like some kind of self-important royalty on a throne staring down at all his underlings.

Cage quickly put a hand over Sammy's mouth before he could tell Britta what he thought of his "throne."

"That's my son, Sammy," Zach told Britta.

Sammy, whose mouth was now free, corrected him, "Samir Abdul Hassim Arsallah."

"You forgot the Floyd in there, big boy." To Britta, Zach explained, "His last name is Floyd, same as mine."

"He looks just like you," Britta observed.

"Huh? He has different hair color," he pointed out.

She shook her head. "Doesn't matter. He's the spitting image of you. Pretty."

So many people called him Pretty Boy, he no longer considered it a compliment. But he kinda liked Britta thinking he was pretty. Sammy, on the other hand, could be heard sputtering his outrage in the backseat. The last thing he wanted was to look like his father. Or pretty.

"Where are you taking me?" Britta asked as he pulled out.

"You'll see. It's a surprise."

"I hate surprises."

"You'll like this one."

"That's what you said that time when you showed me tongue kissing."

He laughed and heard laughter behind him, too, and one "Yeech!"

"Well, not as good a surprise as that." He turned to smile at her before returning his attention to the road.

"Dolt!" she muttered.

Britta had to be terrified over this first ride in a car, but she never showed it as they cruised out of the base and toward the Coronado Bay Bridge. Her knuckles were white where she held on to her knees, but brave girl that she was, she never let out a peep.

The Bay Bridge had a high arch in the middle to allow for oceangoing vessels to pass through. When a tugboat let loose with a loud foghorn under them, Britta jumped as far as her seat belt would allow and muttered what must be a Norse curse, something about Thor's bloody toenails.

Out of the relative quiet, Sammy said, "Scaredy cat!" As if he hadn't practically peed his pants the first time he'd heard it. Then Sammy remarked to Britta's back, "You sure are big."

*Uh-oh!*

Britta turned slightly to look back at Sammy.

"Are those boobs for real?"

A stunned silence met his question. Where did the kid learn this stuff? Well, some of it came from the mercenaries that had lived in the rebel camps in Afghanistan. But some of it had to come from TV or Zach's buddies or, okay, himself. He had to be more careful.

Even Cage and JAM had no smart remark to make, or none they were about to speak aloud, and Britta probably didn't even know what he meant.

She soon proved him wrong.

"Dost know what they do with boylings in my country who misbehave?"

Sammy raised his chin defiantly.

"We boil them in oil."

Sammy's chin dropped, and for once he didn't have a quick comeback.

"I think you should apologize, Sammy," Zach said into the rearview mirror.

After a moment, to Zach's surprise, Sammy murmured, "Sorry."

Zach turned on the radio. He wouldn't be able to carry on much of a conversation with Britta, but then she wouldn't be able to hear Sammy's crude remarks.

Britta remained quiet on the half-hour ride while he pointed out various landmarks. And the country music station told her all about cheating hearts, low-down men, and redneck women.

Soon they pulled into the driveway of Mac and Madrene's modest oceanfront cottage. There were a half dozen other cars around, indicating the party was already in full swing.

He got out, then walked around to help Britta, who was struggling with her seat belt, complaining about being a prisoner. Since it was a two-door, the guys had to wait till they were out first to emerge.

"What does that say?" Britta asked, pointing to a banner that had been draped across the bay window in front. She seemed to have no trouble understanding the spoken language here but apparently could not read. Yet.

He smiled and squeezed her to his side. "Welcome, Britta."

"Well, 'tis past time you offered me welcome to your country. And keep your tempting fingers to yourself."

He kept his tempting fingers right where they were, pressing against the bare, warm skin of her exposed waist, and smiled. "Not me, honey. That's what the banner says. Welcome, Britta."

"Huh?"

Just then, Sammy came up to him, having been released from his car seat by one of the guys. Adjusting the matching Polo for Kids shorts outfit Zach's mother had bought for him, complete with its very own mini-golf shirt, Sammy said, "I look like a dork."

"A cute dork," Cage remarked.

"Bite me!" Sammy replied. "Everyone's gonna laugh at me."

"No, they're not," JAM said. "They're gonna pinch your cheeks and tell you what a handsome little fella you are."

The guys were not helping at all, which was probably their intent.

Sammy snarled and narrowed his eyes.

Zach recognized the crafty gleam in the kid's eyes, which presaged his bolting to parts unknown, like the proverbial roadrunner. Quickly, he grabbed him by the belt of his shorts with his free hand, then wrapped the same arm around his waist, lifting him off the ground.

Thus it was that when he emerged at the back of the house, he had Britta tucked against his one side and Sammy tucked on the other side, his little sandals two feet off the ground, his little butt in the air, his arms and legs flailing wildly.

"SURPRISE!" the crowd yelled. And they looked as surprised at the picture the three of them must have made as Britta was at the dozen or so people waiting for them.

There were people in the crowd Britta knew but hadn't seen for years. They'd gathered to welcome her to . . . California. A surprise!

Britta claimed to be okay with where she'd landed in Coronado, but she had to be feeling lost. Zach's heart ached for her. This party had been the only thing he could think of to help her.

"Smile, you two," he told his two human appendages.

Under her breath, Britta said, "I am going to kill you."

"Kin I help?" Sammy asked.

# Chapter 7

**Hail, hail, the gang's all here . . .**

"Good tidings, Britta! Welcome to Ah-mare-eek-ah!"

"Didja bring yer big-ass sword? Ha, ha, ha!"

"Has Pretty Boy lured you into his bed furs yet? Ouch, why did you elbow me, Alison?"

"Give the lady some room, fellas. Remember me, Britta? Torolf. C'mere, Britta baby, and give me a big ol' wet kiss."

"Mind your manners, husband."

"How does The Sanctuary fare?"

"Oooh, Britta, you look hot, hot, hot."

"Forsooth, give the lady room to breathe."

Zachary had released his hold on her shoulders and squeezed her hand, letting her know he was still beside her. For once, she welcomed his presence.

Britta blinked with confusion. Pressing in front of her was a blur of people—men, women, and children—in colorful clothing that nigh blinded the eye. Leastways, colorful compared to her time where drab brown was the norm for common folks. On some women were knee-length gunnas that left the shoulders and legs shockingly bare. Lips were rouged and eyelids kohled.

Other people were adorned with flowered *sherts*, like Zachary's, but also tanking tops and tea-*sherts*, like hers, of all the colors of the rainbow. On bottom, worn by men as well as women, were braies made of den-ham, a popular fabric in this country, as well as short braies that barely reached the knees.

And the noise . . . what a cacophony of shouted greetings! Lively music . . . a man singing of wasting away in Margaret's villa, having only a last shaker of salt, and a woman to blame. A baby was crying, people laughing, all against the backdrop of the roaring ocean waves. There was even a barely stifled sob!

Then suddenly silence, except for the ocean.

Everyone stared at her, smiling, expecting some response.

Slowly, Britta began to take in the scene before her as faces became separate and in some cases familiar.

There was Ragnor Magnusson. A handsome rascal still, who was surprisingly wed to the sister of the WEALS' dour Commander MacLean, who, not surprisingly, stood looking dour beside his wife Madrene. A little boyling sat on his shoulders pounding on his head; it must be the infamous Ivan the Terrible. Madrene held a sleeping babe against her shoulder.

And, oh my gods and goddesses, waving at her over there was her good friend Hilda, though she could barely recognize her in her new attire: white den-ham braies, like her own black ones, and a fluttery long-sleeved *shert* that was nigh transparent, showing underneath the female harness known as a bra . . . in her case, a black lacy one. Her hair was still long but arrayed in wild curls. Standing next to her was that grinning rogue, Torolf, who had a restraining hold on the hand of a squirming child scarce out of swaddling clothes. The boy had Torolf's mischievous eyes and Hilda's silver-colored hair.

Also in attendance were Geek, whom she already knew, and several others she did not recognize, some of whom must be SEALs, and was that Kirstin Magnusson over there? Sweet Frigg, she had not seen Kirstin since they had both been girlings at a Hedeby Althing. She saw Cage slip an arm around Kirstin's waist, which Kirstin promptly slapped away. But she grinned as she did so.

In the background stood an aging Magnus Ericsson, a giant of a man. Britta was tall. Zachary was taller than she. Magnus was even taller still. His long, light brown hair, threaded with gray, was plaited into thin war braids on either side of his face, exposing big ears. He wore a belted tunic and slim braies. Still Viking to the bone!

It was all so confusing . . . and overwhelming. So many people that Britta had thought dead! More than ten years ago, Magnus Ericsson and nine of his eleven living children had supposedly been involved in a shipwreck in Iceland with no survivors. Ragnor had died in battle; everyone said so. Madrene had been captured by the evil Steinolf and sold as a slave in the Arab lands. And her good friend Hilda, surely she had died in that avalanche that even Britta had witnessed; no one could have survived that disaster.

*What is happening? Could it really be time travel? Surely not! But what other explanation is there?*

Instinctively, she stepped even closer to Zachary.

He squeezed her shoulder, kissed the top of her head, and whispered in her ear. "It's okay. Everything's gonna be all right, babe."

"So you say!"

"Behave yourself." He pinched her bottom.

To which she yelped, then shoved his chest.

Startled, he fell backward onto the sand.

Betimes Britta did not know her own strength.

Everyone was laughing as Zachary stood, rubbing his buttocks.

"I did not mean to hurt you," she apologized begrudgingly.

"That's okay. You can kiss it and make it better."

Her eyes widened. "You want me to kiss your arse?"

Luckily, he was the only one to hear that remark. He grinned and said, "Only if you want to."

"You are making jest of me in front of one and all. I did not mean to knock you down." It was as close to an apology as the brute would get from her. But, really, 'twas embarrassing when she hurt people accidentally, one of the disadvantages of her great size. Hopefully, that great size would prove an advantage in the WEALS.

She held out a hand to help Zachary up to stand beside her. A big mistake.

He immediately put his mouth near her ear again. "After the party's over, I'll take you to my place and rock your world," he told her, then blew a hot breath, which slingshotted all the way through her body, arousing even her pores.

She turned fully, brow creased with a mixture of irritation and confusion. His face was mere inches from hers. In truth, she could smell the mint on his breath and feel his manheat. Her traitorous body reacted with pearling nipples and a pulsing betwixt her legs, the usual response of late to this too-handsome man. Even the spot he had pinched throbbed. Next she would be drooling like Hilda's dog Stig, who had been ever randy.

"Orgasms," he explained, waggling his eyebrows.

*Huh? Oh. So, that is what 'rocking my world' means.* "You could try!" she said with more assurance than she felt, then pushed away from him and headed toward Hilda, who was motioning for her to approach. Why had she ever mentioned the subject of orgy-as-hims . . . rather, orgasms . . . to the man? Now he used it against her.

To her back, she heard Zachary say, "Oh, I'll definitely try. Count on it." There was a smile in his voice.

"Lackbrain!" she muttered as she resumed stomping away.

Magnus was the first to greet her with a tight hug that lifted her feet off the ground. "Welcome to Ah-mare-eek-ah, Britta. Is your father still the greedy bastard he once was?"

She had to smile at Magnus's frank manner. "Worse," she answered as he placed her on her feet. "I do not understand." Britta rubbed her eyes with both hands, then looked at the big man again. "I thought . . . everyone thought you were dead."

"Do not try to take it all in right now," Magnus advised. "Give yourself time to adjust to what you will discover is an amazing adventure."

"Amazing, for a certainty," she agreed.

"I came soon as I heard of your arrival, dearling. My wife Angela would have come, but she is busy with a wine festival."

Britta appreciated the welcome.

"Come stay with us," he urged. " 'Tis a confusing time, I warrant. Best you make a home at Blue Dragon till you decide what to do."

She shook her head. "My thanks for the offer, Magnus, but I know what I want to do."

"The military?"

She nodded.

" 'Tis no place for a woman," he grumbled and would have said more, but a red-haired woman stepped up beside him and extended a hand to Britta, then held Britta's hand in both of hers.

"Don't pay any attention to Papa Ericsson. He is still living in the Dark Ages."

"Humph!" Magnus said, walking away to pick up an amber glass bottle, then putting it to his mouth.

"Hi, I'm Alison MacLean Magnusson, Ian's sister and Ragnor's wife."

Aaah, she should have known by the red hair and the resemblance to Commander MacLean.

"I'm in the Navy, too," Alison said. "We need to talk later if you really are serious about WEALS. You'll need some outside instruction, like Ragnor did when he first came here. English as a second language. World history. That kind of thing. I'll give you a buzz."

Britta wondered what she meant. Was she going to buzz by her, like a bee? Although she was able to understand English, some words spoken here were still confusing.

"You do not try to talk me out of my military inclinations?"

"Good heavens, no! Why would I do that? I'd be in the WEALS program myself if I weren't married. And, hey, I saw you give Pretty Boy a shove. Good for you, girl! He's needed a good comeuppance for a long time."

This was a woman Britta could like.

A short time later, after being hugged warmly by those people she already knew and introduced to others, a stunned Britta sat at the far end of the deck, a wooden ledge attached to the keep, talking with Madrene and Hilda and Kirstin. The men were at the other end, watching an object called a grill as it sizzled meat and drinking from the amber glass bottles. Grown men watching meat cook! Ridiculous!

Even more ridiculous, out on the beach some distance away, Britta saw a man being led on a leash by a dog who pulled him hither and yon, then squatted down to deposit his waste on the sand. The ridiculous thing, though, was that the man used a small metal scoop to pick up the leavings and place them in a bag. Then the dog led him off again. What was the man going to do with the dog leavings? What a strange land this was!

Britta and the three women from her past spent an hour catching up on old news, mostly her telling them all that had happened after Hilda left The Sanctuary or how Norstead and Amberstead fared these days. Britta assured Hilda that The Sanctuary still thrived . . . alas, there would always be women fleeing abusive men . . . but not so many as when Hilda had been there. As to the two estates, they flourished under the Ericsson cousins from Norsemandy, Thorfinn and Steven.

"We wanted to talk to you in private," Hilda began, "about the time travel."

Britta groaned her opinion. *That again!*

"There are some things you need to know," added Kirstin, the sister to Torolf, Ragnor, and Madrene. She worked at a school for adults called You-Seal-Aye teaching ancient history, the turn of the tenth century and beginning of the eleventh century. Dark Ages, Kirstin called it, which Britta could understand. Everything was brighter here, including the buildings with their magic lighting.

"Come inside, Britta," Madrene suggested. "Let me show you some things that should convince you that this is a different time." Once in the scullery, Madrene demonstrated a large box that kept food cold and even made ice, another box with fire circles on top that cooked food without flames, and a loud whirring hole where wet garbage was chewed up and washed away. No middens here, apparently. Off the kitchen, there were two more boxes, one for washing clothes and the other for drying them. There was even an object that sucked up dirt from the floor, as if brooms were not sufficient.

Madrene and her husband must have had great wealth, although Britta was not impressed at all by the size of their keep. Compared to Norstead and the nearby Magnusson farmstead where Madrene and her family had grown up, this dwelling would scarce fill the great halls.

After a tour of the downstairs, they went up to Madrene's bathing chamber, where she showed Britta a vast array of woman products . . . flesh-colored face creams, cheek rouges, lip paints, eye kohl. Laughing, the three ladies sat Britta down on the closed porcelain privy and showed her how to use the various items. Soon they had her hair unbraided and spread out in spiral curls. The faint imperfections in her face—she'd had no idea she even had imperfections— were smoothed out with liquid "makeup." Her eyelashes were curled and colored a dark brown, making them appear extremely long and full. And on her lips they applied red lip gloss.

While they worked on her, they talked.

"I do not understand," Britta said. "Oh, I know, I keep saying that, but how did this come about? I fell off a cliff.

One moment I was staring up at that lackbrain Sister Margaret, and the next I was staring at that lackbrain chieftain Uxley."

"Yea, Uxley is a lackbrain," Madrene agreed. "As for me, I was in a harem in the Arab lands—do not ask, it is a long and not very interesting story—when a fierce lightning storm erupted. Somehow, when the storm ended, I was in a cave, still in the Arab lands, but a thousand years into the future. Ian rescued me." She disclosed that last on a sigh.

"You already know I was caught in a mudslide," Hilda said, squeezing Britta's hand in empathy for her confusion. "When I emerged from the mudslide, I was also in another place and time: Malibu. Except Torolf was there with me. The sweet lout rescued me." Another sigh.

"My family was on board a longship, caught in a strange fog," Kirstin revealed. "We landed on a Hollywood movie set."

"Huh?"

"Never mind." Kirstin grinned. "My uncle Jorund arrived on a killer whale, naked, and ended up in a mental hospital. That is the most bizarre of our means of transportation."

"So, you are saying that I must learn to accept that I have time-traveled."

They all nodded.

"It's important that you don't discuss any of this time-travel business with anyone," Hilda warned. "I barely escaped some madmen two years past. They wanted to cut me open and study my innards."

Britta's eyes nigh popped with horror. "Why?"

"Because they suspected I was not of this world, and they wanted to know how I was different," Hilda explained. "Those particular men are not a danger to us, but there will always be others if word gets out."

"*Are* we different?" Britta asked.

"A little bit. At first." Every so often, while Hilda was talking, she would go to the window and scan the beach and deck area to make sure her husband had their son in tow. He did; they, like all the other males, were watching the meat cook.

Madrene's babe slept soundly in his own cradle in the next room.

"'Tis something about the blood," Hilda went on. "But after we are here several months it seems to become the same. Strange, I know, but then this whole time-travel business is strange, is it not?"

*Strange is too small a word to describe this happenstance.* "How many people have . . . um, time-traveled?"

"We do not know precisely. From the Ericsson family . . . Jorund, Geirolf, Magnus," Kirstin said, "plus all of my father's children. You are the only person outside the family that we know of, except of course when Torolf's SEAL teammates went back with him, then forward again."

*More than a dozen! Good gods!*

"Since we do not make our presence known, mayhap there are others out there who do not talk of it as well," Hilda speculated.

Britta's head spun with all the bizarre details. "Why? I mean, why us?"

"Since they could not come up with an explanation, my father and his brothers decided that it must be a miracle, ordained by the Christian One-God."

"I suppose," Britta said dubiously. "Like many of my country, I accept both Christian and Norse religions. I assumed I was here because Zachary wish-prayed me here."

"Really?" Kirstin clapped her hands together with delight. "My father says he was wish-prayed here, too, by Angela's grandmother."

"You know what this means?" Hilda took both of Britta's hands in her own.

"What?" She did not like the sly looks in all three women's eyes.

"You and Pretty Boy are destined to be together," Hilda announced.

"Soul mates," Madrene concurred. "Best be careful; my

father will have you wedded and bedded in a trice if he hears of the wish-praying."

Britta laughed. "Zachary would turn green and run like the wind if he heard you say that. Oh, he wants to . . . you know, 'rock my world,' but just for a bit. Then he will swagger off to wave his dangly part elsewhere."

"Rock your world?" Kirstin sputtered.

"Dangly part?" Madrene put a hand over her mouth to cover a giggle. "I have not heard *it* called such in ever so long."

"Yea, swaggering is what men do best," Hilda opined.

"Or mayhap you were sent to help Pretty Boy with his son, who is more than a handful, believe you me," Madrene offered.

"Hah! I have already declined his offer to be nursemaid to his bratling."

They all laughed, Sammy's wordfame having traveled far.

She stood as they finished working on her. Looking in the mirror over the sink, she scarce recognized the face staring back at her. "Are you certain I do not look wanton with this face paint?" Britta asked, wanting to reach for a towel and scrub it off but not wanting to offend her friends.

"Honey, you looked hot before," Madrene said. "Now you are a hottie."

Britta was not sure she wanted to be a hottie.

They were walking down the corridor leading to the stairs when Madrene asked, "So what was Pretty Boy saying to you earlier that had you turning red-faced, then stomping off?"

Britta waved a hand dismissively. "Oh, he was goading me, as usual. Said he wanted to give me orgasms tonight."

Madrene and Hilda grinned at each other, then looked back at her. Kirstin just blushed.

"And? Are you going to let him?" Madrene inquired.

"Nay." She was not about to tell them that she had brought the subject up to him first. "In truth, I do not really know what an orgasm is, except the women who share my sleeping chamber speak of it incessantly."

"Oh, sweetling, do I have something to show you!" Madrene said, taking her by the hand and winking at the others.

When they reached the solar, Madrene pressed a flat box she held in her hand. Instantly, yet another box, this one the size of a hearth opening but resting on the floor, sprang forth with light.

Britta gasped.

"It's a television," Madrene explained. "I want to show you something. Check this out."

Britta had no clue what Madrene had just said. But then it did not matter.

There were little people inside the box. One of them, a handsome man with brown hair threaded with white, was standing over a body that appeared to be dead. Leastways, the brown-haired man was cutting open the belly of the prone man, blood spurting everywhere. Was he torturing a prisoner? And the women dressed in white at his side had huge breasts that pointed straight out.

"Oh, my gods! Can we not do something? There are four of us, and they are small people . . . dwarves, mayhap."

Madrene, Hilda, and Kirstin all laughed.

"You find humor in torture?"

"They are not real people," Madrene said, patting her hand. "I wanted to show you this soap opera, *Light in the Storm*, so you could see Pretty Boy's father. He plays Dr. Lawrence Bratton on this show."

"He's really good-looking, for an old guy," Kirstin said.

"I hear he has a mistress who is only twenty," Hilda remarked.

"Well, that is just like a man, is it not?" This from Madrene. "Always chasing the young girlings."

"Wait, are you saying that dwarf torturer there is Zachary's father? I must needs console him, even if he is a lout. To have such a monster for a father has got to be a burden."

The three women laughed again. "I'll explain it to you

later," Hilda said, "But Pretty Boy's father is not really in the TV box. He may be an old lecher, but he is not a torturer."

"Forget about that. This is what I really wanted to show you," Madrene said. "My favorite program. *Sex and the City.* I have twenty shows on tape."

Britta had no idea what Madrene had just said, and she did not care because, whoa, different people were in the box now. Naked people. A man, whose buttocks could be seen pumping up and down, and a woman beneath him who was writhing and moaning and then actually screaming. Before Britta had a chance to ask what *that* was, there were yet again different people in the box. Four women, fully clothed, sitting at a table eating, and one of the women was the screaming one. How had she dressed so quickly? And gotten to this other place?

"Whoa, whoa, whoa!" Britta said. "What was that?"

"That was an orgasm, honey," Madrene said, grinning. Kirstin and Hilda were grinning, too.

"It happened so quickly I scarce had time to study the . . . uh, process."

Still grinning, Madrene pressed something on her hand-held box, and the same naked scene was happening again. This time she saw some kissing, too. Hard, passionate kissing. She would bet her best sword there were tongues involved.

Britta felt the same pearling of her nipples and weeping in her woman place as she did when Zachary touched her.

"Who are they?"

"Samantha and Jerrod."

"Do they not have any qualms about doing it in front of one and all?"

"Apparently not." Madrene was grinning, as if she had some great secret. Over and over Madrene manipulated the magic box till they had witnessed the orgasm six times. "How many times can they do it afore needing to rest?"

"Oh, dearling," Hilda said, "those aren't real people. I know how it must seem. We all felt the same way the first time we saw television."

"As for those orgasms . . . I see no appeal in all that writhing and moaning and screaming! Besides, you must admit, the man looked a mite ridiculous with his buttocks in the air. Yea, methinks I will abstain from that particular exercise in torture."

For some reason, the three other women laughed hysterically.

# Chapter 8

**You want to put WHAT on my penis? . . .**

Zach sat on the edge of the low, rail-less deck with Cage on his right and JAM on his left. Max and Ragnor sat on low beach chairs in front of them. Omar and Slick were down at the Wet and Wild.

They were all swigging down longnecks, having been banished by Commander MacLean to a perimeter of no closer than ten feet from his precious grill. They had been giving grilling advice, which had not been appreciated by MacLean.

Sammy was a short distance away, near a sand dune, blowing bubbles that Madrene had given him, thus giving Zach a short breathing period. Zach figured that should occupy him for, oh, say, five minutes. The kid had the attention span of a gnat.

"How's the WEALS program going?" Max asked. All the SEALs had nicknames. Torolf's was Max . . . short for Magnusson.

Zach rolled his eyes.

"We're treatin' them with kid gloves, and they think we're torturin' them," Cage said. "Wait till next week when we start IBSs." The hated Inflatable Boats, Small, were the bane of every trainee who had ever tried to be a webfoot warrior, though necessary in the field. Some considered that phase of BUD/S even worse than Hell Week. "I 'spect we'll have a dozen DORs the first day. That bell'll be ringin' like a Salvation Army Santa. Talk about!"

"And Britta? How's she doing?" Max asked.

"She's holding up," Zach said.

"Holding up what?" Geek asked with wide-eyed innocence as he joined them. Sometimes Zach suspected that Geek wasn't as naive as he pretended to be.

"Get your mind out of the gutter," he snapped.

"Hah! Like your mind isn't there most of the time," JAM commented. He ducked when Zach tried to swat him with his free hand.

"As to your question, Max, the WEALS will train for one year, under less stringent conditions, and have weaker bodies in general . . ." He shrugged. "Would you want one of those covering your six in a black op?"

"Hell, no!" the rest of them said.

"Still, there might be a place for them. No, there *will* be a place for them," JAM, ever the fair one, said. "This country is in antiterrorism mode, and probably will be for the next century. We need every breathing body we can get to help with the good fight."

JAM's defense of the WEALS program wasn't surprising, and he *was* right. This country needed every able-bodied man—and woman—to fight the ever-increasing tangos in the world.

"Besides, I suspect the one-year WEALS program, if it succeeds, is going to end up being a two- or three-year deal, just like SEALs," Zach speculated.

"What's the latest with Arsallah?" Ragnor wanted to know.

"Still making lots of noise. Our government doesn't deal

with terrorists—at least not publicly—but the Afghan government is now claiming Sammy belongs in his native country. And the Department of State is on my tail, too, wanting concessions to avoid alienating the tenuous government there."

"I'm thinkin' it's a Taliban pride kinda thing," Cage said, tugging at the stupid gold loop in one of his ears. "The U.S. representing some imperial warrior kinda monster tryin' ta destroy Afghan culture."

"In other words, a propaganda nightmare," Geek remarked.

"What kind of concessions?" Max asked. Being a fairly new father, Zach suspected that he was more conscious of the paternal instinct. "Surely not a shared custody, because you gotta know, once they get him, they're never letting him come back."

"I know. Ironically, to Arsallah, Sammy is racially impure. I've gleaned this from bits and pieces Sammy reveals. When Arsallah looks at him, he doesn't see half-Afghan, he sees half-American. No blood bond there."

"And worse," JAM added, "Sammy was fathered by a Navy SEAL, number one on the Taliban hit list."

"I don't think they would use Sammy as a suicide bomber, nothing that drastic, but my greatest fear is that they would use him in some political way. Train him to speak against America . . . and me, representing the U.S. military."

"When do those bodyguards hired by your father arrive?" Geek asked.

"Any time now. Plainclothes, of course. Two in Sammy's vicinity at all times until this whole mess settles down."

They all nodded their understanding of the need for protection.

"You making any progress with your son?" Ragnor asked.

"Not much," he answered honestly. "He resents me for not coming for him the instant his mother died. And he resents me for having abandoned his mother, too, when she was pregnant. Not that he says so in those words. In his potty-mouth lingo, he pretty much says, you humped my mother, then left."

All the guys grinned.

"It's not funny."

They still grinned.

"Dickheads," he muttered and took a long draw on his beer, meanwhile checking out Sammy. He was still blowing bubbles, but he was blowing them at some seagulls that were trying to pick a few crumbs left on the beach. The gulls ignored him.

"I'm ready to ditch this party after we eat . . . if MacLean ever gets that filet done. How about a lift to the Wet and Wild?" JAM was speaking to Geek.

"Yeah, I'm in the mood for a little . . . dancin'." Cage waggled his eyebrows to indicate it was more than dancing he had in mind, though the Cajun did love his two-step.

Geek's face turned red. "Sorry. I'm not going in that direction."

"Oh?" Zach said. "Big date?"

He hadn't really meant anything by his question, except Geek's face turned even redder. Geek gave the impression of being sexually inexperienced, but, hell, at his age he was no virgin. So, why the embarrassment? The other guys must have thought the same thing, because they were all staring at Geek.

"I'm helping a friend set up a website," Geek said.

"And *that* makes yer face turn red as boiled crawfish?"

"Could this friend be of the female persuasion?" Max asked.

"Yes, it's a girl. She has this . . . uh, invention that she wants to market on the Internet. I'm just helping her set up the website."

Ragnor, also a computer expert, tapped a forefinger against his closed lips thoughtfully before he inquired, "And the name of this site would be?"

Geek put his face in both hands.

Now every guy in the group was on red alert.

"*Mon Dieu!* This has gotta be really bad . . . or really good," Cage observed.

Geek mumbled something.

"What?" they all asked.

Geek raised his head and glared at each of them in turn before revealing, "It's www.penileglove.com."

There was stone silence, expect for the ocean sounds.

Finally, Cage exclaimed, "Say what?"

And Zach said, "Uh, I think you better explain, Geek. Otherwise, we're gonna think you're putting a glove on your cock at night to keep the little guy warm."

"Bullshit!" was Geek's reaction to that. "Listen, have you ever heard of hand waxing?"

They all shook their heads, except for Cage, who frowned and said, "Isn't that the crap they have in beauty parlors and spas, where people put their hands in warm wax before getting a hand massage?"

*Amazing!* Zach thought. *Where does he learn this stuff?*

Geek nodded, no doubt thinking that would be the end of the interrogation. Not a chance! Not when there was the mention of penises and something warm. "It's sort of a massage kind of thing, like Cage said. You put your hand in the warm wax, then take it out. As it dries, it shrinks and hardens, but not like a face mask . . . more like a tight, formfitting rubber glove. But the neat thing is when you pull it off, slowly, starting at the wrist, it's a really sensual feeling."

More silence as everyone let what Geek had said sink in. Then there was a communal smile.

"No way!" Cage said.

"Hot damn!" JAM said.

"Formfitting? I like the sound of that," Zach said.

"If it was Cage pulling this stunt, we'd just laugh it off," Max said.

"Hey!" Cage said, pretending affront.

"You're right," Zach said. "Coming from Geek, it must be true. Holy shit!"

"You're not saying that you expect men to put their penises in that crap, are you?" Ragnor asked.

"Oh, yeah," Geek said, no longer red-faced, "and Julie's gonna make a mint on it."

"I for one volunteer to be a test subject," Cage said. "Anyone else?"

They all raised their hands.

"Does she want any investors?" This from JAM.

"You can't tell anyone about this," Geek emphasized.

Hah! The Navy SEAL grapevine would have it on the news by tomorrow night. And they'd have more volunteers than the Navy had swabbies.

Still laughing, Zach glanced over and didn't see Sammy at first. But then, he noticed him going inside, to play with Ivan, he supposed.

MacLean, who'd just walked over, told him, "Ivan has a Playskool Viking ship with about a gazillion little Vikings."

"Little Vikings!" Ragnor and Max exclaimed at the same time.

Laughing, Zach went inside.

He didn't find Sammy right away, but he found something else.


**The little people were naked, and bouncing, and, oh, my! . . .**

"Britta," Zachary called out as he passed through the scullery and into the solar where he came to a halt when he saw what they were watching on the box. "What the hell are you guys doing?"

"Watching an orgasm," Britta said, lifting her chin defiantly.

The four of them—Britta, Hilda, Madrene, and Kirstin— were sitting in the solar, still watching the man and woman having orgasms. What did he think they were doing?

"I can see that," Zachary said, then smiled. "Madrene, the boss is gonna kill you if he sees what you have on the tube." Just then, Zachary seemed to notice Britta's face and hair. "Jesus, Mary, and Joseph!"

She was not sure if that was a compliment or not.

"Nay, Ian will not be upset with me for watching *Sex and the City*," Madrene told him. "He knows that it gets my sap rising."

"Way more information than I need to know!" Zachary laughed.

"Why were you calling me?" Britta asked him.

"Oh. I need your help."

"With what?"

The other women chuckled as if they had a pretty good idea what he needed help with. Orgasms, no doubt.

"Sammy," Zachary said.

*Huh?*

"Come on, let's take him for a walk on the beach."

As they walked upstairs, side by side, to get Sammy, she noticed Zachary gaping at her.

"What? You do not like my makeup?"

"I love your makeup. Especially the wild, sex-tossed hair and the red lip gloss."

"Did you just insult me?"

"Hardly. I'd like nothing more than to kiss your sweet mouth till it was red and glossy, just from my kisses."

More pearling and throbbing, just from words now. Britta was beginning to feel like a sinking ship.

**Sometimes heroes were of the female persuasion . . .**

They were walking along the beach at the water's edge, collecting seashells. There were already a considerable number in their pockets.

Almost like a normal family, she thought. *What would it be like to have a husband to love me, and a son of our loins?* What foolishness! That life was not for her. Still, that soul-ache that had beset Britta of late assailed her now.

Zachary took her hand in his as they watched Sammy drop down to his knees in the surf, digging for sand crabs. The giggle that escaped Sammy's lips surprised them both, and Britta realized how rarely the little boy seemed happy.

She glanced at Zachary and saw the smile he'd flashed at Sammy's giggle quickly fade to be replaced by the worry, something that she was coming to realize was the norm when he was with his son. In fact, his gaze continually darted right and left, as if on alert for some danger.

"Why are you so worried?"

"Sammy's grandfather is a world-class bad guy, an Afghan terrorist, and he wants Sammy."

"Oh," Britta said, beginning to understand the danger.

"Arsallah would be nuts to attempt a kidnapping here where entry could only be by air or sea. He couldn't sneak in by land, undetected, with so many people strolling on the beach and Wilson posted out front. Plus there are a half dozen SEALs here to back me up. And we're all armed." He patted a bulge under his flower *shert*. "Still . . ."

Sammy kept putting his sand crabs into a little pool he had dug in the sand, but the water kept seeping into the sand. He looked up at Zachary. "Where's my bucket and shovel?"

"I left them in the car." Zachary looked at her. "Will you be okay watching him if I run up to get them?" At her nod, he said, "I'll be back in a sec. Don't let him out of your sight."

She went over to kneel beside Sammy. The little sand crabs were fascinating. So engrossed were the two of them in watching the creatures scurry away that she was unprepared for the wave that came up and covered them both. She was laughing as she righted herself and combed her hair off her face. But then she realized that Sammy had been caught in a riptide.

Slipping off her shoes, she dove under an oncoming wave and began to swim vigorously in a diagonal fashion till she was deliberately caught in the same riptide. It was best not to fight a riptide but let it carry you out to its end. Leastways, that's what she had always been taught.

Everything had happened so quickly. How could they be out so far already?

She soon caught up to Sammy, whose eyes were wide and terrified as he choked and spat out salt water, fighting to stay afloat. "Shh, shh, you will be safe now," she said, putting an arm across his front and swimming backward till they were in calmer water. Then he twisted in her grasp and wrapped his two little arms around her neck, hugging tightly.

Zachary was soon beside them in the water.

Sammy clutched her even tighter.

Other members of the party lined the shore, watching, in the event they were needed. Several had taken off shoes and even braies and *sherts*.

"Come on, little guy," Zachary said, trying to take Sammy from her. He was bare-chested, having no doubt shed his *shert* and weapon on the beach afore entering the water.

"Nooooo," he wailed. To Britta, he whined, "My father will beat me."

Britta glanced at Zachary, who seemed both angry and hurt by his son's remark.

"I have never beat you," Zachary said.

"It wasn't your fault, Sammy," she consoled him.

"Now, c'mon. You're too heavy for Britta," his father urged.

"Nooooo."

"He is not too heavy for me," Britta said . . . to Zachary's chagrin, she could tell.

"Okay, let's go back in together then," he conceded through gritted teeth.

As they swam side by side, Sammy told his father, "I was only catchin' sand crabs."

"I'm not blaming you, Sammy."

"You will."

Zachary's eyes connected with hers for a second, and she saw his misery.

"Go on ahead," she told Zachary. "And tell the others to go back to the keep. Let me get him settled down a bit first."

Before he left, Zachary mouthed to her, "Thank you."

**Sometimes love comes not with a bang but a whimper . . .**

Fifteen minutes later, Zach was walking barefooted across the beach, a towel in one hand and a blanket in the other. He was wearing a pair of the commander's jeans and one of his old T-shirts, his own clothing being soaked.

His hands were still shaking, and that was a shocker to him. He'd engaged in some of the most dangerous black ops in the history of special forces and couldn't recall ever having been this scared.

He saw that Britta had Sammy on her lap now, arms wrapped around him to ward off the chill, and was talking softly to him. He wrapped the blanket around both of them before dropping down beside them. She glanced his way and nodded her thanks. Sammy was facing the other direction, probably not even aware of Zach's presence.

If Britta could only see herself holding his son! The reflexive kiss to the top of his head. The soft caress of his back. She would make a wonderful mother. And wife. *Oh, man, where did that thought come from?*

While his mind had been wandering in that forbidden arena, Zach realized that Britta had encouraged Sammy to talk about himself and how he liked living here in this country.

"I don't have no friends," he was telling her. "Other kids don't wanna play with me."

"Oh, Sammy, that is not true."

"Uh-huh. I look different and I talk different. Nobody wants to play with me."

"Being different is not so bad. I am different."

He twisted his head to look at her. "Yeah, you are," he said with a child's bluntness. "Do you have anyone to play with?"

Britta turned slightly, her eyes connecting with Zach's for a brief second.

He winked at her. *You can play with me anytime you want, baby.* He hoped she got that message.

She blushed. *Yep, she got the message.*

"You and I must work to fit in better in this country," she told Sammy, meanwhile brushing his hair back off his face in a maternal fashion. "We need to learn to speak better, to write in this language, to adapt to the way of living here. Because, like it or not, this is where we are both going to stay."

"My father will send me away," Sammy said in a small voice, but Zach heard it.

"No, he will not," she told him.

"He'll whip me like Grandfather did."

Zach's hands fisted, and his eyes watered.

"My father beat me, too," she confided in a voice so low he barely heard her.

Now, not only were Zach's hands fisted and his eyes watering, but he felt a tightening in his chest.

"But *your* father, he will *never* do that," she assured the boy.

"Good," Sammy said sleepily and snuggled up against her chest.

For a few moments, he and Britta sat in silence.

Her blonde hair, which had been wildly sexy with curls a short time ago, now hung in lanky hunks. Her sexy red lip gloss was gone; in fact, her lips were kind of blue. Mascara had run down her cheeks, making black tracks.

Still, she looked gorgeous to him.

This woman was like no other. Instead of screaming for help, like many females would have, this Amazon had not hesitated to dive into the ocean to save his son. Now, she sat Madonna-like, holding the boy, the antithesis of the GI Jane she tried to portray.

He had no idea how it had crept up on him. Somehow, he had always imagined he'd hear bells and see stars. But, quietly and with no fanfare, a remarkable fact hit him square in the face . . . rather, heart.

He was in love with her.

*No, no, no,* he immediately corrected himself. *I am in like, not love. She saved my son. What's not to like?*

# Chapter 9

**The best laid plans . . .**

Zach was going to get laid tonight or die trying.

*Note to self: That was a bit crude. Try again.*

Okay, Zach had a plan to seduce Britta into his bed. And it all depended, number one, on his persuading Britta to come in his town house. No pun intended. And, number two, it depended on his talking Britta into an overnight—hell, a weekend—stay with him. And, number three, it depended on Sammy being cooperative for once, willing to fall asleep. And, number four, it depended on his SEAL buddies not showing up to chat, which they'd threatened to do; yeah, like he was up for a frickin' chat. He'd told them they could go to a chat room if they wanted to chat. And, number five, it depended on Britta being in the mood.

So many "depends"! You'd think he was a bleepin' ad for incontinence.

Yeah, he had allowed the "love" card to enter his brain for a blip of a second back there on the beach, but he was past that now. He wasn't in love. Uh-uh. Nope, lust was the name of the game. Good ol' healthy lust. And it would be healthy for Britta, too, he told himself.

After this weekend, WEALS training would be racheted up. More intense physical evolutions. Less liberties. Focus to the max. This might be his last big chance, and he wasn't about to blow it.

Seduction was a breeze for Zach. Lack of confidence wasn't even in his vocabulary. But this time . . . with Britta . . . he just wasn't sure he could pull it off.

Thus far he'd only succeeded with number one, maybe two if he was lucky, and that was thanks to his son who had wheedled and whined till Britta agreed to tuck him in, telling her some outrageous lie about how his father, meaning him, told scary ghost tales that gave him nightmares. It probably hadn't occurred to her yet that he wouldn't be able to drive her back to the base and leave Sammy alone.

Britta was upstairs now telling Sammy some bedtime story about a young Viking boy named Svein the Short who wanted to go a-Viking but was considered too little. Not a single ghost in her tale, she promised. Sammy probably empathized with Short Svein since everyone was always telling him he was too little.

There was a knock at the front door. Peering through the peephole, he saw Wilson. Beside him stood a guy flashing a Vortex Security badge; he looked as if he could bench-press a bus. Zach opened the door and invited them both in.

"Care for a beer?" he offered. *Please say no.*

"Nah. I'm gonna take off." Scary Larry was already halfway down the steps. "Just wanted to introduce you to one of the guys who'll be taking over for me. This is Jim Butler."

"I owe you for all your help, Larry."

Wilson, as usual, didn't crack a smile, just nodded.

Once inside, Butler shook his hand. "Your dad hired a team of us. We'll rotate shifts, but there will always be a Vortex guard protecting your perimeter. You might not always see us, but we'll be here."

"Appreciate it. Do I need to fill you in on any details?"

"Not now. I got the file you e-mailed me. If there's any-thing new, though, be sure to let me know ASAP. Here's my beeper number. It'll go to whoever is on duty, as well as headquarters." He took out a business card, which Zach put in his pocket.

Afterward, Zach checked the locks on all the doors and windows, set the outside motion detector and the inside key-pad, put some wine in the fridge and two stemmed glasses in the freezer, laid out some gourmet cheese and crackers that his mother had bought last time she was here, made a mental count of how many condoms he had in his bedside table, and sniffed his underarms to see if he was okay in that depart-ment. He was.

After waiting another five minutes, he tiptoed up the stairs, not wanting to set off any alarm bells in the kid if he was still awake, and certainly not wanting to awaken him if he was catching some z's.

First he went into his bedroom at the far end of the hall and put his KA-BAR under his pillow and his Glock on the bedside table. Since Sammy's arrival, he'd put most of his weapons un-der lock and key. Those that he needed at the ready had child-proof safety locks on them, which meant he would need an extra second to be in a firing position in the event of an emer-gency. But it was the price he had to pay with a kid in the house.

He double-checked his beeper as well. All SEALs were required to have their direct-line-to-command beepers near them at all times, and even though he wasn't technically on active duty, he could be called up in an instant, like anyone else.

Next, he went back to the first bedroom and, peeking in, saw that Sammy was sleeping. Bless you, Britta! God, the little snot looked like an angel when he was asleep. Britta must have scrubbed his face and washed his arms, because he smelled of Oil of Olay soap, another left-behind of his mother's.

But then—whoo-boy!—he noticed something else.

Britta's sandals were on the floor on the other side of Sammy's bed, but no Britta. That wasn't where the "whoo-boy" came in, though. Like Hansel trailing Gretel, he followed her clothes to the bathroom. First her red tank top next to Sammy's door. He must have stepped over it, thinking it was Sammy's. Then her jeans out in the hall. Her bra hung over the doorknob of the bathroom which was, thank you, God, open, where her panties lay in the middle of the floor.

"Britta!" he called out, not daring to step inside.

No answer, but he heard the shower running. *Forget that "not daring" crap.* He walked right in. Then. Stopped. Dead.

Through the sliding glass doors of the shower, he saw Britta, her arms raised, combing her hair back off her face, which was raised under the showerhead, eyes closed. She was a big woman, no denying that. At least six feet tall . . . and athletically muscled. But, man, a lot of that size went into mile-long, shapely legs, high curved buttocks, and breasts that were full and just the right size for her body. The pink nipples were the . . . uh, cherries on the cake.

If ever he doubted a man could get an instant, full-blown, wham-bam-thank-you-ma'am hard-on, he was a believer now. Testosterone blasted through his body, setting afire every erotic spot along the way, and there were a whole hell of a lot of them. He leaned on the doorjamb when his knees turned to butter and almost buckled on him.

Hesitating for a nanosecond, he shucked his clothes so fast they were strewn all over the place, even his briefs, which landed on the toilet seat, which was closed for once. Probably Britta's doing. One of his flip-flops slam-dunked into the wastebasket.

Whispering a silent prayer that Britta wouldn't whack him on the head with the long-handled loofah brush, he opened the shower door and stepped inside.

Britta stared at him, wide-eyed with surprise, and backed against the tile wall. She didn't try to cover her breasts or pubic hair, like lots of women would. Nudity probably hadn't been that big a deal in her time, certainly not among warriors. But she did say, "Begone, knave!"

*Knave? I've been called a lot of things, but knave? Stop grinning. Stop wasting time on irrelevancies. Think quick, cowboy.* "Uh, I thought maybe we ought to conserve on water and take one shower together."

"Oh. We do the same in the Norselands, except we reuse the bathwater, over and over."

*Okay, score one for me. But, yeech!*

"The dirtier ones go last," she elaborated, as if that made it all right.

*Double yeech!* He reached for the Olay body wash—his mother again—and squirted a big dollop into one hand, then rubbed both palms together, creating foam. The scent of aloe permeated the cubicle. He sure as hell hoped it was an aphrodisiac.

"Is that soap?" she asked, fascinated by the foam and the scent. Still no false modesty about covering herself.

*Good diversionary tactic . . . the body wash.* "Yep. Soft soap. And you know what they say? 'Cleanliness is next to godliness.' "

"God? Did you say God? Oooh, I knew you were a god."

*Hey, if she wants to think I'm a god, who am I to complain?* "Turn around, baby, let me do your back." *Then let me do you, period.* He bit his bottom lip to make sure he didn't say that aloud.

Britta stared at him dubiously.

"It'll help conserve on soap, too."

"Ah, 'tis a luxury in your land, too?"

"Oh, yeah." *I am so good.*

She turned.

"Put your hands above your head and spread your legs a little," he directed. *Please, please, please.*

She snorted and started to turn around in protest.

Every man worth his salt knew there was not one, but several windows of opportunity in the art of seduction. The rule here was, never allow a woman time to think. So, cool guy that he was, he placed a palm against her back, between her shoulder blades, and shoved, mashing her flat against the tiles.

"Ooomph!"

"It's easier for me to wash your back and sides if you raise your arms and spread your legs." *What a line! I should write that down. Later.*

"Dost think I am a wanton?"

*A guy can only hope.*

Miracle of miracles, she put her hands above her head. That's all. But, hey, that was enough of a start for a guy in lust mode.

"Stubborn wench," he muttered.

"I heard that."

"This will also massage your sore muscles."

They were both silent then as he worked the soft soap into her shoulders, down her back and sides, where his fingertips barely skimmed the sides of her breasts, over her hips. Then he started all over at the bottom, her feet, ankles, calves, and thighs. He was working fast, knowing that any minute now Britta was going to change her mind.

"I should forewarn you," Britta said. "I am no longer interested in any of those orgasms."

"Is that a fact?" He smiled. "Why?"

"I saw one performed by those dwarves on Madrene's black box. Six times, actually. And I am not impressed."

"What exactly did you see?"

"Much moaning and screaming and rocking up and down. It cannot be an exercise to be desired if it involves moaning and screaming. Right?"

"Wrong. There is good moaning and screaming and bad moaning and screaming."

"What nonsense!" She gasped, then squealed, "Yikes!" as she peered over her shoulder and saw him kneeling with his face in front of her butt, soaping her up. She turned quickly and managed to knee him in the funny bone—not *that* funny bone, thank God!—the funny bone at his elbow.

"Ow, ow, ow!" he yelped, clutching his elbow.

"I am sorry, but it was a shock to see you kneeling there sniffing my bottom, like Hilda's randy dog Stig."

"I was *not* smelling your butt. I was lathering you with soft soap, which incidentally smells very nice, don't you think?"

She sniffed several times. "Yea, 'tis nice, but move aside so I can leave this showering box. 'Tis crowded in here."

*Not crowded enough, baby.*

" 'Tis past time I returned to the base."

*Should I tell her now that she's stuck here . . . at least overnight?*

*Nah!*

"Let me shower real quick. Then I'll finish you off."

"I do not think . . ."

He managed to stand under the shower, blocking the door, and took the quickest shower in history. When he finished and used the heels of his hands to wipe the last of the water from his eyes, he saw that she was staring unabashedly at his body. "Do you like what you see?" *I sure as hell like what I see.*

"What is not to like? You are a pretty man. But pretty is as pretty does. Now move aside."

"Not yet, sweetie. I need to wash this side . . . of you." He waved a hand to encompass the front of her body from neck to toes.

"I can wash myself."

"I can do you better." Already his soapy hands were rubbing across her breasts. The nipples were small and pink, and the sensation of them abrading the palms of his hands was beyond pleasurable. If her gasp was any indication, she was enjoying it, too.

Britta was shocked. Not by what the lout was doing to her but by her own reaction to it. And why was she standing here like a knight's pike stuck in the ground, allowing him such liberties?

Gazing downward, she watched as he used his palms to lift and massage her breasts, the whole time his calloused palms abraded her nipples. Then she looked upward, and her eyes connected with his, a bright, stormy, very serious blue. He appeared to be waiting for some reaction from her.

"How does that feel, honey?"

Now he was using his fingertips to tap her nipples, then flick them up and down, side to side.

"Strange. It feels strange."

"Strange how?"

"My breasts ache . . . nay, not ache. Yearn."

"That's nothing. Wait till we wash this soap off. Then I'm going to kiss your breasts and lick you all over. My mouth and your breasts are going to become very well acquainted."

She should have been appalled, but instead she moved a hand to her belly where the yearning had moved.

His eyes followed her hand.

Abruptly, he grabbed hold of her and placed her under the showering water, facing him. Sputtering, she closed her eyes under the onslaught of sluicing water and eye-irritating foam. Once the soap melted off her back, he turned her, and both of them stood under the spray, his one arm wrapped around her waist, the other hand resuming its pleasure-torture of her breasts. She could feel his manpart, hard and long, pressing against her buttocks.

She blinked, able to see now. That yearning that had begun in her breasts and moved to her belly now lodged itself betwixt her legs, where it swelled and pulsed till she was overcome with spiraling sensations. She tried to break away from him, but he held her tight against him and turned her face to the side where his lips met hers in a kiss that began soft and searching and soon escalated into hard and hungry.

And whilst she was preoccupied with all these different sensations—his tongue plunging in her mouth, his fingers playing her nipples—his other hand stole to her female place and dipped into the hot wetness there. She screeched at the invasion, but the sound was caught in his mouth. Her hips bucked outward, but his arm was a vise around her waist, holding her in place.

Thus she was caught by the man's wicked fingers doing wicked things to her down there. He seemed to have found some spot that was particularly sensitive, because when he touched her there, stars burst behind her eyelids in a colorful shower, and her traitorous hips began to undulate against his finger in a rhythm matched by his thrusting tongue.

It was too much. And not enough.

She heard herself whimper. Her body stiffened. She tore her mouth out from under his and arched her neck back over his shoulder, keening.

But the brute would not relent.

"Relax. Take it easy."

She tried to laugh at what must be a jest. How could she relax when her body was rising to some fever pitch?

And then . . . and then, it was like a shower of stars she'd seen one time in the eastern skies. That part of her that he still strummed splintered into a million pieces shooting out to all the parts of her body and beyond.

It was the most wonderful awful experience of her life.

And Zachary was no better. He held her even tighter now and stroked his manpart along the crease of her buttocks and between her legs, faster and faster as he panted for breath, then bit her shoulder, lightly, slammed into her back, hard, and groaned, "Yessssss!"

She was fair certain she bit his shoulder, as well, but she could not be sure, because she lost consciousness for a moment. When she regained her senses, he was toweling her dry, then taking her by the arm, leading her down the corridor. In a daze, she barely noticed him stopping to peek in Sammy's room to make sure the child was still asleep. He turned around then, passed the bathing chamber, the next bedchamber, and then led her into a third . . . his, she presumed, considering the vast size of the bed.

Still in a daze—else she would clout the man for leading

her about like a pet dog—she watched him pull down the bed coverings and take some objects out of the bedside table.

"What was that . . . back in the showering chamber?" she asked.

He glanced up and smiled, and Holy Thor! the man did have a charming smile. "An orgasm."

"Nay! It could not be."

"A small one. To take the edge off." He was moving around the bed toward her.

She frowned. "But that was not like the little people in the box. The woman was reclining, and the man was on top of her. And there was screaming."

"Oh, there will be screaming all right. That's a promise."

" 'Twas interesting, but I am not sure I liked it. In truth, methinks 'twould not merit a repeat."

He arched his brows at her in disbelief. "Maybe we'll have to try it a few more times to get it right, till we get to the screams." Before she had a chance to react to that, he picked her up by the waist, tossed her on the bed, then crawled up and over her.

"Who will be screaming?" she asked. "Me or you?"

"Both of us, baby. If we're lucky."

**In the game of seduction, who's on first? . . .**

Britta lay on her back, naked as a newborn babe, with the most beautiful man in the world atop her, also naked as a newborn babe. But there was naught babelike about this scene.

He probably thought she was being docile because of his overwhelming charm. Well, there was that, but the situation and position she was in now was all of her doing: a hastily concocted plan to seduce the man into thinking he was seducing her. His conceit was excessive enough already, without her handing herself to him on a platter . . . uh, pallet.

After Sammy had fallen asleep, she had realized that

Zachary would not be able to transport her back to the base . . . a perfect opportunity to carry out a plan that had been brewing in her no doubt demented mind for days . . . mayhap even for the past two years.

Still, she had not wanted to appear overeager.

Now, still holding to her plan, she pushed against his chest, using a small portion of her strength, and said, "Methinks this is a bad idea."

He raised himself up on straightened arms, extending her arms overhead with their intertwined fingers, thus pinning her to the bed with his belly and legs. His manpart nudged her womanpart, just to let her know it was there. As if she did not already know that. "No, sweetie. This is a very, very good idea. And I'm not letting you go till I prove it to you."

*Not letting?* Did the idiot think she could not shove him off of her? Yea, he did. Little did he know her true strength, for she was as strong as many a man.

"In truth, I am a mite curious about this whole sex business," she admitted.

He grinned with pure, unvarnished male slyness, as if he were the cat and she the helpless mouse.

*What a lout!*

"You liked your first orgasm, huh?"

" 'Twas interesting."

"Interesting?" he nigh yelled. You would have thought she'd hurled some great insult his way. "It was more than interesting, babe."

She shrugged. "Euphoric then. Like the rush after a hard-won battle. Or the satisfaction of a particularly good meal following a fast, as evidenced by a loud belch. Or a ladle of cool spring water to quench a fierce thirst."

"This has got to be a first for me. She's comparing my sexual prowess with a belch!" He rolled his eyes with mock dismay.

Even Britta saw the humor in those comparisons. And Britta was nothing if not honest. She liked what Zachary had

done to her, and she was curious to see what he would do
next.

Britta had no time for thought then as Zachary began to
lead her on yet another journey into sexual bliss.

"You are so beautiful," he murmured.

"I am not beautiful, and save your slick words. They gain
you naught with me. Do what you will with me and be done."

"Britta, Britta, Britta, there's no rush here. We have all
night for this sexual adventure."

"There may be no hurry for you, but there is for me. This
journey progressses too slow for my taste. Like pouring thick
honey syrup, when what I crave is thin, honeyed mead."

He laughed. "Food again!"

She must have frowned her opinion, because he added,
"The best meal is savored slowly, bit by bit. And I intend to
savor you for a long long time."

"How long?"

"Hours and hours."

"What? I expect to be asleep shortly and up afore dawn to
return to the base."

"All night long. I've been dreaming about this forever,
and no one is going to rush me."

"Oh, for Thor's sake! What can a man and woman do for
so many hours? Nay, do not answer that. You will no doubt
say something coarse."

And he did. In explicit, crude detail. He told her a dozen
and more things he planned to do to her, things she had ne'er
heard of and some she guessed might be physically impossible. Then he told her a dozen things he would like her to do
to him.

He'd stunned her speechless, as he had intended. Then
whilst she was still gaping at him, he leaned down, brushing
his lips back and forth over hers till she became pliant. But
did he then stick his tongue in her mouth like he did afore?
Nay! Not even when she opened her mouth for him. Instead,
he chuckled and moved on, nibbling at her chin and jaw and
moving up to her ear. *Her ear, for the love of Odin!* There he

did some engaging things with the wet tip of his tongue, tracing her whorls, plunging into the canal. The sensations he created in her ear ricocheted down to her nether parts, where warm liquid pooled. *Hmmm, mayhap the ear is not such a bad place to start.* Still, this was syrup, and whilst syrup was fine and good, her appetite had been whetted for ale.

"Do you have any idea how much I want you?"

"Nay, how much?"

"That was a rhetorical question."

"Well, you have dawdled so much I no longer want you."

"Liar."

"I am just curious."

"Liar. Do you want to know how I can tell?"

"Nay."

But he told her, again in explicit detail. Something about erect nipples, slick folds, flushed face, panting breath, and swelling clit. She did not ask what he meant, not about folds, not about clits, suspecting she would learn more than she wanted to know about those signs her body revealed.

"Plus, you haven't smacked me upside the head yet. If you really didn't want me, you would have let me know, in spades."

"There is that."

He released her hands and lowered himself to his elbows. Now he was nuzzling her neck. Her *neck!*

*Frigg's foot! Enough!* She grabbed his face, raised it, then kissed him hard, thrusting her tongue inside of his mouth with the finesse of rusty plow in a cotter's field. He did not resist, exactly, but he choked and lifted his head, evading another kiss.

"You move too slow."

"Slow is good."

"Slow is good for fermenting ale, not for fermenting the female juices."

He chuckled. "Give me some credit for knowing a little bit about lovemaking, Britta."

"And give me some credit for knowing what I want." In

one deft motion, she hooked a leg around his calf, pressed against his chest, and rolled him over so that she lay atop him. "Now do it," she ordered. "I would *do it* myself if I knew exactly how."

He was laughing so hard he could scarce breathe, let alone "do it."

Now she was embarrassed at her daring. He must think her a wanton. She tried to roll off of him but only succeeded in landing at his side and almost knocking them both off the bed.

With much more deftness than she'd employed, he took her by the waist, tossed her back to the middle of the bed, and placed himself atop her again. "Now, behave yourself, Britta. I welcome you jumping my bones, but not this first time. Understood?"

"Nay, it is not understood," she grumbled, turning her face to the side, still embarrassed, not just at her attempt to control the bedsport, but at having failed.

"Look at me, sweetheart." When she refused, he slid down her body a bit and kissed first one breast, then the other, right on the tips.

She squealed and arched her body upward. She was looking now, all right. Good and plenty.

He put a hand at her chest and pushed her back down, roughly. She would no doubt have finger bruises on her chest come morn.

It had been a bare whisper of a kiss, but her nipples rose to attention, wanting more. Then he went to work in earnest, kneading her entire breast, raising it high from underneath, licking all around, but never quite in the center where she most wanted—nay, needed—his mouth to be.

She continued to try to arch her chest upward, offering her breasts to him.

He continued to hold her down. "Tell me what you want, Britta," he said in a voice that was deliciously husky.

"How do I know what I want? I do not know. Yea, I do. I want your mouth on me."

"Oh? Here?" He pressed his mouth against hers in a fleeting kiss.

She shook her head.

"Or here?" He raised one hand and kissed the wrist where her pulse no doubt beat like a battle drum.

She shook her head.

"Ah, I know." He nipped her shoulder with his teeth, then kissed it better.

"Nay, nay, nay, aaaaahhhhh!"

He had taken her nipple into his mouth and was flicking it with his tongue. Over and over and over. And whilst he ministered to the other breast with playful fingers, he began to suckle her, soft, then hard, soft, then hard, in a rhythm that had no end.

She succeeded in arching her body off the bed, taking him with her.

And still he suckled.

She was keening a never-ending response to his breast play, not understanding how his touch in one place could be felt by her in another place. Ripples of the most incredible tension were building there. She feared she was about to have another orgasm, except this felt different than the one in the bathing chamber.

And what did the lout do? He bloody hell stopped. And knelt betwixt her legs. And just sat back on his heels, studying her *there*.

"Look at you, Britta. Curly blonde hairs glistening with honey. I want to taste you, but that'll have to wait. This time when you come, I want to be there for the party."

He made no sense at all, but then Britta was nigh senseless with need.

Zachary reached to a table beside the bed and picked up a silver packet that sat next to his weapon . . . a piss-tol. Tearing the packet with his teeth, he then sheathed himself.

"To prevent pregnancy," he explained, seeing her confusion. "Are you ready, sweetheart?"

"Ready? I have been ready for nigh on . . . oh!"

He'd raised her hips and slowly entered her. Bit by excruciating bit till he was firmly embedded in her woman chan-
nel, which shifted and clutched at him in welcome. Then he
did something, twisting his hips, and she took even more of
him.

He stopped and looked down at her face. His lips were
parted. His eyes were a hazy blue. Perspiration dotted his
forehead. And Britta knew that he was as aroused as she was.

Then he smiled. He just bloody hell smiled at her. "I've
been dreaming about this moment for two years. You've
been the star of more of my wet dreams than I care to mention. And now you're here."

She smiled back at him.

His manpart jerked inside of her, obviously liking her
smile.

Leaning upward, she kissed his mouth . . . a shy, inexperienced moving of her parted lips against his parted lips. He
moaned, which pleased her ever so much. Slowly he thrust
his tongue inside her mouth, and for the first time she understood the significance of his thrusting tongue emulating his
manpart, which was beginning to thrust as well. Long, slow
strokes in both places, at first.

Britta soon learned the rhythm and met him stroke for
stroke, especially when he took her hips and showed her how
to move. "Like that. Yes. No, no, no, I'll slip out. Oh, sweetheart! Put your legs here. Do you like that? How about this?
Sweet mother! I knew you would be magnificent."

Britta kept trying to take over control of this bedplay, but
he would not allow it, even slapping away her hand at one
point when she tried to touch the place where his manpart
joined with her female folds. She was unaccustomed to being a follower, whether in battle or bed.

But what a wondrous thing this mating was! Truly, it was
as if she and Zachary were one being. The joining was more
than physical. Only he and she could fit together so well.
The only key to fit a lock. A fanciful notion, that.

When his strokes became shorter and harder, she wrapped

her legs around his waist, trapping him, or so she thought. She met him thrust for thrust, a rhythm that must be intrinsic to men and women under the lust frenzy, she mused. He grunted; she groaned. Still they could not reach that peak that spelled orgasm.

But then it happened, to both of them at once. Britta knew what it felt like to fall off a cliff. This was the same but different. Whereas her real-life fall off the cliff had been terrifying and deadly, this was an incredible blossoming of the senses. Like flying, soaring high till it was almost unbearable, exploding in a blast of sunlight, then floating downward in the fall.

In a haze, she watched Zachary rise from the bed and remove his sheath, wiping himself with a cloth. Then he returned to the bed and drew her close, her face resting on his still wildly beating chest. Kissing the top of her head, he murmured, "You are all I dreamed you would be."

She thought about replying with some flowery words; most smitten maids would. But this was Zachary, the man of a thousand swivings. They were just words.

So, what she said was, "I did not scream."

"You moaned a lot."

"A moan is not a scream."

"Are you daring me again, sweetheart?"

"And if I am?"

He lifted his head, stared down at her with mirthful eyes, and said, "Hoo-yah!"

# Chapter 10

**Do Vikings ever ride horses . . . uh, men? . . .**

Zach was happy.

Why that thought should strike him, was odd. But not really. His life since discovering Sammy had been nothing but chaos on a personal, professional, and emotional level. Britta, his good ol' thousand-year-old girlfriend, had grounded him but good.

And, yeah, getting laid had that effect on a guy. But this was much, much more than that. When he'd met Britta two years ago, there had been an instant recognition on his part. She was "the one" or as close to "the one" as he'd ever come before. But he'd been too chicken to stay and too chicken to try to bring her home with him.

So what to do now? Maybe the answer was to just be happy. To savor those moments that life throws your way . . . and hope there'll be more.

And, whoo-boy, there was definitely going to be more if Britta's fingers trailing down his chest were any indication. The fingers paused to stir the curly hairs on his chest and test his nipples, then moved over his abdomen, then his belly. When she got to never-never land, she took his half-erect penis in hand and studied it.

He counted to fifty, silently, trying to get himself under control. Otherwise, this movie was going to be over before the previews were done.

"Can we do it again?" she asked.

"Baby, I thought you'd never ask."

Taking her hand, he raised it to his mouth and kissed the palm. Then he tugged her up and over him.

"What do you say we have us a rodeo?"

She frowned in confusion.

But she wasn't confused for long.

And praise God, the saints, and some long-dormant gene for sexuality, but Britta was the most uninhibited lover he'd ever had. Once she'd settled herself in the saddle, so to speak, she smiled.

"I like it."

"I thought you would."

"Can I move?"

"I would hope so."

"Any way I want?"

"Oh, yeah!"

She arranged her legs on either side of him and rose up high. Pausing before she lowered herself onto him, she looked just like a Valkyrie he'd seen in a painting one time riding some otherworld destrier. All wild blonde hair, sharp Norse features, long-waisted and long-legged, beautiful beyond belief.

She was any man's dream come true. She was *his* dream come true.

Then his sweet Valkyrie rode him hard. After that, she rode him gently . . . and slow. She bit his bottom lip, then kissed him boneless. She tongued his ear and whispered what must seem indecent words to her. She played with his nipples and was fascinated by his balls. Then she did it all over again. And again. And again.

He was in sex heaven.

So he fondled her breasts while she leaned over him, and kneaded her buttocks. He showed her how to brush her breasts back and forth across his chest so that the nipples were abraded by his chest hairs.

He fit so tightly inside of her. It was like warm oil caressing him with each stroke. He didn't want it to ever stop, but he didn't think he could stand much more.

And when he felt her inner muscles start to spasm—presaging her upcoming climax—he forced her to stop and not move, to prolong and intensify her pleasure. Three times he did this. And then she screamed.

As she rippled over and around his cock, milking him, he might have screamed, too. At the very least, he bucked up, over and over, making her work extra hard for this rodeo prize.

In the end, they both lay splayed on the bed, holding hands. He glanced over at her and said, "Britta?"

"Hmmmm?"

"You make me happy."

As far as declarations of affection went, it was not all that hot. But then she smiled at him and said, "I'm happy, too."

And then, bless her Viking heart, she added, "Can we do it again?"

### "Baby, I have something to show you," said the Big Bad Wolf to Red Riding Hood . . .

Britta awakened during the night to the sound of rustling.

Raising up on one elbow, she saw the sky was still black outside. And she saw Zachary by the light of a half moon pulling on a pair of small clothes . . . black silk ones with red stars imprinted all over. "What's the matter?" she asked, yawning widely.

"I'm just gonna check on Sammy. Go back to sleep."

Which she did, promptly. It had been a very hard, sleep-deprived week, and this might be her only opportunity to catch up. Of course, she thought with a smile, all that bedplay might give her body better satisfaction than any slumber.

It was still the middle of the night when she awakened again, but a stream of light came from an almost-closed closet. This time she found herself at the bottom of the bed, her bare feet on the floor, and Zachary kneeling betwixt her spread thighs.

"Eek!" she squealed and tried to rise up and shove the lout away.

"Go back to sleep, Britta. I just want to check a few things out."

"Hah! Like I could sleep with you sniffing at my nether parts!"

"What is it with you and sniffing? I am not sniffing. I'm getting ready to taste." He wagged his tongue at her, then dipped down to lick her *there*.

"Nay, nay, nay!" she screeched.

"Shhhh. You'll wake Sammy. And you wouldn't want him to see you like this, would you?"

She held her tongue but still tried to shove him away.

He put a palm on her belly and held her fast.

"Relax, sweetie. You'll like this. I promise."

"This has got to be depraved. Is it depraved?"

"Nah! Oh, Britta! What is this scar here?" He used a forefinger to trace the white line that she knew was visible on her inner thigh, high up. She tried to close her legs, but he wouldn't allow that. "Tell me," he insisted.

"My brother Erlend did it."

He sucked in a breath, his outrage visible. "Did he rape you?"

She shook her head. "Nay. He wanted me to display my nether parts for him and his friends."

His upper lip curled with disgust. "How old were you?"

"Eight. Erlend was twelve."

"No wonder you needed to leave home."

"I was too young then, but when I was eleven, Halvdan did attempt rape."

"Another brother?"

"Yea. That was when I went to our castellan, begging for fighting skills. Halvdan ne'er tried again, I tell you that."

He nodded.

"The final indignity came from my father, who gave consent to a Danish jarl for rape as an incentive to force me to wed, a rape I managed to evade."

"The bastards! What did your father do about that?"

"A fist to my chin. Nigh knocked me out. My jaw still aches on occasion, a lifelong reminder of his rage, as he intended." She saw the expression on his face and added, "Do not pity me. I survived."

"That wasn't pity, babe. It was admiration." He leaned down and kissed the scar.

She sucked in air and tried to push him away. "Let me up."

"No, no, no! No getting up yet. Have you ever looked at yourself down here, honey?"

"Nay! Why would I?"

"I want to show you something. Do you promise to sit still?"

"I am not going to promise . . . yikes!"

He'd put his tongue between her folds and was flicking it back and forth, like a pendulum.

"I will sit still if you stop that . . . that perversion."

"Okay, scoot your butt back a little."

When she'd moved back far enough that her feet were on the bed, he quickly, all in one deft move, raised her knees, spread them wide, then pulled her forward so that her knees and buttocks rested almost at the bed's edge. "This is definitely depraved," she said.

"Now look down," he ordered.

She rose to a sitting position. *Nothing there to make such a fuss about,* she thought.

"See this here?" he said, pointing to a little rose-hued nubbin.

She nodded.

"It's the center of everything to make a woman have fun with sex. It's called a clitoris . . . or clit." He touched it lightly, and she about shot off the bed, so intense was the sensation. "Now, I'm going to make you come, just by touching you there, but you have to sit still. Promise?"

"Come where?"

He laughed, even as he pulled out another of the silver packets and sheathed himself. "Climax. Have an orgasm."

"Why are you putting that thing on if I am to orgasm on my own?"

"Because, sweetheart, at the tail end of your first climax, I plan to join in for the show. To see if you can have an endless orgasm."

"Ah, multiple orgasms."

"Bingo. But here's the deal, babe. Let's make this game more interesting. How about this? If you move, I get to tie you up and do whatever I want with you."

"What kind of deal is that?"

But the rogue was already at work down below, touching her slick folds with his fingers, then his tongue and teeth. He fluttered the nubbin with a finger, even as he had two other fingers inside of her.

She tried to close her legs against the too-intense sensations he was creating.

"Are you moving?" he asked, almost with glee.

"Nay, I am not moving, lout."

"Lean back on your elbows and let your heels touch your butt."

He used each of his thumbs to separate her folds, then put his tongue against her and licked and licked and licked until she was keening her pleasure. Orgasm after orgasm rocked her body, a never-ending pulsing at that one spot, but then he slid his manpart inside of her and started the orgasms all over again. When one ended, another started, over and over till Zachary grunted and arched his neck back, blue veins nigh popping out. He peaked inside of her with a roar of triumph, and she orgasmed around him one last time.

So depleted was she that she was hardly aware of Zachary pulling her up to the pillows and cradling her in his arms.

She thought she heard him murmur, "I am so screwed."


## Oh, brother! . . .

"Well, well, well!"

In that hazy state of half sleep, half awake, Zach became aware of himself splatted out on his back on the bed, with Britta's face mashed down on his chest, her hair spread out all over like a wild bush, and her hand on his cock.

"Well, well, well!"

"Holy crap! Not again, Britta. You gotta give me a chance to regroup."

"Oh, I think you've regrouped plenty, Brother."

*Brother! That isn't Britta.* He jackknifed to a sitting position, shoved Britta behind him, and had his weapon aimed at the doorway in a split second.

It was his brother, Danny, who had the good sense to duck outside the open doorway where he had been leaning.

"Sonofabitch!" Zach muttered. "You should know better than to sneak up on a military man. Especially one who has a jihad out on him. I coulda killed you."

"Is it safe to come back in?" Danny inquired, peeping around the doorway. The idiot was grinning, not having the sense to realize that he could have been stepping into a land mine of his own making.

Britta was sputtering groggily behind him, a combination of outrage over his having shoved her behind him and confusion over his motive. When she noticed the man standing there getting a grinning eyeful of her naked body, she squealed and tried to hide her large body behind Zachary's body, which was large but not large enough. He laughed and tossed her a blanket, even as he stood and walked toward the door. "It's just my dickhead brother who doesn't have the sense God gave a . . . dick."

"Does he not knock?"

"Hardly ever," Danny answered for him, peeking over Zach's shoulder. "A guy misses a lot of good stuff if he announces himself. Right, Bro?" Danny chuckled, then murmured, "Whoa! That is one hot mama. Wanna share?"

"Get out of here, idiot." He shoved Danny out in the hallway. Before he closed the door after himself, he told Britta, "Go back to sleep, honey. It's not even dawn yet."

Then he put both hands on his hips and glared at his brother. Danny was still in uniform—he was an Air Force pilot—and his duffel bag sat on the floor at his feet.

"How'd you get in?"

"I have a key. Had to practically wrestle some goon outside, though. Is that one of the guards Dad hired for you?"

"Yeah."

"Probably some stunt man Dad knows on one of his sets."

"Nope, this is a top-notch security firm. Great reputation. Expensive as hell."

"The old man can afford it. Is he still boffing that Lolita that plays his daughter on the soap?"

Zach shrugged. "What the hell are you doing here, Danny?"

"Tsk-tsk-tsk! I'm just gonna crash here for a night or two. I've got a one-week pass. Thought you could use some help with the kid, but . . ." He jerked his head toward the closed bedroom door, ". . . maybe you've got all the help you need."

"I can always use help, and Britta will be going back to the base."

Danny raised his eyebrows at him.

"She's in that new WEALS program—"

"A military babe? Since when do you go for ball busters? Man, oh, man, you attract all types, don't you?"

"—which I am assisting Commander MacLean with. WEALS, I mean."

His brother hooted with laughter. "Your punishment for various and sundry crimes, I assume."

"You got that right."

"Anyhow, Bro," Danny motioned his head toward the closed bedroom door, "you hit the jackpot this time."

"Yeah, I did," Zach agreed with a grin.

"Listen, we'll talk in the morning, okay? I'm beat." Danny reached over and gave him a hug. "Yeech, that is taking brotherly love a step too far. Hugging a naked guy."

Zach just realized then that he was still naked. He would have blushed if he were a blushing kind of guy.

"By the way, nice war wounds!"

"Huh?" As Zach reentered his bedroom and looked in the full-length mirror on the closet door, he saw a bite mark on his chin. A hickey on his neck. Scratch marks on his shoulders. A bruised elbow where Britta had clocked him in the shower. And his cock looked as if it had been through a battle.

War wounds, for sure.

*Hoo-yah!*

## He wanted her to spend all day doing WHAT? . . .

Britta had dawdled long enough. Time to go down to Zachary's great hall and face the object of her humiliation.

She had pretended to be asleep when he rose soon after dawn, even when he came back from bathing and dressed in his bedchamber. To say she was having morning-after regrets for her wanton behavior would be a monumental understatement.

Oh, 'twas not that she had not enjoyed herself. Far from it. Not even the things Zachary had taught her. Not even the fact that his brother had seen her nude body. Nay, what embarrassed her most was the wicked things she had initiated herself. Ne'er would she have guessed there were so many ways to tup. Ne'er would she have guessed that she would have such enthusiasm for the bedsport.

If Zachary dared laugh at her, she was going to clobber him over the head with the nearest heavy object.

She combed her still damp hair off her face and plaited it into one single braid. Her long hair was a hindrance in the military exercises of WEALS, and she was seriously considering having it all chopped off.

Then she pulled on pant-hees and the breast harness. After that the black braies, red *shert*, and red shoes, which were ridiculously open-toed and open-heeled. Mayhap there was a shortage of leather at the cobbler's when these were made.

She heard voices as she went down the steps and headed toward the scullery. Delicious smells permeated the air, and she realized how hungry she was. They had left Madrene's afore the meal was served last night, following Sammy's near mishap.

Everyone stopped talking and turned to her when she entered the scullery . . . Zachary, his brother, and Sammy.

"Good morning, sweetheart," Zachary said, rising from his chair and offering it to her. When she sat, he kissed her shoulder.

She made a hissing sound to indicate his behavior was inappropriate in front of others. And besides, all he had to do was touch her, and the sap began to rise in her traitorous body.

He just ignored her hiss and pulled out an empty chair for himself.

"This is my brother, Danny." Zachary waved a hand to the grinning rogue across the table.

"We've met," Danny said, winking at her.

Danny was as different from Zachary as night from day. He had brown hair and brown eyes, compared to Zachary's blond hair and blue eyes. And whilst of the same height and build, Danny could not be described as pretty by anyone's definition.

Zachary shot his brother a warning glower for the wink, which daunted him not a whit.

"And you already know Sammy."

"Are you gonna tell me 'nother Viking story?"

She nodded. "Later." *Good gods, I hope I am gone by then.* "Take me back to the base," she told Zachary. "Now that your brother is here, there is no excuse—"

He patted her thigh. "Now, now. Eat some breakfast first." He was piling food on a plate in front of her: ham, sausage, eggs, some kind of round cake with syrup on it, and buttered bread that had been toasted. Then he poured an orange substance into a clear glass and the black, bitter beverage known as coffee into a cup.

"Who cooked all this?" she asked, already having taken three mouthfuls of the delicious food.

"Danny started it, and I helped when I came down," Zachary said.

"Me, too," Sammy interjected.

"Sammy, too," Zachary agreed, rumpling his son's hair, which caused his son to frown fiercely at his father.

"What's that mark on yer shoulder?" Sammy asked Britta around a mouthful of food.

"Don't speak with food in your mouth," Zachary advised.

Sammy stuck out his tongue, covered with half-chewed food.

"It looks like ya got bit by a bear," Sammy observed, back to the mark on her shoulder.

Britta glanced sideways to her shoulder, saw Danny look, too, then turn to his brother, Zachary, and pump one arm in the air.

"Yep, a big bad ol' bear," Danny told Sammy.

The conversation veered then toward a discussion of WEALS, Sammy's tutor lessons, which would start on Thursday, Zachary's father having hired guards, and the lovely sunny weather outside.

The whole time Danny was watching her and Zachary closely, as if trying to puzzle something out. "I'm taking Sammy for the day," he announced of a sudden. "An uncle's prerogative," he added, seeing that Zachary was about to protest. "You need a day to yourself, Bro." He patted Zachary on the arm.

"That's nice of you to offer, but—"

"We're going to Disneyland," Sammy announced. Then, addressing Britta, he said, "Wanna come with us?"

"Oh, nay, I do not think I could go to Dizzy Land today. I . . . I . . ."

"Your dad and Britta are gonna spend the day together," Danny explained to Sammy.

"The whole day? What're they gonna do for a whole day?"

She looked at Zachary, saw the hot regard in his eyes, realized he was not about to return her to the base any time soon, then turned back to the others.

"I would love to go to Dizzy Land."

# *Chapter 11*

**Heigh-ho, Heigh-ho, it's off to Disneyland they did go . . .**

"I can't believe I'm wasting a day off going to a glorified kiddie park."

" 'Tis not my fault."

"Oh, yes, it is, sweetheart. Danny gave us the perfect opportunity to stay home, alone."

"Nay, 'tis your fault. You are the one who gave me a hot look."

"Hot looks are bad?"

"They are when they make me do lustsome things."

Zach glanced over at Britta in the front seat and smiled.

Danny was sitting in the backseat with Sammy, enthroned in his car seat, playing a game of I Spy. The roar of the motor and traffic noises through the open windows made their front seat conversation relatively private. They were halfway to L.A. and a blasted day at Disneyland. At least they had VIP passes, thanks to his dad, which would move them around some of the time-sink lines.

"You were incredible last night, Britta."

"Oh, do not speak of that again." She put her hands to her cheeks, which were nicely flushed. "I was a wanton."

"God bless wantons."

"That is profane."

"Ya think? Why would God create great sex if he didn't want men and women to enjoy it?"

"This is not a conversation we should be having in front of a child. Or your brother."

"They can't hear us back there. I had our whole day planned out."

"I wager you did! How much of it would have been spent with me on my back on your mattress?"

"Actually, I have a checklist of all the ways and places we were gonna have sex, and only a few of them took place with you on your back." He grinned at her.

"A checklist? Where is it?"

He tapped his head. "In here, baby. Wanna know what's on my list?"

"Nay."

"You on my lap in the vibrating La-Z-Boy. Me nailing you against the mirror on my closet door. On the kitchen table. You straddling a bench. On the deck. In the bathtub. At the top of the cargo net, back on the grinder. Here in the car. With your legs over my shoulders. With me bending over you, doggie style. Hanging from the chandelier."

"Enough!" she said.

"Hey, I was just getting started."

"You make my woman's fleece get damp when you talk like that," she hissed at him in an undertone.

Her words hit him right between the legs. Slam dunk! Erection. "Britta, you are priceless."

"You should have taken me back to the base. I must needs prepare myself for this upcoming week. Even you have said it will be brutal."

"Tomorrow's gonna come soon enough, baby. And, yeah, last week was a piece of cake compared to what's coming up."

She groaned.

"The whole point is to weed out the weak ones. If a trainee, man or woman, can't make it during these evolutions, they'll never make it out in the field. I for sure wouldn't want someone covering my back who's gonna bail at the first sign of disaster."

She nodded her understanding.

"I have been told all this afore. I am not going to drop out, Zachary. Where else would I go? And, nay, do not offer me a position as nursemaid for your son again. 'Tis not what I am trained to do."

"Duly noted. Well, maybe I can give you some tips on surviving then. Number one, don't call attention to yourself. Number two, take each step one at a time. There's a famous Navy SEAL motto: 'The only easy day was yesterday.' It's absolutely true, but you can't allow yourself to think about what's ahead, or you'll give up. Number three, rest whenever you can. SEALs learn something called REM sleep, where they can sleep standing up, eyes open. Even if it's only for five minutes at a time, it can energize you, get you over the next hump. Number four, make close friends with your buddies. The SEALs and WEALS are all about teamwork. You're as strong as each one of you, but also as weak as any one of you. Number five, we've got to get you some private tutoring—reading, English, math, history—before someone discovers you're not the missing Norse officer."

Britta was grinning at him.

"What?"

"You make a good teacher."

He grinned back. "Don't you dare tell anyone that, or I'll be stuck here on base forever."

"You would rather be fighting?"

"Absolutely. There's so much bad stuff happening in the world. The government needs every specially trained man to fight the good fight. The demand for SEALs far exceeds the supply."

"Then why are you on the base?"

He motioned his head toward the backseat.

"Sammy?"

"Yep. I took him out of a foreign country illegally. His grandfather is a terrorist, and he wants him back. That's why there will always be bodyguards around till this is resolved. It's a world-class snafu." He was glad she didn't ask him what snafu meant, not sure she would appreciate *situation normal all fucked up*. He decided to lighten the subject. "Hey, you could be Sammy's babysitter with an AK-47. Then I wouldn't need any bodyguards, and you could utilize your fighting skills."

"What is an achy-forty-seven?"

"A whoop-ass weapon."

"Thank you for the offer, but nay."

"There would be benefits."

"As long as I am stuck in this strange land and this strange time, I will train to be with the WEALS, I will survive whatever torture is thrown my way, and then I will go off and kill bad people. And that is that."

"We'll see," Zach said and took her hand in his, lacing their fingers.

She glanced down at their intertwined fingers, then up at him.

"Why didn't you want to be alone with me today?" He hadn't realized that he was going to blurt that out. How pathetic did that make him sound? She didn't answer at first. So of course he blundered on like a needy teenager. "I thought you liked being with me last night."

She made a snorting sound. "Pfff! I liked it too much."

That made him feel a little better. "And?"

"I wanted to know how to have an orgasm, not how to set a record for swiving till my eyeballs rolled back in my head."

Unfortunately, he'd just pulled to a stop at a red light and her voice carried to the backseat.

Zach heard his brother choke in the middle of telling Sammy, "I spy something—*cough, cough*—red."

"My father's face," Sammy answered.

*The snot!*

"Didja know my father has a magazine with naked wimmen in it? He hides it under his mattress."

*The sneaky snot!*

It was Zach's turn to choke now. Looking in the rearview mirror, he saw a smirk on Sammy's face that was pure one hundred proof Dennis the Menace.

"There was this one picture where a lady was bending over and ya could see—"

"That'll be enough, Sammy," Zach said. He would have to be even more careful with what he had in the house. "Besides, I think it belongs to Uncle Dan."

"Yeah, right!" Danny was smirking, too.

"A tattoo," Zach lied. "On her thigh. That's probably what Sammy saw."

"No, I saw—" Sammy started to say, but Danny clapped a hand over his mouth and said, "Haven't you ever heard that children are to be seen and not heard, short stuff?"

"Who said that?" Sammy demanded to know. "Musta been a grown-up."

"I am thinking of getting a tattoo," Britta said.

*Oh, boy!* He turned to look at her. "Where?"

"On my buttock."

*Friggin' A!* "My name?" he suggested.

"Why would I do such a thing? Nay, I am contemplating either a longship or my favorite sword."

"What's the name of your favorite sword? Ballbuster?"

"Ha, ha, ha! My best pattern-welded sword was called Head Lopper."

"That's just peachy."

"'Twas a jest, lackwit. My sword is named Wound Maker."

"Oh, that's better. If I had a sword, I would name it Whoop-Ass."

"Must you always be so vulgar?"

"Listenin' to you two is more fun than sex," Danny observed. "Almost. And to think I was feelin' sorry for you, all alone here, celibate, practically a prisoner. What a laugh!"

"We're almost there," Zach said. *Thank God!*

Glancing over at Britta, he did a double take. Her mouth was parted, her eyes wide, and she let loose with a long sigh. It was the kind of glazed expression a guy fantasized about seeing on a woman's face the first time he dropped his drawers. But that was not the case here.

" 'Tis the most beautiful castle I have ever seen." She was staring at the gaudy pink Cinderella castle in the distance. "What kingdom is this?"

He grinned. "The Magic Kingdom, baby."

Her belief, reiterated over and over in the next fifteen minutes, that they must have entered a totally new and enchanted land was reinforced when he read the entrance sign to her:

HERE YOU LEAVE TODAY
AND ENTER THE WORLD
OF YESTERDAY, TOMORROW,
AND FANTASY

### Splash this! . . .

The first clue Britta had that a Splash Mountain adventure was perchance not a good idea was when they made her sit down in a hollowed-out log that immediately wet her bottom.

She had been shamed into going on the ride, not by Zachary but by his son, the taunting little devil. People scared themselves nigh to death for entertainment in this country, as she'd soon learned on entering this Magic Kingdom. The more they screamed, the greater the fun, apparently. Rolling coast rides that turned a body upside down and inside out. Animals walking about hither and yon, though they were not really animals but people dressed as animals, which was even stranger. And the animals had names, too. Mickey the Mouse. Donald the Duck. Goofy Dog.

In the midst of all this confusion, the little boyling, aptly dubbed Sammy the Snot, whom she had mistakenly considered angelic in the past, had been jeering at her, "Scaredy cat! Scaredy cat!"

How could a Viking not react to such a challenge?

The log was big and long, situated in a trough of low water. It held six bench seats, one behind the other, for a single person each. Danny sat down in front, followed by Sammy, two rowdy boylings of about ten winters, her, and finally Zachary.

Zachary had explained earlier that this ride would show the adventures of a mischievous animal called Brrrr Rabbit as he left his home in the briar patch to search for the laughing place. That sounded barmy but harmless, she had thought. But, wait a minute. "Why are they strapping us in?" she turned and asked Zachary.

"So we don't fall out."

"How could we . . . oh, do not tell me they intend to turn us upside down?"

"Nope. But they are gonna drop us off a mountain that's, oh, let's say, five stories high." He flashed her one of his rascal grins.

"Whaaaat?" she shrieked, but the log had already started moving, and she was busy staring straight ahead, holding on, white-fisted, to the bar in front of her.

Almost immediately, music starting blasting out of the scenery that they passed, weird songs about "Zip-it-he-dodah," all sung by animal creatures. She soon got the flow of a saga being told about Brrrr Rabbit and Brrrr Fox and Brrrr Bear and a briar patch. There was even a "laughing place," and those in the log were told that everyone had a laughing place. Hah! If anyone dared try to find a laughing place on her, they would be minus a hand, she vowed silently. Mayhap it was the same as the funny bone Zachary had said she hit on him in his showering stall yestereve.

Nothing frightening was happening yet . . . just peculiar creatures singing barmy songs about it being a small world, and, of course the zip-it-he-do-dah. And some mild dips of the log, accompanied by mists of water. And the clackety-clack of the log rolling along the track.

Zachary, taking advantage of the lull, leaned forward, lifted her braid, and kissed the back of her neck.

"Do not distract me," she grumbled. "I must concentrate on what is ahead."

"Too bad I didn't have you sit on my lap." He was licking her ear now.

The lout! She would have slapped him away, but she was afraid to take her hands off the bar.

"We could have been having the first ever orgasm falling off Flash Mountain. Betcha we'd set some kind of record."

*If he keeps on licking, I may have one anyhow.*

"This place got that nickname, you know, Flash Mountain, because women were flashing their breasts, not just at the waterfall, but—"

"Waterfall? What waterfall?"

Danny turned around then, winked at her, and gave Zachary a signal involving a circle made by a thumb and forefinger. It was no doubt something obscene.

They entered a dark tunnel in the mountain now.

And of course the rogue behind her took advantage. She felt two hands creep around to cup her breasts from underneath, the thumbs strumming the nipples into aching points. "How does that feel, sweetheart?"

She did not speak, but she moaned her answer.

"That good, huh?" He used thumbs and forefingers now to pull at the nipples and roll them till she felt a soft thrum of pleasure between her legs. "Touch yourself between your legs, sweetheart. Come on. Do it. Please."

She did, and within seconds she was coming apart, her lower body stiff and arched up off the seat as far as the belt would allow her to go.

He kissed her neck and whispered, "Zip-it-he-do-dah, baby!" With the braid back in place, he said something ominous. "Prepare yourself. See that white light at the end of the tunnel?"

"Prepare myself? For what? Oh, you louse, you were trying to distract me when you . . . when I . . . aiyeeeeeeeeeee!"

The log shot out the tunnel into the light, then straight down from a huge height, with water spraying them from all sides. Meanwhile that blasted song was still playing.

When the log came to rest, a crowd cheered, whilst waiting for their turn. She was soaked from the top of her head to her toes, as were others in the log, who were laughing as if it was great fun to be tossed off a mountain and nigh drowned.

Once she was on her feet and had swept wet strands of hair off her face, she searched for Zachary. He stood laughing, like all the rest.

But then she saw he was looking somewhere else. As were some of the men. At her chest. She looked down and saw that her nipples were standing out like sharp pebbles against the wet tea-ing *shert*, due to the cold water and Zachary's wicked fingers.

"You lecherous, loathsome, perverted, odious son of a troll!" She walked over, swung her arm like a windmill, then punched him, missing her mark on his chin and instead landing on his chest. Surprised, he lost his balance and fell flat on his back. If there were not so many people around, she would have jumped on his too-flat belly and pummeled his too-pretty face. As it was, she had already created a scene, with people all around them laughing.

The laughter died down immediately when they became aware that Sammy was on the ground behind them trying to beat on the boy that had sat behind him in the log.

"Raghead! Sand eater! Stinkin' Arab!"

"I am not an Arab. I'm . . . I'm . . ." Sammy seemed unable to come up with a description of exactly what he was. He did have an eastern cast to his features, but his eyes were blue and his cheekbones sharp, like his father's.

Two men who had extraordinary muscles and height, one

blond, the other black-haired, rushed into the area, and one immediately held out his arms, barring people from getting closer. One of them was yelling, "Secure the perimeter! Secure the perimeter!"

She thought she heard Danny mutter, "Good ol' Dad!"

Sammy's boyling target was twice his size, but Sammy was getting in punches here and there. That was before his father picked him up by the belt, leaving the scamp to flail and kick about, using words that brought a blush to Britta's face, and she understood but half of them.

Meanwhile, a bald man—presumably the boyling's father—pulled his son up. Instead of chastising him, his lip curled with disgust on viewing Sammy. The father and son swaggered off. The other boy who had been in the log shot them an embarrassed shrug of apology and went away, too.

The black-haired muscleman followed the trio. The other blended into the crowd directly behind them.

Zachary set Sammy on the ground then and used a white linen he pulled from a pocket in his braies to wipe the dirt off Sammy's face and the blood off his nose and cut lip. "You okay, tiger?"

Sammy nodded and stifled a sob. The brave little thing did not want to cry in public. She knew the feeling well.

Glancing over at Danny, she saw that he appeared equally touched by the scene.

Zachary made a silent signal to someone in the crowd, presumably the blond muscleman. Then he did just the right thing. He swung his son up into his embrace and forced the bloody face into the crook of his neck. He made soothing sounds, like "Forget about them."

"They were jerks," Sammy choked out.

"Yeah, they were. You want me to go beat the crap out of them, the kid and the father?"

Sammy raised his head and grinned at his father. "Would you?"

"If you really want me to."

After a moment, Sammy shook his head and allowed his

father to kiss him on the cheek. But then the boyling followed up with, "I still hate you."

"I know," Zachary said. "Wanna go over to the arcade?
Betcha I can win you a few prizes. You, too, Muhammad Ali,"
he said to Britta. "I'm pretty deadly with the rifle game."

So, still carrying his son, Zachary extended a hand to her.
Danny looped an arm over her shoulder from the other side.
As they walked away, they could have been mistaken for a
family.

And something deep in Britta's soul stretched and sighed.

# Chapter 12

**Like sand through an hourglass, or some such crap . . .**

It was only a matter of time.

Samir knew he would be leaving this country and his father shortly. If he hadn't been certain before, he was now, after seeing Hakim and Daoud, his grandfather's men, hovering behind the merry-go-round, watching for an opportunity to grab him.

That was why he started fighting with that boy. Not that the jerk didn't deserve a beating, but Samir sensed that the two Afghan men were about to pounce. This way Samir drew a crowd, preventing them from taking him without notice.

But Samir was no dummy. The time would come soon.

And his grandfather was going to be so maaaaad. He would blame him for leaving the country. He would say that he could have fought his father and escaped. He would say he was a stupid American. He would say his father was a killer and his mother a whore. What would his punishment be this time? No food for days, probably. Much shouting and insulting, for sure. But the whip? Would the whip be used?

He shivered.

"Hey, kid!" his father said, still holding him. "You're shaking. It's over now."

For a brief moment, Samir allowed himself to be held, nestled against his father's broad chest, his face buried against his neck, which smelled of shaving cream and soap. Then he pulled away and said, "I'm hungry."

His uncle Danny groaned behind them, then tousled his hair. "Kid, you must have a tapeworm."

"I am hungry, too," Britta said.

Sammy smiled at the lady who was big as a tree but told good stories.

"So, what'll it be this time?" his father asked, setting him back on the ground.

He pulled at his shorts and wiggled his butt. Those stupid underpants were up his crack again.

"Cotton candy," he and Britta said at the same time.

## If you think that's crazy . . .

Britta and Sammy had eaten so much cotton candy, they were probably going to piss pink.

But it had been a good day, Zach decided as they left the Disneyland park. Even if he hadn't gotten to screw Britta's brains out, as had been his original plan.

There was hardly room for anyone to sit with all the stuffed animals and other crap he and Danny had won. He'd earned some Dad points with Sammy when he showed him how to hold a rifle at the pigeon-shooting game. That was, until the owner kicked them out for winning too many times.

He'd lost a few points with Britta when he rocked their seat at the top of the Ferris wheel, asking, "Do I rock your world, baby?" She didn't punch him that time, though. And he did please her when he won her a gold heart on a chain; it was junk, but she kept looking at it as if it were some precious jewelry. *Note to self: Buy Britta something nice.*

It was barely five o'clock as he drove back toward San

Diego, but Britta, Danny, and Sammy were dozing. A long day in the sun. And a lot of walking. He wouldn't offer to stop for dinner. Hell, in addition to a ton of cotton candy, they'd had hot dogs, cheeseburgers, French fries, waffle cakes, pizza, popcorn, fudge, and ice cream in the course of their day. He wasn't a gung ho health nut, but he hadn't eaten so much junk food since he was a kid.

Britta moved restlessly, and she turned to look at him through slitted eyes. "Are we almost there?"

"Pretty soon."

She shocked the hell out of him then by reaching over and lacing her fingers with his.

A bit choked, he said, "I'm crazy about you, babe."

She frowned. "Dost mean I turn you demented?"

He laughed. "You could say that."

"Then I am crazy about you, too." With those words, she closed her eyes and fell asleep again.

And thus a thousand-year-old woman managed to rock his world.

**He lured her with the ultimate female temptation . . .**

Britta was sitting at the scullery table, playing a game called poke-her with Danny, whilst waiting for Zachary to take her back to the base. He was upstairs putting an exhausted Sammy to bed.

"How long have you known my brother?" Danny asked the question, then took a drink from a long-necked amber bottle of mead. She was sipping from a glass of the same substance, Danny having told her that ladies usually drank from glasses rather than long-necked bottles, because the bottles gave men wicked ideas. Whatever that meant! And was it not odd that glass was squandered in this country for mere drinking vessels, when a horn or wooden mug would do as well? It must be a prosperous country, indeed.

"Um, two years, but I have not seen him in all that time till this past sennight. I have three of those asses. Are they

worth more than your three kings?" They played games in
her country, too. Dice and the board game *hnefatafl*, but
ne'er had she heard of games using hard parchment "cards"
with pictures and numbers on them. They would wear out
too easily to last long, she would think, but then this was a
wasteful country.

"It's a-sez, not asses," he said, smiling at her. "But, nope.
Kings beat a-sez. I win." With a mischievous grin, he drew
the round chips toward his already impressive pile and began
to shuffle the cards again. Then he studied her for a moment,
as if an idea had come to him, unbidden. "Aha! So, you're
the one."

"Which one?"

"Zach hasn't been the same since he came back from
Norway two years ago."

For some reason, she felt pleased at that news. "How is he
different?"

"For one thing, he's more selective in . . ." He let his
words trail off, mayhap having second thoughts about dis-
closing such intimate details about his kin.

"More selective in which women he swives?" she finished for him.

Danny choked on his mead, spraying the table. After he
got a cloth and wiped the table and the cards off, he studied
her with speculation. "You talk peculiar."

"Hah! Methinks you are the one who talks peculiar."

"*Touché!* No, I wouldn't say he was more selective about
*who* he got involved with. He was always picky that way, and
let's face it, with a face like his, he always gets the pick of
the crop. No, he cut way back on . . . um, relationships, period."

She narrowed her gaze at him. "Surely you are not saying
he became celibate."

Danny laughed. "Hardly. But he stopped setting world
records."

"As if that is an achievement to be lauded!"

"You're pretty hard on Zach. Why is that?"

"My father and brothers were evil fornicators. They tupped every girl or woman who caught their eyes, willing or not. Bastards abounded, so many I lost track years ago. In their opinion, women were property, their only worth in the breeding of heirs and coin from prospective husbands."

"Wow! And you place Zach in that same category?"

"Well, nay, but 'tis best for a woman to steer clear of comely men with the morals of a goat."

Danny laughed and reached across the table to squeeze her hand. "Babe, you are gonna be so good for my brother. Don't be hard on him, though. There's a good reason why we're both so screwed up. We come from a dysfunctional family."

"Diss-what?"

He smiled. "Screwed up. Broken. Our mother, divorced long ago from our dad, and our grandmothers are like female Attila the Huns. Our grandfather is a pole-up-the-ass rigid military man. Our father has been married five times. Right now he has a girlfriend who's practically a teenager."

Britta shrugged. "The *more Danico*. Many wives. We have that in my country, too. I knew one Viking jarl who had four wives, eight concubines, and ten female thralls to serve his needs."

Danny's eyes went wide. "Not all at once. My father divorces one before marrying another. Geez, where are you from?"

"The Norselands," she answered, though she could see it was not explanation enough for him. "So, mayhap Zachary has learned his lessons from his father?"

"Zach is in no way like Dad, and you're a fool if you can't see that."

"Your defense of your brother is commendable. I was not being insulting, just seeking explanations."

"Listen, bottom line. Zach has—or has had—so many women for one reason only. He can."

"Are you talking about me?" Zachary said, coming into the kitchen and sitting down in an empty chair.

Britta and Danny both smiled, not about to disclose their conversation.

"What are you playing?" he asked.

"Strip poker," Danny said.

Zachary glared at his brother, but she was not sure why.

"Will you take me back to the base now?" she asked Zachary. "Your brother is here to watch Sammy. There is no excuse."

"Do I need an excuse?"

"Um, I think I'll go shave, maybe go down to the Wet and Wild for a little action," Danny said, rising and making his way to the door. "If you want, I can drop Britta off on the way."

Zachary looked at her and took her hand. "Don't go," he urged. "You don't have to muster till oh five hundred. I can get you there in plenty of time." Meanwhile, his thumb drew circles on her palm, which caused the fine hairs to stand out all over her body, deliciously so. She felt light-headed with instant arousal.

"How do you do that?" she asked.

"Do what?"

"Make me want you."

He smiled, one of those glorious you-please-me-sweetling smiles that would melt even the chastest maid. "Stay with me. Please."

"Why?"

"Because we won't have any private time for the next three weeks. Because I don't think I can stay away from you that long. Because I'll risk my career and yours if I go sniffing after you on duty."

She couldn't help but smile. "See. I told you that you have a habit of sniffing."

He squeezed her hand in admonition for her teasing. "Will you stay?"

As much as she wanted to, she hesitated. "I am fearful."

"Of me?" He was clearly shocked.

She shook her head. "Nay. Of myself. I cannot grow too

attached to you, because no matter what you or Hilda or the others say, there is always the chance I will be sent back." *Or you will move on to some other woman.*

He nodded in understanding. "Just like Sammy."

"Huh?"

"Sammy tries his best to hate me, or pretend to hate me, because he's convinced that I'll either send him back or that his grandfather will take him away. If he doesn't care, there is no risk of being hurt."

Much as she would like to disagree, he made a point. "Ne'er have I avoided hurt," she said hesitantly, thinking as she spoke. "'Tis a coward who would do that."

He shrugged, and afore he was able to mask it, she saw a gleam of victory in his mischievous blue eyes.

"You have tricked me with your web of words," she accused.

"That depends on whether you've agreed to stay or not."

"We have a saying in my land. 'Beware of rogues with lustsome charms; they lure maids with their honey words.'"

*"Honey,"* he said, standing and pulling her into his arms, "we have a proverb here, too. 'Beware, ladies, who withhold your honey; men will eat you in the end.'"

"I like my saying better than yours," she said on a moan. He had his hands on her buttocks, pressing her into the cradle of his hips, and he was nibbling at her ear.

"Whatever you say, sweetheart."

She was not fooled by his false submission. "I have not yet agreed to stay," she still insisted.

*So said the fly to the spider, just before being caught.* He, meaning the spider, put the final knot in her noose—uh, web—by offering her the ultimate temptation.

"How would you like to take a bubble bath?"

**Even _he_ had never tried THAT before . . .**

Zach was a regular sex machine. Or at least he planned to be. Once he got off the frickin' phone.

He had seven hours before he had to get Britta back to the base, and he grudgingly admitted that he would have to allow at least three hours for sleep. Otherwise, she would be dead on her feet in the grueling rotation of exercises this week.

With his cordless phone in hand, he checked his messages as he walked Britta up the stairs. *Thank God for multitasking!*

"Mayhap this is a bad idea. Mayhap I should return to the base and get some sleep. Mayhap—"

"No, no, no! This is a very good idea. It'll make you relax and smell good and, did I tell you, bubble baths give soldiers stamina to fight on the field? Something about proteins or minerals or extra oxygen in the bubbles." *What a load of crap!*

"They do?" She narrowed her eyes with suspicion. "Do you take bubble baths?"

"All the time."

"Methinks all these orgasms are draining my body of strength, and I will be unable to keep up with WEALS for the next sennight."

"Baby, this is the God's honest truth," he made a sign of the cross over his heart, "orgasms are good for the body. I can show you some books on the subject, once you learn to read. Too much sex is never a bad thing."

"Well . . ." She was still unconvinced.

*Man, I must be losing my touch.* He held the opened bottle of the Calgon bubble bath under Britta's nose. His mother's habit of leaving all her beauty products in her wake was finally bearing fruit for him.

"Lavender." She sighed.

*Well maybe lavender, not fruit,* he joked with himself.

"Well, mayhap I can stay a little bit longer."

He did a mental high five.

"Okay, honey, take off your clothes while I run the water in the tub and pour in the bubble crap . . . I mean, liquid. Once you get in, let the water go up to about an inch from the top."

He glanced away as Britta eased her nude body into the

old-fashioned, freestanding tub. If he looked, he'd be in there with her, and then he'd never complete a few urgent tasks before hitting the sack.

He got Britta settled in the tub overflowing with bubbles. He'd poured a half bottle of the Calgon in before reading the directions. She was half-asleep before he even left the bathroom, her neck resting on the back lip of the tub, her long hair hanging over the side.

Then he rushed downstairs, removing his clothes in the process. While he walked through the house, checking on locks and dimming lights, he studied the display window on his phone and groaned. Twelve more calls to check! Calls that had been made to his house, not cell, phone. He listened to all the messages and knew that he had to answer a few of the more urgent ones.

"Jack Delaney here."

"Zach Floyd. You called earlier?"

Delaney was the hotshot lawyer his grandfather had hired. He was considered the F. Lee Bailey of international law and high-profile legal disputes, well worth his exorbitant fees. "Yes, glad you got back to me tonight. Listen, can you meet with me tomorrow morning? I can come in on the red-eye."

"Yeah. Sure. I suppose. Is there a problem?"

Delaney laughed. "Boy, there are problems and then there are *problems*. Arsallah is playing hardball. I won't go into details over the phone, but you need a contingency plan in case things don't go the way we want . . . at first."

Zach knew exactly what he meant by a contingency plan. They'd discussed it before. Taking Sammy into deep hiding on a short-term, or maybe even long-term basis. How the SEALs command would feel about that was a given. Zach's ass would be fried.

"Your grandfather's coming with me."

Zach groaned.

"I can tell him you'd rather speak with me alone, if you want. You're the client."

"No, that's all right. I just don't want this to spiral into a lot of other personal shit." *Why don't you quit the SEALs and come to the Pentagon? When are you going to settle down? How could you have gotten a woman pregnant in this day and age? The usual.*

Delaney laughed. "I'll steer the conversation in the right direction."

Next he called his grandmother.

"Zach-ar-y Frank Floyd! Why is it I had to hear about this special woman in your life from Daniel?"

"When did you talk to Danny?"

"An hour ago."

*I'll kill him. Did he have to be on his cell, even on the way to the Wet and Wild?*

"Sooooo, are we talking wedding bells here, darling?"

"No, we're not talking wedding bells. Or engagement rings, if that's your next question."

"It's not too soon to get registered at Neiman's."

"You are *not* registering me anywhere. Do you hear me?"

"When can I meet her?" This was so like his grand-mother; she heard only what she wanted to hear.

"I don't have a clue. At least not for a few weeks, assuming she's still around by then. She's in that new WEALS program, and—" *Oh, God! Did I just admit there is a woman.*

"A military woman! PopPop will be so pleased." His grandmother was the only person in the world who called the general by that ludicrous name.

"Listen, I have to go."

"Where's she from?"

He barely stifled a laugh. *Eleventh-century Norselands.* "Norway."

"Oh, that's nice. Some of your ancestors were from Nor-way, did you know that? The Floydsson family, but they pro-nounced it Flewed-son."

*That's it!* "Gotta go. Call you later." He clicked the phone off before his grandmother could blather on . . . or ask him where Britta was at the moment.

Before he had a chance to put the cordless down, it rang again. His mother.

"Who is she? Is she pretty? I hear she's tall enough to be a model. Make sure you don't flub this one up."

"Flub? What's a flub?" *Is it anything like that other F word?*

"You know exactly what I mean."

"So, who did I flub before?"

"Every relationship you've ever had was a flub. You're like a bee buzzing from one flower to another. Be careful, or you'll lose your stinger someday, and then where will you be?"

*My stinger is just fine, thank you very much.*

"I bought the cutest Muppets underpants for Sammy today. I'll mail them tomorrow."

Zach had to smile at that. The kid was already unhappy about superhero briefs . . . and the wedgies they gave him. What was he gonna think about Miss Piggy riding his too-too?" Too-too had been his mother's word for *penis* when he and Danny were kids.

He figured he better return his father's call, as well. Not wanting to play favorites with the other family members.

"Hiiiii!" a female voice answered, sounding about sixteen years old to his father's fifty-six. Actually, Bridget was more like twenty-five. Women were attracted to his dad because of his wealth and influence in the television industry, but Zach had to admit, his father was also a good-looking man for his age—and very charming. Genetic traits, he liked to think.

"Hi, Bridget. Is my father there?"

She giggled. "He's . . . uh, sleeping, ya know." *Giggle, giggle.* "I could wake him up, ya know, if it's really important."

"That's all right. Just tell him I called."

The lights off, he went up the stairs, first checking on Sammy, who was dead to the world. It had been a long day for him. He leaned down and kissed the brat's forehead. He smelled of cotton candy and kid. In so many ways, Zach missed being free, as he had been a few short months ago, but he realized now that he wouldn't give up his son for all the freedom in the world.

The cordless phone rang again, and he rushed out of the room before Sammy awakened, closing the door halfway behind him. He recognized the security company number on the caller ID.

"Elliott Samboro here. Exeter Termite Control," one of the partners in Vortex said in a gruff voice befitting the former Marine. Elliott Samboro was his code name; his real name was Tony Siliano.

"What's up?"

"Mr. Floyd, you have a serious roach problem."

"How serious?"

"I think we should talk about it in person. Better I should show you."

Uh-oh. Siliano's words told him, in code, that the line was being bugged. How that happened when they'd done sweeps twice a day was scary. Arsallah's men were better skilled than he'd imagined. "Okay. Tomorrow?"

"Sure thing. There'll be three reps there, early."

Three reps meant that Vortex was upping the security surveillance.

"And, by the way, you should check over anyone entering or leaving your house till we get the problem corrected. Roaches can attach themselves to clothing or things, like grocery bags or briefcases or stuffed animals."

*Stuffed animals? Oh, shit! Arsallah's goons followed us to Disneyland.*

"Can they be here early . . . like seven thirty? I've got some other appointments."

"Yep."

Zach quickly called the commander's house and left a message for Madrene not to come tomorrow to babysit, that he'd made other plans. He figured it would be safer to have Wilson and Danny inside, with the Vortex guys on the outside, for the time being.

He was down to his briefs but decided to backtrack to the

kitchen and grab a bottle of wine, a corkscrew, and two glasses before heading to the bathroom . . . and paradise.

Britta was in the same position, lying back, asleep, in the tub, which was surprisingly still full of bubbles. There was a frown on her face, though, and occasionally her body jerked as if she was dreaming about something unpleasant.

He opened the wine, poured some into the two glasses, and set them on a low stool near the tub. Then he shucked his briefs, dimmed the lights, and eased himself into the tub behind Britta. "Move forward, honey," he said, even as he extended his legs on either side of her hips.

"Nay. Desist, you maggot! Ahhhhh, nay, not Sister Efreda, and Sister Seraphina and . . . ! You beasts! Such rape and carnage!" Water was splashing all over the place, against the wall, on the floor, in both their faces.

Britta had come awake, startled and disoriented in the tight grasp of his arms. She must have thought she was back in her country and time, not a pleasant place to be.

"Shhh, it's okay."

Once she settled down, he loosened his hold on her, and she turned slightly to peer at him over her shoulder. "What . . . where?"

"You fell asleep in the tub."

"Oh." She still frowned. "I had a horrific dream. But it was not really a dream. More like I was floating between two worlds. Being tugged in different directions. I was back at the nunnery, where my father's hird of soldiers were—"

"Shhh, it's okay now." He kissed her lightly on the lips.

Her eyes widened then. "What are you doing in this tub?"

"Joining you?"

"Why?"

He laughed and reached for the two glasses, handing her one. "Drink. It'll relax you and make the bad dreams go away."

She took several sips, sighed, then leaned back against his chest, seemingly unaware of his erection prodding at her butt and his one hand pressed against her belly.

He used his big toe to turn the hot water on to a slow

trickle. Any excess would go out the top drain, thus preventing an overflow. They were swathed in steam and bubbles
and a slow-building sexual lethargy that would soon turn to
sexual frenzy. He hoped. He was already halfway there.

When she emptied her wineglass, he poured them both
another.

"Methinks this wine is more potent than Sister Margaret's mead," she murmured. "It makes me feel strange. As
if parts of me are melting away."

"Your inhibitions?"

She made a small snorting sound. "Pfff! My inhibitions
were lost with you on our first meeting."

"I had you on hello, huh? Too bad I didn't know that you
trying to lop off my head was a form of foreplay."

She slapped at his hand, the hand that was fondling her
nipples. Setting his wineglass down, he continued to use his
left hand to tease her nipples, first one, then the other. At the
same time, he burrowed the fingers of his right hand into her
hair on the one side, turning her into his kiss, which was wide-
mouthed and hungry. He took her whole mouth in his, over
and over, as if he were eating her whole with his lips. Then he
used his lips to widen hers as far as they would go before
tonguing her inside . . . up, down, around the roof and over
her inner jaw. His never-ending wet kiss allowed her no opportunity to reciprocate. He was bruising, demanding, devouring in his intensity.

When she moaned into his mouth, he slowed down.

She moved her hips on him, and he realized that his erection was no longer prodding her butt. She was sitting on him,
perfectly aligning his hard-on with her crack, back to front.

"I have an idea," he whispered into her ear.

"More ideas? How many more ideas can one man have?"
Her voice was thick and sultry, and he didn't think it was because of the wine.

"Thousands," he answered.

Raising them both up on their knees, he said, "Hold on to
the two faucets with your hands, and brace your arms."

"Whaaat?"

Before she could guess what he was about, he entered her from behind and rose in one smooth sweep till he was standing. The only thing keeping her from falling into the water was her hands on the faucets and his hands on her hips.

She squealed and tried to flail her legs to dislodge him. "Are you barmy? Upside down swiving? Surely sane people do not do this."

"Oh, yeah, they do. This is one of women's favorite positions. Besides, you aren't really upside down. You're more like on an incline. Yeah, I like the sound of that. Inclined sex."

"Put. Me. Down."

"Not. A. Chance."

"I feel ridiculous."

"I don't know. You look pretty good from this angle. And I can't believe I'm capable of talking above a croak when I'm inside you, practically to your tonsils."

She said some things to him in Old Norse, probably not flattery.

"Put your knees on my hips, sweetie. That's the way." He helped her adjust herself so that her inner knees pressed against his hips, and her ankles crossed behind his ass. "Good thing we've been working you WEALS on upper arm strength this week. You could probably stay like this for hours."

"I swear, you will pay for this, you lout."

"Whatever you say, baby. By the way, do you know what the best thing is about this position? I get to do whatever I want with your body, and you can't do a damn thing about it."

She was silent for a moment, digesting his words as she realized that she was in fact wide open to whatever he wanted to do. And there were lots of things he wanted to do. *Where to start, where to start?*

"And your point is?"

"I'm going to make you come, and come, and come."

She groaned. "What have I done to deserve such punishment?"

"Not punishment. I'm putting my mark on you, baby. No matter what happens with us in the future, it'll never be as good for you with another man. You'll always remember this night and know we had something special."

"And you? Mayhap I will spoil you for other women as well."

"Sweetheart, that's already a given."

Then words became useless, except for one long whimper of ecstasy, on both their parts. First he brought her to climax just by playing with her dangling breasts. When her inner folds began to milk his cock, he immediately moved his hand to her clit, strumming it to full-blown, swollen attention. Only then did he begin the long strokes that would bring them both to completion. But he didn't want that to happen too soon. So he strummed her inner folds till they were swollen and dripping against his fingers. With her in this kind of frenzy, he used his other hand to touch her in that place between them, nestled against his stomach, that spot most women did not like to have touched, or thought they did not like to have touched.

So, stroking her from both sides, as well as inside, she began to cry out her orgasm . . . an orgasm that went on and on and on, stronger and stronger, as his strokes became shorter and harder, and his fingers became ruthlessly demanding.

He had no idea how many times she came before he was unable to hold back any longer. With the cords standing out against his arched neck, his hands on both her hips holding her in place, he bellowed out his coming, nipping at her shoulder like a wild stallion.

Afterward, he picked her up and sat back down in the tub, with her straddling his lap, her face in the crook of his neck. They were both panting, unable to speak. Half the water from the tub was on the floor, but who the hell cared! In that afterglow of good sex, he kept caressing her shoulders and back, rocking forward and backward, more in a soothing than sexual manner. He was murmuring, "Omigod. Omigod."

When his pulse came down to about a thousand beats per minute, and his brain began to clear, he realized something important.

He'd forgotten to use a condom.

# Chapter 13

**And then the fun began . . .**

It was still dark when Zachary drove her back to the military base. Danny had come back to care for Sammy after his "night on the town," whatever that meant.

She glanced about at her surroundings. Lights on poles illuminated the roadways and metal vehicles they passed or saw parked along the side. Some of the buildings were dark, but there were lights in many of them. Even though it was the middle of the night, there was still activity going on at a military base. They had to pass through a special, guarded gate even to get onto the base.

She was a different person than the one who had left here two nights ago on the way to her welcoming fete at Madrene's keep. For one thing, she felt a not-unpleasant ache betwixt her legs. For another, her lips and breasts were no doubt swollen from Zachary's unrelenting erotic ministrations. And she for a certainty knew what multiple orgasms were now.

When she had time to think about it, she would blush at

some of the things she had allowed the rogue to do to her. Hah! She would blush even more over things she had done to him.

She had slept intermittently through the night. In the tub. And betwixt bouts of bedsport. But every time she fell asleep the most gruesome dreams—rather, night terrors— came to her. All taking place at the abbey. All involving her father and brothers and hirdsmen torturing the good nuns to reveal where she was supposedly hiding.

"Why so quiet, babe'?" He reached over and took her hand in his. The other steered the wheel on the car.

"These images keep flickering through my mind."

"Of us having wild monkey sex?"

"Nay! I need no mind pictures to recall *that*." She squeezed his hand tightly in reproval. "I believe I am having visions of things happening right now, in the past."

"Are you talking about the nightmares?" He'd had to shake her awake from one of them.

She nodded.

"Maybe it's just guilt or something."

She shrugged. "Mayhap. But I am beginning to think there was some method to this madness of my time travel." *And it is a madness in itself that I am accepting the concept of time travel.*

"And that would be?"

"Perchance the gods sent me here to learn modern fighting techniques so that I can gather an army and go back to fight against evil . . . in particular, the evil perpetuated by my father and his followers."

Zachary was oddly quiet.

She turned in her seat to look at him. "What?"

"I don't want you to go away."

A thrill of pleasure coursed through her at his words.

By the light of the dashing board, she could see his face grow grim. "I don't want you to go away . . . *yet*," he amended.

She had to smile at that halfhearted amended statement

of his feelings for her. "Dost think I could? Go back, I mean?"

"I have no idea."

"Something is happening to me. Something even stranger than the time travel. I sense being tugged back."

He flashed a quick glance of alarm. "It was just a dream. You can't just go back," he insisted.

She shrugged. "You and Torolf's men went back."

"That was an accident."

"Are you sure about that?"

He arched his brows at her.

"Mayhap, where there is a need for a hero, the gods—or your One-God—send warriors hither and yon to fight the good battles."

"You think I'm a hero, huh?"

She could tell he was trying to change the subject. "Would you go back with me?" she asked softly.

He drew back, taking his hand away.

She had surprised herself, not having planned to ask such a question. Not even sure she wanted to go back herself.

"Absolutely not! Are you crazy?" He must have realized how he sounded, because he immediately tried to take her hand again, which she would not allow. "I can't risk going away, not with Sammy's situation."

She stared at him, unblinking.

"No way! I wouldn't try to go back in time *with* Sammy, either, if that's what you're thinking. Even if I could. He's in enough danger here without me putting him in the middle of some Dark Age uncivilization."

He pulled up in front of the women's sleeping quarters. When she tried to open the door, he pressed a lever that locked her in. She turned her face away from him, not wanting him to see her tears. Tears, for the love of Loki! She was not a weeping woman, or ne'er had been till she met him.

"Don't go away angry," he urged, trying to pull her into his arms. "You're going to hate me enough during the upcoming

WEALS rotations. At least let us keep this special bond we seem to have separate from the military crap."

"You mean sex?"

"Well, yeah, you must admit we're incredible together."

"And that is everything to you?"

"Don't put words in my mouth," he snapped, then immediately regretted his words, tugging on her arm to pull her closer. "Come on, give me a good-bye kiss. I don't want you angry with me, not after what we've shared these past two days."

She knew better than to allow his embrace, knowing the effect he had on her. In a trice, she would be in his lap, rubbing their nether parts raw. "I am not angry. Just disappointed."

"I enjoyed being with you, Britta." He used a forefinger to trace circles on the back of her neck. "I care about you."

Minutes later she was tiptoeing into the chamber she shared with the three other women, who were thankfully sleeping. She knew she'd hurt Zachary when she declined his kiss and pushed out of his arms. She knew she was being unreasonable in expecting him to grant her such a great favor, putting his son at risk. She knew he'd just given her the best two days of her life, and for that alone he deserved a token of her thanks. But she was in a contrary mood. And she was very worried about what might be happening back in her own time.

It took her a long time to fall asleep.

It was just past dawn when she and the other women throughout the sleeping quarters, not just their room, were awakened by a loud ruckus. First a shrill, loud, long blast of a whistle. Men—the instructors, it turned out—were banging on the doors and yelling into objects held up to their mouths that magnified their voices. Weapons were firing out in the hall, and flares of light were going off.

"Fall out! Fall out!" one person screamed. "Out of your racks!"

"On your feet! On your feet!" someone else yelled.

"Get up, you lazy maggots," the instructor known as F.U. hollered through the now-open doorway.

"Go, go, go!" It was Cage—rather, Instructor LeBlanc—joining in the yell-fest.

Thus far, none of them had entered the sleeping chamber, just opened the doors, presumably respecting the privacy of the women. At first, that was.

"Oh, great!" Terri whispered. "Do they have to use those bullhorns? I have the hangover from hell."

"I just hope those aren't live rounds they're firing from those machine guns," Donita remarked, even as she jumped out of her sleeping pallet and stood at attention, like the other ladies.

"Nah. They're blanks," said Marie. "And firecrackers."

"You are the sorriest group of pretend warriors I have ever had the misfortune to meet," Commander MacLean said, storming into the room. So much for privacy! He needed no bullhorn to increase the volume of his voice. It was ear-splittingly loud on its own.

Disoriented, Britta was having trouble rising to her feet like the other women. Her brain told her to follow what the others did; her aching body had other ideas.

"Petty Officer Asado, either ring out or get your lazy butt in gear," the commander yelled, right in her face. For a brief second, Britta thought about saying that she would tell Madrene on him, but that would mean she expected special treatment, which she did not.

Instructor F.U. looked at her in passing. Then his head snapped back to look at her more closely. "What the hell have you been doing, Asado?"

There was a brief lull in the yelling and noise as everyone, including the women, turned to look at her, then smile. She was wearing the finger sleeping *shert* that covered her with a modicum of modesty, so she had no idea why they were all gawking.

"Way to go, girl!" Terri whispered behind her hand.

"Guess she knows what an orgasm is now," Donita added in a low enough voice the men couldn't hear.

"Ya look lak ya been wrestlin' a gator, *chère*," Marie added.

Obviously, what she'd been doing the past two days was evident in her appearance.

The commander just shook his head, as if she was a hopeless case. Or more likely that opinion was directed at Zachary.

Master Chieftain F.U. was not about to remain silent, though. "Well, well, well. Someone in this room got laid this weekend. And laid. And laid. And laid. Dare we ask who the lucky fellow was, Asado? Or was it a woman?"

"What a jerk!" Terri murmured.

"Enough of that, Uxley," the commander said, motioning for the chieftain to leave the room. But to Terri, the commander said, "Did I hear someone complain? Was that you, Evans? Did you dare to complain? Drop and give me twenty and make it quick."

Terri dropped to the floor and began doing pushing-ups.

Master Chieftain Simms, the black-skinned instructor, shoved his way into the little room, too, passing F.U. on the way out. While he shouted, he was firing his weapon at the ceiling. They could barely hear him say, "Are you giving me a look, Ms. Leone? Are you giving me a look? I think a little cargo net, carrying a fifty-pound backpack, might be just the thing."

Donita glared at him, and Master Chieftain Simms grinned at her, flashing white teeth against his dark skin.

"I'll give you ladies three minutes to dress and get yourselves down on the beach for some surf appreciation," Commander MacLean said, glancing at the timing bracelet at his wrist.

They were already rustling into their exercising clothes when the box on the wall started to crackle.

"Attention, attention!" she heard a familiar voice announce. It was Zachary. "Welcome to week two of WEALS. It will be my pleasure to show you a little torture, Navy SEAL style."

Zachary had warned her that he would be one of her tormentors in the next weeks. She just hadn't realized it would happen so quickly.

**This is the way the big boys play, honey . . .**

The grinder had been made to resemble a war zone, designed to scare the spit out of the newbies and force some of the weaker ones to quit.

The predawn darkness was illuminated in an eerie fashion by flames blasting out of M60 machine gun muzzles. Red and green smoke created by M18 grenades. Noise of bombs bursting blared out of the speakers. While at first glance, it might all seem like a cruel Halloween fright-night tableau, it was in fact a replica of what they might face in battle. If they couldn't handle the shock here, they sure as hell couldn't survive on a live op.

Not all the trainees were shocked or amused. He heard one of them remark, "Men and their silly war games!" That one would be spouting a different tune come nightfall, if she hadn't already rung out, Zach guessed.

Another one said, "It's gonna take more than firecrackers and a Freddy Krueger SEAL to scare me off."

He mouthed to Cage, "Me, Freddy Krueger?"

Cage laughed. "Nah, you too pretty. Mus' be F.U. she's talkin 'bout."

First thing up for the women was a quick tour of the O-course . . . also known as the Oh-My-God obstacle course. *Quick* being a relative term. There were more than a dozen different obstacles here that had to be climbed, crawled, lifted, or shoved, all to use every muscle in the body. The cargo net, the Tower, a tire sequence, the Weaver, and lots of other good stuff. Everything was timed, though those times were reduced for the WEALS. Some SEAL trainees not-so-lovingly dubbed this the "Kiddie Playground from Hell."

And it wasn't just trainees who used this course. Well-seasoned SEALs were required to run the evolution before any live op. An oft-quoted saying around the compound was: "The more SEALs sweat in peacetime, the less they bleed in war."

An hour later, and the women were being marched down to the beach by the commander and by F.U., and a half dozen other instructors, for a quick, cold dunking, a roll in the sand, and a five-mile run along the shore. Just for a wake-up call. The instructor-to-trainee ratio would be high during the next week or two to ensure safety during exercises that could be unsafe.

Most of them didn't like inflicting pain on the trainees but knew there was a reason for the torment to come. F.U. yelling into a bullhorn, on the other hand, just enjoyed it.

Even the cold water, irritating sand, and energy-draining runs might seem like wasted exercises, but they also replicated battle scenarios where comfort was the last thing a warrior might have. Just how long could an operator stand in water or remain immobile when being driven crazy by the itch of a sand rash? And the constant running, well, everyone knew it developed stamina and leg muscles.

Zach walked at the tail end, talking to Cage, Sly, JAM, Geek, and Max, who had agreed to help him with WEALS till they got called up to a live op. Which might be any minute.

"Way to go, dude!" Cage said to him.

"Huh?"

Glancing around in the dawn light, he saw that all the guys were grinning at him.

"What?"

"*Cher*, you look lak ya been pulled through the sex keyhole, backward," Cage said, giving him a good-buddy jab in the upper arm. "In the bayou, we calls it the sex flush."

He tried to pretend ignorance but felt his face heat.

"The boy can still blush!" JAM hooted with laughter.

"I don't know what you're talking about," he tried to say.

"Man, have you looked in the mirror today?" Max asked. "Your lips are swollen, like you got a freakin' collagen injection."

"More like a tonsil hockey injection," Cage interjected. "Talk about!"

"You got a bite mark on your neck," Max continued. "In fact, I could swear that's a bite mark on your inner thigh."

He glanced down. There was nothing there beneath his shorts, but it was too late. He'd revealed the possibility that there might have been.

"Actually," Geek began, "there really is such a thing as a sex flush. During sex, blood rushes to the genitals and all the other body extremities, including the face. The flush, which mostly resembles a measles-type rash, usually goes away after orgasm. Except if a person has an excessive number of orgasms in a short period of time. Some people even take niacin or vitamin $B_3$ a half hour before sex to increase the blood flow to the skin and mucous membranes. There was even a guy in China who—" Geek stopped midsentence, noticing that everyone was staring at him. The boy did astonish them sometimes with his font of knowledge. "I'm just sayin'," he concluded with his own blush.

"Open your mouth and show me your mucus," JAM requested of Zach with fake seriousness.

"Bite me!"

"I'd say you already had way too much of that," JAM shot right back.

"So how's the love glove comin'?" Cage asked Geek.

"It's a penile glove. Sheesh!" Geek corrected, then realized that Cage was just ribbing him. "Great. The website is up, and Julie had five thousand hits the first hour. They can't make the product fast enough to fill orders."

"Amazing!" Zach said, not because the concept was so outlandish. Hell, they had everything on the Internet, even . . . well, everything. The amazing thing was that Geek was involved. He was beginning to think that Geek's naive-and-inexperienced persona was a big scam.

"Back to Big Mama," Cage said to Zach. "How ya gonna separate WEALS from yer love life, *cher*?"

"I don't know, but I have to. I can't treat Britta any differently than the others."

"Oooh, boy! This oughta be good," JAM remarked. "Pretty Boy restraining his libido!"

Did everyone really think he had that little control over his sex life?

Probably.

They must think his dick was on autopilot every minute of the day. For the first time in his life, he was embarrassed by his reputation.

He and his guys put the bell on the back of a pickup truck and drove it to the grinder so that it would be visible and readily available to the women who were ready to quit. Then they pulled out the heavy kapok life vests, which had been around since Moses was a kid . . . or at least before World War II. The vests kept even an unconscious person floating in turbulent waters. They also pulled out the women's personal helmet liners, preparing for the next rotation. Two dozen helmet liners of already rung-out trainees were arranged beside the bell . . . a graveyard of sorts.

Every class of Navy SEALs painted their helmet liners with the class number on the front and back, along with their last names. Green for first phase, blue for second phase, and red for third phase. These ladies had made their own personal statement by painting theirs pink with #1 on front and back.

After that, they lugged out the heavy IBSs. Inflatable Boats, Small, were among the most hated training tools in all SEAL training. They weighed several hundred pounds even without being packed with equipment, and they had to be carried on the heads or extended arms of the trainees at almost all times. This rotation alone should result in a dozen women ringing the bell.

"Listen up, ladies," Zach told the group when they came back. "This is your new best friend. Inflatable Boat, Small. Better known as IBS. Or 'that frickin' boat.' From now on, you will carry it almost everywhere, even to the chow hall, mostly on top of your heads, six persons to a boat, three on each side. Now, some of our SEALs have been known to develop permanent bald spots from their IBS experiences." He waited till their protests died down and till they watched two women walk over, take off their helmets, place them in the line, then ring the bell. "But we are going to make a concession to your female sensibilities." Some of the women made disparaging remarks about the likelihood of that, which he chose to ignore. "So, you may wear one of these pretty little bathing caps." He twirled a red, butt-ugly, thick rubber cap on a forefinger up in the air. Or you can wear your helmet liners all the time, which could be uncomfortable. Or you can risk baldness. Your choice." They all took the caps, muttering as they did so.

"Another thing," Commander MacLean interjected. "I've been hearing way too much muttering. Next mutter I hear, and the whole group of you will be punished. One for all and all for one."

Donita Leone, once a famous Olympic swimmer, made the mistake of muttering, "Sadistic bastard."

Simms, who seemed to have an attraction for his black "sister," stepped forward gleefully, motioning with a forefinger for her to follow him back to the grinder. "How do you feel about Helen Kellers?" everyone heard him say. Helen Keller was a politically incorrect name for an exercise in which half sit-ups were done holding the back off the ground at a forty-five-degree angle and hands cupping the ears. A leg was lifted a few inches off the ground, then a knee brought up till the leg was ninety degrees to the hip. Only then was the elbow of the opposite arm brought over to touch the knee. Over and over. Alternating sides. Supreme balance, muscle control, and stomach muscles of steel were required to do them properly, which most people didn't. Instead, they flailed around like . . . well, Helen Keller. Donita was doing a pretty good imitation now of the famous deaf lady immortalized in that movie with Patty Duke.

"Let's start with surf appreciation," Zach ordered the

others. "Into the water, ladies. Pronto." When they had waded into the surf, shivering despite the temperature, which wasn't all that cold today, about seventy degrees already, he yelled out, "Line up and lock arms. All fifty of you. Now, march into the surf zone and sit down. You heard me. Sit the hell down." Instantly the icy waves came crashing over them.

He made them sit there for three minutes, but it probably felt like an hour before he shouted for them to come to shore. "Up boats, ladies. Time for a short run to warm you up."

Britta was visibly shivering, her teeth chattering, when she came out.

"Are you cold, Asado?" he inquired. "I can get you warm real quick. All you gotta do is ring out."

She said something in Old Norse that he was pretty sure equated with "Get a life, bozo."

After much clumsy scrambling, they got the knack of holding the IBSs on their heads. Little did they know that quickly they would experience an almost unbearable pain in the neck and jaws, even the ankles and knees, just from the weight of the rubber boat as they ran.

He had to give them credit when they began calling out what had to be a quickly improvised series of jody calls. Anyone who had ever seen the movie *Stripes* knew how ridiculous they could be. These particular ones seemed to be prompted by a woman from Nashville that someone had told him was a country western singer. Her name was Alda Sue Perry.

*"I don't know but I been told,"* Alda Sue sang out.

*"I don't know but I been told,"* the rest of the women repeated.

*"Navy SEALs aren't all that hot."*

*"Navy SEALs aren't all that hot."*

*"Of women, they know diddly squat."*

*"Of women, they know diddly squat."*

*"That's the truth, we swear to that."*

*"That's the truth, we swear to that."*

*"Now WEALS may be hot to trot,"*

*"Now WEALS may be hot to trot,"*
*"But not for a webfoot hotshot."*
*"But not for a webfoot hotshot."*
*"Keep it up, SEALs cannot."*
*"Keep it up, SEALs cannot."*
*"Sound off, one, two . . ."*
*"Three, four."*

"Very funny," the commander said. "Enough slacking off. Pick up speed here, ladies, or ring out. This isn't a turtle race. We have something fun planned back on the grinder. Betcha that bell will be ringing then."

A communal groan followed his words.

They ran five miles, which was a lot for some of these women. Halfway back to the command center, they were really dragging, the weight of the boats and length of their run catching up with even the fittest of them. He knew from experience that their muscles were screaming by now, especially the back of the neck.

Britta was in the middle of the line, struggling, but no more than the others. He tried to stay away and let the other instructors pick on her, but he couldn't help but glance her way every five minutes or so.

"Are you still mad at me, honey?" he inquired, jogging along beside her.

She stared straight ahead, panting like a woman in labor. Was she still upset because he wouldn't agree to her preposterous suggestion that he travel back in time with her? As if!

"You didn't really expect me to time-travel with you, did you?"

She glanced his way for a brief second. "I'll find someone else to help. Now begone, lout! You will scare the other men away."

"Huh? What men?" He slowed down his pace, dropping to the back of the pack. She'd planted an uncomfortable idea in his head. She wouldn't go out seeking some other man, would she? For orgasms or a friggin' time-travel buddy? Not if he had any say in the matter, and he had plenty to say.

F.U. got in the faces of some of the women then. Jogging backward, he taunted Alda Sue, "Well, Mzzz. I-Am-a-Country-Singer, yer not singin' now, are ya? Yer sweatin' like a pig. It's a wonder ya don't jist fall down. Come on, baby, I'll help ya to the bell. Ya kin be in Nashville before dark."

"F.U.," the woman choked out.

F.U.'s eyes about bugged out. "Wh-what did you say?"

Alda Sue just widened her eyes innocently and replied, "I said, 'Yes, Master Chief F.U., sir.' What did you think I said?"

The commander jogged up then, and F.U. gave the woman a look that pretty much said to watch her back.

Meanwhile, Petty Officer Evans, Britta's swim partner, began to chant:

*"Eeney meany miney mo."*
*"Eeney meany miney mo."*
*"Catch a jerk by the toe."*
*"Catch a jerk by the toe."*
*"If he hollers, grab his cock,"*
*"If he hollers, grab his cock,"*
*"Teeney-tiny on a know-nothing jock."*
*"Teeney-tiny on a know-nothing jock."*
*"Sound off, one, two,"*
*"Three, four."*

The grody jody was clearly aimed at F.U., which was undoubtedly going to merit Evans some sort of retaliation. She would probably say that his embarrassment was worth it. Zach and the commander would have to watch F.U. a little closer to make sure he didn't cross any lines.

Zach's eyes caught Britta's just then as she passed. He smiled. She frowned.

He studied her from the back as she continued to jog back to the command center. She was sex in motion. The sinews of her long legs stretched with her stride. Her butt cheeks moved up and down. Her single braid swung side to side.

"Hey, buddy," Cage said, loping up to him as he brought up the rear of the joggers, "your lust is showing."

"Huh?" he gazed down to his shorts.

"Not there, you idiot." Cage laughed. "I meant you have hungry eyes every time you look at Britta."

*Great! That is just great!*

"Down boats! Down boats!" F.U. screamed into the faces of some of the trainees who were too numb to respond in the proper manner, which would be "Yes, Master Chief, sir." Instead, they just let the boats drop wherever, their shoulders sagging with relief.

But only for a second.

"On your backs, sweetie pies," F.U. continued with glee. "Give me twenty flutter kicks. Hurry, hurry, hurry. Start knockin' 'em out."

They were the most half-assed flutter kicks he'd ever seen, despite him and all the other instructors leaning over the trainees yelling encouragement or directions or mostly offers to help them DOR.

A couple of the women walked off to the side and hurled into the sand. Overexertion did that to a body.

"I have a good idea," Zach yelled out then. "Let's play volcano."

The women were too exhausted to mutter aloud, but the glowers they shot his way spoke volumes, Britta's more than any of them.

The class was gathered in several big, tight circles on the beach, backs to the center, and ordered to keep tossing sand up in the air and over themselves, like what else? Volcanoes.

"There's a point to this exercise, snuffies," Zach explained. "Out on an active op, with artillery, demolitions, and shells exploding all around you, sand and dirt are going to be tossed in your face and ears and other body cavities. You're going to have to learn to work despite the discomfort and fuzzy vision and impaired hearing."

No one was buying his logic.

"And now," Commander MacLean said, "we're going to show you whistle exercises. Over and over and over during the course of your program, no matter what evolution, you must adhere to the whistle directives. Come over here and demonstrate, Instructors Floyd, Uxley, and LeBlanc." A loud blast came from the commander's whistle. The three of them dropped to the ground, face-first. "This is the same position you would take if there were real artillery rounds coming at you or bombs being lobbed in your vicinity. Notice how they face away from the sound, hands behind their necks to keep their heads from bouncing on the ground, open mouths to keep their ears from blowing out, ankles and legs crossed to protect"—he grinned—"their private parts."

The women for once seemed to understand the need for this battle replica drill and paid strict attention.

Two blasts from the whistle, and the three of them began to crawl toward the sound. Three blasts and they recovered, getting to their feet and brushing the sand off their fronts.

"Now, let's see you do it." At least twenty times, the commander played the different whistle blasts till they seemed to get the routine. Drop, crawl, recover, drop, crawl, recover. Over and over and many different patterns. It was a Pavlov exercise in the extreme. "Remember, you're going to hear this whistle at random times during all different exercises. And always, ALWAYS, the whistle routine takes precedence. It might save your life someday. Understood?"

Dozens of heads bobbed. Four women walked off to ring the bell.

"Remember, snuffies. No pain, no gain."

"If a barrel of lutefisk were nearby, I vow I would stuff it into the commander's mouth to prevent him from uttering another of his lackwit sayings." Luckily, Britta's remark wasn't overheard by MacLean, or she would be in Gig Squad tonight.

As it was, Zach told her, "Asado, watch your mouth. It's going to get you in big trouble."

She glanced his way, checked to see that no one was looking, then stuck her tongue out at him.

The commander and half the instructors then herded the staggering women, carrying the IBSs again on extended arms, toward the swimming pool for drownproofing exercises. At least a dozen of the trainees would ring out in the midst of that horror by the end of the afternoon, guaranteed. Their arms and legs would be tied, and they would be tossed in the pool where they were expected to remain underwater and survive for a full five minutes. If they attempted to rise to the top, an instructor was there to shove them back under.

Zach made his way into the command center to meet with his grandfather and his lawyer.

His grandfather, General Floyd, was standing at the window observing the progress of the WEALS. Even though he was at ease, his backbone was straight as a board. His high and tight showed not a gray hair out of place. His face was rigid and unsmiling, as if he was ever at attention. His uniform was immaculately pressed with five rows of ribbons to indicate combat tours, along with various medals and of course the stars. His shoes were spit-shined. Army lifer to the max. He extended a hand formally to Zach. It was a wonder he didn't salute.

After shaking hands, the general asked, "Which one is she? The tall blonde?"

He shook his head at the hopelessness of his blabbermouth brother. "Which one what?" he pretended innocence.

"Don't play games with me, Zachary Frank Floyd."

"My personal life is my business."

"Hardly," he scoffed, motioning to the lawyer sitting at the conference table.

Zach nodded at Delaney, who was trying his best not to be a party to this private conversation.

"I meant my sex life." Sometimes he had to be blunt to get through to his grandfather.

"I would say your sex life is pretty much public fodder these days, wouldn't you?"

"Listen, Britta has nothing to do with this."

"Britta?" His grandfather raised his eyebrows. "Are you going to marry the girl?"

He released a whooshy exhale. "Number one, Britta is

twenty-seven years old, not a girl. Number two, marriage is the last thing on my mind . . . or hers. Number three, even if I wanted to get married, and I don't, it would be the kiss of death for Britta in WEALS."

His grandfather nodded. That was one thing he understood: military obligations. "Just don't get the lady pregnant. That's all you need is another—"

"Don't even go there," he warned with an upraised hand. He might not have married Esilah, but he'd deck any person calling his kid a bastard.

His grandfather's face flushed, but he had the good sense not to say anything more on that subject. "I'm going over to the XO's office to relay a message from Admiral Jenner. Let's have dinner tonight." What a piece of work his grandfather was! You'd never know they'd just exchanged barely civil words.

He shook his head. "I have to be home with Sammy."

"How is the boy?"

"He's fine. Correction, he's not fine, but he will be."

The general gave what for him was a grin. "Still cursing up a storm?"

"Yeah, but he's toned his repertoire down a bit. He's trying." *What a crock!*

"You could let him come back to D.C. with me. Your grandmother and I could care for him till this whole debacle blows over. He'd be safe in our gated community."

*Not in a million years! Sammy is screwed up enough.* "Thanks, but he stays with me."

After his grandfather was gone, making arrangements to drop by the house before leaving town, Zach and Delaney got down to business. He signed legal documents giving the lawyer power of attorney to access his confidential files and act on his behalf in legal matters where privacy laws prevailed.

"Arsallah wants to arrange a meeting between himself and your son."

"Absolutely not."

"Not even in a secure setting?"

"No. It can serve no purpose other than to intimidate Sammy and give Arsallah information about how to access the boy."

"The courts might say he has a grandfather's right to visitation."

"Then he'll have to fight for it in the courts. And that means he'll have to explain some of the scars on the boy's body and some of the things Sammy has inadvertently revealed about his treatment in the mullah's camps."

"None of this is going to be easy."

"I know that."

"And not just because of Arsallah's threats. The State Department has Lebanon and Iran breathing down its neck. They're urging diplomacy."

"Bullshit! What they're urging is that we sacrifice the boy for the sake of goodwill with a bunch of terrorist nations."

Delaney shrugged. "That's the way the world works."

"It's not the way I work."

"The Vortex Security guy talked with you today, right?"

He nodded.

"They think you should find a safe house for Sammy and yourself for the short term."

He shook his head. "Sammy's lived with nothing but turmoil practically since he was born. I have to give him as close to a normal life as I can. And, yeah, I know my home is no Brady Bunch paradise, but it's better than he's ever known before."

Delaney reached across the table and squeezed his forearm. "You don't have to convince me, Zach."

After his meeting with the lawyer, it was past noon, and he decided to catch up with the WEALS class in the chow hall. When he got there, he saw a bunch of ragtag women who looked as if they'd been put through the ringer. It was hard to tell whether they were eating or sleeping as they sat on the benches. Wet, scrawny hair from the pool. Sweaty bodies. Grimy clothing. Exhaustion and pain etched on their faces. But wait, there was a group of women who weren't sitting down, and in the middle of that bunch, he saw Britta holding center court. She was holding something up to the women who surrounded her. Whatever it was, it caused the other women to laugh. Even some of the instructors standing nearby were smiling.

When she saw him, despite all the military protocol to the contrary, she stomped up to him and held out a dish. "Do you know what this is?" she demanded.

"Uh, chocolate pudding?"

"Covered with?"

"Whipped cream?"

"And how does one eat whipped cream, pray tell?"

"With a spoon?" Uh-oh! He knew where this conversation was going.

"Do not dare to smirk at me, lout. You told me there was only one way to eat whipping cream. By licking. And, for a certainty, it was not on a bowl of pudding, either, you son of a codsucking camel."

He couldn't help himself from joining the crowd. Everybody was laughing.

Except Britta. She tossed the dish of pudding in his face.

### MEMO

**From: Captain Lenore Feldman**
**To: Commander Ian MacLean**
**Subject: WEALS**

**Whipped cream and other food products can be a form of forbidden sexual fraternization.**

# Chapter 14

**Who hid the red paint? . . .**

They had just completed the fourth week of WEALS training, and only thirty-five of the original ninety-five women remained. Fortunately, Britta and her three sleeping-chamber companions were still in the race.

Despite how hard they had been worked, from before dawn to dusk every day, and sometimes in the middle of the night, Britta felt good. And she was proud. Not just of the strength and stamina she was building in her body, but how much she was learning. How to use weapons, like rifles and KA-BAR knives. How to maneuver in close-quarter fighting. How to infiltrate an enemy's territory. How to survive a nigh-drowning. How to work as a team, not an individual fighter. How to ride a rub-her boat on the waves without swallowing an ocean of salt water. How to jump off exceedingly high towers without breaking a limb, an exercise preparing them for jumping out of metal vehicles in the sky, something she chose not to think about.

Zachary, with his overconcern for her well-being, had

approached her several times, trying to coax her into ringing out. Mostly, she just ignored the lout. Yea, they had enjoyed great bedsport, but now 'twas time to move on to more serious matters. Not that he didn't still make her blood heat and her nether parts thrum when he was near, but any other passably fair man would probably affect her in the same way, and she had told Zachary so. Which had caused his pretty face to flush with anger. Now he was the one ignoring her, or trying to.

In the midst of her busy schedule, she was even learning reading, writing, geography, math, and history in classes arranged over her dinner hour each night. This instruction was provided for her privately, probably at Zachary's urging, under the guise of her being a foreigner unfamiliar with the language and customs of America. The history lessons were the most illuminating to her; they drummed home more than anything else that she really must have traveled through time, as unbelievable as that was.

But now, it was Frey's-day afternoon, and Britta and her fellow trainees were about to have their first free time in weeks. "At ease, snuffies," the commander hollered. Everything he ever said to them was delivered in a holler. "Be back here by oh seven hundred Sunday morning. Clean, pressed uniforms. Be prepared to strut your stuff for the powers that be." A contingent of far-famed governing people from a place called Con-grass was coming to inspect their progress. "And be prepared to start survival training and simulated combat exercises on San Clemente Island starting Monday. We'll play some Sims. Get in a few tracking, patrolling, ambushing, concealment, first-aid, and night-movement exercises. That's it. Fall out! Class secured for the day!" You would think he could at least have told them they did good so far, but nay, praise from him would be considered a weakness.

*Two whole days.* She sighed.

The first thing any of them wanted to do was shower away the day's sweat and grime. By the time Britta was done, she smelled of apple hair, strawberry skin, and floral armpits. In other words, delicious. Once back in the sleeping quarters, all four women sank down on their cots, planning to rest for a short time afore going to a shopping mart, which they promised Britta would be a real treat. However, the women were dead to the world for a full five hours, only rising after their stomachs rumbled with hunger.

Except for Britta, to whom sleep these days meant horrific dreams taking her back to a time and place where sword dew was being spilled aplenty at the abbey . . . and the good nuns' virtue was forfeit to every passing man. She could no longer think of the dreams as products of her imagination. They were peek holes into the past as it was happening. She was sure of it. Which meant she must return and help.

Or did it?

She would have to ask Hilda and Madrene the first chance she got. Both women had called several times on a magic box called a telephone during the past three sennights, inquiring about her well-being and progress in the WEALS.

When she rose from her cot, stretching with a wide, lusty yawn, she told her three chamber companions, "There is something important I must do afore I even think of eating or going off to a shopping mart."

"What's that, sweetie?" Terri asked while she towel-dried her short, curly hair.

"Bet she wants to call Pretty Boy and arrange a few more of those mind-blowing orgasms," Donita teased.

"Nay, I do not. Zachary has been as cruel as the other sadistic instructors these past sennights. What I want—"

"I know, *chère*, you want a Brazil wax, yes?" Marie interjected, also teasing.

Britta had to laugh. She'd already become accustomed to this country's female ritual of shaving the legs and underarms, but shaving her nether region held no appeal and, truth be told, made no sense. Besides, she would not wear a bikini in public under any circumstances. She'd rather go naked.

"I want to cut my hair," she told them, combing her fingers through her waist-long hair, damp even after five hours.

"Oh, honey, I don't know," Terri said, running a hand over the wet swath. "You have beautiful hair, like gold silk."

"I agree," Donita said. "If I had hair like yours, I'd leave it the way it is."

"What does Pretty Boy say 'bout ya cuttin' yer locks?" Marie inquired.

That question surprised Britta. "Why would his opinion on my personal grooming matter a whit to me?" Oddly, it did matter, but that was neither here nor there. "My long hair is becoming a hindrance, even when in a braid. It catches on wood objects in the obstacle course. It is heavy and warm, causing me to perspire more. It takes too long to shampoo and dry." And she felt different than the other women.

In the end, Britta sat before a full-length mirror Donita had inside her metal closet, and all three women, laughing and chattering away, began to cut her hair and dry it with a blowing apparatus.

"So, Marie, I saw you talking to that Cajun hunk," Terri said, spreading a towel around Britta's shoulders. "You two got somethin' going?"

Marie shook her head. "I've had enough of Cajun men, growing up on the bayou. I would feel like I was getting it on with my brother. Talk about!"

"And you?" Terri glanced at Donita. "I've seen you and Sly exchanging looks."

"Hah! The only looks I been exchangin' with that too-full-of-himself black brother are glowers. Did you know he used to model men's underwear? I asked him if he had a life-time supply of briefs, and he told me he doesn't wear underwear. And that he'd be willing to prove it to me sometime."

"That sounds lak interest to me," Marie said. "In Southern Loo-zee-anna, we'd say that boy's been flashin' ya his widow-bait smile."

"Hardly! He also asked me if I was still on steroids. The jerk!"

"Well, then, you can have Cage, and I'll take Sly," Marie said saucily.

"Honey chile, the last thing this black woman wants is a redneck boy with a pointy hat."

"Oh, that's not fair." Marie's face flushed. "Not all Southerners are bigots."

Donita patted Marie on the shoulder. "I know that, honey. I was just kidding. A bad joke!"

The two women hugged.

What had just transpired, Britta had no idea. All she knew was that she was becoming close to these woman friends. As close as she had once been to Hilda. It would be hard to leave them if—or when—she had to leave.

They braided her hair first, then cut off the long plait to be sent someplace that made wigs for women who had lost their hair to a wasting disease. They did not cut it short-short as she'd originally requested, telling her that would be too drastic. Instead, her hair was cut in layers down to her shoulders, framing her face. When she shook her head, the strands all fell in place neatly. To her surprise, she had natural waves, which her lady companions described as "sexy."

"It's too late to go to the mall," Terri said then. "Anyone wanna go to the Wet and Wild?"

At Britta's arched brows, Terri explained, "It's a local watering hole. Good food, cheap booze, great music, and a lot of the Navy guys hang out there."

*A watering hole? Terri wanted to go to a place where animals watered?* The other women all voted yea, and Britta wasn't about to ask yet another question, so she agreed, too.

"I for one plan to get me some tonight," Terri said. "It's been ages since I did the dirty."

"Same here," Marie said. "My IUD, she is gettin' lonely."

"I just want to eat and drink with my friends," Donita said.

Terri and Marie looked at Donita and said as one, "Bull!"

"You know, honey," Terri told Britta, "I suspect you've led a sheltered life when it comes to men. You had to if you never heard of orgasms before coming here. Maybe it's time you tested the waters, to see if what you had with Zach was all that great."

Britta had no doubt it had been great. She had no need for multiple partners to prove that fact. Still, there was appeal in seeing what could happen with other men. Besides, Zachary had been a pig in his role as instructor these past sennights. Not loverlike at all. She did not want special treatment, but making her do endless pushing-ups was not necessary, in her opinion. Yea, she would find another man, one who would be eager to please her not just in the bedsport but mayhap even in her trip to the past, if that became necessary. Not that she would tell anyone about the time travel . . . at first.

She turned to Terri and smiled, "Perchance we can both *get some* tonight."

Soon they were off, driving over the bridge in Marie's horseless carriage . . . a pick-me-up.

"Let's make a pact," Terri said. "We're gonna paint the town red or die trying."

Britta glanced around the vehicle. Not a brush or container of paint in sight. With a sigh, she wondered if she would ever understand this strange country.

### MEMO

**From: Captain Lenore Feldman**
**To: Commander Ian MacLean**
**Subject: WEALS**

**Provide Tampax dispensers and air fresheners in all toilet facilities.**

## His son, the sex advisor . . .

Zach was not a happy camper.

It was Friday night, but was he out on a hot date, or at least out trolling for a hot date? Nope. He was sitting in an Italian restaurant in San Diego with his son, the sulker; his father, the celebrity show-off; his father's girlfriend, Bridget, the dumb twit; and enough security guards to give the leader of a small nation heartburn.

"Yoo-hoo, Dr. Bratton!" a woman three tables over called out.

Bridget giggled—for about the hundredth time—and squirmed in her seat, which was a feat in itself, considering how tight her red silk slip dress was with the deep scooped neck.

His father flashed his twenty-thousand-dollar smile and gave a little Hollywood wave to his fan at the other table.

Meanwhile, Zach's security squad, along with his dad's, circled the wagons—uh, tables—a little tighter. What a great way to have a nice quiet dinner with family! Not!

People thought his dad really was the doctor from the soap *Light in the Storm*, a part he'd been playing for fifteen years. Hell, he probably considered *himself* that toney doctor from some daytime dynasty. He certainly dressed the part. Tweed sport coat with leather elbow patches. A sissy white scarf wrapped casually around his neck; he'd probably seen Cary Grant wear one. A hairstyle with just the right sprinkling of gray at the temples; it had probably cost five hundred dollars or more. And a George Hamilton suntan, of course.

A woman had tried to kidnap his father five years ago, believing Dr. Bratton could cure her husband of Alzheimer's. Thus, his father always traveled with some well-dressed grunts who looked like they were straight out of *The Godfather*, whereas Zach's security detail resembled special forces guys, which they probably had been at one time. His father employed his guards for show as much as safety. He'd certainly gotten a pig load of publicity over the kidnapping episode.

Meanwhile, his dad was talking to Bridget about an upcoming story line where he would be doing a liver transplant on his wife, who had been in a coma for five years after having been cloned into her own twin sister.

Bridget giggled.

His father smiled.

Sammy slouched and muttered something about assholes. Zach wasn't exactly sure who he was referring to and wasn't about to ask. Just then, he noticed that Sammy was wearing as much spaghetti sauce as he'd left on his plate. Dipping a napkin in a glass of water, he proceeded to put Sammy in a neck hold and wipe his mouth and nose and chin. With all the squirming, the napkin slipped from his hands and floated to the floor.

Bridget bent down to pick it up, and he and his son—five going on twenty-five—got a gander at a set of world-class hooters. She gave new meaning to cleavage.

"Behave yourself," he whispered to Sammy, who he could tell was about to say something inappropriate.

"Did ya see that?" Sammy whispered loud enough for everyone within five yards of the table to hear. "Her nipples're big as marbles. Uncle Dan sez big nipples, easy pickin's."

Zach rolled his eyes and clapped a hand over the kid's mouth.

Lips twitched on a couple of the guards.

Luckily, Bridget was talking to his dad and didn't hear Sammy's remark.

"Uncle Dan said he would bring me a new video game," Sammy whined to him.

"I know he did, but he was held up. He might not be able to come at all this weekend."

Sammy's eyes teared up. The least little disappointment seemed to set him off these days. He was getting spoiled, but it was hard not to spoil a kid who, until recently, had nothing.

"I can get you a video game," he offered. "We can stop on the way home."

Sammy's blue eyes, which matched Zach's own, lit up. No more sulks. "No *Dora the Explorer*."

"Okay. But no blood and guts either."

"Oh, I forgot. I got a little present for you, Sammy," Bridget said, laying a square box on the table.

"You didn't have to do that," Zach said.

"I wanted to, but, really, I just happened to see them in one of those Rodeo Drive boutiques, and they screamed Sammy to me."

Sammy was giving the box the evil eye. From a kid point of view, a square, flat box usually meant clothing.

Opening the box hesitantly . . . as if a snake might pop out—or clothing—he removed the tissue. Then Zach and Sammy stared incredulously at the tiny briefs with Hotshot printed on the butt and flames all over the black background.

"How come everyone always gives me underpants? Do I smell?" Sammy asked Zach.

"No, you don't smell. At least not all the time," he told him, then turned to Bridget. "Thanks, that was really nice of you."

He squeezed Sammy's hand under the table till he, too, thanked Bridget for the "really cool ass covers."

Just then, Danny, with perfect timing, plowed his way through the Odd Squad. "Dad, sorry I'm late. There was a mother of a traffic jam on the freeway. Oops, sorry for the language, Sammy old man." He squeezed Dad's shoulder, then leaned down to kiss Bridget on the cheek. "Hey, Bridge!"

In that blink of a second, Zach noticed Danny noticing Bridget's breasts. That was confirmed when Danny looked his way and winked.

Bridget just giggled.

His dad beamed, pleased as always to have his two sons with him, like a familial entourage.

And Sammy was happy as a hog in a mud hole now that Danny was here. He probably figured Danny would buy him any kind of game he wanted. Little did he know that Zach was going to have a heart-to-heart with Danny. Big nipples, easy pickin's, were among the subjects he expected to cover.

"Boys," his father started, "I have a really good idea, which should solve all our problems."

They waited as the old man paused dramatically.

"I think we should have a family compound. Like the Kennedys. Stones fences. Guard dogs. The works. That way no bad guys—or loony women—could enter. What do you think?"

"Cool!" Sammy said. He didn't know what a compound was, but he liked dogs.

"Maybe you could build a moat, too," Zach offered.

"That's a thought," his dad said, not getting the sarcasm.

"Here's a news flash, Dad," Danny said, barely stifling a laugh. "We are not the Kennedys. There are only four of us."

"And your mother and your grandfather and grandmother."

"Oh, that'll happen." Zach couldn't believe he was even discussing this ludicrous idea. "Remember the last time Mom was in the same room with you, Dad."

"*Hmpfh!* It's about time Lillian got over herself."

"Remember to tell her that next time you see her," Danny suggested.

"We're not having a compound," Zach said. The idea of being locked up anywhere with his father and his bimbo du jour made his skin crawl. One time he stayed at his father's Hollywood pad and heard him making loud sex through the thin bedroom walls. Yeech! "Eventually this situation with Arsallah will be resolved, and we can go back to living normally."

Sammy peered up at him with a mixture of hope and disbelief.

"So, pip-squeak, I'm starving." Danny poked Sammy in the arm.

"Me, too," Sammy replied.

"You just ate a pound of pasta," Zach pointed out.

"So? I'm growin'. I need lotsa food."

"What say we go over to Pizza Pizza for a few slices and a game of pinball?" Danny suggested.

"Cool!"

"Whoa, whoa, whoa! You can't go out in public without a guard detail."

"Sammy and I will let them hold all our winnings," Danny said. "Last time we got five hundred tokens."

"And only spent fifty dollars," Zach pointed out.

"What's your point?"

"And what's with the you-and-Sammy business? What am I? A potted plant?"

"A *pretty* potted plant. Jeesh, are those leather pants you're wearing? I didn't think anyone other than rock stars and gay men wore leather." Danny smiled at him.

"They're faux leather, and they're the latest style."

"I have a pair," his father said.

Forget faux leather; that was a designer faux pas he and Danny could not imagine, as evidenced by their exchange of horrified looks.

"Anyhow, Sammy and I are giving you a break," Danny continued. "Go out and take a breather. Drink a beer. Relax." He checked his watch and added, "I give you five hours before curfew, big boy."

"I don't know."

"This is the last time I'll be able to help out for a while," Danny said. "My leave is over tomorrow."

"Take him up on the offer," his dad advised. "He can take two of my guards with him. You need some free time, son."

"I think you should go find Britta and boink her a bunch of times," Sammy said around a mouthful of garlic bread.

The entire table went silent.

Finally, Zach choked out, "I beg your pardon."

"What? Why's everyone starin' at me? You and me need someone to take care of us, Dad."

Zach's heart lurched. It was the first time he'd heard Sammy call him Dad.

"You're grouchy all the time, and Britta tells good bedtime stories, and she's nice-looking, even if she is big and talks funny." Sammy was on a roll. "And Uncle Dan says the best way to make a woman fall for you is to boink her till her eyeballs roll."

His father stopped chewing his chicken cacciatore.

Bridget giggled.

Danny grinned shamelessly.

"Oh. My. God!" He wondered with hysterical irrelevance if Sammy even knew what boinking was.

And soon found out.

Leaning in close to Zach's ear, Sammy told him, "Boinking is lotsa yucky kissin'."

Everyone turned to stare at Danny, who shrugged. "From the mouths of babes."

# Chapter 15

**Who needs you, baby? I got chums . . .**

It was nine o'clock before Zach arrived at the Wet and Wild, and the bar was rocking in its usual Friday-night, wall-shaking, yee-haw style.

Bypassing the T-shirt spraying machine at the door, a politically incorrect attraction that drew women as well as men, he made his way through the crowd toward the bar. The band, Bad Love, a favorite of patrons from the naval base, played a mix of country and classic rock. Right now it was a raucous version of Garth Brooks's "I've Got Friends in Low Places," to which the customers sang along, taking particular delight in the low octaves of *low places*. Next came "Working for the Weekend," then "We Gotta Get Outta This Place." It was a wild bunch tonight, singing, shouting, and of course drinking.

He found a spot at the bar and waved at Bo Anders, a bald-headed weekend biker fanatic who had been a bartender at the Wet and Wild for as long as Zach could remember.

"Hey, Pretty Boy, haven't seen you around lately."

"Been busy."

"That gives the other guys a better chance with the chummies."

"Yeah, well, they can have 'em." *Chummies* was a less-than-flattering name given to SEAL groupies who hung around Coronado, the name based on chumming, a strategy fishermen used to draw fish into an area where they could be easily hooked. It was an effective method for prize fish as well as arrogant men who preferred a free meal to one requiring expended energy and time. Hey, no one ever accused SEALs of being Alan Alda sensitive.

"What'll it be?"

"Sam Adams, in the bottle."

Zach slapped a few bills on the bar, then turned, longneck in hand, and leaned his elbows back on the bar. He took a long pull on the cold beer and surveyed the room, noticing right away the gorgeous babe standing a short distance away. She had long, mussed, black hair, a model-thin body encased in a skintight minidress, and a siren-red mouth that conjured all kinds of images. Slanting her silvery eyes his way, she winked. A chummie, for sure.

Britta had been driving him nuts the past three weeks. He was sick of chasing his tail over her. Sick of teaching women how to run and breathe at the same time. Sick of being on inactive duty. Sick of whacking off himself at night. Sick of being a nonplayer in the dating games. Time to get back to his old modus operandi. Time to forget, at least for a few hours, that he was a father in a pig load of trouble with every frickin' government official from here to Afghanistan. Time to stop hitting on a thousand-year-old girlfriend who didn't want to be his girlfriend. He had little free time these days, and he was damn sure going to make good use of this gift from Danny.

He smiled at the woman, and she walked over. "Hi," she said in a Marilyn Monroe breathy fashion.

A good start. He liked breathy.

"Hi," he said back. "My name's Zach Floyd."

"Linda Lowery."

"Can I buy you a drink?"

"Sure. Double shot of VO, straight. Over ice. No water."

*Okaaaay.*

When Bo handed her the drink, he gave Zach a silent message, as in *Whoa boy! This is a hot one.* Which soon proved true. She downed the drink in one swallow, then licked her wet, red lips.

*Double okaaaay.* He put his arm around her shoulder and tucked her into his side, making room for her to squeeze in at the bar.

"Is it true what they say about SEALs and their . . . uh, stamina?"

"Oh, yeah." *Typical groupie question.*

She smiled.

*Yep, easy breezy fishing here.* He wondered idly if they should cut the crap—uh, small talk—and just take it out to his car for a wham-bam roll in the backseat.

Oddly, that prospect didn't appeal to him. Before he had a chance to contemplate why, he saw Cage and the gang on the far side of the tavern, waving at him to come over. "Care to join my friends?" he asked Linda.

"Sure."

He led her by the hand through the crowd, with her hand on his ass . . . marking her territory, he supposed, but who the hell cared? Soon they arrived at the large round table where Cage, Sly, Geek, JAM, Slick, and Omar were sitting. Slick's presence was a surprise. He usually didn't socialize with them, but maybe things had changed since his divorce seemed to be final now. Omar rarely went out, either, being in the same predicament as Zach; he had custody of his seven-year-old daughter.

He introduced Linda to everyone. They all noticed her hand on his ass, if their grins were any indication.

They sat down.

"Man, you're the only guy I know who wears designer duds to a lowdown bar," Slick remarked. "And, shiiiiit, are those leather pants?"

"Faux leather," he replied, used to their teasing.

"I think he looks good," Linda remarked, rubbing a hand over the sleeve of the silk shirt, then the material at his knee.

"If I wasn't already Mr. *GQ*, I'd say you fit the bill," Sly said to Zach. "I used to model underwear for *GQ*."

Linda listened attentively, as if Sly had just told her he invented oral sex.

"I was out to dinner with my dad," Zach explained.

Linda turned to chat with JAM on her other side about a doctor they both knew at the naval base hospital, and Cage leaned in close to him. "No more Britta on your mind, buddy?"

"Gone, gone, gone," he said. And he meant it, too. For some reason, Britta had stuck in his craw for the last two years, probably because she hadn't given in to him. Then the last few weeks, after she *had* given in to him, he'd convinced himself it was something more than lust. Well, he was over her now. And, to be fair, she was over him, too, as evidenced by her telling him more than once in recent days to "Be-gone!" Usually after some particularly brutal rotation in WEALS, which she was taking personally.

"Who's watchin' the kid?" Sly asked.

"My brother, Danny, again. He's building up brother points."

"And he doesn't mind you being gone?" Omar asked, rubbing the shin that Sammy had bruised a few weeks ago.

"Hah! You know what he told me to do tonight? To go boink Britta till her eyeballs rolled."

A bunch of the guys, overhearing, laughed. They got a kick out of Sammy's antics. He did, too. Sometimes.

"So, why aintcha takin' Sammy's advice, *mon coeur*? About Britta, I mean?" Cage was staring at him as if he saw something that Zach didn't realize was apparent.

"Number one, Britta won't have me. Number two, so the hell what? Number three, out of sight, out of mind. Number four . . ." Glancing at Linda who was still talking with JAM, he shrugged. "Enough said!"

"Number five, bullshit!" Cage laughed, not buying his story at all.

The waitress showed up then. Not Bawdy Maudy, but an older woman he didn't recognize. He ordered another Sam Adams, and Linda ordered another Double VO. Yee-haw! No longer talking with JAM, she placed her hand on his thigh, high up, licked those tempting red lips, and began to suck the salt off a stick pretzel she picked up from a basket on the table.

Seven sets of eyes observed intently.

*Life is good . . . or about to get good,* he thought.

Until he saw who was entering the tavern.

## Looking for fresh meat . . . uh, men . . .

The Wet and Wild was an eating and drinking establishment that had an odd showering device just inside its front door. Women who were willing to have their *sherts* showered went in free.

When an explanation was given to Britta for this odd practice, she exclaimed, "Men! They are e'er the same, drooling over a woman's udders. Would any right-minded lady e'er suggest wetting down a man's breeches to ogle his manparts?"

"Men would jump at the chance," Terri pointed out, and they all agreed.

"I'd have to be half-blitzed before I'd go in here with a wet T-shirt," Donita said.

"I doan know," Marie mused. "Depends on who I'm tryin' ta impress."

Britta and her friends chose to pay the entry charge.

It was hard to hear each other speak over the loud music and hum of conversation, clinking of glasses, and laughter.

Immediately, they were accosted by men offering them drinks and places to sit at their tables, or requesting that they dance with them. One particularly persistent fellow identified himself as Dill-land Overdorf, a Navy pilot. That was a person who steered those metal objects flying across the skies. He wore a wide-brimmed hat similar to the one Cage wore betimes . . . a cow hat for boys, she thought it was called, although Dill-land was far from a boyling. He wore carved leather boots with heels and a belt with a large brass buckle. He pressed a glass of mead into her hand and remarked on how good she smelled.

"Fruit or flower?" she asked, sipping at her mead.

"Uh . . . flower?"

"Ah, my armpits." She raised an arm so he could get a whiff of the floral scent.

At first, the guy seemed surprised by her action, but then he grinned, "That would be the one. Hey, I love a gal with a sense of humor."

Britta gave him another look. He was tall and lean with dark hair and eyes and a most alluring dimple at one side of his mouth. He really was an attractive man. Not as pretty as Zachary, but then no man was.

"Are you Navy, darlin'?" he asked.

"WEALS."

"Ah."

"What does that mean?"

"That I'm impressed. You must be one . . . uh, fit woman."

"Fit where?"

"Huh? Where you from, darlin'? You have an odd accent."

"The Norselands."

"Norway?"

"'Tis what I said. But you are the one with an odd voice. Where are you from?"

"Texas."

"A country called Tax Us? How odd!"

He gaped at her for a second as if questioning whether she was barmy or not. She probably was, especially since she was actually considering finding herself another man for bedsport, just to see if what she had experienced with Zachary was the usual way things went betwixt men and women.

"How do you feel about orgasms?" she blurted out.

He choked on his mead. Then he smiled, a slow, lazy exercise that drew the dimple out nicely. "Did you say orgasms?"

"Yea, that is what I said. Dost have an ear wax problem?"

"No problem at all, sugar."

"So, how do you feel about orgasms?"

"Mine or yours?"

She pondered that question. "Both. But I must have multiple ones, or it would not be worth the effort. Would it?"

"Baby, you and I are gonna get along just great. Let's dance."

"Oh, nay. I could not do that."

People were flailing their arms and shaking their hips in a ludicrous manner to loud music that spoke of twisting and shouting.

"I'm not much for fast dancing, either. Oh, here comes a slow one." Without a pause, the musicians started into a slower melody, with the one singer announcing, "Let's get it on."

Dill-land pulled her into his embrace and out onto the dancing arena. He immediately began swaying them back and forth in a shocking manner. Her breasts were pressed into his chest, and she could feel the ridge of his manpart against the joining of her braies. She felt nothing at all. Not the thrill of pleasure that surged through her body at just a look from Zachary. Not the ruching of her nipples at the brush of his *shert*. Not the wet pooling betwixt her thighs that she associated with foresport from Zachary. And this close dancing was definitely foresport, in her opinion.

She was doomed, Britta realized with a sigh. Zachary had ruined her for other men.

Dill-land was humming in her ear . . . in an attempt to make her grow lustsome, she supposed. All she wanted to do was laugh. His humming was unmelodic.

Smiling, she looked over Dill-land's shoulder. Then looked again.

Zachary was sitting at a far table with his comrades-in-arms. And, most important, at his side was a black-haired woman staring at Zachary as if she'd just had multiple orgasms.

*The loathsome lout! The randy jackass! The womanizing fornicator!*

And he was staring back at Britta with equal dismay, glaring at Dill-land's back. She saw him start to rise, but Cage and Slick took hold of his arms and shoved him back in his seat. They were talking earnestly to him. The black-haired wench was looking back and forth betwixt her and Zachary with a questioning frown.

Britta did the only thing a right-thinking woman could in the circumstances. She nuzzled her face into Dill-land's neck and kissed his ear.

Dill-land growled his appreciation. And began to hum some more.

She hoped she didn't hurl the contents of her still-empty stomach.


**The froggie turned a lovely shade of green . . . uh, red . . .**

Zach heard a loud buzzing in his ears, and he literally saw red. The feeling was not unlike the berserk rage that sometimes overcame SEALs and other special forces operators before a battle.

Luckily, or not so luckily, Cage and Slick had moved Linda's chair aside, and they stood on both sides of him, forcing him to stay put.

"Doan even think it, *cher*," Cage warned.

"Buddy, you're already in deep shit. Do you wanna land in the brig, end your career, lose your pretty looks?" That last was said by Slick with a grin.

"I don't give a rat's ass about the frickin' brig, the frickin' SEALs, or my frickin' face. That dickhead has his hands on my girl."

"Your girl?" Linda squealed. "You have a girl?"

"He means that in a collective sense, as in Britta is in

WEALS, as in Britta is *our girl*, to all of us SEALs," Geek explained . . . with a straight face, yet.

Zach snorted his opinion of that bullshit, but Linda seemed satisfied with the explanation.

"Calm down, boy." Cage patted his shoulder. "Looks lak she's the one got her tongue in his ear and his nuts in hand . . . so ta speak."

"Yeah, but Overdorf has his hands on her ass," Sly pointed out. "And it looks to me like, yep, he's making Mr. Happy . . . well, happy, rubbing against her belly like that."

The roaring in Zach's head got louder.

He studied Britta for a long moment. She'd cut her hair. Dammit! But it was nice. Kind of wavy blonde down to her shoulders, framing her face. Feminine. She wore regular straight-legged blue jeans, silvery high-heeled sandals—Lordy, Lordy! Britta in high heels!—and a floaty type of blue and silver long-sleeved blouse that appeared transparent in spots. Pink lipstick glistened on her mouth, and mascara lengthened her eyelashes. What bothered him most was that Britta no longer stuck out with her waist-long braids and scrubbed maiden skin. She was changing.

"She should be careful with Dylan Overdorf," Linda broke into his thoughts. "He's got hands like an octopus, and he doesn't take no for an answer. I heard he keeps a record of all the women he's slept with, and a rating beside each name. He even makes notations of kinky stuff he convinces his partners to do."

That did it. Zach stood, knocking back Cage and Slick's hands. "Back off," he warned the two of them. Then he headed for the dance floor.

Britta saw him coming. He noticed her body go stiff and her eyes widen with surprise. *I'll give you a surprise, all right. With your butt pointing north, right over my knee.*

"Britta," he said, forcibly lifting her hand off Overdorf's shoulder and hauling her out of his arms.

"Unhand me, knave."

Surprised at first, Overdorf let her go, then tried to pull her back. "Whoa, who the hell are you?"

"Your worst enemy. Let go of Britta."

Overdorf glanced at Britta and cocked an eyebrow. "Darlin'?"

"*Darlin'?* Listen, cowboy, fun's over. Time for Cinderella to go home."

"And you would be Prince Charming, right? I don't think so. I know who you are. One of those Navy SEALs who thinks his shit don't stink."

People were stopping their dancing and staring at them. All his buddies were behind him, urging him to come back. Somewhere in his testosterone-broiled brain he knew he was making a fool of himself.

The band launched into a new song. Toby Keith's "How Do You Like Me Now?" For a blip of an insane second, he thought about asking Britta how she liked him now.

"Come on, cupcake, let's get out of here. Start on one of those orgasms." Overdorf was addressing Britta, whose face had the good sense to turn pink.

Zach saw red again. His eyes cut to Britta, telling her silently that she'd betrayed him. She was only supposed to have orgasms with him. At least, that's what his male pride told him, and a little part of his heart that felt wounded.

"What is the cause of your ill humor, lout?" Britta inquired sweetly.

"You," he snarled.

"Me? You jest. I just got here."

He inhaled and exhaled to tamp his temper down. "Come with me, Britta. Please."

"Why should she, froggie?" Overdorf sneered. SEALs were sometimes referred to as frogmen, an appellation from World War II days.

"Because she's my fiancée." He hoped God didn't strike him dead for the lie.

"Oh. Well. Why didn't you say so?" Overdorf gave Britta an accusing look, as if she'd led him on, which she probably had. *How could she discuss orgasms with anyone but me?* Before anyone had a chance for second thoughts, he put a hand around her waist and practically frog-walked her to their table. An apt thing for a frogman to do, he joked with himself, a sure sign of his mental state.

He stopped just before they got to the table, where seven people, including Linda, were watching him expectantly, wondering what he would do next. Hell, *he* wondered what he would do next.

Turning her to face him, he pulled her close, leaned forward, and gave her what he intended to be a kiss of conciliation, to make up for his rude behavior. Instead, he aligned their bodies from knees to chests, easy to do when Britta matched his height in her high heels which, incidentally, gave him all kinds of ideas, most dealing with bare skin. It quickly morphed into an intimate kiss of wild, hungry, public-be-damned exaltation. He was like an oversexed hound dog marking his territory.

He heard clapping before and behind him and hoots of encouragement. Britta stared at him as if he'd lost his mind.

He had.

When they finally sat down at the table, there were six sets of laughing eyes gawking at them and a not-so-laughing pair from Linda.

Britta nodded to each of them in turn, knowing most of them already, except Linda, whom she shot a glower. Then she asked him, "What is a fee-aunt-say?"

# Chapter 16

**Mead turns men's minds to sex . . . the same throughout the ages . . .**

Right off, she told the oaf what she thought of him. "You are an oaf!" she said.

"Yeah, but a loveable oaf."

"Why did you tell that man we are betrothed?"

"Quickest way to get rid of the jerk."

"Jerk?"

"Loser."

"Loser?"

"He was unworthy of you."

"Oh. And you are not?"

"Nope. I'm very, very worthy of you. I deserve you. We are a match made in heaven."

"So, now we are betrothed?"

"Well, no. Not unless you wanna be."

She laughed. "I release you from that false promise."

"What if I don't wanna be released?"

She laughed again. "Zachary, to become betrothed, you would have to be smitten with me, which you clearly are not."

"Hah! I'm smitten all right."

"So you say!"

"Ask anyone."

"The boy, he is smitten, all right," Cage said, and the others, all of whom were listening with great enjoyment to their conversation, nodded their agreement. The woman whom Zachary had introduced as Linda did not look happy.

"Besides, I was rescuing you from a guy with a very bad reputation," he told Britta.

She arched a brow with disbelief.

"Ask Linda. He makes his sex partners do perverted things." She could tell that Zachary regretted making that statement. But Linda nodded.

"More perverted than incline sex?"

Zachary red-faced, gawked at her as if he could not believe she had said that. She realized why when she saw all the men go silent with interest, waiting.

"So, Zach, *mon coeur*, exactly what is incline sex?"

"Is it on an inclined plane, like a skateboard ramp?" Merrill the Geek asked.

Before Zachary could speak, she said, "It is rather like upside-down sex. Well, not really that. More like a wheelbarrow. Hmmm. How would you explain it, Zachary?"

"I wouldn't."

"Do you blush, lout? Odin's breath! You do," she hooted.

Everyone at the table was laughing, so hard some were holding their sides, even Linda, who seemed to have moved her affections from Zachary to Luke the Slick, who paid her no nevermind.

"Zach, Zach, Zach!" JAM said, wiping tears from his eyes.

"And here we were all thinking you'd lost your touch!" This from Sly.

"It would appear that our pretty boy has a bit of the nasty in him. Hoo-yah!" Cage teased.

"And you guys make fun of my penile glove!" Geek added with affront.

Linda turned slowly to gape at Geek. "You wear a glove on your penis? Do you mean a condom?"

"No, I don't mean a condom, and that's all I'll say on the subject in mixed company." He glowered at his friends.

Zachary was looking pleased that the attention had moved away from him.

But then Sly said, "Back to sexual perversions. What other kinky stuff does Pretty Boy do, Britta?"

"Well—"

Zachary slapped a hand over her mouth.

"Spoilsport!" JAM complained.

She had no idea what they were making such a fuss over.

"You wear a glove on your penis?" Linda persisted with Geek.

"Yeah."

"Why?"

"Sometimes it gets cold. And lonely. You want me to show you?"

"You men are crude and rude. I've heard that SEALs are nuts, and now I believe it." Linda rose from her chair and walked away.

No one seemed to care much. Leastways they did not try to talk her into staying.

But then JAM said, "We *were* crude. Maybe you should go after her, Pretty Boy."

"Hah! She was feelin' up my family jewels under the table. She can't be too offended by crudity."

Britta turned to Zachary. "You have family jewels?"

Once again, everyone at the table laughed, presumably at a joke she did not understand.

"Oh, yeah," Zach replied.

"Can I see them?"

"Oh, yeah."

The laughter increased.

Zachary leaned close to her ear. "Family jewels refers to my . . . uh, package."

She frowned. "Package. What package?"

Zachary rolled his eyes, took her hand, and placed it over his manpart, which began to grow under her fingers. She jerked her hand away.

"Linda was correct. You are all crude."

The men, including Zachary, grinned as if she'd given them a compliment.

"The best sex I ever had," Sly related, as if that had aught to do with the subject at hand, "was with a showgirl who could stand against the wall on one leg and lift the other leg straight up in the air, perpendicular to the floor." He paused. "Naked, of course."

Zachary looked at her.

"Not in a million years!"

"We'll see."

"We will not see."

"That's nothin'," Cage added to the conversation. "I got it on one time with a gymnast who could stay in a backbend position, like forever, and—"

"What did you say about gymnasts?" Terri asked. She and Britta's other friends had just walked up to the table, waving to Britta and the others. "I used to be a gymnast."

"No kidding!" Cage smiled, but before he could say more, JAM said, "Have a seat, honey." He gave her his chair, saying something teasingly to Cage in the process, something about 'You snooze, you lose, bow-zo.' " Soon the men were pulling another table closer so that their now large group could sit together.

Even Dill-land, whose name was actually Dylan, came over to join them, much to Zachary's displeasure, even though Dylan gave most of his attention to Donita, which seemed to annoy Sly, who had done naught but goad and taunt Donita in the past. In any case, Dylan greeted one and all by saying, "How-dee," and winked at Britta. That, too, brought a growl out of Zachary's tight mouth.

They all dined then on a feast. Two large rounds of manchet bread covered with a red sauce and cheese. Wings— and only the wings—of a chicken, but so hot one needed tons of ale to wash them down. A large tray of salted sticks called French fries made from the potato, a vegetable she'd never heard of afore, although it apparently came to this country from Frankland. A big platter of notch-hose, which were crispy thin chips covered with melted cheese. And two racks of pig ribs swimming in a sweet and sour red sauce, which was very messy to eat but delicious.

After that, the musicians began to play again. First off was a raucous song called "That Old Time Rock 'n' Roll," which prompted Cage to yell across the table, "Yo, Marie."

She glanced up with surprise from a conversation she'd been having with Dylan.

"Wanna show these Yankees how ta dance?"

She looked skeptical.

"Yer Cajun, aintcha?"

"Yeaaaah."

"Enough said! We Cajuns have an extra dance gene, ain't that so, *chère*?"

She smiled. "Oh, yeah. My mama, she was dancin' in the cradle, and Papa, that man been playin' the washboard since he was knee-high to a crawfish."

The two of them did not walk out onto the dance area; they danced out.

"Wait till you see this," Zachary said in her ear.

And what a show Cage and Marie put on! One song ran into another and yet another. No longer about rocking and rolling, but one about a love shack. *Do they have special shacks for loving here?* Then, another with the oddest lyric, "honky tonk badonkadonk."

"What is a honky tonk badonkadonk?" she asked Zachary.

"Female ass."

"That remark is sorely lacking humor."

"It's true."

She glanced around the table, and those who had overheard nodded their heads.

Not for the first time, she thought, *What an odd country!*

As ribald as Viking men were wont to be, even they did not sing about arses. Leastways, not in mixed company.

Cage and Marie were doing the most suggestive dance moves, all to the rhythm of a pounding beat of music. They circled each other, never quite touching, sometimes undulating in unison, with Cage spooned up to her backside. Britta could only describe their movements as a game of seduction. And she didn't think Marie even liked Cage all that much.

Then, one of the band of musicians yelled out, "Have we got any cowboys in the crowd?"

There was a wild roar of yeses and yee-haws.

In response, the musicians launched into a song called "Save a Horse, Ride a Cowboy," and Marie actually appeared to be riding Cage's extended leg as if it were a horse. Still not touching, but everything but.

Britta shook her head at the absurdity and outrageousness of it all.

Other couples moved onto the dance floor, too, including everyone at their table. Dylan and Donita. JAM and Terri. Sly and Geek, with other ladies. Omar and Slick had already left, claiming other places to be.

"Wanna dance?" Zachary asked her.

"No."

"That was blunt."

"If you think I am going to engage in sex in public and call it dancing, I have a longship you might want to purchase."

He smiled and squeezed her shoulder. His arm was draped casually over the back of her chair, and his fingers played with the edges of her newly shorn hair.

Why was it that she was so aware of him when he merely smiled at her, whilst Dylan, and any other men in the tavern, could be stumps for all she cared?

"I have not talked with you for sennights."

"Not for lack of my trying. If I recall correctly, you pretty much told me to go do something physically impossible to myself. More than once."

She had to think a moment to figure what he meant, then said, "Tsk, tsk, tsk! I ne'er said those words. Besides, every time you attempted to talk to me it was after having nigh drowned me in those bloody rub-her boats, or in the midst of dousing me with sand, or mostly after a brutal assault on my body by excessive exercising."

"I warned you how hard it would be, Britta. It's my job to push you and the other WEALS as hard as you can stand. I haven't treated you any differently. Besides, you can always—"

"—ring out," she finished for him. "I have not struggled this far to quit now."

He nodded. "How are the tutoring classes going?"

"Very well, but as much as I learn, there is so much more I realize that I do not know."

"Hey, that's life."

"Do I have you to thank for the classes?"

"Me and the commander. Next month WEALS will go into half-day sessions in the classroom. We knew you'd never make it with your . . . background."

"I feel so lackwitted."

"No, don't say that. You're just in a new culture. Anyone would be the same. In fact, you and Sammy are in the same boat. He's being tutored, too, but on a rudimentary level. Reading, writing, basic numbers. Even at his age, he's aware that he's different from other kids. He should be okay by the time school starts next semester, though, assuming he'll be able to go to school."

*Yea, there are similarities betwixt me and the boy. Lost souls in a new land. Struggling to fit in. Not sure what the future will hold.*

"Who cares for your son tonight?"

"Danny."

"Does your brother come to help you often?"

"Actually, no. I usually don't see him for months on end. He's probably worried about me."

"Because of the danger?"

All the guys were there watching JAM, who was already on his cell phone to the command center. JAM was nodding his head and saying, "Yes, sir. Sly, Cage, Geek, and Pretty Boy are here with me. I understand, sir. Right away, sir." JAM handed the phone to Zach. "He wants to talk to you."

"What's your home situation, Lieutenant?" the XO asked him. "Are you able to go on a live op?"

"Yes, sir. A contingency plan is in effect."

"Good. See you in two hours for the predeployment workup. Geared up. No uniform."

Zach closed the cell and handed it back to JAM.

He was elated. He was back on call. Maybe his life would get back to normal now.

The guys were already leaving, paying their bills, saying good-byes to the women, and heading for the door.

"What is happening?" Britta asked him.

He realized that he was still holding her hand. Lifting their clasped hands, he kissed her knuckles. "We're to report for duty. Walk me out to my car?"

She nodded.

With his arm over her shoulder and her arm around his waist, they walked outside and toward the back lot. Since he'd arrived late, he hadn't been able to find a parking space anywhere close to the entrance. She was a little wobbly on her feet, the high heels digging into the gravel, so he held on extra tight, inhaling the smell of her apple shampoo.

But he was distracted, his mind racing with all he would have to do before going wheels up. He didn't know where they would be heading yet, but that didn't matter. The security force his father had hired for him would continue to watch over his home, and a female guard would stay inside. Sammy wouldn't be a happy camper, but he would be safe. Zach kept his weapons in good condition . . . broken down, cleaned, and lubed on a regular basis. No problem there. His will and other legal documents were stored at his lawyer's, just in case.

He grinned. "Nah. Because having a child is crimping my social life."

She smacked his arm for making jest with her.

"Still having the dreams?"

"Yea, but they vary now. Betimes the blood and carnage I see is from the good nuns. But, in other dreams, it is my father and brothers and their evil cohorts who lie lifeless at the hands of a band of warrior nuns, led by one particular nun."

"Like Boudicca?"

Britta was familiar with the Celtic warrior queen, as she'd once told Mother Edwina. "In some ways, but Boudicca was not a nun."

Zachary stiffened. "Is that nun in the dream you?"

She understood his dismay. If she saw herself in that dream, it must mean she would be returning. "Nay, 'tis not."

He relaxed visibly.

"Still, the dreams are horrifying and confusing. And they are pulling at me."

"Pulling?"

She nodded. "As if I could be pulled into a dream."

"I still say that you need to talk with Madrene and Hilda. They might have insight, having traveled the same path."

"I will . . . when I get a chance."

He stood, took a big swallow from his long-necked bottle, placed it on the table, then took her hand, pulling her to her feet. "Come on, let's dance. The music is slow now."

"I cannot dance."

"You were dancing with the dickhead."

"Who?"

"Dylan."

"I was just standing still. He did all the moving."

Zachary made a growling sound low in his throat. "Do the same for me, then." Without waiting for her response, he led her out onto the dancing arena. He put both arms around her waist, then advised, "Put your arms around my neck, sweetie."

She did.

He then yanked her hard against his body so they were

aligned breast to chest, belly to belly, thigh to thigh, and some interesting places in between. With her high-heeled shoes, she was eye level with the rogue.

"Surely this is not a dancing position for normal folks."

"It is for lovers." He put his face against her cheek and began to sway from side to side.

"We are not—" she was about to say.

"Don't you dare belittle what we have between us."

"I was about to say, we are not lovers *anymore*."

He chuckled softly. "Sweetheart, you are so full of it."

They remained quiet then, just swaying and occasionally turning. It was like a soft embrace, with the backdrop of music. He smelled good, like mint and his distinctive manscent. She liked the feel of his arms enveloping her possessively, especially since she was enveloping him just as securely. And his ardor, blessed Frigg! His ardor for her was enough to turn a saint lustsome. What woman wouldn't feel complimented by that?

"I missed you," she murmured before she had a chance to stop herself.

"I know," he said, drawing his head back to look at her and smile.

She smacked his arm. "Your ego far exceeds your worth, lout."

"Ya think?" He leaned forward, a hairsbreadth from her lips, and whispered, "I missed you, too, baby. So much it scares me."

And then he kissed her.

**When smart women turn the tables on clueless men . . .**

Women were right. Slow dancing was foreplay to a guy. Not the best kind, but still, a prelude to sex . . . or at least a chance for seduction.

The question was: Who was being seduced? Him or her?

There was no explanation for the way he felt about Britta.

She had him from the moment she'd called him a lackwit. Didn't matter that it was two years ago, or that she'd been holding a big-ass broadaxe at the time.

Every time he kissed her, like now, he felt an incredible sense of rightness . . . that he'd been dog-paddling all his life to reach this woman. He couldn't—he *wouldn't*—let her go.

"Come home with me," he urged, breaking the kiss but not his hold on her.

She shook her head. "I cannot."

"Don't you want to be with me?"

A choked laugh escaped her lips. "I want to. Too much."

"Then why?"

She sighed. "Zachary, why do you pursue me?"

"I don't know. I just know I have to."

"I but wish . . ."

When she didn't immediately continue, he prodded, "You wish what?"

"I wish I had met you long ago. Afore my life path was set in another direction."

"What life path?"

"The one that dictates I be a warrior. Not a wife or mother. Oh, do not get your loincloth in a twist. I am not suggesting you would want me for a wife."

"Don't make assumptions about me, Britta. And I don't accept that life paths, or fate, or destiny can't be changed. In fact—"

Just then, he felt a vibration in his back pocket. He pulled his beeper out and couldn't believe his eyes. He was being called to active duty. Glancing around the bar, he saw his fellow SEALs doing the same thing. It must be something really critical if they were willing to overlook his recent transgressions.

"Uh, I have to go, Britta."

"Go? Where?"

"That was my beeper. I'm on active duty, as of this minute." He took her hand and led her over to the table.

They were almost to his car. He hadn't realized it was this far back. He would drive Britta around to the front when he left. No way would he let her go back alone, not with a tavern full of half-drunk horndogs.

He noticed her staring at him then . . . and that she was especially quiet. "What's wrong?"

"Nothing," she said. "I am just thinking."

"Uh-oh."

She didn't smile . . . or smack him upside the head. "Where you are going tonight . . . will it be dangerous?"

"I won't know till I get back to the command center, on a need-to-know basis. But yeah, there's always a risk of danger on any mission. You know that."

She nodded. Still serious. Still staring at him in the strangest way. "Dost know how long you will be gone?"

He shook his head, frowning now.

Suddenly, he knew.

*Holy shit! Britta is planning to offer me a pity fuck. Or more precisely, a good-bye fuck.* He shouldn't be surprised. Women got all teary-eyed and softhearted when a soldier was about to deploy. Yo-yo panties were the norm on any military base the night before the troops went off to war. Men had been taking advantage of that perk since the beginning of time.

But this was Britta.

Should he take her up on the offer . . . when she makes it? Or should he be noble and not take advantage?

But then she surprised the spit right out of him. She didn't make the offer. Nope. Before he could say "Hallelujah" or "No thanks," like that was ever gonna happen, she slammed him up against the trunk of his Firebird, bent him backward, and began to rip off his shirt, buttons flying everywhere.

He was laughing and protesting, "Whoa, whoa, whoa!" at the same time.

"What?" She stopped.

His chest was bare, his shirt pushed back over his shoulders and halfway down his arms. *Man, she's strong.* Her blouse was off. *When did that happen?* He grabbed her upper arms to hold her in place. "Wait just a minute, honey." *I sure hope I have a condom in my wallet.*

She went still, even before he released her arms. "Are you not feeling lustsome tonight?"

*Oh, yeah. I'm feeling lustsome, all right.*

But she didn't wait for him to answer. She put her hand over his erection, checking for herself.

Talk about a kick-start hard-on. He went from mild interest to full-blown boogie in a nanosecond.

She smiled and stroked him several times.

He was pretty sure he gurgled something out. And in that split second where his eyes were rolling back in his head, she'd begun caressing his chest with her breasts, back and forth.

"I like how that feels. Do you?"

*Are you kidding?* "I don't know. Do it again."

She did. Again. And again. Then she plucked at his nipples, which had a direct line to sex central. "Now your nipples look like mine," she murmured.

"Huh?" *I don't think so.*

"They're all pointy and hard."

*Okaaaay.* "Let me see." His fingers played with her breasts then, fluttering the engorged peaks, twirling them between a thumb and a forefinger, then fluttering again.

She moaned and arched her back so her breasts stuck out even more. What a picture! Like a hood ornament. Which gave him an idea.

He sat up, then stood. Picking her up by the waist, he carried her to the hood, which faced the woods behind the lot, and placed her on the cool metal so that her head was almost to the windshield. "Don't move." He pulled off her high-heeled sandals, tugged her jeans and bikini panties off, then put the high heels back on, spreading her legs slightly in the process. "Raise your arms."

"Like this?"

His you-know-what gave a mental shout of "Hoo-yah!"

He, on the other hand, was unable to speak at first. Then, "Don't move," he repeated.

Damn, he wished he had a camera. This was a picture he'd like to have. But, no, he didn't need a photograph. This image was imprinted on his brain for life.

He shook his head to clear it, which was almost impossible with testosterone barreling through his body, sizzling his gray matter.

In the blink of an eye, he was nude, covered, and ready for action. He crawled up and over her, kissing his way, till he was on his elbows facing her, and they were belly to belly, with his cock pressing against her clit. Sex heaven.

She lifted her belly, trying to make him enter her. "Not yet." He panted for control, sweat beading his forehead.

He kissed her softly, once he was reasonably sure he wasn't going to embarrass himself. "You didn't have to do this for me, you know." *Am I nuts?* "But thank you anyway." *I'm carrying on a bleepin' conversation on the hood of my car with a naked woman. How amazing is that?*

*I better be careful, or there'll be a dent in the bodywork. Hah! Who the hell cares?*

"Do what for you?"

"Make love."

"Oh, I am not doing this for you."

*WHAT?* his brain squawked. "For the team then," he joked.

"Do not be a lackbrain. I am doing it for me. I want to have another orgasm."

"In case I don't come back?"

"You better come back. I am not being stuck here in the future without you."

"You sweet talker, you."

"Nay, I need a comparison."

"With what?"

"Other men?"

"You've been with other men?" *This is unbelievable. She's having sex with me so she can rate my prowess.*

"When would I have time to be with other men? Nay, 'tis just that I felt nothing when Dylan touched me, and I wondered—"

*Okay, so it hasn't happened yet.* "Dylan touched you? I'll kill him. Where?"

"In the tavern."

"I meant, where on your body? He copped a feel, didn't he?"

She tilted her head in confusion. "You speak in riddles. I just meant that when he touched my hand or danced with me, I did not feel that tingle that I do with you."

A big ol' smile started to spread across his mouth, and he didn't even try to hold it back. "I make you tingle?"

"Hah! All you have to do is look at me, and I tingle."

"I tingle, too," he admitted, though that wasn't quite the word he would use. "Are you tingling now?" he asked as he rocked against her clit, then thrust inside in a long, slow stroke.

She gasped out, "Like a bell."

He started to tell her that bells tinkled, not tingled, but stopped himself. Actually, he liked the comparison. "How do you like my gong?" He moved from side to side.

"Nice."

"Nice?"

"That was a compliment."

"No, babe, nice is not what a guy wants a woman to say about his favorite body part. More like, 'Wow!' 'Huge!' 'Yikes!' "

She started to laugh, then stopped abruptly as her inner walls began to clasp and unclasp him in a hard rhythm. She closed her eyes and stiffened.

"No, open your eyes. I want to see your orgasm. I want you to see me enjoying your orgasm."

Meanwhile, he was still embedded in her, to the hilt, trying his best not to move, because to move would mean instant, way-too-quick ejaculation.

When her body stopped its delicious squeeze on him, he

leaned down and kissed her parted lips. "Babe" was all he could manage to say.

But she said nothing.

He soon found out why.

She spread her bent knees wider. "If you do not start moving, I am going to smack your arse to get you moving."

He would have laughed if he could have. Instead, he began long, slow strokes against her friction. Sweet torture. He kissed her as he moved. He caressed. He murmured his appreciation of all she did to make this better for both of them. When he came, she came with him. They shattered apart but at the same time seemed to melt together.

Every time he made love to Britta it was different.

Every time he made love to Britta it was better.

When he was able to breathe without gasping for breath, he raised his head, still half limp inside her. She stared up at him, wide-eyed, with parted lips. She looked stunned.

"That's what I call ringing your bell."

She remained dazed, gazing at him. "Is it always like this betwixt a man and a woman?"

"No." He traced her lips with the tips of his fingers, then kissed her softly. "No, it's not. It seems you and I have something special going on. I'm not sure what it is. Chemistry. Emotion. Probably both."

She frowned, not understanding a word he'd said. "Can you do it again?"

"What?"

"Ring my bell."

"Oh, Britta, you are priceless. No, we don't have time. I've got to get back to the—"

She rocked her hips against him, which of course caused his half-limp cock to come to life inside her again and protest in manly sign language, *Who doesn't have time?*

Then she did something so uninhibited, even a little kinky, that caused him to almost swallow his tongue.

He checked the glowing face on his watch.

"Maybe a little ring," he said.

A short time later . . . a *really* short time later, Zach was dropping Britta off in front of the Wet and Wild.

"Are you sure you don't want me to take you back to the base when I report for duty?"

She shook her head. "Nay, I must needs return with my comrades. We made a pact afore coming here that we would stick together. Unless one of us got lucky." She was deep in thought for a second. "What does 'getting lucky' mean?"

He was about to say, "Getting laid," but figured she wouldn't understand that, either. "Getting their bells rung."

Her mouth formed a perfect O, then she giggled. Zach realized then that he'd never heard Britta giggle. Hell, with the childhood she'd had, she'd probably never ever giggled before. He put an arm around her shoulder and squeezed.

"Don't go away, Britta," he blurted out. *Where did that come from?*

"I must go back to the base."

He shook his head. "Not there."

"Oh. I see. Well, I may not have a choice about going back."

"Just don't. Please. Wait till I get back, and we can talk."

Her friends were coming out of the tavern now. Britta called to them out of the open window, telling them she would be with them in a moment. Then she turned to him, and there were honest-to-God tears in her eyes.

*Tears? From Britta? What next?*

"Be safe," she whispered huskily, kissed him quickly, and was gone.

Zach sat behind the wheel, unmoving, trying to fathom what had just happened. His heart felt funny, sort of achy. There was a buzzing in his head. He wanted desperately to call her back and ask what she'd really meant, because what he was thinking was impossible.

One thing he did know. There was no way that little sexercise in the back parking lot was Britta taking notes to compare him with other guys. Nope. Britta had been telling him in her own way that she cared about him.

He had a lightbulb moment then, the kind that makes a guy wonder how he could be so dense.

As he drove home to pick up his gear and make last-minute arrangements, he was alternately smiling and frowning about this particular epiphany. And it wasn't related to Britta turning the tables on him sex-wise, or not entirely.

*I'm falling in love.*

*No, no, no! I can't be falling in love. Falling in love is a bad thing. Bad time. Bad in every respect. Bad, bad, bad!*

*Like love waits for the right time. Like love is bad.*

*I. Am. Not. In. Love.*

*But what if . . . what if, for the first time in my friggin'— literally friggin'—life, I'm falling in love?*

*It's just lust, and some mind-blowing sex. That's all.*

*Ha, ha, ha!*

**MEMO**

**From: Captain Lenore Feldman**
**To: Commander Ian MacLean**
**Subject: WEALS**

**Fraternization between Navy SEALs and WEALS is to be discouraged.**

Commander Ian MacLean glanced at the memo in his hand and passed it to Floyd, whose face immediately turned red.

"This is just great! Now they expect me to be the sex police." He glared at Floyd, who didn't have the sense to keep his skivvies under lock and key. Too bad the Navy didn't make chastity belts . . . for its men.

"It's not really fraternization. It's just that I've known Britta for a while, and I feel responsible for her. Like a brother . . . or something."

"That doesn't even pass the giggle test, boy."

"Yeah, it *was* pretty lame."

"What next?" He threw his arms out in disgust.

He found out the next day, just before the team went boots up, when he got another blasted note from his female ombudsman.

### MEMO

**From: Captain Lenore Feldman**
**To: Commander Ian MacLean**
**Subject: WEALS**

**Sexual encounters between SEALs and WEALS in the parking lot of the Wet and Wild are expressly forbidden.**

*"WHAT?"* His outraged exclamation could be heard down the corridors of the command center.

Luckily, a certain SEAL was out on assignment and was not expected back for several days. Otherwise, a certain SEAL might be minus a certain body part.

# Chapter 17

**From the Dennis the Menace book of tricks . . .**

Samir was bored. He was scared. He was pissed. And, yeah, he might be five years old, but he knew what pissed meant.

His father had been gone for almost a week. And he had had eight . . . EIGHT . . . babysitters so far. Not family members like his grandmother or Uncle Danny, not even family friends, except for once in a while the witch Madrene. Nope, these were big ol' scowling giants with arms the size of Frisbees and grumpy voices . . . even the women. They didn't let him do ANYTHING . . . not anything fun, anyhow, like play blood-and-guts video games . . . or play catch outside. The only thing they would let him watch on TV was *Sesame Street* or *Noggin*. *Like I'm ever gonna play with someone like Dora the Boring Explorer! Or Ernie the Dork!* They wouldn't even let him have Pepsi and Twinkies for breakfast. *They probably give prisoners that shredded hay stuff with milk and no sugar.*

The only visitor he was allowed to have was a tutor . . . that was the name for a teacher with bad breath who forced him to read silly books, like *See Jane Run. If I was Jane, I would run, too . . . right out the door.* And numbers! *My brain hurts from doing all those numbers.* He liked studying geography, though, especially when he could see on a map how far away Afghanistan was. And history, he liked that, too. That Ben Franklin was a cool guy; he wrote a book called *Fart Proudly. Farts are awesome.*

Mostly, though, he was scared. They wouldn't be having all these big goons watching him if they didn't think that his grandfather was close by.

*What would Grandfather do if he got me? Would he lop off my head like I saw him do one time to Taj's cousin's uncle? Probably not. But he would beat me. I am certain of that. Maybe with a whip this time.*

And he was scared that his father would not come back. Just like his mother. She had gone on a mission, too. And got killed.

Samir needed to do something, but he was only a little boy. He needed help. From someone who could be coaxed into stuff.

Suddenly, he knew.

Britta.

## From caterpillar to babysitter, all in one day . . .

A week had gone by since Britta had made a harlot of herself . . . and, yea, that was how she increasingly viewed her performance on the metal frame of an automobile with Zachary.

Not that she had not enjoyed herself.

Not that she would not repeat the exercise, if given the chance.

But Zachary and some of his cohorts had been gone for almost a sennight now, and not a word about their whereabouts, or even if they were still alive. She'd tried to ask the commander about the mission on several occasions, but he'd merely glowered at her, muttering something about stupid men and stupider women.

"Okay, snuffies, I think it's time for a new game," the chieftain named F.U. said with an evil glint in his eye, mostly directed at her.

For some reason, he had taken a dislike to her and picked on her constantly. No doubt because she had dumped him on his arse that first day, but he had more than deserved his comeuppance. Since Zachary and some of the other instructors were away on a mission, Chieftain F.U. was in charge, backed up on occasion by Commander MacLean.

The performance that the WEALS had given for the visiting law persons five days past had gone well. In fact, one of the female governing persons—a senator, just like the ancient Romans—had taken her aside and asked, "How are they *really* treating you?"

Taken aback, she replied, "Our training is difficult, but less so than SEALs. No need for complaint." Britta was being generous. She would have liked to tell her of the incessant running, the incessant surf passages, and all the other incessants, but she had held her tongue. "Choosing battles" was a tactic she'd learned this week in battle theory class, and a good lesson it was, too.

"I like your attitude," the white-haired woman had said. Then she had put a small parchment item in her hand. "That's my telephone number. A private line. If there's ever a problem, just call me."

Now, five days later, they were deep in physical training . . . again. Incessantly.

She and the other WEALS had just returned from a five-mile run on the sandy shore carrying that heavy rub-her boat. To say they were hot, tired, dirty, odorsome, and in pain would be like saying that boars had bad breath . . . a large understatement.

"Okay, snuffies, here's the deal," the commander told them. "Next week we go to San Clemente Island again for survival training and Sims. The week after will be rock portage, the gateway evolution for SEALs and WEALS. Doesn't mean you're on easy street after that, but it is a major hurdle. Now I'll turn the program over to Instructor Uxley, and I'll see you early Monday morning."

"Yes, Commander, sir!"

Chieftain F.U. waited till the commander was out of hearing range, then yelled, "I'm thinkin' it's time to play caterpillar, sweet things, and guess who's gonna give head . . . I mean, be the head?" He winked at Britta. If ever a wink could be construed as malicious, his was.

No doubt this would be another exercise in torture designed to make the women ring the quitting bell. Her assumption soon proved true.

In truth, everything they did these days was torture. And the hollered orders all ran together. "A-ten-shun!" "Listen up!" "Run, run, run!" "Recover!" "Hydrate!" "You weak-as-piss maggots!" "A-ten-shun!" "Fall in!" "Fall out!" "A-ten-shun!" "Drop!" "Drop and give me twenty . . . thirty . . . fifty!" "Hydrate!" "Recover!" "On your backs, scruffies!" "On your feet!" "A-ten-shun!" "Up boats!" "Down boats!" "Hydrate!" "Hit the deck!" "You can always ring out!" In between, they kept hearing that blasted whistle and must needs react in the correct manner.

Now they were going to be bloody caterpillars.

Wearing heavy life vests and helmets, the trainees were forced to sit in the water in a line, breasts to backs, snugly placing the legs around the person in front, thus becoming a water-going caterpillar. They could paddle out to deeper waters with their hands but not kick their legs. The vests kept them buoyant, but they were nigh drowned after a half hour in this position. When they staggered back to shore, vomiting, several instructors helped those in greatest need. Chieftain F.U. just smirked. Three women wobbled up to the bell to ring out. Leaving only thirty of the original ninety-five, a number that did not surprise those in authority.

The caterpillar nonsense was a not-so-great ending to a not-so-great week, with a two-day liberty looming ahead, but all Britta could think about was sleep. That plan was cut short when Commander MacLean intercepted her on the way to the women's quarters.

"Madrene wants to talk with you," he said, handing her a telephone.

"Greetings!" she said.

"Britta, how do you fare?" Madrene asked. In the background, she could hear Sammy clamoring, "Let me talk, let me talk."

"How do I fare? I am sore. I am tired. I am dirty. I am hungry. And I smell. Other than that, I am just wonderful."

Madrene laughed. "Well, I can take care of one of those. Wouldst join me and Hilda for dinner tonight? Ian could drop you off here at Pretty Boy's on his way home. I am watching Sammy today, but one of the guards will be taking over."

The thought of getting into a small vehicle space with the dour commander was daunting, but Britta relished the idea of meeting with these two old friends. Plus she yearned for news of Zachary, and going to his home might provide the information she wanted.

Several hours later Britta braved the guards surrounding Zachary's keep, whilst Madrene brought her two children out to the automobile for the grumbling commander to take home so she could enjoy a "girls' night out." She noticed that the commander kissed Madrene sweetly afore leaving, which made her think that mayhap he was not as bad as he appeared.

Besides, on the drive there, the commander gave her news of Zachary and his comrades-in-arms. They might be home in a few days, she was told. Plus, she found out that they had not left the country but instead were fighting terrorists at a football stadium. Football was a ludicrous game in this country where grown men threw a leather ball and tackled each other with great force, often causing serious injury. Viking men would love it. In any case, Zachary could not be in such great danger at a game, she told herself.

The second Britta entered Zachary's keep, Sammy launched himself at her, arms wrapped tightly around her neck and little legs hugging her waist. He was sobbing and talking a garbled message that seemed to indicate he was lonely and scared and wanted her to stay with him.

Madrene, who had been watching him that day, just shook her head with dismay. "I don't know what to do with the boyling. The longer Pretty Boy is away, the more frantic he becomes."

Madrene went to open the door for Hilda, who had just arrived. Britta sat down on a soft fabric, cushiony chair and pulled Sammy onto her lap, drying his eyes with the hem of his tea-ing *shert*. At the little-boy scent of his skin and the feel of his tightly clinging arms, Britta fought to control her tears . . . and a yearning for something she had never thought possible for herself: motherhood.

"Stay with me," he wailed.

"I cannot, dearling. I must needs do my military training."

"All the time?" His words were alternated with hiccups.

"Well, not all the time. Most times."

"Stay now."

"I am going out to dine with Madrene and Hilda."

"You're leaving me here . . . alone."

That set off a new round of crying. And more aching in the region of her heart. "You are not alone. There is always someone here with you."

"But they are different all the time. The only one who's the same is Madrene, and she's a witch."

She and Madrene exchanged glances and grins.

"Come into the scullery, my little man," Hilda said, taking him by the hand. "I brought you a surprise."

She thought she heard Sammy mutter something odd— "It better not be more stupid underwear"—as they left the room.

"What was that all about?" she asked Madrene once they were alone and her friend sat in a chair next to her.

"The poor kid is distraught over his missing father. Thinks he's never coming back."

"Has he not been told this is his father's job? That he has every intention of returning?"

"Yea, but the little boy has experienced much loss in his short life. He is convinced that Pretty Boy is going to die and leave him alone in this country. Plus he has had a parade of guards here to watch over him. They are good people but strangers. In time, I am sure Pretty Boy will find help that is steady and reliable, but for now at least the child is safe."

"How about you?"

"I help when I can, but I have my own home and children to care for."

"And Zachary's family? I have met Danny."

"They help when they can, but they all have jobs, too."

"And danger looms still from the grandsire?"

"More so than ever with Pretty Boy gone."

"Why does he cling to me? I am almost a stranger, too."

"Methinks he senses your common backgrounds. Both lost in a new country. Both stumbling with the language. Both a little lonely. Both facing some danger. Both caring deeply for Pretty Boy."

Britta was about to argue the caring for Zachary bit but held her tongue. Instead, she pondered Madrene's words and offered hesitantly, "I could stay with him tonight and mayhap tomorrow night. Try to calm him down and explain things to him. But then I would have to return to the base."

"Would you?" Madrene asked with great enthusiasm. "Praise the gods, would you, please?"

"I would."

"I will be so appreciative, and so will Pretty Boy. I know this is cutting into the little free time you have."

"'Tis no bother." And that was the truth. "I have no inclination to join my women friends in shopping for clothing I do not need. Who needs more than two pairs of braies and two pairs of shoes? Dost know, my friend Terri has twenty-five pairs of shoes back at her home? How can any one woman wear that many shoes?"

Madrene smiled, no doubt having been as dumbstruck as her on first arriving in this country. "You will learn to love shoes, believe me."

"Nor am I inclined to go clubbing again 'to get lucky.' I have been lucky enough, thank you very much."

At first, Madrene's eyes went wide, then she flashed her a huge grin. "Now this is a subject we must discuss over dinner."

"Getting lucky?"

"Sex."

"Ah. One and the same, am I not correct?"

"Holy Thor, mayhap I could learn a thing or two from you."

"Mayhap," Britta said, with a surprising lack of humility. She leaned toward Madrene then and whispered, "Dost know about multiple orgasms?"

Madrene blinked at her, then burst out laughing.

They were both laughing when a puzzled Hilda and Sammy returned to the solar.

Sammy did smile when she told him she would be returning later to stay the night with him . . . and that she had a special bedtime saga to tell him. "The Loathsome Lout Prince and the Beautiful, Brave Viking Warrior Maiden."

## Give me an S, give me an E, give me an A, give me an L . . .

Zach was standing in the empty press box at the Penn State Nittany Lions football stadium, preparing for tomorrow night's homecoming game with Notre Dame.

He was connected by lip mike and earpiece to the other eight members of his team scattered about the 110,000-seat steel edifice. They were all jacked up, but nothing was happening . . . so far.

It was a great architectural marvel, situated here among the beautiful Nittany Mountains in Happy Valley, but it could very well be a bitch to empty if terrorists had their way.

In addition, it was an especially attractive setting because of all the colorful hot-air balloons there in the near distance, part of the homecoming celebration. The ballonists, many of them Penn State alumni, met here every year to show off their latest babies to each other and the grateful crowds. The parade and pep rally had been held the night before.

The government was keeping this threat low key, but the rumor mill had it that terrorists were targeting this stadium on this particular weekend. Americans in large numbers made a tempting target. If they could take down a hundred thousand people in one pop, it would make 9/11 appear like a minor blip on the terrorist tally board. Still, it was only rumors at this point.

"Everyone in place?" asked JAM, head of this mission.

"Roger," said Cage, who was lying flat atop the roof of the VIP suites.

Sly, Max, Geek, Slick, Scary Larry, Omar, Travis "Flash" Gordon, and Cody O'Brien also reported in from their various positions . . . in the two tunnels leading to the locker rooms, outside the concession stands, the massive parking lot, and even tailing Coach Paterno. They were all dressed to blend in with the expected crowds, wearing blue and white or blue and gold jerseys with school emblems, except for a cursing Flash, who'd picked the bad luck short straw. He was dressed as the Nittany Lions mascot, complete with sweaty lion's head. It was a tradition at Penn State that every time a touchdown was made, the Nittany Lion had to go out on the field and do a push-up per point, including those previously earned. By the end of the game, the lion could conceivably do more than a hundred push-ups in that heavy costume, not to mention dozens of front- and backflips. Occasionally, he was passed up through the bleachers by rowdy, sometimes drunk students. All in all, a pain-in-the-butt assignment.

Geek was the only one who thought it was cool to hit on college coeds, although Cage had been eyeing one of the cheerleaders who had "a bootie to die for." Cage's words, not Zach's. They'd been there all week, twiddling their thumbs, way too much time to think.

And of course Zach was thinking about Sammy. And about Britta . . . way too much. But then, she'd given him a going-away present to beat all going-away presents.

"You've got that look on yer face again, *cher.*" Cage had just slipped into the press box with him.

"Would that be my 'I'm bored to death' look or my 'I'm past ready to rumble' look?"

"It would be the love-struck look."

"Don't you mean horny?"

"Nope. I'm seein' love, baby."

"Seriously, dude, I've gotta make some decisions about Britta when I get back to the base."

"Why?"

"Because . . . I don't know, just because."

"Dum-dum-de-dum."

"Please. It's just that I feel responsible for her being here. And I do care about her. And . . ."

"And?"

He grinned.

"Great sex, huh?" Cage prodded.

"Really great sex."

"Let's face it, you've been hooked on her since you met her two years ago."

"That's another thing. Do you really believe this time-travel crap? Do you really think *we* traveled back in time? I know we don't talk about it, but I got used to telling myself that it was our imaginations, that it was just some kind of reenactment crap."

"Me, I tell myself it was a joke that Max pulled on us, and one of these days he's gonna say, 'Gotcha!' Except he hasn't . . . yet."

Zach bit his bottom lip, then confided, "I'm thinking about quitting the teams."

"No way! You love being a SEAL."

"I do, but maybe it's time to move on. I don't think

Arsallah is ever going to give up. Unless he dies—and I can only hope—but, barring that, Sammy is going to be in danger forever. Living with guards and babysitters is no normal way to raise a kid."

"Shiiiit! I kin see yer point, but, man, ya blindsided me. What would ya do? Would ya stay in the Coronado area?"

"I would need to go in hiding of some kind. New name, persona, job, everything. And I'd have to cut off contact with all my family and friends, totally. Like witness protection, except done voluntarily."

"Jist doan do anythin' hasty. Talk it over with someone who knows somethin' about this hiding in plain sight business. Your grandad, maybe, with all his government contacts."

"It was his idea."

Cage whistled. "I doan know what ta say, then. Let me ask ya this, wouldja take Britta with you?"

He thought for a long moment. "I don't know."

But deep inside, he knew. And the answer was no.

**Girl talk . . . same thing through the ages . . .**

Britta sat with Madrene and Hilda in Tony's Bar & Grill where they laughed till they cried, then they cried till they laughed. The fact they were drinking pitchers of mead did not help the situation.

Wiping her eyes with the back of her hand, Britta glanced at Hilda. "I still cannot believe you lived in a place called Hog Heaven."

"How about me? I lived in a bloody harem for two years. *Me?* In see-through gunnas, with rouged nipples!" Madrene was a far-famed shrew—a *nice* shrew—who had a talent for nagging.

Britta and Hilda put hands over their mouths to stifle their giggles. Britta could not imagine Madrene being subservient, which would surely be required in a harem. Or that she would stand still while someone painted her nipples.

"And you both believe you have time-traveled?" Britta

asked. "I cannot credit any sane person accepting such nonsense, and yet . . ."

"Most of us have concluded that it is a miracle of some type. A God-ordained thing," Madrene said.

"But mostly we try not to think about it at all," Hilda added. "Searching for logical explanations is a futile exercise."

"Tell me why . . . how . . . you decided to stay here in the future," she urged them both.

"I no longer had any family there. I had no desire to go back," Madrene said. "Except for a need to avenge myself against that evil Steinolf, but then my brother Torolf took care of that."

"'Twas different for me," Hilda said. "I was drawn two ways, wanting to stay here but believing I was needed in the past, at The Sanctuary."

"And what decided you?"

"Love," they said as one.

Britta's heart wrenched at that message. Partly because she suspected she was falling in love with Zachary and partly because she feared he only lusted for her. "I am so confused. I do not want to go back, but I keep having these strange dreams. My father and brothers are attacking the abbey in some of them, and there is so much blood. But in other dreams, it is the nuns who are attacking my father and brothers, led by some warrior nun, and the ruthless men are the ones lying in their own sword dew. Either way, I feel almost a physical pull to return to the abbey."

Madrene and Hilda stared at her. It was a compelling dream . . . and obviously different from their own experiences.

"Dost think the warrior nun is you?" Hilda asked.

"Nay. She has coal-black hair. And unusually vivid blue eyes."

"How does Pretty Boy fit into all this?" Hilda asked.

"Like a thorn in my backside." Her flip answer garnered

grins from her friends. Then she added, " 'Tis his fault I am here. I think. He wish-prayed me here."

"My father believes he was wish-prayed here," Madrene told her, "and look how well things turned out for him and Angela at the vineyard." Madrene's father, Magnus Ericsson, was married to a woman who owned Blue Dragon Vineyard somewhere here in California.

"You say that you blame Pretty Boy, but you aren't unhappy to be here, are you?" Hilda inquired.

"I am content to be here. Mayhap I was destined to travel here to learn these new military tactics, as I originally thought. But what if Zachary is the reason for my being here?"

"Would that be so bad?" Madrene asked.

"Yea, it would. Who would I be then, except an appendage to some man? I have always identified myself as Britta the Warrior. If not a warrior, what would I be?"

"Lover, wife, mother . . . or any job you choose," Hilda said. "This really is a remarkable country for women."

"Lover? I am already that. I think. But wife . . . or mother?" She shook her head decisively. "Ne'er did I expect to see myself in those roles. I always considered myself too big and unfeminine, with none of the maidenly graces." Although an image flashed into her mind of her holding Sammy earlier that night.

"I don't know." Hilda grinned. "Pretty Boy does not seem to have a problem with your size or femininity." She turned to Madrene and told her, "Pretty Boy was smitten with Britta from the start. Could not keep his eyes or hands off her."

"Pretty Boy?" Madrene glanced Britta's way. "Pretty Boy does not chase women; they chase him. You must have something."

"Well, I do let him perform perversions on me," she admitted.

Both women choked on their glasses of mead.

Some ladies at a neighboring table stopped eating and gazed at her with sudden interest.

"You better explain yourself," Hilda said with mock severity.

And Britta did, much to the ever-dropping jaws of her two friends . . . and their neighbors.

"Oh, I do not think that is so perverted," Hilda said, "except mayhap for that wheelbarrow business." She leaned closer to Britta and Madrene and confided, "Torolf taught me how to pleasure myself. In front of a mirror." Seeing the interest she had garnered, Hilda continued with glee, "And one time he made love to me as I was bound and gagged."

"Do not dare stop now," Madrene said.

Already, Britta was picturing herself in such situations . . . with Zachary, of course.

"And you both know about chocolate body paint, do you not?" Hilda inquired.

When she finished relating the purpose and method of chocolate body paint, Britta said, "Can we stop to purchase some on the way back?"

"I'll second that, and mayhap strawberry, as well. Ian is partial to strawberries." Madrene had a considering expression on her face. "And, by the by, I think my brother Torolf wins the prize for most perverted."

"I will tell him that." Hilda smiled.

"Oh, no, please do not," Madrene said.

They all stood up, preparing to leave, when Hilda said, "So, anyone game for The Horny Toad?"

"The *what*?" Madrene inquired.

"A sex shop."

"Hilda!" Madrene was laughing. "You shock me."

"Hah! There is naught that could shock you, Madrene," Hilda contended. "You are the one who gave me edible underwear for a bridal showering gift."

*Edible underwear? Eeeew! A sex shop?* "Uh . . . I do not think I am interested in purchasing sex," Britta said. "I get enough from Zachary."

Everyone laughed at her then, including the people at nearby tables.


## The plot thickens . . .

Mullah Ahmed Arsallah sat in a San Diego hotel suite watching a TV screen showing remote-access pictures of that bastard Floyd's home, twenty miles away.

"Everything is in place?" he inquired of his assistant.

Daoud nodded. "Our operatives are in place in the house across the street. Six of them."

"And the occupants of the house?" He addressed Hakim, who was sometimes referred to as The Executioner.

"Disabled and will not awaken for hours." Hakim would have preferred killing them all, including their hostages-to-be, something which might yet happen.

"And Lieutenant Floyd . . . are we certain he will not return in the midst of our . . . um, mission?"

"He and seven other SEALs are occupied with that bomb threat we devised. In a place called Pennsylvania. Even if he were warned now, it would take half a day for him to return. By then, we will be gone, including the boy, Allah willing."

Arsallah nodded. "Number of guards inside and outside?"

"One inside, two outside," Hakim said. "Plus there is a woman inside with the boy, as well. A military woman from WEALS."

Arsallah frowned his confusion.

"Rather like a female Navy SEAL." This explanation came from Daoud, who exchanged stony looks with Hakim. The two men had no love for each other, which was just as well. Arsallah did not like his comrades to develop strong bonds with each other. Their whole allegiance should be to him. "It is a new military unit for women," Daoud elaborated.

Arsallah and Hakim both sneered, as did others sitting about the lavish three-bedroom suite where they had been staying these past two days, waiting for the right opportunity. "American women are immodest. Harlots for the most part," Arsallah postulated. It made no difference that they had all watched an X-rated movie on the television the night before. Actually, it probably contributed to that opinion if all American women behaved in that manner. "Take the female SEAL, too," he ordered.

"We will use silencers on our weapons outside," Hakim told him. "Inside, shall we use drugs or Tasers?"

Arsallah shrugged. "Just do not harm the boy and woman in any way that will show on the outside. Once we are on the return flight, a reporter and cameraman from Aljazeera will interview me. I do not want any human rights or U.S. government officials crying mistreatment."

"Shouldn't we wait a day or so then, till we are certain the boy and the woman will say what we want?" This from the more logical Daoud.

"They will do as told," Hakim answered for Arsallah with a harsh laugh.

Arsallah agreed with his henchman. "Especially that spineless grandson of mine. I should have had him shot at birth, along with his traitorous whore of a mother. At least now Samir can be used for our benefit. First off, we use him for a bargaining tool to have every al-Qaeda prisoner released from CIA prisons."

"Can we threaten to kill the boy, or cut off a body part, if the Americans do not comply?" Hakim practically licked his lips with anticipation. Not so long ago, Samir had kicked Hakim in the balls when ordered to get rid of a mongrel dog that had been bothering his sleep.

"Threaten, yes, but get my permission to follow through."

Both Daoud and Hakim studied him carefully, probably thinking that he was getting soft on his grandson. He was not. As far as he was concerned, Samir's diluted blood merited no familial consideration. But he did want to rein in control of this volatile situation.

"And then . . . after the negotiations are complete?"

Daoud asked. "What happens to the boy . . . and the woman soldier . . . then?"

Arsallah knew, but he was not about to share all information, even with these old comrades. No one could be trusted, really.

# *Chapter 18*

**Being conned by a mini-con . . .**

Britta didn't have a maternal bone in her body. Leastways, that had been her opinion till today . . . and tonight, with Sammy.

They were propped up against pillows in his small bed, looking through picture books. The way he leaned against her, smelling of boyling skin and minty soap from his bath, the way he seemed to be drawn to her, and she to him . . . well, her heart nigh swelled with strong emotions she had ne'er felt before.

Her reading was still not very good, despite the tutoring lessons, so she and Sammy were making up stories to fit the pictures, some of them absurd, some poignantly telling of both their pasts.

His favorite of the children's books was *The Poky Little Puppy*; apparently, he yearned to have a pet dog someday. She would have to mention that fact to Zachary when he returned. Her favorite was *Snow White and the Seven Dwarves*, although she was a mite suspicious about the goings-on betwixt the pretty lady and the seven little men. Men were men, no matter their size, in her experience.

"That is enough, do you not think? Time for sleep."

"Just one more."

"That is what you said three books back."

"I could show you my father's magazine." There was a sly look in his blue eyes . . . eyes that matched Zachary's.

"Why would I want to . . ."

Sammy had already jumped off the bed and was digging under a pile of shoes on the floor of his closet. "He hid it under his mattress, but I found it there. Then he hid it under the towels in the bathroom."

He tossed the magazine to her. A magazine was sort of a book, but bigger, with no hard cover. This one, with the title *Penthouse*, seemed to be filled with lots of words and lots of color pictures.

*Penthouse? I wonder what kind of house that is?*

She flipped the magazine open, gawked, then immediately flipped it shut. *Oh, my gods and goddesses!* "Sammy! This is not appropriate fare for a child."

"How am I ever gonna learn stuff?"

"I do not think you need to know, close-up, how a woman's nether parts look."

"Why not?"

"Because . . . because it will be a long, long time afore you would find that information of any use."

He cocked his head to the side. "What kind of use?"

"That is enough." She stood and told him, "Slide down so I can cover you."

"I dint say my prayers yet."

She let out a long sigh. More delays.

Sammy slid down to the floor, on his knees, put both hands together, then said, "Dear God, thank you for another day without my grandfather findin' me. Thank you for Britta stayin' with me. Thank you for not lettin' anyone know about what I put in the blender today. God bless my great-grandfather Floyd, my great-grandmother Floyd, my grandfather Floyd, Grandfather's bimbo girlfriend, Bridget, my grandmother Floyd, Uncle Danny, and . . . and . . ." He gulped. "Keep my daddy safe and bring him home. Amen."

Britta choked up.

Until he added, "And please let Britta become my mother."

"Sammy," she tried to say, but he had already crawled into bed, pulled up the blanket, and pretended to be asleep.

She was shaking her head with dismay when he cracked open one eye and said, "You kin give me a good-night kiss."

Smiling, she leaned down and kissed his forehead.

The imp was grinning with his eyes closed.

### Then, all Muspell broke loose . . .

Britta was sitting in the bed in the guest chamber, flicking through Zachary's magazine, which was . . . interesting, incredible, outrageous, perverted . . . she could not think of the right word.

The breasts on some of the women were huge, and yet they managed to stay uplifted. On some of the pages, she angled her head right and left, studying the naked women portrayed, legs widespread, their inner workings detailed. *Is that how women . . . how I . . . look down there?* She was repulsed and fascinated at the same time.

She came to a page titled "Penthouse Forum" and sounded out some of the words in what appeared to be a letter. "My . . . girl . . . friend . . . loves . . . anal . . . sex," Britta said slowly, frowning with confusion. When understanding came, she slammed the magazine shut. "Perversions! Is that all men think of?"

Just then, Britta heard some odd popping noises outside, like the sound made when pulling the stopper from a container of overfermented wine . . . except louder. She threw the magazine to the floor and got up off the bed, but before she could go to the window and investigate, she heard a banging noise at the front door. Alarmed, she ran out into the hall, just as the door was smashed in. Several men, all in black, including black hoods, called balaclavas, with only the eyes showing, rushed in. She stepped back before they could see her, then ran to Sammy's room where she closed and locked the door. Moving quickly, she shoved a chest of drawers away from the wall and in front of the door. It would only delay the attackers.

Going over to the bed, she picked Sammy up and whispered in his ear, "Sammy, wake up. Quick. Hurry, dearling, we've got to get out of here."

His eyes shot open, then he whimpered as he realized the situation they were in.

"Here," she handed him a hockey stick and picked up a metal bat for her own pitiful weapon. Adapt, adapt, adapt . . . that is what they were taught in WEALS.

Men could be heard conversing in a foreign language outside, down the hallway. Sammy's room was the last one in the corridor. They would be here soon.

"It's my grandfather's men," Sammy told her, eyes wide with fright.

"I'm going to open the window and try to climb out on the roof with you," she told him. "Once I open the window, we should both start screaming for help, loud, very loud."

He nodded his understanding.

Someone was trying the doorknob, and the tone of voice she heard on discovering the lock indicated some swearing going on. Just as she began to raise the window, two hands came up. A man, also in a balaclava, must have crawled up the drainpipe to this second story. They stared at each other for a startled minute.

He put his hands on the windowsill, about to come in.

She slammed the window down on his fingers.

He cursed loud and long as he pulled his hands out, then fell off the roof ledge.

That small amount of time wasted gave the attackers a chance to enter through the hall door. But, before they did, she and Sammy rushed over to stand behind the door. The first man through got the baseball bat across his face, causing him to scream. Even through the hood, blood spurted everywhere. She must have broken his nose. Meanwhile, another miscreant came in, and Sammy, bless his little soul, brandishing the hockey stick, whacked him across the knees. That man went down with a scream of pain, too.

Unfortunately, four more men followed, jumping over their comrades. Britta and Sammy stood, backs against the wall now, "weapons" raised overhead. But then, a man with an evil glint in his eyes aimed a two-pronged instrument at Sammy. With a gasp followed by rolling of the eyes, Sammy dropped the hockey stick and slid to the floor. In that brief second, whilst she turned to Sammy with dismay, a similar instrument was aimed at her shoulder. The most intense pain shot through her body, like the pain one got when striking one's elbow, but a hundred times worse. After that, she felt boneless and disoriented as thousands of needles seemed to be pricking her body.

The last thing she thought as she lost consciousness was, *Zachary is going to be devastated.*

**Even when you win, you sometimes lose . . .**

The game was about to begin.

A small aircraft flew over the field, and a serviceman parachuted out to hand the referee the game ball. It was Sly, who had taken over this traditional role, which usually fell to one of the university's ROTC students. They weren't taking any chances with anything.

With a blast from his whistle, the drum major began an exaggerated strut across the field, starting at the student end of the stadium and ending with a series of front flips midstream. The Penn State Blue Band followed after him, instruments blaring out the school's alma mater.

Soon the field was filled with coaches, players, and news media. A hundred and ten thousand spectators had shown up for this homecoming event, made extra special because it was the Fighting Irish they would be playing. Thank God the game was in the afternoon and not at night.

By halftime, nothing had happened, and they were all nervous. There was always a chance this would be a dry hole . . . not the first time a mission had been unsuccessful, but it was too early to make that call.

In the midst of the usual hubbub in the press box, a *Philadelphia Inquirer* reporter had been bugging Zach for the past fifteen minutes. "You're not a reporter; I can tell."

"Oh, yeah? Why? Because I don't have acne and a flatulence problem?"

The reporter's face flushed, but still he plodded on. "You're government, aren't you? FBI? CIA? No, that's wrong. With that body, you've gotta be military. Holy shit! You're a Navy SEAL. Don't deny it. My second cousin was a SEAL, and I recognize the signs."

He had to give the guy credit for some good reasoning skills. He was probably a top-rate reporter, which was what they didn't need here at this time. "You're delusional," was all Zach said, and he walked away to pour himself a cup of coffee.

The reporter, of course, followed him. "Your body is ripped. You've got the right haircut. You're stoic. You've been watching this field like a guard dog. You've got that ear mike. I heard the word *terrorist* more than once. Yeah, you're a SEAL. What's up, buddy? Is al-Qaeda gonna blow this football crowd all the way to Philly? Ha, ha, ha." He made the mistake of getting right in Zach's face. Even worse, some other of the media were starting to take interest in their "discussion."

"Buzz off, newsboy." Zach picked him up and shoved him aside.

Undaunted, the jerk followed him outside, motioning for a cameraman to follow. "Sonofabitch! There's gonna be a terrorist attack, isn't there?"

The cameraman raised his equipment. A big mistake.

"You take one single friggin' picture of me, and I'm gonna ram that camera down your throat. You'll be shittin' parts for weeks." Into his ear mike, he said, "Cage. A little help here, buddy."

Within seconds, Cage had flipped himself down off the roof and stood beside him.

The two news dorks were staring at Cage with mouths gaping. He guessed they had never seen anyone do a front flip off the roof of the press box.

"We have a situation," Zach said to Cage.

"I can see that, good buddy."

The reporter and cameraman didn't know what hit them. They soon found themselves in a private VIP restroom, bound and gagged, with the door locked tight. There were a few VIPs who might have to take a piss like the rest of the world in the plebeian stalls down below.

Up on the roof of the press box, he and Cage scanned the area with binoculars.

"Is it possible this was all a false alarm?" he asked.

"I doan know. I got a funny feelin'," Cage said. "My maw maw would call it the heebie-jeebies."

"Same here. The hairs are standing out on the back of my neck like porcupine quills. But, man, we've swept this stadium top to bottom; we've screened everyone who came in; we've done everything possible to make this perimeter secure. There's got to be something we've missed. In fact, I . . ." Zach's words trailed off. His heart began to race, and his blood went cold. "Omigod! The hot-air balloons."

"What?"

He put the binoculars to his eyes again.

Cage did likewise.

"Check out my three o'clock. They've got something planned in one of those balloons. Watch. One of them will break loose soon and sort of drift this way."

"*Black Sunday*," Cage said.

"Huh?"

"Remember that old Bruce Dern movie where terrorists were gonna attack from a blimp over the Super Bowl stadium."

Within seconds, they contacted the rest of the team, CENTCOM, aircraft in the region, bomb control, and every other military and police unit within a twenty-mile radius. He and three other SEALs were in an SUV headed toward the balloon site, but already they could see one of the balloons starting to drift. Ironically—or perhaps not so ironically—it was one with an American flag motif.

During the next hour, helicopters dropped down bomb specialists into the unmanned balloon to disable the explosives. It became apparent that the plan would have called for a gunman to shoot the balloon with a long-distance weapon, probably from over by the expressway. Once the balloon started to deflate, the clock would have started. The bomb had been set to go off during the third quarter, as close to center field as possible. Fans would have thought it was a special planned entertainment. University officials would have thought it was a balloon gone astray.

None of the terrorists could be found, but they did find evidence in a local motel room, amid the piles of fast-food debris, all of which was gathered for fingerprint analysis. Maps of the stadium and surrounding area. Details of explosives. And an odd reference on a scrap of discarded paper that hadn't completely flushed down the toilet to Navy SEALs . . . him, in particular.

Did Arsallah have something to do with this?

How did he know Zach would be here?

Suddenly, Zach pulled out his cell phone and called the commander at home. "Zach here. Hey, Mac, quick question. How come you put me on active duty?"

"I had nothing to do with it."

"*What?* What do you mean?"

"Your timing stinks, Lieutenant. Aren't you supposed to be cleaning up after this near–bomb attack?"

Zach bristled. "That's just what I'm doing. Where did the order come from to put me on this op?"

"How the hell—"

"It's important, Mac. In fact, it's urgent. Check it out, and call me right back."

Zach's body was on red alert as he filled the rest of the team in on his suspicions.

Fifteen minutes later, Mac called back, and his tone of voice was ominous. "The call to put you on this op came from a low-level secretary in the Department of Defense . . . a secretary who has suddenly disappeared. This is a royal FUBAR. I'm sorry, Zach—"

"Dammit! Get to my house right away."

"I'm already on my way. The police are ahead of me."

"Call and—"

"I already called. There's no answer."

Zach swore a blue streak.

"Settle down, boy. You're not going to accomplish anything in that frame of mind."

"How would you feel if one of your kids was taken by someone like Arsallah?"

There was silence.

"Keep me on the line till you get there," Zach ordered, followed by, "please."

He could hear the commander talking on another phone to someone. Whatever he heard was causing him to curse, too.

"We're here. There are three guards disabled. Not dead, but they must have been given a huge zap from a Taser. The tangos operated from the house across the street."

"The Lehmans'?"

"Yeah. Tied up the husband, wife, and two teenagers in a basement closet for about twelve hours. They're scared shitless, as you would imagine."

"Someone needs to take Arsallah down. The bastard is a walking target from now on. I don't care what the 'play nice' diplomatic service says, or the two-faced State Department."

Mac ignored his rant. "Listen, I'll call you back once I'm inside, but Zach, there's something you need to know."

"What?"

"It's bad."

There was an increasingly loud buzz in Zach's ears.

"Britta was here, and she's gone, too. There was a struggle. And . . . and blood."

The buzzing exploded in his head, and he went off to the side of the parking lot where he puked his guts out. Once he rinsed his mouth with the bottled water Cage handed him and was reasonably calm, he told the men, "Get us on a transport ASAP. Arsallah has fucked with the wrong guy this time."

"No, dude," Sly corrected, putting a hand on his shoulder, "Arsallah has fucked with the wrong guys, as in plural. We are Navy SEALs, and we are covering your six, all the way."

**I am woman, hear me . . . kick your butt . . .**

The plan was to take her and Sammy out of America immediately after their capture.

They were taken to a parking arena of the airport. Sammy cowered behind her, his arms wrapped around her thighs. Arsallah and a half dozen other men were there, wearing long Arab-style gowns and head coverings. Two of the balaclava-covered men were there, too, including the one whose nose she must have broken. When he yanked the hood off his head and glared at her, she saw that his nose still dripped blood. All of them, except Arsallah, carried weapons.

Face rigid with anger, Arsallah snapped some foreign words at Sammy, who whimpered to Britta, "I do not want to go to him. Help me."

Arsallah repeated his order, and Sammy walked up to his grandfather, feet dragging with reluctance.

The grandfather stared with contempt at his grandson, who came only as high as his thigh, then spat on him.

Sammy, bless his brave little soul, just stood still, tears welling in his eyes.

When Arsallah yelled some other words at Sammy, the boy replied but apparently made the mistake of speaking English, not the Afghan language. For his sin, his grandfather slapped him hard across the face, knocking him to the ground.

"You son of a camel's arse!" Britta tried to go to the boy, but two guards held her back. One of them punched her in the shoulder, causing her to bend over and go unseeing for a moment.

Upright again, she heard Arsallah snapping questions at the boy and Sammy answering him back in the "correct" language. Arsallah obviously did not like the answers and shoved him aside, stalking up to her.

Glaring, he asked in broken English, "You are the whore of the infidel?"

"Which infidel?" That answer merited her a slap as well. Being taller and stronger than Sammy, she at least was able to stay on her feet. She bit her bottom lip to prevent herself from telling this evil troll what she thought of him.

"The infidel Floyd who soiled my daughter and bred this American cur." He nodded his head toward Sammy, who was at her side now. Why he saw only the American half of his bloodline and not the Afghan side as well, Britta did not understand.

"I am no whore."

"You were found in his bed."

"A guest bedchamber."

He waved a hand as if it was the same thing. "Has he fucked you?"

Britta knew that he used such vulgar language to insult her. Still, she flinched. Then she made the mistake of revealing, "We have made love."

Arsallah grinned maliciously and told a man at his side, "We will use them both, the harlot and the mongrel, as hostages."

They were then pushed and punched, even kicked repeatedly, for the next hour or more, but nowhere that bruises

could be seen by outsiders . . . outsiders being members of
something called Aljazeera, who talked at length to Arsallah and pointed black boxes, called cameras, at her and
Sammy.

At one point, they brought Sammy forth and forced him
to say he hated America, hated his evil father, and wanted to
go home to Afghanistan. They took pictures of Britta with
their cameras but did not ask her questions, no doubt sensing
she was unwilling to speak the words they fed to her.

In the end, Arsallah and the Aljazeera people shook hands,
like old friends, and the Aljazeera people left "to catch a
plane."

Some new people came, clearly Arsallah's followers, to
report a problem. Sammy whispered to her, "They can't get
us on an airplane to Afghanistan. They need to find a hiding
place till they can hire another private plane to take us
away."

For that reason, they were brought to a basement room,
and their stay grew longer and longer as the problem of getting out of the country continued. And their treatment grew
increasingly worse, as well.

Now, after three days, they were still bound but no longer
gagged in the basement of an abandoned house near the airport. Incoming and outgoing flights could be heard overheard, day and night.

Sammy wore his sleeping outfit, which was called pee-
jays: loose braies and a *shert* with little bears imprinted all
over. She wore one of Zachary's Navy SEAL tea-ing *sherts*,
which barely covered her undergarments. They were barefooted.

And now, here was Arsallah again with his crew of camera people. Not Aljazeera, just his followers clicking away.
Also accompanying him was the vicious Hakim, who took
great pleasure in hurting her and Sammy; the gentler but still
cruel Daoud, the man whose nose she had broken and who
had taken revenge on her numerous times; and several other
of their captors. With neatly trimmed beard, Arsallah was

dressed in a pristine white gown and neatly pressed and folded head covering. Unlike her and Sammy, who wore the same clothing and reeked.

When they untied their arms and ankles, pain pricked Britta's body like a thousand pins and needles. Sammy's groan indicated he was in similar straits as blood began to circulate in their limbs again.

Sammy was first to speak for the cameras. The little boy looked gaunt from lack of food and fear. Bruises marked his skinny arms and legs, and there was a bad cut on his cheek. He could have been much worse. Britta had taken many of the blows intended for him. As a result, she had a black eye, which had swollen till her lid was closed, a cut lip, bruises and cuts marring most of her body, finger marks on her neck, and an ankle that very well might be broken; at the least, it was badly sprained. Betimes, she wished they would just kill her, but it was a momentary lapse. She must needs stay strong for the boy.

In a docile voice, he repeated all that he was told to say. "Please, father, do what they ask. America is evil. Do the good deed they demand, and I will be free. Please."

Britta was resigned to repeating their hateful words by now, but she did so with a raised chin and defiant eyes . . . well, one defiant eye. Her words were somewhat slurred due to the swollen and cracked lip, but intelligible enough, she supposed. "Zachary, we are being treated well." That was a jest, of course, that the cameras would surely reveal. "You must do as they demand. 'Tis the moral thing to do. Release the holy warriors in the name of Allah. Do as they say, and we will be released." She would have blurted out more, but she was certain they would cut out that part.

After Arsallah and Hakim left, Daoud proceeded to retie their arms and legs. He was done with Sammy and finishing up Britta's wrist restraints when Hakim shouted from the top of the stairs, "Hurry if you want to come for lunch."

Hakim's shout startled Daoud, and he jerked up from his bent position behind her. This instant of distraction allowed

Britta the opportunity to flex her wrists, causing Daoud to think he was done, when in fact the rope was a little looser than usual.

"Behave, and you will be given food and water shortly," Daoud remarked as he climbed the stairs.

"And after that, will we be killed?"

Sammy gasped at her question. Apparently women didn't question in their culture.

"Not if you do as you are told," Daoud replied.

The door was closed and locked. Much activity seemed to be taking place upstairs. Talking, laughter, doors slamming, cars starting and taking off. Presumably, at least some of them were going out to lunch.

This might be their one and only opportunity.

"Sammy, we're going to try to escape."

His eyes went wide, and he whimpered.

"I'm going to turn around. I want you to untie the ropes around my hands. They are a little looser than usual, and your fingers are small. Now, don't start crying. This is the time to pay attention. Be focused."

It took him longer than she would have liked. But once untied, she quickly untied the ropes around her ankles and undid Sammy's restraints, as well. After breaking a wooden chair, keeping one of the legs for a "weapon," she propped the chair back up at the little table so the damage would not be noticed.

"Listen to me, Sammy. This is all going to have to take place quickly. I'm going to lay the ropes loosely around our ankles, and we will put our hands behind our backs, pretending that we are still tied up. Are you listening?"

He nodded.

"When one of our captors comes in, I will wait till he comes close, then hit him over the head. You must go over and lock the door. I will break the window. Can you do that?"

He nodded again, gulping. "I'm scared."

"I am, too, dearling, but we can do this."

"It is a small window," he pointed out.

"Big enough, even for a giant like me."

He did not even smile at her mirthsome remark.

"I am going to shove you through that window first. I want you to run as fast as you can and do not look back. Do not wait for me. I will follow, but if I do not, you are still to run till you find someone. Tell them to take you to the police. Tell the police to call your father, Zachary Floyd, a Navy SEAL, and that you were kidnapped. Can you remember all that?"

"Yes, but I don't wanna go alone."

"I know you do not, and mayhap I will be with you. But if not, you must needs run as fast as your legs can carry you. Can you run fast?"

He smiled for the first time in days. "I run like hell. That's what Uncle Danny says."

Their opportunity did not come till early that evening when Daoud finally came with a tray of food for them: hamburgers, Frankish fries, and fizzy drinks from that Scottish place, McDonald's. Daoud placed the tray on the table and said, "I will release the arm restraints. Samir first." Daoud's English was excellent compared to Arsallah and the others. "While he is eating, I will hold a gun to your head, Miss Asado. The least wrong move by Samir, and you will be dead. Likewise, when he is tied up again, you will eat while a gun is to his head. Do you both understand?"

The second Daoud bent down to untie Sammy's ropes, she, still sitting, smote him over the head with the chair leg. He went down, unconscious, immediately. Sammy ran to the door to lock it. She tore off a piece of Daoud's *shert* and stuffed it in his mouth. Then she tied his hands behind his back and his ankles together. Quickly, she moved the table over by the window and put Sammy on top.

"Are you ready?"

He nodded.

"Once I hit the window, the noise may attract the others, so there will be no time to hesitate. What are you going to do, Sammy?"

"Run like hell."

She tried to smile and cracked her lip even more.

"If I am not able to follow," she said, her voice choking up, "tell your father . . . tell Zachary that I love him."

She cracked the window open then, shoved Sammy through, and immediately heard shouts upstairs. It took her a bit longer to get through the window, and by then the basement door had been broken down and there were orders to go after them.

Britta began running in the opposite direction from Sammy, what she had planned all along. It was not an easy exercise with her injured ankle. She could hear the men coming after her, the distance closing between them. Then there was the sound of gunfire.

She glanced right and left. On the one side was a steep hill, which would only slow her down more. On the right side was a steep incline leading to a rocky beach. The ocean or a lake, she could not be sure.

Her best choice lay in running forward, but then she felt a sharp pain in her back. It must be a bullet from one of the weapons. The pain drew her up short. She stumbled. Fell. Then rolled over and over and over, each rock and sharp bramble digging into her already bruised flesh. She could feel a warm substance—blood?—running down her back. She crashed to the bottom, striking her head on a boulder. The pain was excruciating, but soon it eased.

She thought she saw a flock of black birds flying overhead. A sign of death in Norse legends. The ravens of death. Berserk warriors often saw the vultures in the midst of battle.

With a long sigh, she surrendered to her destiny. The Norns of Fate had won.

*So, this is death.*

# Chapter 19

**You win some, you lose some . . .**

The next day, Cage drove Zach to the small Bella Rosa police station near a private airfield fifty miles from San Diego. Cage drove because Zach's hands were shaking so badly.

Cage's Jeep was first in a caravan, followed by vehicles holding other SEALs, police, FBI, CIA, State Department, and Department of Defense reps, and Zach's family: his father and mother, who had put aside their differences for this occasion, Danny, and his grandfather and grandmother. And the news media, of course, who couldn't be kept away.

Zach had gone through absolute hell the past four days. The first twenty-four hours were bad when Aljazeera had shown an interview with Arsallah, who played the meek-and-injured-party card, pleading for some of his evil cohorts to be released from prison. Like that was ever going to happen. The tangos in question were the worst of the worst. Arsallah had forced Sammy to repeat his demands, interspersed with anti-American insults. Britta had sat in the background, looking a bit bruised but not too bad. He had assumed by the tilt of her chin that she'd declined Arsallah's "invitation" to speak that time.

But then yesterday, Zach had received a manila envelope containing photos and a tape. These were bad. Really bad. But at least they were not body parts, as he had feared.

They must not have fed Sammy and Britta much or given them more than a minimum of liquids since their capture, because their faces were drawn and haggard. Sammy had bruises over every inch of exposed skin. Britta . . . poor Britta . . . had one eye swollen shut, a bleeding, puffy lip, cuts and bruises, and possibly a broken ankle. Her chin had still been raised defiantly as she gave her canned bullshit talk to Arsallah's cameraman.

On the day of their escape, Britta had somehow managed to get herself and Sammy out of the basement they had been kept in. Sammy had hidden in the garage of an abandoned gas station till the next morning, fearing that he would be caught by Arsallah's men. Which gave Arsallah's men time to leave the area. Hell, they'd probably left the country by now. And Britta, well, she had not yet been found. Zach had been warned to expect the worst.

When they got to the police station, Zach told Cage, "Hold everyone off. Let me have some private time with Sammy first. Okay?"

Cage nodded and squeezed his shoulder.

Zach opened the door.

Sammy saw him first and screamed, "Daaaa-ddyyyyy!" as he rushed forward and launched himself into his arms, hugging him tight with his legs straddling his chest. The boy was squeezing so tight that Zach could barely breathe. But who the hell cared about that! Tears ran down Zach's face and onto Sammy's neck. Sammy's tears wet Zach's neck, too.

Pushing his way into an interrogation room and slamming the door with his foot, Zach sat down and just held Sammy in his lap, head pressed against his heart. His clothing was filthy, and he smelled like he'd wet his pants a time or two, or worse, but he was whole and alive, and that was all that mattered.

Finally, Sammy pulled his head back and said, "I escaped."

"I know you did. You're a brave boy . . . I mean, little man."

He shook his head. "No, I'm a little boy." He hesitated, his bottom lip quivering. "Britta didn't escape."

"Well, now, we don't know that for sure. We just haven't found her yet."

"They hurt her bad. Real bad." He began to weep again. Between sobs, he revealed, "Sometimes . . . sometimes she let them hit her when they was aimin' for me."

That didn't surprise Zach. Still, his eyes welled with tears again.

"She broke Daoud's nose with my baseball bat when he came to capture us."

*Ah, so that's whose blood it was.*

"Her ankle mighta been broken. Do you think she coulda run with a broken ankle?"

"I think Britta could do anything she wanted."

"We're gonna get her back," Sammy said, patting his shoulder as if he sensed his father's despair. "I jis' know we are."

Zach wasn't so sure.

"Oh, and I forgot to tell you. I hit Hakim across the shin bones with my hockey stick."

"You did? What a brave boy you were!"

"Oh, I forgot another thing," Sammy said. "Britta said to tell you somethin' if . . . if she didn't come back."

It felt as if a vise were squeezing his heart. He didn't want to know. Because if he listened to the message, it would be like admitting she was dead, and he wasn't ready to accept that.

"No, Sammy, don't tell me. Let's wait for Britta to tell me herself."

Sammy brightened at that scrap of hope.

Zach only wished there were someone to give *him* hope.

## Home, not-so-sweet home . . .

Britta attempted to open her heavy lids, despite the pain that ravaged her body.

"Britta! Britta! Can you hear me?"

Son of a troll! It was Mother Edwina of St. Anne's Abbey.

Either Britta was being plagued with that bloody dream again, or she had reversed her time travel. Both notions posed great threats to her sanity. So she did the only sensible thing: She succumbed to the pain-sleep again.

Whether mere hours or days had passed, Britta did eventually open her eyes again, and this time wider than a slit. She was still on an abbey cot, still in pain, but not so much as before. "Thirsty," she choked out.

With Mother Edwina's help, she sat up, propped against some rolled-up blankets, and drank thirstily from a cup of water. "What happened?" she asked through cracked lips.

"You fell off a cliff when you and Sister Margaret were on your way to Jorvik."

"No, I mean this time."

Mother Edwina tilted her head in confusion. "There was only the one time."

"What? When did I fall off the cliff?"

"Three days past. You have been in a pain-sleep since you were brought back here."

"Three days? That's impossible. I was in WEALS for more than three sennights."

"Wheels? What wheels?"

The blood began to drain from Britta's head as the certainty of her situation hit her. She was back in time. It was as if all the other had never happened . . . the time travel, WEALS, and most of all, Zachary. Had she dreamed it all?

If so, how could she have dreamed in such detail? No, it had been real. Britta's heart constricted at the enormity of her loss. Dazed, she shook her head to clear it, and it felt as if knives were cutting into her scalp. Her brain could not handle the strain of unraveling the turmoil, not now, and she fell back into the pain-sleep.

Days went by, and Britta was able to sit, then move about with a makeshift crutch. Her face and body were battered and bruised. She had a broken ankle. But she was alive. The trouble was, she felt no joy in the living.

One sennight after her "return," whilst still bedridden, her father sent a message informing her of a new groom he had procured for her . . . *procured* being a key word. The man was a Norse merchant of much wealth but no lands . . . Tume Ivarsson. The young man delivering her father's message warned that this would be her father's last effort to deal with her amicably—as if he had ever been amicable to her—and the consequences would be on her head if she did not yield. Later, Britta realized that her crafty father deliberately put none of his threats to parchment.

Britta yearned for normal family life, due to that blasted Zachary, no doubt. So, despite the danger, trying to be amicable, she went to Father Caedmon and asked if he had ever in his travels made the acquaintance of Tume Ivarsson.

Father Caedmon recoiled at mere mention of the man's name.

"What?" Britta wanted to know.

"Amongst other things, he is a slave trader."

She told her father's emissary no, but told him to ask her father if he would accept a groom of her choosing. She received a reply later that day via the red-faced messenger, "Never!"

The fact that she'd received the reply so quickly gave Britta fair warning. Her father was nearby. Oh, he would not attack the abbey outright, not wanting the powerful Papacy on his back, but her father was the master of deceit. She recalled the attack on Sister Bernice that had prompted her initial flight from the abbey and her time travel.

The next day, Father Caedmon set off for the minster in Jorvik for some priestly duties and to seek church backing if her father should dare breach the nunnery walls. The ringing of the bells and constant chapel services were lessened in his absence. Thank the gods for that.

It took more than a month for Britta's ankle to heal, and by then her other injuries were fading. Not so her heart. She missed Zachary and Sammy and her life in the future. At night, she wept for all she had lost.

Britta soon learned what her father had meant by "consequences" if she failed to surrender to his sinister matchmaking. A young nun named Sister Gloria had foolishly left the abbey courtyard to fetch a stray lamb. She had only gone a short distance when captured by her father's men. Her body was returned to the gate the next day. She had been repeatedly raped, but that was not the worst part. They had slit the tendons behind each knee so that the young woman would be a cripple for life. Days later, when she was able to speak, Gloria told them that Britta's father had personally said this was the condition Britta would be in when she wed, if she did not yield soon. A woman did not need to stand to be mounted or to give birth, her father had said.

"Is there no one we can approach to protest?" Mother Edwina asked Britta.

Britta shrugged. "We have no proof. My father has friends in high places. The only weapon we have is the Church, and he has made sure there are no witnesses to his sins. Even if we were able to get an audience before King Aethelred's court, believe you me, they would make Gloria sound like a delusional lackbrain, especially since she suffers those screaming fits. There are two Norse noblemen, Thorfinn of Norstead and Steven of Amberstead, who might help, but how would I contact them? And how long would it take?"

A week later, Britta, now physically healed, had an idea.

"We must needs prepare for an assault from my father."

"*What?*" Mother Edwina was in the abbey kitchen supervising the harvesting of honey from the hundred and more cone-shaped hives on the abbey grounds. Honey was an important product here at the nunnery, their only source of income . . . or rather, the honeyed mead that they produced from a long-ago Margaret's recipe.

Right now, there were a dozen nuns working on at least a hundred honeycombs. Cutting off the caps with heated knives. Draining the honey into pottery jugs. Placing the remaining honeycombs over coarse cloths bleeding into pots near the hearth fires; this would be the second extract of lesser-quality honey. Then the honeycombs would be washed, saving that water rinse for sweetening in the kitchen. Finally, they would mash the clean wax combs for winter candle making. It was a long, messy, arduous process.

"I have had dreams," Britta began.

"Do not speak of the dreams again. Nor time travel. Nor any of your fever-induced fantasies. 'Tis not proper for a nun."

"I am not a nun."

"You will be if you stay here much longer."

The other nuns and novices, working diligently, remained silent but interested in the conversation. Not much happened in a convent, and she was giving them much fodder for talk when they were back in their cells.

"Heed me well, Mother. Danger looms. And it is not just because my dreams tell me so. We live daily with what he did to Sister Gloria. I have gainsayed my father at every turn. He will not give up."

Several of the nuns shuddered.

"Let me give the women here some defensive training in the military arts."

Mother Edwina cringed. "Well, mayhap you could do a little training."

"We would not have to kill anyone, would we?" one young novice asked.

"Only if they try to kill or rape you first."

Mother Edwina looked rather green at the prospect.

"I have been trained as a warrior, and lately, whilst I was at . . . well, just lately, I have learned new fighting skills. In the best of battles no one dies, but I tell you, my father and brothers must meet the raven, or they will ne'er stop. You are not to worry. I will take care of them."

"You would kill your own blood kin?" Mother Edwina inquired.

"I would . . . if necessary."

More gasps.

For the next two sennights, Britta tried her best to teach fighting skills to nuns and novices from age thirteen to sixty, with little success. It was one thing to teach the women at The Sanctuary how to fight; they had incentive. These nuns would rather turn the other cheek, no matter the affront. Also, they had been sedentary for a long time and got winded just throwing spears made out of broom handles . . . and then only several paces away.

"No pain, no gain," a motto she had learned from the commander back at WEALS, meant naught to these ladies.

Sister Conception muttered in a most un-nunlike manner, "The only pain here is you . . . a pain in the arse."

Nor did they understand the SEAL refrain, "The only easy day was yesterday."

"I mucked the stables yestermorn, scrubbed the stone floors of the scullery, changed bed linens, and hauled firewood," Sister Egbert said, not even bothering to lower her voice. "What is so easy about that?"

Finally, she stuck with the age-old "God helps those who help themselves." There was naught they could say to that.

Then everything changed when a group of ten nuns came riding into the abbey courtyard. That they had passed through her father's ranks was amazing. They were riding horses, which was a surprise in itself; most nuns had no coin for such an extravagance. But the biggest surprise was the woman leading the pack.

She wore the drab garb of a nun, except no head covering. Her hair was coal black, and her eyes a strange shade of blue. It was the nun warrior of her dreams. And she was beautiful.

Britta put a hand to her heart in shock as well as thanks. How many miracles could one person sustain in a lifetime?

But then the biggest shock of all came.

"My name is Angelique. We have come from Frankland to help you," the woman said, loud enough for all to hear. Then she rode her horse a little farther so that she was right in front of Britta. "Greetings, Sister."

**Good-bye is the saddest word . . .**

For two months, Zach ranted and raved and made himself and everyone around him miserable.

Not only had Arsallah and his evil cohorts gotten away, they still stirred the diplomatic pot by demanding that Sammy be returned to his native country.

Most of all, Zach was devastated by the loss of Britta. After extensive searches, there was no body, but he figured Arsallah had disposed of that, wanting there to be no connection to his evil deeds in the basement of that abandoned house. At first, he had even hoped that Arsallah had taken her back to Afghanistan to use as leverage, but he would have made mention of that by now. Zach had to accept that she was dead.

He was on leave from the SEALs, with good cause. There was no way he could focus, not even on training WEALS. Besides, the class was down to a manageable twenty now. Actually, twenty was more than had been expected to make it through the rigorous training. There would be no Britta, though, and that saddened Zach even more. She had wanted so badly to succeed in WEALS.

Sammy had been very clingy at first, but then, with the resilience of childhood, he settled into his normal routine and hardly ever mentioned the ordeal he had been through.

Still, Zach knew that Sammy was worried about his grandfather Arsallah and whether he would try again.

And now his family was pulling an intervention on him. An intervention! Like he was a friggin' addict or something. They had him trapped in his town house living room, with Sammy upstairs playing video games with Scary Larry.

His grandmother was serving them tea . . . tea, for Pete's sake . . . using a silver tea service and bone china, both of which he hadn't even known he had. *What is bone china anyway? Crushed bones? Yeech!* It was a scene right out of *Alice in Wonderland*. There were fancy-pancy little cookies the size of quarters she'd brought from a bakery that probably cost a dollar a piece. Danny was flicking them into his mouth like popcorn.

His mother and father, divorced almost twenty years, were glaring at each other. They made *The War of the Roses* look like kindergarten.

"Shape up, boy," his grandfather said after putting his teacup down. "Everybody loses someone sometime. Get yourself a new assignment. Lose yourself in work. Uncle Sam needs you."

*Yada, yada, yada.* He'd heard this spiel a dozen times.

His grandmother gaped at his grandfather as if he'd sprouted two heads. "Nonsense. He needs time to grieve. He may never get over the girl, but in the meantime he must think about Sammy and move on."

*I wonder if there's any beer left in the fridge.*

His mother, romantic that she was, despite having been two-timed by his father numerous times, sighed. "It's just a shame that you had to find the woman of your dreams, only to lose her. Do you think a person can have two loves?" The latter she addressed to her ex-mother-in-law, his grandmother.

*Is that a push-up bra my mother's wearing? No, no, no, I am not noticing my mother's assets.*

"Of course," his grandmother replied.

*Geez, grandma looks good for her age, too. How old is*

*she now? Seventy-five? No, seventy-six. Wonder if she's had a face-lift? Hah! Who am I kidding? Everyone in my family has probably had plastic surgery, except my grandfather.*

"Come to Hollywood with me," his dad offered. "You and Sammy can stay in the guesthouse. I'll introduce you to some women who'll make you forget your own name, let alone a woman you only knew for a few weeks. Hey, I know, Lori, my housekeeper on *Light in the Storm*, is between husbands, and she used to be a Playboy bunny." His dad leered at Zach, something a grown man did not want his father to do.

*Are you kidding? I've seen Lori. She might have been a Playmate, but it must have been thirty years ago. Besides, I'm not into silicone.*

Everyone glared at his father for his insensitivity.

"Isn't that just like you, Victor?" His mother sneered. "Thinking with your zipper as usual."

*Oh, boy, here we go.*

"Maybe if you'd paid more attention to my zipper, we wouldn't be divorced."

*This is just like watching a Ping-Pong match. Duel of the divorcees.*

"Grow up, Victor. You're not sixteen anymore. And, by the way, your hair looks silly with those gray streaks."

*I was thinkin' that myself.*

"You know what's silly, Lillian? You. Modeling for that geezer magazine. If that's what acting my age is all about, no thank you."

*I think her new career change is cool.*

The two of them were practically shaking with anger. A minute more of this, and they'd be clawing each other's carefully made-up faces. Really, there was a reason why his mother and father were rarely in the same room together, and they were just witnessing it.

"Whoa, whoa, whoa!" Zach stood, then sat down on the couch between the two of them. "This is accomplishing nothing."

"I hate to say it, but Dad has a point." Great. Danny was joining the other side. "You need to get laid."

*I do not believe he said that in front of our parents and grandparents.* "You think the answer to everything is sex."

His father, Danny, and Cage and Sly, who were leaning against the wall, all looked at him as if he was crazy. His mother, grandmother, and grandfather all got into a tsk-ing match.

"Seriously, Zach," Cage said to him. "Britta is gone. Accept that, buddy."

He hesitated, then nodded. "This whole freakin' intervention crap is ridiculous . . . and unnecessary. I'm already making plans to move on."

"Uh-oh," Sly said.

"I'm quitting the teams." He put up a hand to halt the protests that erupted. "I'm selling the town house. And I'm going into hiding with Sammy."

"Where?" his mother wanted to know.

"I can't say."

"What do you mean, you can't say?" His grandmother's eyes narrowed with suspicion. Then she turned and glowered at his grandfather. "Did you have something to do with this?"

His grandfather's cheeks flushed, but he raised his chin. "Zach asked for my advice. This isn't what I would recommend, but if it's what he wants, I can point him to the right people for help."

Pandemonium broke loose, everyone talking at once.

"Hear me out, people. I'm leaving. Until Arsallah is out of the picture—and I mean dead—I can't give Sammy a normal life. And he deserves that. So we're going to disappear."

"Will we see you sometimes? Can we call?" his mother asked.

He shook his head. "Cold turkey."

"For how long?" His father's voice was cold with disapproval.

"As long as it takes."

"Years?" His mother looked as if she was going to cry.

"I hope not, but yes, maybe it will be a long time."

"When are you leaving?" Danny's face was expressionless, but he was clearly upset. He would talk to him later.

He couldn't tell them that it would be in a mere three days. Otherwise, there would be a flurry of suspicious activity around his house. They wouldn't be able to stay away.

So he just shrugged.

Later, he told Sammy of his plans.

The boy was frightened, but more frightened of losing him than losing a familiar home. He became more enthused once Zach mentioned all the things they would be able to do together in the downtime till he found a new job . . . or they were able to return, whichever came first.

Before they went downstairs, though, Sammy tugged on his arm to stop him. "Does . . . does this mean Britta is dead?"

Zach closed his eyes briefly. "Yes. Yes, she is, Sammy."

Sammy gulped, probably having already suspected the worst. "Now can I tell you what she said?"

Bracing himself, he said, "Sure."

"She said, if she didn't make it back, I should tell you," he slipped his hand in Zach's, "that she loves you."

It was probably the worst moment of Zach's life.

**Who says medieval ladies didn't have balls? . . .**

Britta and Angelique got along like . . . well, sisters.

Turns out that their mutual father, whilst on a trip to Frankland some twenty-three years past, went into the Frankish countryside where he raped a number of women, including Angelique's mother. Like Britta, Angelique had trained to become a warrior, but unlike Britta, she had trained to be a nun as well.

While Britta had reason to want her father dead, Angelique had even more. Not only had he planted his seed in her mother, but he'd also planted a disease in her nether parts . . . a disease that led to her death at the age of fifteen.

Angelique's life had been hard, to say the least, but Britta loved her already for her wonderful sense of humor despite her travails.

"So, you are like Boudicca?" Britta asked her as they sat on a stone wall surrounding the abbey courtyard. They were both panting and sweating, having just completed some swordplay. "That's not very nunlike, is it?"

Angelique grinned as she wiped her forehead with the sleeve of her gunna. "We are a different breed of nuns . . . nuns who enjoy the bedsport."

Britta's eyes went wide.

"Do not look so shocked. Are you a virgin?"

"Well, nay, but—"

Angelique wagged a forefinger at her. "Judge not, lest ye be judged." She grinned as she spoke. "In truth, I am not really a nun. 'Tis a disguise that has worked well for me and my followers."

Britta laughed and slapped the forefinger out of her face. "I was not judging, and you well know it. I was just surprised. But, believe you me, I know how to wipe that smirk from your face, Sister."

A short time later, Angelique's jaw dropped nigh to her bosom. "Multiple orgasms? Clits? You jest with me?"

" 'Tis no jest. The women of our time are being cheated."

"Our time?"

"Let us save that story for later."

"One last thing. Was it some special man who taught you these things?"

"Yea, but he is far, far away, and we will ne'er meet again." Leastways, Britta did not think they would meet again. "Let us speak of our battle plan instead of lost loves."

"I like your idea of gorilla warfare, though I ne'er heard that word afore. Nor 'Look and See,' 'Growl and Prowl,' 'Escape and Evade,' 'double-backs.' "

"We must needs take the advantage out of our father's hands. We will choose the site where the fight will take place. He has left the area, but he will return."

So it was that two sennights later, several aged nuns went begging alms to one of her father's Northumbrian keeps; he had several here and in the Norselands, and still he wanted hers. The aged nuns were performing their own lackwit version of 'Look and See.' Whilst there, spying, they spoke of a nunnery in Northumbria where they had stayed overnight . . . a nunnery where two sisters, Britta the Big and Angelique of Frankland, were plotting the takeover of some castle or other owned by their father. "Is that not odd?" Sister Clementina inquired through rheumy eyes. "Women fighters?"

"And they with only slingshots and broomsticks for weapons," Sister Mary added, also blinking her rheumy eyes in innocence. "And they will be leaving the abbey grounds as they march to battle. Imagine!"

The men in the great hall guffawed and made coarse jests, even in the presence of the good nuns.

The two nuns reported back to the abbey that even before they had left the bailey, men-at-arms were being called forth. A small band because, as her father had remarked, "How many men does it take to topple a few lackbrained women?"

A sennight later, her father's small hird of ten men on horseback, including himself and his three sons, was on the move. When they were several hides from the abbey, Britta and Angelique's band surrounded the two forward outriders and offered them the opportunity to surrender. The men laughed and attacked. A mistake. The women soon hid the severely wounded bodies and rushed away from the scene. Escape and Evade.

The nuns at St. Anne's would be used for nonviolent activities, because they were reluctant to take anyone's life, even a man as evil as her father. Caring for the wounded. Preparing arrows and boiling oil, a contingency plan.

Closer to the abbey, they maneuvered and reined their horses in at the far end of a tight pass where there was a hillock on one side and a rocky cliff on the other. Laughing, they taunted the hirdsmen, rode off, then did a double-back to the other side of the pass, thus blocking them in. With the element of surprise, they managed to kill one brother, Trond, and three other men, which left her father, two brothers, and one hirdsman. Looking down at Trond, all Britta could see was her brother laughing as he held up her skinned cat all those years ago.

No longer able to ambush, the eleven of them faced the men, full-on, swords and spears raised. The men probably thought these split-tail bitches, as her father ofttimes referred to females, would be easy pickings. But they had not counted on their expertise, as meager as it might have been in comparison to the battle-hardened warriors. Their downfall was over-confidence and surprise.

Her father smirked at the nerve of these women thinking they could best him. But then he recognized Britta, and his eyes narrowed with hatred. "So, Daughter, you think to send your own father to Valhalla?"

"Not just me, but my sister, Angelique, as well. Your other daughter." She indicated with a jerk of her head Angelique at her side. "And know this, you scurvy cur who does not merit the name father, you will not go to Valhalla. That is for noble warriors who die in battle. Today you will burn in Muspell."

It was an even fight, despite the odds of eleven to four. In the end, both Britta and Angelique put their swords through their father's chest, coming at him from two sides.

Some of Angelique's band were retching at the side, now that the fighting was over. It may very well be true that warfare was contrary to a woman's nature.

"Do you have any regrets?" Britta asked Angelique as they both knelt before a small pond, washing the sword dew from their arms as well as their blades.

Angelique shook her head vehemently. "He was a bastard. He needed to be put down like a rabid dog. Do not tell me you are feeling sorry after all he has put you through."

"Not sorry, exactly. Just sad. He was our father. They were our brothers. Blood kin. Why were they so . . . mean?" She had told Angelique about their father's pressure to wed, her one brother's attempt at rape, and another's displaying her private parts to his friends.

"Some men—some women, too—are just born bad, to my way of thinking." Angelique shrugged. "Methinks our killing them was a good thing. Leastwise now other women, not just us, will be spared their cruelty."

Britta nodded. "Best we get back to the abbey. There is much work to be done."

The nuns and novices had already brought all the dead back. Father Caedmon would be performing death rites for the men, a service Britta and Angelique declined to attend.

Later, having bathed and eaten, Britta and Angelique were sitting on benches in the back garden, sipping from horns of Margaret's mead.

"I have an idea," Britta said.

"Should I be afraid?"

Britta punched her playfully on the upper arm. "Nay. You know that Everstead and all the surrounding estates now belong to me?"

Angelique nodded. "So I am in the exalted company of a wealthy woman. Shall I bow?"

Britta said a foul word rarely used by women.

Angelique just laughed.

"I want naught to do with Everstead, and yet I know not where my place in life is now. Let us go to Everstead and rule it together."

"Huh?"

"I have not been to Everstead in more than fifteen years. It is in the far northern reaches of the Norselands, but beautiful, as I recall. We could put it forth that we are both of my mother's line, and the odal rights belong to both of us. It is my understanding that all the old retainers are gone; none will know different. Let us go there till we decide what our future holds for us."

Angelique eyed her warily. "Are you thinking to leave me at Everstead and go off to find that lost love of yours?"

Britta shook her head. "That is impossible, I think."

"In truth, now that my mother is avenged, I have no desire to continue fighting . . . or be a nun."

"The frightening thing is, I no longer see myself as a warrior, either. There are other roles I must needs play now."

Angelique put her hands on her hips and glowered at her. "What is it you are not telling me?"

"I am with child."

**Home, home on the range . . . the very cold range . . .**

"Holy crap! It's colder'n a pig's butt in a poop parade."

"Sammy! What have I told you about your language? No video games tonight."

"Daaaaad!"

"No video games."

"Maybe I shouldna said it like that, but, geez, Dad, you gotta admit, movin' to Alaska wasn't a great idea. Even my snot is frozen."

"You do have a colorful vocabulary."

"If I had a dog, I prob'ly wouldn't be so cold."

Zach pulled the ear flaps on his son's cap down lower, then handed him two more pieces of firewood. Once he loaded up, as well, they walked back to the cabin that had been their home for the last three months. And, yeah, it *was* really cold—twenty below today—but chances were Arsallah and his men wouldn't be dogsledding out here any time soon.

The cabin was actually a two-bedroom log house, with all the modern conveniences—electric heat, plumbing, updated kitchen—but it was still nice to have a fire in the fireplace at night. Cozy.

And there was a school two miles away that Sammy went to every day via the county school bus. He balked and claimed to hate it, but his mind was like a sponge, and he was learning so much. Zach suspected he liked school. And he'd made some friends there. They were almost a normal, single-parent family.

Of course, they'd changed their names to Smith, and Zach was using his middle name of Frank. Frank Smith and Sammy Smith, whose mother had died last year. Sammy never slipped with his real name. He knew how important their hidden identities were to their safety, which was sad, really, that a child would have to worry about such things.

That evening, Sammy lay on the floor doing his homework before the fire.

Zach was working on his computer at the desk by the window. He'd decided to try his luck at writing a suspense novel while in hiding. About Navy SEALs, of course. It might never sell, but he was enjoying the writing . . . for now.

"Will we ever go back?" Sammy asked suddenly.

Zach sighed. "Yes, I think so. Eventually." And actually, he didn't want to get Sammy's hopes up, but Arsallah hadn't been heard from in weeks, and rumor had it that he'd been murdered by one of his followers. *I can only hope!* Zach's only link to his old life was a secure phone line to Commander MacLean's office that only the two of them knew about.

"I miss Danny," Sammy said.

*I miss Britta.* He didn't say that aloud because he didn't want to add to Sammy's misery. Though, truthfully, Sammy had adjusted better than he had.

"But I prob'ly wouldn't be so lonely if I had a dog."

Zach shook his head. "Give us a chance to settle in ourselves first."

"Then can we get a dog?"

"I didn't say that. A dog is a big responsibility." Especially when they might have to pack up and go on a moment's notice.

"I'm responsible."

"You don't even know what that word means."

"Are we gonna go to the Thanksgiving dance at the Grange barn on Thursday?"

*Great! A diversionary tactic.*

"A party in a barn?" *Hoo-yah!* "Do you wanna go?"

"There's nothin' else to do," Sammy grumbled, then glanced up at him with a crafty gleam in his eye. "'Specially without video games."

"Forget about the video games. What does a person wear to a dance in a barn?"

"How do I know? I'm just a kid."

"When it's a convenient excuse."

"What does convenient mean?"

"Maybe I should buy us some new clothes?"

"No. You always buy me dorky stuff."

"I resent that." He laughed. "What have I bought that's dorky?"

"Kermit the Frog pajamas with web feet, for a start."

"It was all they had in your size."

"A bow tie. When am I ever gonna wear a bow tie?"

"That was your great-grandmother who bought that, not me. Besides, maybe you'll go to a wedding or something where you have to dress up."

His little eyebrows arched. "Are you gettin' married?"

*Hardly.* "What do you think?"

He shrugged. "You could marry an Eskimo, and we could live in an igloo."

"And you're complaining about the cold now. Besides, how many igloos have we seen since we arrived?"

"None. Okay, another dorky thing. The hat with the ear flaps."

"You've got a point there, but they do keep you warm."

"At least I don't have to wear those dorky superhero underpants anymore, now that we're wearin' long johns."

They were both quiet then as they returned to their respective work. Zach's mind had drifted, though, and he logged off the computer. Overall, he should be thankful. They were safe. Sammy accepted him as his father. And they were alive. And someday, he was sure, they'd be able to return to family and friends.

"Sammy . . ."

"Oh, no! You're gonna say somethin' mushy. I can tell by your voice. It's all soft and gooey."

"I love you."

"Yeah, I love you, too," he finally said. But then he added, "I'd still like to have a dog."

# Chapter 20

**Maybe she should go a-Viking . . .**

Britta was cold, and damp, and lonely, and miserable, as she stared out over the vast, snowy estate that was Everstead. Being landlocked here for more than a month in deep winter, she began to understand why Norsemen went a-Viking every year at first thaw.

"Britta! Britta, is that you?"

Britta rolled her eyes. As if it would be anyone else! Why did Jarl Rolf Thorsson, a visitor from a neighboring estate, continue to pursue her when she had made it more than clear that she was not interested?

And he was not the only one. It was strange, really, what had happened on her journey here with Angelique from Northumbria. For years, she had held no appeal to men. Too tall, too big-boned, too manly. But now, 'twas like she was honey and the entire male race a horde of randy bears. She suspected there was something in her bearing since she had engaged in bedsport with Zachary that shouted to men: Here is Britta Asadottir. She is one hot bedsport companion. And she had not even mentioned multiple orgasms to any of them.

"Yea, I am here, Rolf," she said with a long sigh.

"What are ye doing, wench?"

He only called her wench to get a rise out of her, so today, she refused to rise to the bait.

"Just admiring the fjord." *Trying to evade you.*

"Why?"

*Wondering how I might escape.* "Does there have to be a reason?"

"Well, I would think so." His handsome face brightened. "Have ye given any more thought to my proposal? Really, dearling, it makes sense for us to wed. We could merge our two estates and—"

Rolf was a fine-looking man. Huge in stature. And fairly young, having seen only thirty winters. If her father had offered him as husband, mayhap back then she would have accepted. But her father had never chosen him because Rolf would not have played puppet to her father. Rolf's first wife had died childless five years past. He would be a prize catch for most women. Perchance Angelique would be interested.

"I have gifted Angelique half of Everstead."

Rolf inhaled sharply. "Why would you do that?"

She had not told Rolf she was increasing. She would have to soon. Being five months gone, she did not yet show much because of her height and size, unless she was naked, and she had not been naked in many a month. Not since . . . *I must stop myself from dwelling on the past. 'Tis not healthy for me or the babe.*

"'Tis only fair that I share with Angelique. I owe her much."

In truth, marriage to Rolf might not be so bad. And speaking of fairness, she had not given him a chance. She leaned up and gave Rolf a gentle kiss, to test the waters, so to speak. Both of their lips were ice cold.

Rolf was surprised, but not for long. He was a Viking, after all, and Viking men did not have to be invited twice. When she started to pull away, he yanked her into a tight embrace, taking command of the kiss, which was no longer gentle but devouring.

Britta tried to be objective, which was telling in itself. It was not a bad kiss. His breath was sweet. Fresh-shaven, his skin smelled of hard soap and the outdoors.

And she felt nothing.

She was not repelled, but she was not aroused, either.

Had Zachary ruined her for other men?

That thought caused her blood to rise, and she shoved Rolf away gently. Truly, not only had Zachary got her with child, but now it appeared she would never find joy in the bedsport with another man.

Rolf's head was tilted to the side in question. "Come back to my bed furs with me, dearling, and we will warm each other up." He was not being forceful in his request. More like inviting, as any virile man would do in the circumstances.

Britta thought briefly of telling Rolf of her pregnancy to test how great his yearning was to wed with her, but, really, it made no difference. She would not have him in any case.

She shook her head. "I am sorry, Rolf."

He was about to argue but then caught himself. Pride was great in Norsemen, and he was no different.

She watched him go, then decided to walk down to the fjord. It was a clear day, and exercise was supposedly good for breeding women.

Was it really only five months since she had last seen Zachary? Did he miss her as much as she missed him? Hah! A man as pretty as him would have women lining up to take her place. Not that she had had a place, precisely, other than as a bedmate.

*Aaarrgh! Always it comes back to Zachary.* Placing both hands over her stomach, where even now a part of him grew, she wondered if motherhood would be enough. Well, it would have to be.

A niggling thought tugged at her mind, though. Zachary

had laughingly said that he had "wish-prayed" her to the future.

*Could I do the same?*

*Nay, I could not risk the babe.* Whether in the womb or already born, a human life would be in her hands. Whilst she could step freely into the magic of time travel herself—not that she had a clue how to do that—a child was frail and dependent on her. It was selfish of her to be unsatisfied with her lot. A small part of her wondered if mayhap sometime in the future, when her child was born, they might both travel to the future. But, nay, that was wishful thinking, and she must needs be practical, resigned to her fate.

Tears filled her eyes, a common and vexing malady of her pregnancy, and she decided she'd best go back to the keep where cook would have a hearty broth prepared. Angelique, who loved Everstead already, was doing inventory of all the supplies for winter.

And yet she lingered, miserable beyond bearing.

Britta eased down to her knees and did pray then, whether to the One-God of the Christians or to the Norse gods, it mattered not. In truth, they were probably one and the same.

"Please, God, help me. I know not what to do. A miracle, that is what need. Barring that, help me to be content with my lot."

She stood and, as if in a trance, began to walk closer to the water's edge. In fact, she placed a booted foot into the icy water and shivered. What kind of lackwit put a booted foot into a winter fjord?

But wait, it did not feel so cold. It was rather warm. And soothing. Without thought, Britta walked into the water, which first seeped over her ankles, then knees, then hips and bosom.

*Have I finally, truly gone barmy? Am I going to take my own life? The babe! Remember the babe. I must go back.*

A voice in her head whispered to her, *You are taking your*

*own life, yea, but into your own hands. Go home, Britta.
Take the babe home with you.*

*Where is home?*

*You know, Britta,* the voice said. *You know.*

And she did.

Standing stock-still, she was like a statue, unmoving, as a
wave lapped up and covered her head. There were no waves
in this fjord, or never had been before.

*Amazing!*

With a sigh, she sank into a deep, seagoing sleep.

And that was that.

God was calling her home.


## I see dead people . . .

"I saw Britta today."

*"What?"* Zach slammed on the SUV's brakes and
pulled over to the side of the road. They were on their way
to the grocery store, but that could wait. "That was not
funny."

"I wasn't jokin'. The school bus was goin' down that road
by the sea, and I saw this lady walk out of the water. She was
soakin' wet, an' her hair looked like snakes, an' she wore this
long fur coat, and—"

"Stop it, Sammy! Just stop it!"

Sammy awakened from dreams at night on occasion, crying. Apparently, Britta was alive and well in those dreams
and holding out her arms for him to come to her. But those
were dreams. Was he now fantasizing in the daytime? That
was not healthy. "Britta is gone."

Sammy ducked his head. "I know," he said in a small
voice.

"Besides, no one could survive a dunking in the cold
Bering Sea, even for a short period. It's frigid."

"I know," he repeated, "but it sure looked like her. Honest. She even had a frowny face on, like she did sometimes."

Zach shook his head but couldn't suppress a grin. Britta with her frowny face. Yeah, Sammy had gotten that right.

"Maybe it was just a walrus."

*Yeah, right.* "Can we change the subject?"

"Can I have a dog?"

## The ice woman thaweth . . .

For two days Britta lay shivering in a cot piled high with woolen blankets.

At first she feared that the babe would die from the shock of the ice-cold near-drowning, and she believed she was back in the Everstead keep. But neither of them died. Nor was she at Everstead.

Britta had walked out into the Norse fjord, but she came out of the Bering Sea in another part of the world, frozen nigh solid. Out of her mind with fever at first, she'd eventually discovered that she was in a land called Alaska, which was part of America.

A wonderful couple had taken her into their home . . . Daryl and Dottie Woolever, lawyers here in Alaska. The young couple had even called a doctor to come care for her. To everyone's surprise, she had not only survived her foolish dunking, but she had not even gotten hypo-therm-ia, a condition where body appendages often fell off. She was rather fond of her fingers and toes and especially her nose.

Once the confusion of her fever wore off, Britta realized that she had time-traveled forward again and survived, along with her unborn child. And if she had her way, this time-travel business was ended for her, in either direction.

The bad news was that she was cut off and isolated from anyone and anything that was familiar to her. Why she was sent here to Alaska, she had no idea, but then she had had no idea why she had been sent to Coronado, either. Mayhap Zachary was here, and he'd wish-prayed for her again.

Almost immediately, she discarded that foolish notion.

Already she had asked Daryl and Dottie to inquire if there was a Zachary Floyd or Sammy Floyd anywhere in the region. There was not. The only Sammy was a child named Sammy Smith, and his father's name was Frank.

"It's Thanksgiving, Britta, we should celebrate," Dottie said as the two of them set the dining table.

"I am thankful. I just wish I had been able to contact Zachary by now."

Daryl and Dottie had helped her dial Zachary's telephone number, which she had remembered, thank the gods, but when she called, someone told her, "This number has been disconnected." Her friends explained that it meant he had probably gotten a new number.

Everyone else that Britta tried to call had unlisted numbers: Hilda, Madrene, the other SEALs.

Daryl knew someone who knew someone at a telephone place, and they told him that there was no new number for Zachary, that he must have moved, whereas the other numbers were merely unlisted for privacy and safety concerns.

So her only choice was to travel to California next week, with the aid of her new friends, and see in person what was happening. In the meantime, she was tired all the time, weepy, hungry, and ready to relieve her bladder every other moment.

After a fabulous turkey feast, Britta needed a nap. She was still sleeping on the sofa in front of the fireplace in the solar when Dottie shook her shoulders gently. "Britta, it's time to get up. We're going to the dance."

Britta blinked to clear her head, then sat up, yawning widely. "Methinks I should stay here and tend the fire."

"Now, you promised," Dottie cajoled.

"Besides, I doubt anyone but you two would dance with me," Daryl said.

Britta smiled at the devilry in his dancing eyes. "I have naught to wear."

"Ta da!" Dottie tossed a pile of clothing at her. Another pair of Daryl's den-ham braies, a white tea-ing *shert*, a flannel over-*shert*, thick wool hose, and a pair of Daryl's boots. Daryl was her height and thin, whilst Dottie was short and well-curved. A pair of Dottie's braies would come only to her calves.

So it was that a resigned Britta went to her first-ever Thanksgiving dance in a barn. These Americans were very strange.

## Oooh, wait till I get my hands on you . . .

Zach and Sammy had been at the Thanksgiving dance at the Grange hall for an hour, and he had to admit it was fun . . . the first time he'd smiled in what seemed like ages.

Sammy was off chasing some of his friends, rather than dance to the country band playing what he called "dorky music." Zach had been teaching Sammy how to dance the last few nights, and the two of them had laughed more than learned any new steps. Besides, Sammy said he wasn't going to touch any stinky girls anyhow, not even their hands.

Zach leaned against the wall and watched. There were at least two hundred people here, of all ages, and about half of them were out on the dance floor. As his eyes scanned the crowd, he saw Francine Doucet, Sammy's schoolteacher. He smiled at her, and she smiled back.

Okay. Zach had been a player for too long not to recognize the message given by her particular smile. In the old days, they would have called it a "come hither" smile. He called it a "come on over here, cowboy, and let's rodeo" smile.

He hesitated, then figured, "What the hell!" It was only a dance. He did in fact dance with her. Then he danced with her again, and again.

Sammy came over to ask him if he could stay overnight with a friend. As he stood talking to the boy, his hand wrapped around Francine's waist, tucking her into his side. It felt good to be with a woman again. And she got along well with Sammy. Not that he was planning anything . . . yet. He and Francine were both laughing at Sammy's long-winded explanation for why he really, really needed a dog.

In the midst of their laughter, he glanced across the room and saw a blonde woman dancing with a tall guy who had one arm around her waist, and her right hand held up to his chest in one of his hands. The woman matched the man in height, probably six feet tall. She was slim, but she filled out the tight jeans very well.

Then she turned.

And the blood drained from his skull.

It was Britta.

"Oh, my God!" He clutched Francine's waist tighter.

Francine asked, "What's wrong?"

"Sorry. I thought I just saw . . ."

". . . a ghost?" She laughed.

"You could say that." Zach's heart was beating so fast he feared it might burst.

Then the woman, who resembled Britta, but couldn't possibly be Britta, noticed him, and she stopped dead in her dancing shoes . . . boots.

He started to smile.

She bared her teeth. And then she bolted.

By the time Zach made his escape, rushing across the room and to the doorway, there was no one there. It couldn't have been Britta. This woman had been pure Alaskan with her flannel shirt, heavy jeans, and boots. His eyes must have been playing games with him. Wishful thinking.

But he had no heart for the dance, or Francine, anymore. After going in to give permission for Sammy to stay with his friend, and saying his good-byes to a clearly disappointed Francine, he left the hall and headed for home.

He had thought before tonight that he was getting better, but he was right back to step one. He missed Britta so much he could almost cry.

And, yeah, there were tears in his eyes.
He almost hated her for how she'd ruined his life.
Almost.

## Life does not always have happy endings . . .

Britta was so miserable and angry that she could scarce keep her balance as she stomped along the icy road, heading toward the Woolever home.

*The lecherous, traitorous, slimy, fornicating maggot!*

Here she was getting bigger by the day with his child, and he had his paws all over that woman's body. A painful thought occurred to her. *Oh, my gods! Mayhap he has married the wench in the months since I have been gone.* That hurt.

Knuckling her eyes so that she could see better, she plodded on. She needed to get back to the Woolever home and make plans to leave as soon as possible. She could not stay within such close proximity to Zachary. She just could not.

Her heart felt as if it were being crushed.

*It could have been someone else.*

*Hah! It was him.*

*Why would he leave the warm lands of California for this frigid place?*

*Arsallah. He must be hiding from Sammy's grandfather.*

*He is not hiding that much, if he thinks naught of public displays of affection with a woman.*

*The randy cur cannot help himself. He is a man, after all, a prisoner to his lustsome inclinations.*

*I wonder if he gives her multiple orgasms.*

*Of course he does.*

More tears flowed from her eyes. She had never been a weepy woman afore. It must be the pregnancy.

Which prompted her to reach inside her fur-lined cape and cradle her small belly. *It is just you and me now, baby. We must needs find a place in this new world.*

*Mayhap I can go to Hilda and ask her for help.*

*Nay, she would tell Zachary, and then he would feel obligated to come to me.*

*Not if he is married to another woman.*

The headlights from a car came at her from behind, and she stepped farther off the road's edge to give it room. After it passed, she continued her walk.

Once she was calmer, Britta had to admit that she wanted to be here in the future, even if it was alone, without Zachary. She fingered the amber pendant hanging from her neck . . . one of the few pieces of her mother's jewelry that had been left at Everstead. Mayhap it could be exchanged for coin so that she could set up a home for her and the child. Far from Alaska.

Her heart was breaking, but that would pass, she promised herself. She was not about to sip the bane drink over the worthless whoreson. She had a child to think of. Enough!

Yea, that was what she would do. No pining after the clodpole. No contacting Hilda or Madrene . . . leastways not till after the babe was born. She was proud, and she was strong. She would survive.

A new chapter in her ever-chaotic life!

## There are the bonds of love, and then there is BONDAGE . . .

Zach was halfway home when he passed the figure walking alongside the road. He should probably stop and offer a lift, but he was in no mood for company.

He had driven a mile farther when an unbelievable thought entered his mind. It was crazy. He was crazy. But still he turned his SUV around and headed back.

Yep, there was the person still walking along the berm of the road. Which was nuts with the slippery ice. But then, in the clearer focus of his headlights, he saw that it was a tall figure wearing a long black cloak with a hood, which seemed to be lined with fur. An odd garment, even for Alaska.

Holy crap, it was a woman, he realized, when a long strand of hair blew out of her hood. Blonde hair.

*What did Sammy say about a woman in a long fur coat?*

He felt almost light-headed as he drove a few yards past the woman, turned around, then came up alongside her. It was impossible to see exactly who it was. But his body was on red alert, and it had never let him down before.

The woman refused to even glance his way or slow down. He pulled over to the side of the road and got out. Quickly he caught up with her.

"Britta!"

The woman didn't even look at him but snarled, "Begone!"

*Oh, my God! Oh, my God! It is Britta.* The how and why of it didn't matter right now; he just knew that all his prayers had been answered. She was back.

"Britta, honey, you're back. Thank God, you're back."

She muttered something that sounded like, "Slimy maggot."

"Britta, stop, you're giving me a stitch in my side."

"I'd like to give you something, but it's not a stitch."

"What's wrong? Why won't you talk to me?" He was in front of her now, walking backward as he tried to see her face.

She refused to answer him.

"I have missed you so much."

Still no response.

Finally, he caught her by the upper arms and made her look at him.

She was crying. For chrissake, she was out-and-out crying.

He didn't even ask her what was wrong; he just pulled her into his arms and hugged her tightly, not loosening his hold, no matter how hard she squirmed. But then she wasn't squirming anymore. But he was still holding her.

Leaning back to look at her, he said, "You're back."

"Smart-brained, as always."

He ignored her sarcasm and gave her a quick kiss on the mouth before she could slap him. "Where have you been?"

"Where in bloody hell do you think I have been?"

"I thought you were dead." He began to back her in the direction of his car. With the cold and the wind, she was shivering, even with that strange cloak. Or maybe she was shivering because of him. He could hope.

"Did Sammy get away?"

He nodded.

"Unharmed?"

"Perfectly unharmed, thanks to you."

She made a harrumphing sound as if to dismiss his compliment. "Well, that is one good thing in this whole sorry mess."

"I missed you so much, Britta. Honest to God, there were times I wanted to die, too."

"Hah! You were not missing me much in there with your hands on that woman's arse."

*Francine? She saw me with Francine.* "My hands were not on her ass. Besides, you were in the arms of a man, and I don't like seeing another man's hands on you."

"He is married."

"Like that matters!"

"He is married, *and* I have been staying with him and his wife the past sennight."

*Oh. Well, okay then!* "Where were you before that?"

She closed her eyes for a minute as if seeing some painful memory. When she opened them, she said, "I killed my father."

He let those words sink in. "Oh, Britta."

"I have no regrets. My father was a *nithing*, less than nothing."

"Are you saying you traveled back in time, and are now back here again?"

"It would seem so," she grumbled.

*The time-travel crap again!* "I'm never going to let you go again."

"You have no say over what I do."

"Wanna bet?"

They stood glaring at each other, a stalemate. But they'd arrived at his car.

"Do you remember the last time we were together, Britta?" His voice came out raw and husky. Probably due to the cold air.

She seemed to notice her surroundings for the first time and sucked in air at the reminder of that other time. "If you think I am going to give a repeat performance in this cold on top of that car, you are more demented than I already think. My nipples would probably freeze and drop off."

"I can't believe you just said that."

"What? Do you not know about hypothermia?"

"I know about hypothermia. God, I am so happy to see you."

"I am not happy to see you."

"Too bad. Get in the car, Britta." He opened the passenger door for her.

"Nay."

No longer amused by the delays, he took matters into his own hands. He picked her up, hitting and flailing, but he finally got her into the car, strapped in, and engaged the child locks on the doors. He turned the car on but stared at her before pulling out.

"Stop smiling at me."

"I can't help it. I'm so friggin' happy to see you."

"You no longer have any obligation to me."

*Is she the most stubborn woman in the universe, or what?* "Why is that?"

"I have decided to go off on my own."

"And do what? The military again?"

"Nay, I am going to try something different."

"Like what?"

"Will you stop asking me questions? I do not know. Mayhap I will be a cattle woman. I have been riding a horse of late."

He laughed. "Do you mean cowgirl?"

"That is what I said, lackwit."

"I am a lackwit . . . for ever doubting you would come back."

"I did not come back to you."

"Liar."

"Where are we?"

He had pulled into his driveway and turned off the ignition. "My home."

"If you think for one instant that I will share bed furs with you and your wife, you are in for a good thumping, you perverted son of a snake."

"You think I want a ménage à trois?" He grinned. "I'm not married, Britta."

"Oh." She turned slowly to look at him. "And the woman you were drooling all over?"

"Sammy's teacher. And I was not drooling."

"Mayhap you will have more children with your new love."

"Aaarrgh! I am not married, engaged, or involved with Francine in any way. And the last thing in the world I need is another child in my messed-up life. Sammy is enough, thank you very much."

Britta flinched.

An odd reaction, he thought.

"Is Sammy here?" She checked out the well-lit cabin.

He shook his head. "It's our lucky day . . . rather night. He's sleeping overnight at a friend's. We have the place to ourselves."

"I will not be having sex with you."

*Ha, ha, ha.* "Whatever you say. Come on. It's cold out here."

She followed him meekly into the cabin, or as meekly as was possible for Britta. While she walked around, examining the place, he added more logs to the fireplace. "Take off your cloak, Britta." She was sitting on the sofa now, still enfolded in the voluminous, fur-lined garment. He was pretty sure it was sable. PETA would hate it. *God, that thing must be worth a mint, even if it does smell like wet dog.*

"I do not want to remove my cloak."

"Wanna tell me what's bugging you?"

"You are."

*Okaaaay.* He went to sit down beside her, and she shooed him aside.

"Did you wish-pray me here again?"

"Probably."

"Why?"

"Briiiitta! I've told you I missed you like crazy. Sammy has missed you like crazy, too. What more do you want?"

She shrugged. "I thought I wanted you. I called your keep, and the number was disconnected. Everyone else has an unlisted number . . . Hilda, Madrene, Cage. I was going to find a way to go back to Coronado next sennight."

"But . . . ?"

"But I saw you with that woman, and I realized how tenuous this bond is betwixt us, and I cannot take the chance . . . What are you doing?" That last came out on a squeak.

"Taking my clothes off."

"Well, do not."

He continued to remove his clothes and was down to his long john bottoms.

She watched him closely, her eyes glazing over. He hot damn knew what that meant, but he needed to play his cards close to his chest. This was Britta, not his average targ—uh, prospective partner.

"I am not taking *my* clothes off."

"Not even your cloak?"

She shook her head. "Especially not my cloak."

Something strange was going on here. Meanwhile, his emotions were banging off the walls. "I was kinda hoping you would toss it on the floor, and we could make love the first time on the fur."

"The first time?" She whimpered and stood, backing away.

He took one step forward. She took one step backward. A losing battle for her, if she was thinking straight, which she must not be. Praise God and bring on the ammunition!

Speaking of ammunition, time to bring in the big artillery. "Britta. Honey. Sammy gave me your message."

Her blush told him that she knew exactly what he meant. She didn't try to deny it; he had to give her that.

"It is not chivalrous of you to bring that up to a lady."

"*Lady*, I'm fresh out of chivalry." His frustration was turning into anger. "Do you or do you not love me?" He had her backed up against the wall now. She had no place to hide or escape.

"There is so much more involved than . . . than . . ."

"Love?" He licked her neck, and for a brief second she sighed before putting her hands to his chest and holding him at arm's length.

Britta stared at the too-handsome rogue and felt as if she were drowning in quicksand. Warm, tempting, sensual quicksand. She wanted him so much it hurt, but what she decided now would have implications for not just her lifetime but the lifetime of the child she carried. She needed time to think. Hah! She could not think when under the influence of searing arousal. "Zachary, there is so much you do not know. So many things to consider."

He took both of her hands, which were pressing against his bare chest, and raised them, kissing first one wrist, then the other. She barely suppressed a moan. How could a mere butterfly of a kiss, and not even on her lips, inflame her so? "We need to talk."

"No, we need to make love. And make love again. And then maybe talk."

"Your persistence is to be commended."

"It's one of my better talents."

"That was sarcasm, lout."

"C'mon, Britta, come with me into the bedroom. I want to lay you down and show you how much I've missed you."

"You fight dirty. Another of your talents?"

"For sure." He took her hand and tried to tug her along with him.

She dug in her heels, fighting an inner battle. She, too, wanted to make love. She, too, had missed him desperately. But she could not let him know about the babe . . . not till

other issues were resolved. Like his stated opinion that he
wanted no more children. Like his womanizing habits . . .
leastways, in the past. Like what kind of future they might
have.

An idea came to her, a way to have what they both wanted
and not reveal her secret . . . yet.

"There is only one condition under which I will engage in
bedsport with you."

He halted in his tugging exercise and raised his eyebrows
at her.

"You need to allow me to do some things to you."

He let out a hoot of laughter before he could catch himself. "Baby, you can do anything you want to me."

"Be serious."

"I am."

"Turn around and do not look at me when I tell you
my . . . uh, conditions."

"You've got to be kidding. Man, your face is red as a beet.
This must be really good." He turned his back on her, but he
still held her one hand in his.

"You must allow me to tie your hands to the bed so you
cannot touch me."

She heard the hiss of his indrawn breath and the reflexive
squeeze of their joined hands.

"And you must let me blindfold you."

Silence was her only response.

Then, slowly, very slowly, he turned and gave her his hot
regard. "Are you freakin' for real?"

She tried to back away, humiliated.

"No, no, no! You don't make that kind of offer to a guy,
then back off."

"Dost mean you would like . . . um, what I offered?"

His smile now was pure, unadulterated lustsome male.
"Bondage? Baby, I'm game."

And Britta wondered if she might have entered a trap of
her own making.

# *Chapter 21*

**Beware of women with secrets . . .**

Okay. So, Zach was lying on his bed, nude, his arms spread and tied to the headboard posts. There was a lamp lit in the room, but he couldn't see it because a folded knit neck scarf covered his eyes.

This should have been Sexual Fantasy Number One, but it felt weird. Not that weird was bad. No. It was just that something felt odd with Britta.

But, hey, he was a guy. He wasn't about to argue.

"If you're not going to let me see you, or touch you, at least talk to me, honey."

He felt the mattress move as Britta crawled up beside him.

"Have you taken off the frickin' fur shroud?" he grumbled at her continuing silence. Was she looking at him, or what? If she was, he had a flagpole standing at attention, and growing, even as he thought about it.

"Yea, I have taken off the cloak . . . and everything else. I intend to make bold with you, knave."

"Make bold, huh? Promises, promises." He laughed, but she was quiet. "What are you doing?"

"Just looking. You are so beautiful."

A certain part of his body nodded its thanks for the compliment.

She chuckled. "I want to touch you all over."

"Feel free."

"And I want to lick you all over, too. To see if you taste as good as I remember."

"Holy crap, Britta. Keep that up, and the opera's gonna be over before the fat lady sings."

"Are you saying that I am fat?" There was genuine indignation in her voice.

"Are you kidding? You don't have an ounce of fat on your body. It was a saying."

Her fingers traced his mouth, and he latched onto one finger, sucking.

He felt her soft gasp of pleasure against his face as she replaced her fingers with her mouth. This he could handle blindfolded. Over and over, they shaped each other's lips, relearning each other. Openmouthed, wet, tongues and teeth. They were both panting when she lifted her head.

"I like kissing you," she said and moved downward. He could tell she was still kneeling at his side.

Her fingertips stroked his neck and shoulders and arms, then his nipples, which were supersensitive.

"You are gritting your teeth. Does that mean you liked that?"

His answer was short puffing noises designed to haul in this raging freight train of an arousal before it crashed.

Taking his puffing for a yes, she flicked him some more with her fingertips, then took him in her mouth and suckled.

He about shot up off the bed . . . or at least as far as his restraints would allow him to go.

"You did not like that?"

"I liked it too much. Take it easy or—" His words were cut off because Britta had moved even lower, her hand cupping his balls, her fingertips stroking him lightly, as if she were petting a dog. A dog!

"Dost know you have blue veins sticking out of your manpart?"

He gurgled, especially when it felt as if she had just kissed the tip. "Britta, bring yourself up over me. I mean it. Do what I say, or this game is over."

"And how would you stop . . . this game?" she asked, even as she straddled him, then leaned over.

*By pulling the damn bedposts out of the headboard, that's how.* Every nerve in his body, in fact every inch of his skin felt raw with arousal. He needed the deed done, and soon. But what did the witch do? She was stroking his chest with her breasts. Lightly. So that the nipples grazed his chest hairs.

"That feels wonderful," she revealed breathily.

"Bring your breasts up to my mouth, sweetie," he urged.

He latched onto one breast and licked and flicked and sucked on her till she was keening. Then he moved to her other breast, not letting her move back, even when she tried. Her body stiffened then. He could feel her buttocks clenching against his belly. "What?" he asked.

"I just orgasmed."

His cock jerked against her butt, and he could swear it grew some more. He'd like to see that. "That's just great, baby, but you better climb up on me and take me home, or you're gonna be tied to this bed for a week. My love slave."

It was Britta who gurgled now. "And that is a threat?" She laughed.

But then she was in the saddle, and he was filling her tight, hot sheath. Amazing how the senses intensified when one of them, like eyesight, was withdrawn. For example, he could feel Britta's wetness pooling around the base of his erection.

"Do me now, baby," he encouraged. "Do me good."

And she did. Had he taught her how to move like that? Had he shown her that slow was good at first, but short and hard was even better? It didn't last long. It couldn't have. But they both came together in an excruciatingly intense orgasm, him howling with neck and chest arched, her whimpering a long, "Oh, oh, oh, oh, oh . . ."

Then there was silence, except for the beating of their two hearts against each other, with Britta's face nuzzled into his neck. She raised her head, kissed him gently, and said, "I love you, Zachary."

He felt about ten feet tall then and told her, "I love you, too, Britta. And before you say anything, I have never said those words to another woman."

"Good."

"Untie me now. I want to touch you."

His words prompted her to lift herself off of him.

"What now?"

"Mayhap I will let you touch me tomorrow. For tonight, methinks I will sleep in Sammy's bed, and we can talk in the morn." The mattress dipped and rose as she stood up.

"Like hell!" he roared, and with one mighty pull, he yanked his hands free, carrying the drapery ties and the broken bedposts with him. Within a second, he had the blindfold off and was removing the ties. Only then did he glance up and see Britta standing beside the bed with that bloody fur cape held in front of her.

"Enough, Britta! This is enough! What is it that you're trying to hide? What did Arsallah and his men do to you?"

" 'Tis not what Arsallah and his men did to me. 'Tis what you did to me."

"Huh?" He sat up in bed and was about to go yank the friggin' cloak off of her when she dropped it herself. Chin raised, diamond tears glittering in her eyes, she waited for his reaction. It came quickly. First his jaw dropped, his eyes widened with disbelief, and then he smiled. "You're pregnant."

"How can you tell?" she inquired with sweet sarcasm, putting both hands over the swell of her stomach.

He smiled even wider, then opened his arms wide for her. "Come here and let me hold you, sweetheart."

She knuckled the tears off her face and moved closer. "You are not angry?"

He frowned. "Why would I be angry?"

"You said you did not want any more children," she reminded him.

He lunged for her and hauled her onto the bed and under him. He kissed her forever, then settled his new hard-on between her legs. Raising himself on his elbows framing her face, he told her, "I didn't mean I never want children. If I had a choice, the timing would have been different, but children with you would be wonderful. How do you feel about it, though? I know you wanted a military career, and now you'll never be able to go back to WEALS."

"It does not matter. Whatever else the Norns of Fate hold for me, I want this child. And I want you."

"You've got me," he said huskily. "And now, about that love slave business."

"Hah! As if you could ever make a thrall of me!"

"Was that a dare? Oh, baby, you should never challenge a Navy SEAL. Never."

She laughed, but not for long. And much, much later, she was heard to yell out in surrender that favorite Navy SEAL word, "Hoo-yah!"

# *Epilogue*

**Another one bites the dust . . .**

In springtime, Zachary and Britta Floyd, now married, had a baby girl. Her name was Angelique . . . or Angel for short.

When Zach asked why that name, she just smiled. She still had too many secrets for a married woman, Zach told her. And, again, Britta just smiled.

At the christening, all of Zach's SEAL buddies—Cage, Max, Sly, JAM, Geek, Omar, and Slick—claimed the rights of godfather, but that honor was given to Danny, the proud uncle. The christening was held in off-hours at the Wet and Wild, of all places.

Sammy was ecstatic, both over Britta being his mother and over his new baby sister. Right now, he was teaching one of Madrene's kids how to belch on cue.

Arsallah was dead these past three months, having fallen to the greed of his own followers. Which was always the case with men of power, whether they be politicians, presidents, or religious men.

Zach's grandmother practically had a stroke over the choice

of reception places, but with true class, she managed to hide her distress and provided foie gras, caviar on toast points, little cucumber and pâté sandwiches, and strawberries in clotted cream. Zach's father provided the beer. A great combination, everyone agreed.

Zach's mother got something going at the reception with the owner of the Wet and Wild, who happened to have seen her photo spread in the latest AARP magazine. Zach's father was hitting on Bawdy Maudy.

Later, when Hilda was cooing over Angel, with Madrene leaning over her shoulder, Zach realized that Britta was missing. He found her in a back corridor.

"What is it, sweetie?" Zach asked.

"I am just so happy. I fear my happiness will make the gods jealous and take me back."

"No one is ever taking you back," Zach assured her.

"How do you know?"

"I just do. There are some things you know right here." He patted his heart, then took her hand and led her over to the door. "Look there," he said, pointing through the door window to the back of the parking lot where his red Firebird was parked. Then he waggled his eyebrows at her.

Britta's jaw dropped. "You would not dare . . . not in the light of day."

"Britta, Britta, Britta," Zach chided. "Never dare a Navy SEAL."

But she did.

And he did.

And six months later, they were living happily ever after, or as happy as a thousand-year-old Viking warrior maiden with a big belly and a too-pretty, virile SEAL could on a cattle ranch in Montana.

Hoo-yah! Or was that Yee-hah?

# Reader Letter

Dear Reader:

I hope you liked Pretty Boy and Britta's story. I had fun creating a big woman with muscles who could bring down a gorgeous man. And didn't you just love Samir, better known as Sammy the Snot, Pretty Boy's son?

In the past, I have said there was nothing like a Viking man. Well, that goes for Viking women, too. Who do you think ran the farmsteads and jarldoms when the Norsemen were off a-Viking? And, although it was rare, there were women warriors in history. In particular, Boudicca, the Celtic queen who led an army against the Romans, had to be an inspiration to all females who needed to defend a home.

As our country continues its fight against terrorists worldwide, I am increasingly impressed with the service so many military men and women give and the sacrifices they make. That includes the Navy SEALs I write about, but it also includes all military wives and lovers left behind who tell me over and over how much my books mean to them . . . a bit of laughter in troubled times.

Next up will be Thorfinn's story in *Fast and Furious*. Thorfinn, a secondary character in *Rough and Ready*, is a dark and brooding Viking man whose wife left him, taking with her his infant son. He is on a quest to find them—or at least his son—and that quest will take him—where else?—into the arms of Lydia Denton, the widow of a slain Navy SEAL.

After that, it's up to you fans who vote with your dollars when you buy the books we romance authors write.

Do you want more Viking Navy SEAL time travels? After all, there is still Thorfinn's brother Steven, who is left in the past. Or all those other Navy SEALs who merit their own stories: Cage, Slick, Sly, JAM, and Geek.

But perhaps you'd like a straight historical romance. John of Hawks Lair, Jamie the Scots Viking, Tyra's four sisters, Alrek the clumsy Viking, and dozens of others are dying to tell you what's been happening to them.

Maybe it's time for another modern character to go back to antebellum Louisiana and the Creole family created in *Frankly, My Dear* and *Sweeter Savage Love*. I'm thinking a female who owns an Internet dating service gets shot back to Louisiana where she sets up an 1870 version of a matchmaking service. After all, there was a dearth of men after the war.

Or do you want something entirely different, like, for example, a Viking vampire?

As a special gift to those of you who have been supporting my Viking books for years, please check out the free novella on my website, *Bolthor's Bride*. It is not currently available anywhere else.

Please know how much I appreciate you fans and all the feedback you give me. I continue to wish you smiles in your reading.

Sandra Hill
P.O. Box 604
State College, PA 16804
www.sandrahill.net
shill733@aol.com

# Glossary—SEALs

**boondockers.** Heavy boots.
**BUD/S.** Basic Underwater Demolition/SEAL training.
**Budweiser.** The trident pin worn by Navy SEALs.
**CENTCOM.** Central Command.
**collateral damage.** Inadvertent casualties and destruction inflicted on civilians in the course of a military operation.
**Coronado (California).** The West Coast site of the U.S. Naval Amphibious Base and the Naval Special Warfare Center, where BUD/S are trained. The other SEAL training center is located in Little Creek, Virginia. Coronado is also home to the famous Hotel del Coronado.
**cover your six.** Cover your back.
**DOR.** Drop on request.
**FUBAR.** Fucked up beyond all recognition.
**Gig Squad.** A punishment inflicted during BUD/S where a SEAL trainee is forced to spend hours, after the evening meal and a long day of training, outside the officers' headquarters, doing many strenuous exercises, including the infamous duck squat.

**grinder.** The blacktopped area where PT takes place, along with the O-course, on the SEAL training arena at Coronado.

**high and tight.** Standard military haircut.

**Look and See.** Reconnaissance mission whereby the operators penetrate enemy territory, identify the targets, and depart without being seen.

**MRE.** Meal ready to eat.

**NSW.** Naval Special Warfare.

**O-course.** Obstacle course on the training compound, also referred to as the Oh-My-God course.

**PT.** Physical training.

**scruffies.** Lowest of the low in military training.

**SEAL.** Acronym for Sea, Air and Land, est. 1962.

**Sims.** Short for Simunitions, paint bullets that emulate live ammunition, down to short-range ballistics and cyclic rates of fire.

**snafu.** Situation normal all fucked up.

**SOCOM.** U.S. Special Operations Command.

**SOF.** Special Operations Forces.

**tango.** Terrorist or bad guy.

**UA.** Unauthorized absence, modern version of AWOL.

**WARCOM.** Warfare Command, as in Naval Special Warfare Command.

**XO.** Executive officer.

# Glossary—Vikings

**Althing.** An assembly of free people that makes laws and settles disputes. It is like a Thing but much larger, involving delegates from various parts of a country, not just a single region.

**Birka.** Market town where Sweden is now located.

**braies.** Long, slim pants worn by men, usually tied at the waist; also called breeches.

**drukkinn.** Drunk.

**gunna.** Long-sleeved, ankle-length gown for women, often worn under a tunic or surcoat or long, open-sided apron.

**Hedeby.** Market town where Germany is now located.

**hird.** Troop, war band.

**Hordaland.** Norway.

**jarl.** High-ranking Norseman, similar to an English earl or a wealthy landowner; could also be a chieftain or minor king.

**Jorvik.** Viking-age York in Britain.

**Jutland.** Denmark.

**karl.** One rank below a jarl.

**nithing.** One of greatest of Norse insults, indicating a man is less than nothing.

**Norsemandy.** Vikings ruled what would later be called Normandy. To them, it was Norsemandy.

**odal right.** Law of heredity.

**sagas.** Oral history of the Norse people, passed on from ancient history onward.

**sennight.** One week.

**skalds.** Poets or storytellers who composed and told the sagas, which were the only means of recording ancient Norse history, since there was almost no written word then.

**straw death.** To die in bed (mattresses stuffed with straw), rather than in battle, which was more desirable.

**Thing.** An assembly of freemen called together to discuss problems and settle disputes; forerunner of the English judicial system; like district courts of today.

**thrall.** Slave.